It's Better To Be From Yale

It's Better
TO BE
From Yale

Memoirs of an Ivy League Doctor

PRESTON T. STONE, MD

Langdon Street Press | Minneapolis, MN

It's Better To Be From Yale

Memoirs of an Ivy League Doctor

Copyright © 2010 Preston T. Stone

Langdon Street Press

212 3rd Avenue North, Suite 290

Minneapolis, MN 55401

612.455.2293

www.langdonstreetpress.com

ISBN - 978-1-936183-50-0

ISBN - 1-936183-50-1

LCCN - 2010936332

Cover Photo © 2010. All rights reserved - used with permission.

Cover Design and Typeset by Nate Meyers

Printed in the United States of America

Chapter 1

I can't remember the exact color of the interviewer's suit as he sat across from me. Gray or blue, I think. Each outfit was interchangeable with the next. The science of interview suits was reputed to be an exact one amongst our advisors in the college. Sodom and Gomorrah faced but a mild penalty compared to the applicant who dared wear a black suit rather than the more subtle option of gray.

"That's too striking!" warned friends and family as I considered the apparently unthinkable option. I was never one to quite follow the rules. My tie was always a touch less than conservative, and on this occasion, my suit touted a double-breasted and olive green cut. Not the olive green you would expect to see on a sofa from the '70s, truthfully. It was classy and modern but green nevertheless.

All together, seven applicants waited in the room at Mon Gracia Medical School, including myself: three females and three other males. While they all looked somewhat professional, it did not seem quite right to think of them as men and women. These were the same guys and girls I would have caught a movie with if we were attending the same college. The suits did not seem reason enough to graduate, or retire them, rather, to the ranks of men and women.

Today, the guy across the table from me decided to strike up a conversation.

The dialogues were always similar and similarly awkward, like a crowded elevator ride that lasts thirty minutes. Everyone tried to ignore the unspoken tension, but we all knew we were competing for the limited number of medical school positions. And we all shared the fear that "the person I befriend today may be the one who gets my spot tomorrow."

"So, what college do you come from?" the guy asked.

I told him. When I caught the expected look of confusion, I explained that it was just north of San Francisco.

"Oh, I'm from..."

I am sure I remembered the school he said for a little while, but this process had become so routine that everything, even conversations, had become kind of an act. We each put on a face of almost British etiquette while speaking to one another, all the while silently quizzing ourselves on the ethics of removing a dying loved one from a ventilator. Each of us was largely just an artificial caricature of intellect and morality. The Miss America candidates in each of us, with their pearly smiles and ambitions to bring world peace, were revealed. We eager young candidates would erupt into dreams of nothing less than curing the world's devastating diseases and insuring the poor, even when asked by the interviewer only if we wanted diet or regular soda.

Some women have argued that having a swimsuit competition is a humiliation to the candidates and does nothing to show who beauty contestants truly are. I would argue that medical schools have Miss Oklahoma beat when it comes to humiliation through wardrobe. It was standard practice to have medical applicants wear large stickers with our names etched in bold black marker.

"Gary," as his nametag declared, leaned over to me and introduced himself. "Hey, I'm Gary. How ya doin'?"

"Doin' good," I replied. "I'm Jeff."

"I don't know how they expect us to look professional when they make us wear these nametags."

"At least they wrote the names for us," I whispered back. "I always look like a retard when they make me write my own name on the tag."

"You think that's bad? One school on the east coast really wanted to make us look like schmucks, so they made us write our names with freaking Crayolas!"

"I don't know, man. I bet you could mistake 'Gary' for 'Gucci' if it was written in a nice aquamarine."

He shook his head. "Not so lucky. They only sported for the small box of crayons, and I got stuck with magenta."

"Eww."

We both cringed, knowing that there was both hyperbole and truth in our banter.

After everyone had remarked about how sick they were of these medical school interviews, the tension had broken. We exchanged stories about the most impressive schools we had seen, the worst interviews we had done, and the scariest urban legends we had heard regarding med school interviews.

"Do you know that one of those schools in the Northeast has you come into the office and sit on a kindergarten-sized chair?" said one of the girls. "And once you sit down, they have you get up and open a window that is nailed shut, just to see how you handle the pressure."

"I heard about that place," Gary piped up. "It was Columbia. Or was it Cornell? Anyway, I heard they were thinking about stopping that practice after some guy last year apparently had a breakfast that didn't agree with him. He strained so much to get the window open that he crapped all over himself. And it was not one of those self-assured, formed craps. It was the nervous, liquid kind that you can't hide."

"Oh, God." We all winced and turned away in our seats.

"The real funny thing is, they accepted him, I guess out of pity. But the senior class got wind of the story. So on his first day, a group of them jumped him and took his pants, then forced him to go to class in a Depends diaper."

Legends were in no shortage among those applying to medical school. I didn't know whether it was the fear, excitement, or anticipation that inspired them. Perhaps it was just premedical students' vast experience bullshitting their professors to get the grades they needed.

"I heard that place has the highest suicide rates of all med schools," Gary said. "It got so bad that they had to put a phone booth that connects directly with the suicide hotline on the nearby cliff everyone jumped off of."

"I didn't find that place so bad," I interrupted. "The professor took me downstairs and bought me coffee during our interview."

One of the guys at the far end of the table smirked and said, "Ah, they gave you the coffee test, huh?"

"What coffee test?" I asked skeptically.

"Did you put cream in your coffee?"

"Yeah, why?"

"Obviously, that tells him that you are not a serious, stable person. Not someone he thinks can tough it out."

"Get the hell outta here," I scoffed.

No one else in the room seemed to share my disbelief—or perhaps it was denial.

"How about sugar?" muttered the guy down the table, whose nametag introduced him as Brian. "You can't tell me that he can figure anything out by my sweet tooth."

"Oh, dude! Please tell me you didn't use sugar. You have to know better than that. Or worse yet, Sweet-n-Low. The little packets alone are designed to make you look like a dork."

I sat there silently in my own thoughts for a few minutes, second-guessing each of my recent interviews, trying to ferret out the hidden personality tests I had likely failed.

Gary told of an interview in the Midwest that had taken him a week to recover from emotionally. Halfway through the questions, he had caught the distinct odor of rotten eggs, and within seconds, the interviewer got a terrible scowl on his face. Then he stood up and accused Gary of passing gas in his office. Gary's impression of the professor's face was reminiscent of Robert De Niro's in one of those *Godfather* movies. Gary had to survive two more questions before the professor revealed that he had opened a jar of something from the anatomy lab just to see how he would react.

"What about this place?" said Sue, who sat next to me in a dark blue pantsuit. "This place is supposed to be the only religious medical school in the country."

I nodded slowly. "There *was* one other. But the FBI shut them down when they found it was just a cover for training religious freaks and suicide cult members."

"I hear that they make the med students go to church every week and take religion courses as part of the daily curriculum." She sounded frightened as much as shocked when she contemplated her own words.

"That's not the worst part," Gary added. "They make you sign a contract promising that you won't drink or smoke or a list of other things they don't believe in. And if you do any of those things...Bam! You're kicked out. Not to mention the more-than-likely trip to hell."

~~~

The application process for medical school is nothing less than grueling, and this is especially so for those in California. The theories of supply and demand say that when the number of Californian applicants rivals the national debt, the medical schools are within their right to go so far as to cup the applicants' genitalia, as they do in dog shows. I had endured most of this and was growing beyond weary.

Mon Gracia was one that I considered a "fallback school"—which is to say, I would take them if all else failed. When the economy is booming, scholars go into business, computers, and those areas of society that can make millions. When the economy is not so grand, students tend toward those careers that their parents always told them to choose. With the economy in a constant state of flux, students were looking for some sense of job security. I happened to be in the mob that flocked to med school. Some of my friends resorted to attending Mexican and Puerto Rican medical schools. This fate seemed like the kiss of death to a blossoming medical career. I imagined the foreign medical school grads as the lepers of the profession. Everyone assumed that their anatomy cadavers had been stolen from nearby cemeteries. We feared the cold shoulder from specialties like neurosurgery and others with a similar elite mystique.

Despite how it must seem, I am not one of these people born with two physician parents and a stethoscope in my playpen. My mother and father named me Jeff. Not Jeffrey T. Triton III. Just plain Jeff Triton. As a boy, I was into sports, girls, and music, like everyone else. This certainly doesn't seem like the formula for the standard premedical student. The one thing I had in common with the students that seemed like geniuses was a sense of drive. I was always motivated toward some goal. I played the jock role for a while, then made the transition to band geek, always finding some spark that made me want to excel. The jump from musician to premed came in that universal meeting with the career guidance counselor when she handed me the ten-pound book of jobs and salaries. Needless to say, music teacher did not rank among the most lucrative. Starting from the front, the first job I came across that impressed me was anesthesiologist, which averaged $250,000 per year.

"You realize that doctors have to study a lot, don't you?" my mother said to me when I broke the news of my new career goal. "Maybe you should just be a pharmacist or something."

"I know how to study, damn it," I growled. "I am not going to be a pharmacist. I am going into medicine." And that is the less-than-globally-benevolent birth of my medical career—the birth I do not mention in interviews, that is.

I was actually pretty familiar with Mon Gracia Medical School. I grew up in a town ten minutes away and remembered all the times I would see it from the freeway when my family would drive to one of my sporting events. The beautiful building stood almost alone in a basin of the three neighboring cities. Grand mountains shielded this basin from the Southern California desert to one side and the Pacific coast to the other. The topography was perfect for trapping the Los Angeles smog, leaving an ever-present gray-brown haze. The Empire of Smog, they called it. While visitors would invariably remark on its equivalence to a pack a day, the locals had long since become oblivious to the smog's comings and goings.

The hospital itself was well regarded by people in the Empire, many of whom were familiar with the medical and historical trivia of the hospital. I recalled my dad mentioning that some celebrity had an eye removed and was fitted with a glass eye there and had since donated the giant cross which would shine through the valley during the holiday season. The religious affiliation, although largely taciturn in the Empire, was well known to those considering a medical education there. Although I was pretty sure that gross anatomy was not going to be taught while speaking in tongues, I was worried that the emphasis on religion might become annoying after a while. But my primary concern was that it might not be prestigious enough to make me stand out.

I had set my eyes on the big-three schools: Harvard, Yale, and Hopkins. I pictured myself a world-famous neurosurgeon, perhaps even Nobel laureate. One day I would be teaching other doctors, developing new procedures, and pushing boundaries. Nothing great was ever accomplished by settling, and I knew I could not settle for less that the best medical school. My father would say, "If you are the best in your school, it doesn't matter whether you are at Yale or Mississippi."

My reply was always, "No one ever won the Nobel Prize from the University of Backwoods, USA. It's always better to be from Harvard or Yale."

"I heard they're, like, vegans or something out here," Brian said. "Is that true?"

I shook my head. "Not vegans. Just vegetarians. The funny thing is, they sorta fool themselves into thinking that what they are eating is healthy because it has no meat, but they create these synthetic pseudo-meats that are genetic hybrids of alien vegetables, only to deep fry them in a bunch of fat. They give them cute little names like Wham or Grass-strami, but you feel like you're chowing down on the Frankenstein of the culinary world."

"Sounds perfectly delectable," Brian said.

"Oh, and don't think you're going to make it taste better with mustard or pepper. Those are banned as well. Apparently those are considered stimulants, so they aren't allowed around here."

"Are those in the contract, too?" Brian asked.

"I don't know about that. But your coffee might be in it. That's one of the biggest stimulant no-nos."

"No coffee? That's it. I'm getting the fuck outta here." Brian rubbed his face in disbelief.

Just as Brian got up to refill his glass of water, an older man wearing a charcoal suit and tie walked in the room. Brian sat back down quickly, as if hiding his sins. The man had a gray mustache and a big smile from his first step through the door until he addressed the group.

"Hey, everyone, I'm so glad you could come down here. I am Dr. Johnson, Dean of Admissions, and I want to welcome you." The man spoke for about five minutes, telling us about the history of the hospital, reaching back farther than some 1970s celebrity and a glass eye. Astonishingly, his talk involved very few references to God.

A few minutes later, an assistant called me back into a room where Dr. Johnson sat at his desk. Thankfully, a comfortable chair was positioned directly across from him.

"You have a very impressive application, Mr. Triton. Your grades, your MCAT scores, and your research are all fantastic."

The MCAT was the entrance test to medical school, which tested a student's ability to answer difficult questions in subjects only remotely related to medicine.

This was one of the first times I had ever heard anyone compliment my achievements. Prior to this, everyone had either seemed unaware or unimpressed.

"Thank you, sir."

Words like "sir" and "certainly" subconsciously replaced words like "dude" and "fuck, yeah!" when I was in an interview. I always wondered if the other people I met were "dudes" or "sirs" in their real lives. I also wondered if it was polite and professional to put on this façade, or just phony.

"There is just one thing, though," Johnson said as he leaned forward, looking with puzzlement at the papers in front of him. "This says here that you don't go to church . . . Do you want to explain yourself?" The sound of his voice and the terrible dismay in his expression reflected his feeling that I had not only committed the greatest sin but must have suffered the greatest tragedy.

I realized instantly that I should have prepared for such a question.

Fuck, I thought. The adrenaline percolated off my palate and onto my tongue, left dry by his insinuation. "Well, sir, when I was young, my family was very religious. Then something happened within the organization of our church that made my father feel alienated. I don't exactly know what, but it must have made him truly angry, because we never went back to church and never even approached the subject of why we did not go."

"Wow. That must have been troubling for you to watch," Johnson said, offering his consolation.

I fought back the smirk as I wondered what kindergartener would rather go to church than watch cartoons on Sunday. "Yes, perhaps it was a bit. But I credit my close family with hiding those shallow conflicts from me so that I might one day find a faith of my own." That was about as much crap as could be fit into one sentence.

"Don't you feel you have missed out on something important by not attending church?"

"I actually don't think so, sir," I replied. "Would you agree that some of the greatest things taken from church are a source of hope and positive direction? Perhaps inspiration and instruction to treat each other right?"

"Yes, that is a significant part of it."

"My family has always provided me with those values. I never lacked hope. I never questioned their unreserved love. So, for that reason, I never felt I was lacking in the things that religion promised."

Anytime I bullshitted my way out of a tough situation, my vocabulary sounded like it came straight from a mediocre thesaurus. My sentence structure became convoluted like the dialogue I had seen on those British mystery shows. This time, I threw in the spice and flavor of those TV evangelists. *Can I get an "Amen"?* I thought.

The remainder of the interview went without a hitch. All the rest of the standard questions were asked. The dean seemed intrigued with most of my answers. But I could not be positive that he was showing genuine interest and not simply humoring a person whose soul was almost certainly doomed for eternity.

An hour later, I was on the road back up to my tiny dorm room in Northern California. I wondered if I had a shot of getting into Mon Gracia after essentially admitting I was an atheist. I did have a few connections at the school from the research and volunteer work I had done there over previous summers. Research and volunteer work were the bread and butter of every applicant's résumé. Hopefully my returning home each year to Mon Gracia implied a dedication to family and the school itself.

When I got back to my room, it was late, and my exhaustion got the best of me. I collapsed into bed immediately without even checking the mailbox. The mailbox ritual had become an obsession over the past few months. But not even the adrenaline rush of opening the box in the hope of an acceptance letter could divert me from my glorious pillow.

As usual, my alarm chimed, and I woke an hour before the sparrow rolled over and farted in his nest. It was time for my daily game of racquetball with Jim. He and I had been roommates all through college and had similar goals in the health-care profession. Jim had picked a field just outside of medicine that closely tied to his extreme attention to physical fitness. He had the look of a body-builder without the exaggerated veins. This made him both athletic enough to beat me at almost any sport and a magnet to the ladies. His charm was also undeniable, as women seemed to flock to him.

"How was the interview?" Jim asked as we walked toward the gym. There was no hint of sunlight at this hour.

"It was fine, I guess."

"Just fine? After all the shit you've done down there? You would think they would be jumping all over you. Or at least hire you as a janitor."

"Jim, you've been living next door to me for almost three years now. Have you ever known me to keep anything clean?"

"Good point. You better hope they think you would be better at cutting people open."

"What did they serve you to eat at the interview?" Jim was well aware of the interview routine, since he was in the thick of the interview process himself. He theorized that you could tell how good a program was by the quality of the food served.

"Dude, it was another one of those schools that just brings in a freaking five-foot-long sandwich."

The staples at these interviews were sandwiches and semi-cold pasta from the cafeteria. Often the hosts would make a feeble attempt to woo the applicant with a rock-hard cookie, also from the cafeteria.

"And here is the real kicker," I added. "The sandwich was a veggie sandwich. Why can't anyone just bring in a pizza or two? It might even be cheaper, and it sure as hell would be a lot tastier."

"You know it would be crappy pizza anyway, and just full of grease." Jim tried to set me straight.

"Screw that nutrition and health stuff, man. If everybody starts doing that, there isn't going to be any need for someone like me to cut into people's hearts. Then, bam! Before you know it, I'm out of a job before I'm out of school. I say they should keep the veggie shit in your nutritional side of the building and bring the good old American pizza to mine."

"I don't think you can call pizza American."

"Oh, shit, I guess that's something you have to learn from a nutritionist. All right, how about a nice thick steak? That would do. Or... wait! I've got it. Ribs!"

"You're out of your mind."

"No. That would be killer. To be sitting across from the admissions committee at one of these schools and tell some head dude that he has barbeque sauce on his chin."

"And you are going to look sooo *GQ* with that stuff all over your suit, aren't you?"

I gave in. "Okay, maybe not the ribs."

"Yeah, maybe not."

We trekked the quarter-mile as the chill bit into my exposed arms. I looked over at Jim, who was comfortable as ever. "I don't know how you can wear shorts and a tank top out here every morning. It's freezing."

"Easy, man. I keep my metabolism up by being in shape. We've got to get you working out more. We could make you look like a stud."

"What do you mean, assface? I am a stud."

"And furthermore, I have to keep my arms exposed in case there are any hotties at the gym."

"Hotties? At six in the morning?" My voice rose up an octave. "The only ones dumb enough to be out at this hour are us. And I sure as hell ain't gonna get all turned on by your sweaty arms."

"You will after I beat your ass at racquetball. Oh, and speaking of hotties, did you see that new chick working the front desk in the student office?"

"Yeah, she was okay."

"Okay? Okay? Did you see the set on that one?" Jim was not a pervert by any means, but he did have this one fetish.

"Yes, but I couldn't see past them. They were too big."

He looked up at the ceiling. "God, if you're listening, he didn't mean it. You are wise beyond us and superb in your artistry. There is no such thing as too big. Just keep on going making them bigger and bigger, as we agreed the other day." Jim turned back to me. "I don't know how you can not like boobs. Are you an ass man or something?"

I pleaded my case. "I like boobs just fine. I love boobs, in fact. I just like them a particular size."

"A-cup is not a size. It's a lack of size. I've heard of this problem. It starts off like this, and before you know it, you start liking guys instead."

"Fuck you. No one is going for guys. I just like the fashion-model body style."

"Well, I hope you end up with a girl who will starve herself for you. Let's play."

We began our typical session, and, as usual, Jim repeatedly smashed the ball within inches of his target and sent me running from one side of the court to the other. His strokes controlled me as much as the ball. If I hadn't been willing to throw myself around like a rag doll to get a single hit, the game would have been done before it started. Today, though, I was a little more winded than normal. I made a desperate dive to salvage a point as the score was tied. My racquet got to the ball, but my swing wasn't quite enough to get the ball to the front wall.

Panting, I turned and slowly walked back to receive the next serve. "You know, I almost had that one."

I heard his racquet hit the ball, but it sounded like it was in the next room over. I considered this only mildly strange. All at once, I felt a sense of intense weight from my head on my shoulders and a sensation of my head floating above my body. The ball sped toward the wall but seemed to leave plenty of time for me to focus on the warm, comforting feeling within my stomach and to consider how wonderful it would feel to close my eyes for a nap. Although I had no difficulty seeing the ball whiz past me two feet away, it might as well have come directly at my head. The warm euphoria of my lightheadedness had completely distracted me. I considered the likelihood that I was going to pass out, but not even something as simple as sitting down occurred to me.

For a moment, fatigue overwhelmed me, and my racquet seemed mountains heavier. But to drop the racquet took more concentration than I could muster. I was in a parallel dream state so blissful that I had no desire to snap out of it, despite the likelihood that I was about to fall on my face. A whisper repeated itself in a voice that I remembered incidentally from a childhood television show. A young girl of thirteen whispered, "If you don't panic... If you don't panic..." The words meant nothing to me, but the voice was unexpectedly familiar to me for some reason. It clicked that hers was the voice of a Holly, from *Land of the Lost*, a show from my childhood.

"Dude, are you okay?" Jim asked startling me from my daze. "You look totally gray."

I could hear his words, but the cloud around my head filtered them like a drunken stupor.

I was slow to respond and may have even answered the wrong question. "Yeah, I'm just tired. I got back late last night."

"Okay. Well, we should get you a drink and then some food." Jim gave me a minute, then helped me out of the glass playing area.

I reclined onto the bench, still pale. My eyes demanded that I close them, and I fell almost immediately into a semi-sleeping state. To my surprise, I was no longer nauseated. In fact, the sensation in my stomach now was almost preorgasmic.

"Wow, I have never fainted before," I mumbled.

"Yeah, you didn't totally faint, but you were pretty out of it. Drink some Gatorade. We'll go back and get some breakfast before class."

I would eventually discover the unwelcome cause of this bizarre euphoria, but for now I got my bearings and headed for the cafeteria with Jim.

~~~

The dorm food was not bad by cafeteria standards. Jim and I had been eating there together for the past three and a half years. The food had been, at one time, leftovers from nearby San Quentin. Students were forced to eat dry, overcooked meat and bland casseroles day after day. It had gotten so bad that students would often walk down the cafeteria line and not take any food. This created a fantastic opportunity for the school, because they could simply put the same dish out the next day. It wasn't long before students became savvy to this ploy and began mangling the food as it lay in the trays. This way, they at least had a shot at getting something edible the following day.

But things improved over the years. The food got better, and they added a grill for hamburgers and eggs, and more importantly forced some element of freshness into the cuisine.

"That guy can make a hell of an omelet," Jim said, sitting down at the table.

"I like the girl who works back there on Saturdays better. She puts, like, three extra slices on my grilled cheese."

"You just like the way she winks at you and bends over when she flips the sandwich."

I shrugged. "You can't beat that."

My mouth was no longer dry, and my body did not feel like the empty shell it had been thirty minutes before.

"You're looking better," Jim said with his mouth full of egg.

"Better? Why, did you think I had lost my girlish figure?" I snapped back in a typical sarcastic tone.

"You didn't let me finish, punk. What I was going to say was, 'You look better than all the times we actually finished the game and I kicked your ass.'"

"Oh, I see. And I suppose you think you would have won *this* game had I not suffered from malnourishment or dehydration or whatever you nutritionists call it?"

"Let's just say the Red Sox have a World Series record even you can admire."

"Oh, crap. I gotta go to class. I'll see you later."

"Wanna get your butt kicked at pool this afternoon?" Jim asked.

"Um, I think I'm going to be feeling faint then," I muttered. "Actually, I have class and then tutoring all afternoon."

"Okay, later, man."

Before I ran to class, I checked my mailbox for any good news. There was a jitter to my hand as I turned the dial. Inside was nothing but an announcement of the month's intramural sports events. "Damn it!"

Each day was almost identical in pattern. Racquetball, eat, CHECK MAILBOX, class, sleep. Sure, the day was spattered with some leisure time, seeing my girlfriend or watching TV. But during class, and even when I was with my girlfriend, these days I was thinking ahead to the mailbox. I needed that letter. Harvard, Hopkins, Yale, someone.

And so the routine went for days. Waiting-list offers, frank rejections, all were equally sickening in tone and implication:

We were very pleased to have had the chance to meet you and were very impressed with your qualification. We regret, however, that we are unable to offer positions to all those we feel are qualified. We will therefore be unable…

The idea that these schools took the time to regret anything that happened to the plethora of applicants they turned down was ludicrous. It was getting close to the end of the application season, and my compassion for my fellow applicants had waned. So I couldn't have cared less for "all those they felt were qualified." I was sweating for that acceptance letter.

It had been about seven days after my most recent interview at Mon Gracia, and my spirits were as low as I could remember them ever being. Again, I dragged myself to the mailbox of bleak despair, as I had come to know it. That morning, my girlfriend was walking past the box, and our eyes met.

"Hey, sweetie, how's it going?" Mina asked. "I haven't seen you in ages."

"Hold that question for thirty seconds while I check the box, and I'll be able to tell you better."

"Frantic" aptly describes the way I rummaged through the credit-card applications and cell-phone offers.

"They should ban all junk mail from being sent during the application period," I griped. "Not only does it freak me out, it makes it harder for me to get to my acceptance letters. And what if it's slowing things down at the post office? Or worse yet, maybe it confuses some poor postal worker who is *this* close to taking an AK-47 to work, and now my acceptance letter is on the floor, covered in blood."

I obviously wasn't the nicest guy or best boyfriend during this time. But I cared for Mina deeply, and there were still times when I could abandon my fears of no future and enjoy the relationship we had. And Mina was more devoted and supporting than I had any right to expect during this time.

"Anything?" Mina asked.

"Shit, another small envelope!" I shouted as I opened the envelope from Columbia University.

Mina was wringing her hands as she watched the paper being torn recklessly. "Don't worry. The size of the package doesn't mean anything."

"Don't say that too loud," I said, putting my hand over her mouth. "Who knows what people will think we're discussing?" Come to think of it, I don't know which of the implied packages I more feared being small.

After fumbling with the envelope, I finally got to the letter. "Goddamn it. It's another wait list." I threw the letter to the ground.

"It's better than a rejection. They might call you in a few weeks and tell you they have a spot for you." Mina was always the embodiment of encouragement.

She was a tiny Indian girl with an innocent cuteness. Throughout childhood and school, she had planned to become a doctor. She came from a traditional Indian family who lived by Hindu principles. Her dreams of being a pediatrician did not fit into the cultural paradigm of arranged marriages and housewifery. She had left the security of her family to pursue an education on her own. I don't know if it was her boldness or her paradoxical innocence, or just her beautiful olive Indian complexion that I was attracted to. But our romance had been going on for two years now, and despite the Shakespearian nature of a romance in the wine country of California, now that we were so consumed with our careers, our lives seemed almost completely business.

"These wait lists are a load of crap," I muttered. "This is the eighth wait list that I have been put on. I don't think there actually is a real list! I think this is just their way of telling me to fuck off, while putting it gently."

"I don't think that's it," Mina said in her soft-spoken way.

"No, it's like that whole 'let's just be friends' thing that women do when they dump you."

Mina laughed. "At least they don't do it like some jerky guy would. You know, say they would call you in the morning."

There was more rummaging to be done, and then I came to a letter from Mon Gracia.

I sighed. "Another small one." I opened the envelope and fell silent in disbelief.

We would like to congratulate you and invite you to attend the Mon Gracia school of medicine… We must ask you to place your first semester's tuition as a deposit within one week to reserve your position…

"Holy shit, I got in!"

"That's great, sweetie. I knew you would."

"They want me to put down, like, $8,000 as a deposit. I've never heard of putting down a deposit on med school. It's like I'm buying a used fucking car. And shit, I forgot to kick the tires while I was there."

"So? Your dad will give you the money. He was going to pay for your school anyway."

"You don't understand." I sighed and felt my jaw clench as this piece of success somehow seemed like a failure. "I've only got a week before I have to commit to this place, and I still haven't heard from my number one and number two choices."

"You will hear from them," Mina assured me. "Just chill out."

"Okay. You're right. I'm being a dumbass. I've got to go to class. I'll catch you at about five." I gave her a quick peck on the cheek and swung around 180 degrees. With the deep breath I took, I actually felt as much relief enter my lungs as oxygen. I settled down. I was going to be a doctor after all.

My walk across Sonoma State University's campus was a beautiful one, but I often found myself distracted by some idle thought. This time I was considering what might have been keeping me out of all the medical schools I was getting turned down from. Wrong pedigree? Not wealthy? Affirmative action?

It's said in some cultures that the assassin named "rationalization" often disguises himself as the servant named "explanation" in order to attack his prey.

I wondered if coming from such a small university was holding me back. No one had heard of my school or any of the professors writing my letters of recommendation. Just a year before, a recent SSU graduate was the first to make it to the NFL. During an exciting Monday night game, as the center for the Dallas Cowboys, he pummeled the opponent's defense like few had seen before. John Madden, quite impressed, said, "This rookie is amazing! He shifts and moves like a veteran. And his strength is incredible. Now, it says here that he is from Sonoma State. Who ever heard of Sonoma State?"

I had to laugh, because Madden had played for and coached the Oakland Raiders for many years, just one hour south of SSU.

Another thing holding me back was the lack of a great hook. A girl I had met at a San Diego interview was conducting research with AIDS at the age of twenty. Her father had discovered the HIV virus a couple years before—a nice connection, to say the least. Other applicants I had met told touching stories about becoming interested in medicine after a sibling suffered a terrible illness growing up. Med schools seemed to drool over these stories. My touching story was about being a band geek who realized he was not going to make any money as a musician.

But despite my shortcomings, I had been accepted. I was going to be a doctor. I walked across the parking lot feeling something I had not felt in years, if ever. Relief. Satisfaction. It's difficult to describe or even perceive the constraints and burdens that stress and worry can place on us. It's nigh impossible until something liberates you. I had been liberated in such a way by hope.

The fragrance in the air was striking. Actually, more striking was the fact that I smelled anything at all. How many days, weeks, and months had I gone through this life without noticing any scent of any kind? On this day, I walked slowly, noticing the briny essence with the slightest cleansing trace of sand in the scent blowing in from the ocean not too far away. How many times had the cut grass or shrubs eluded me? Now the blossoming honeysuckle was sweet enough to remind me of cool sherbet on a picnic.

For so long, life had been about working and achieving and then working again. Once one exam was finished, I simply studied for the next. In the midst of working and achieving, I had forgotten to appreciate—to appreciate my successes, yes, but also to appreciate the exquisite beauty around me. To appreciate the purple hues that peeked out of the bushes just below eye level. To appreciate the song of the gulls that had been without an audience for so long. To appreciate the smells that mingled so intimately with memories and the imagination. Experiencing the aromas that I had forgotten for so long invited me to reexperience emotions that I had similarly forgotten. How liberating a simple scent can be. Only after stopping to appreciate and love these subtle pleasures around me did I realize that I was more than satisfied. I was happy and thought that somehow with this new understanding of what was important, I could be happy forever. Such insight and hope are, quite possibly, the keys to happiness themselves.

Chapter 2

What is learning? Merely the cramming of data or information into our heads so that it can be leaked out at the exam time? And what was the first thing that we learned as infants? Was it our *ABC*s? Was it that crying helps us get fed faster? Or was it that squeezing our head and body through a ten-centimeter hole into a bright room is a pretty arduous and uncomfortable task? Perhaps that's why we spend the whole of our lives avoiding that proverbial walk toward the light.

As for what it means to learn, I have never been a believer in the idea that all those little facts and dates that I rehearsed in the wee hours of the morning were ever learned—although I have been guilty of this crime on more than one occasion. I think that learning is more a matter of placing a piece of information into the frame of logic that we already have, so that when we forget this memorized factoid, we simply reason, "Of course, the answer is…" Even four-year-olds have some pieces of knowledge, so that when they are asked certain questions by their parents, they reply, "Daaaad, everybody knows that." Whether it is that balls roll down hills or that bees sting, kids have a knowledge base that allows them to infer not to stand in front of rolling cars or try to catch bees in their hands. Somehow, it's obvious. And somewhere along our path growing up, so many more things become obvious. When something gets added to that "obvious" column in our minds, there is a little rush of adrenaline or a little high. That's when I think we have actually learned something.

I suppose I've come up with these explanations of learning because, as long as I can remember, my memory has been atrocious. This statement itself has an element of irony, but I never had the memory that everyone assumes that premeds must have, even as a child. At least, I don't think I had a great memory as a child; I don't quite recall. But despite that deficiency, I was able to pick up enough knowledge to do pretty well. I was lucky, actually, that my crappy memory forced me to rely on simple mental models of how things worked. This left me well suited to teach others, and I had been a tutor at the university for about a year and a half.

At some point in time many years back, the academic board of California realized that they had packed way too many students into classrooms, especially in the state schools in cities like L.A. and San Diego. As a solution, Sacramento bureaucrats funded tutorial centers at each of the universities so that students could get free assistance in their learning efforts. A job at these centers looked great on the résumé of an education student becoming a teacher, so there was an abundance of tutors. Usually they assisted in subjects like English, history, or some forms of math. The sciences, however, like physics or chemistry, tended to make them break out in a cold sweat, and I was hired immediately when I volunteered in these areas.

I loved the job. I scheduled myself to work at various hours in between my classes, not only to make money whenever I could but also to save me the walk back to my dorm room between lectures. When I wasn't scheduled, I found myself in the center, helping stray students try to figure out what their physics professor was talking about as he wrote the formulas in Greek. If that mental connection was made when they were sitting with me, I sometimes thought I could actually hear the click in their mind, perhaps through their ear. Later, in medical school, I learned that this probably was not anatomically accurate. I imagined that they were feeling the same high I described earlier. Perhaps there was a part of me that was addicted, not just to the money, but to being needed by these other students.

Hailee Connor was one of these students I developed a consistent academic relationship with. She was twenty-six, a few years older than the average junior at the university. She was planning on going to vet school, and her coursework closely paralleled the premed schedule. She was the secretary/treasurer in the Pre-health Professions Club at the time I was its president. Both of these titles were somewhat misleading, in that there was no paperwork or funds for her to handle, while there were similarly no wars for me to declare upon other clubs (although my finger had to be on the red button at all times, with the president of the Future Actors Guild claiming to have weapons of mass destruction. If there was one thing I learned from my term, it was never trust a FAG with a WMD). So our friendship was fairly close, as was our academic relationship. We had a regular tutoring schedule, often meeting three times a week. Sometimes we would spend as much as half the scheduled time actually discussing the organic chemistry, while the rest focused on applications, relationships, or movies, all the while "on the clock."

Hailee was an extremely optimistic girl. She was slightly older because she had taken the "nontraditional academic path" (which, to some, included anything other than getting a 4.0, going to your father's alma mater, and finally taking a quick breath before going to medical school). She had taken two years off after her second year of college to be with her estranged father, who passed away soon afterward due to cancer. She occasionally spoke to me about his death. Although her spirits always seemed up, I could hear the sorrow in between the words. Somehow she always concluded the story with a tone that reflected some sort of inspiration from the experience. I found myself amazed by this strength. I had never lost anyone close to me and could not imagine finding either strength or inspiration from such a tragedy. She told her father before he died that she wouldn't settle for just any job. She promised that she would become a veterinarian like she had wanted since she was a little girl. And if I was two steps from being a doctor, she was but a third step—an achievement I found miraculous.

"Okay, Jeff, we *really* have to study this time," Hailee said as she pounced onto the chair and dropped the stack of books on the table. "I have an Organic Chem test this Friday, and I know it's going to suck."

"No problem. I'll have you dreaming of benzene tonight," I reassured her.

"Oh God, no!" she cried out. "Forget it. I'll take the *C* plus."

"Do you want to study in here or go to our usual spot?"

"With the weather being this nice, it would be a waste to study in here. Besides, if we go study by the pond, maybe you'll come up with some amazing chemical analogy using a duck."

We grabbed our books and strolled out to the pond as pink blossoms floated across our path.

"Any word from the schools?" she asked.

"Mon Gracia said yes." I was about to follow the statement with a "But..." when she cut me off with excitement.

"That's fantastic! Wow, you would be right next to your family. You could visit them after exams or go out to dinner with them. And you would be close enough that we could call or visit once in a while."

I almost shared all my fears of going home for medical school. I wanted to tell her that it was almost certain that I was going to be living at home with my parents, notifying them when I was going to be home from class like when I was in third grade. I was worried that I would develop a steadfast study regimen, far-fetched as the idea may have seemed, only to be summoned to take a "family trip" to the post office. I worried that the nicknames that had haunted me through my childhood were eagerly awaiting my return. The scenario was clear. I would be in the ICU caring for a terminal patient, my nurse looking to my next action, when overhead I would hear the page, "Doctor Dickens. Paging Doctor Dickens. Please pick up line three. Doctor Dickens." Of course, upon picking up the line I would be informed that I was a "hunkle-head" for not going to the post office with them the night before.

All this I wanted to confide in her, but I saw that she so missed her family, and I couldn't.

"Yeah, that would be great," I said. "You're right."

"What about Mina?" she asked, knowing that I was a little bit nervous about my relationship with Mina. "When is she going to apply?"

"I'm not sure. When we first got together up here, things were great. We took the same classes. We hung out. We thought we were going to succeed together. Then she had to start working more hours to pay her way through school, while my parents paid my way. She started falling behind me in courses. Now, whenever we talk, it's awkward, and I just feel like she isn't challenging me. I feel like she is not going to be able to live up to the life that we planned together. I just don't know."

Hailee had a way of comforting me in a time where she probably should have been chastising me for being a selfish prick. "That's normal. People grow apart sometimes. Especially when they're learning different things at different paces. It's too bad, though. I know you guys were happy a while ago." She put her hand on my shoulder as we walked. "You'll figure it out, and it won't seem as bad as it feels now." And with that, I was forgiven. The pope offering the four points to my forehead in forgiveness could not have made me feel more at peace.

"Thanks," I sighed. "I feel like such an ass, because these were her goals first, and it's almost like I stole them. And when we first got together, I felt like I was the knight in shining armor who was going to step into her life and protect her from the oppressive entities in the world like her father. I wanted to be the one to fix things—to be the hero."

"It sounds like you were the hero when she needed one. I told you that sometimes people's goals change. When I told my husband that I wanted to go back to school, he couldn't understand why. His business was making enough to keep me sitting in our beautiful house in Marin. 'Why on Earth would you want to go to school or get a job?' he would say. It took him months to ease up on the idea."

"How is he with it now?" I asked.

"Ehhh. He thinks he is being a tremendous person in supporting me. And I guess he is being kinda supportive. He just doesn't understand the effort that I need to put into this. He comes home from work and wonders why I'm reading my textbooks instead of cooking for him. Or he wonders why I wouldn't want to go to a movie on a Wednesday just because I have class the next day. Little things like that make me feel like he has no concept of what I am doing, or doesn't take it seriously."

"That's got to be rough on you."

I had met her husband once before when she had invited Mina and me to a barbeque a few months earlier. He was an upstanding guy who owned his own carpet-cleaning business. He had started it ten years before, doing all the work at that time with his brother. Since then, he had built it up to ten employees and enough clients to keep him busy. When I was at their house, I couldn't help but be amazed that cleaning carpets was such a lucrative industry. When I was a boy, my mother would threaten to beat my behind if I didn't clean up the juice that I spilled on the carpet. I guessed that the affluent children of Marin County were hiring people to clean the carpet for them or opting for the punishment and simply subletting the ass-beating out to neighboring Napa County kids for the right price. Nevertheless, I could see that he was a local man with a strong work ethic, who perhaps had a bit of husbandly entitlement because of his earning potential.

On that particular day, the four of us took an afternoon out on their motorboat for some waterskiing. The occasion was momentous. I would remember it as the only time that I had seen Hailee's amazingly fit body in a bikini. While I understood where she got her motivation for academics, she had another passion for exercise that gleamed from every oil-soaked inch of her Rodin-like physique. Such a sight would be a recurring fantasy to any self-respecting college male, but I dutifully buried the memory deep in my brain so it would only rarely pop into my mind during a tutoring session.

We finally reached the pond as I carried her textbooks. Whether they recognized the two of us from previous sessions or just knew that college girls were suckers for the pitiful quacking plea of a duck, I don't know, but the flock sprinted in formation across the water. At first, their mission seamed one of stealth as they swam silently, their tails marking time. But as we sat down, they reached the shore near us, and the onslaught of quacks and squawks began. Hailee's reach into her backpack only intensified the pursuit as the satin-feathered masses huddled around her. Then she pulled out her chemistry book and flopped it on the ground. The bang of the mammoth text on the ground scattered the masses as they went about finding residual bread crumbs around the pond on their own, no longer intrigued by us.

"I always feel so guilty when I don't have anything to give them," Hailee said.

"Don't feel too bad. The pond is right next to the art department, and they throw bread out to these guys all the time so they'll pose for an oil painting. It's amazing what cute feathers can add to a beggar's charisma. The beggars in the city should take lessons."

"Didn't some celebrity wear swan feathers to the Oscars or something a couple years ago?"

"Yeah. Come to think of it, that didn't help her Oscar chances. I think it just made her look like more of a psycho homeless beggar than before."

We worked out some of the chemistry issues that had been troubling her, and I got my fix of academic endorphins. Before our hours together, I had often heard despair in her voice when she mentioned her troubles with a subject. Now she was much more relaxed.

"I still remember when you told me that confidence was the first step toward competence." She bundled her books into her backpack then hugged me as we turned away from the pond.

"Are you sure that I said something as cheesy as that?"

"Of course it was you." She paused and adjusted her sweater and backpack. "Okay, I'm ready," she said with a deep breath of determination.

"I know you are. You are going to kick ass on this test." I knew she was not a swearing lady as I said it. But I saw the slight renegade appeal of an academic guy who had a bit of "bad boy" in him.

"So have you been down to Tibouron yet?" she asked as we walked back to the tutorial center together.

"No, not yet. I haven't gotten around to it."

"My God! You've been here this long and you still haven't been to Tibouron?"

"Nah, I haven't even been down to San Francisco much since I've been here."

"Tell you what. If you don't have any tests Friday, just skip class for a day, and I'll show you some places down by the city. I have got the coolest things for you to see. You'll love it."

"Sure, why not?" I replied without hesitation or consideration. In actuality, I had not ever missed a single class other than to interview for med school, perhaps including elementary school. Somewhere in that time frame, I had gone from obedient to disciplined to paranoid. Yet her disarming manner was so immediately convincing that I had to acquiesce.

"Great. That settles it," she said.

I knew the "date" would be harmless enough. She was married, and I was quite obviously taken. And she was such a sweet girl that there was no way this could be taken as other than a virtuous expedition. Regardless, I still expected I would not tell Mina. Girls, and especially girlfriends, have a way of misinterpreting things and taking things out of context. It was better to just leave the topic untouched, or, if forced, lie. It seemed best for everyone.

The day was ending as the sun set in front of us. I offered a final "Good luck" as we parted to undertake our private tasks. Hailee had to battle it out for one last night of studying. I had to struggle with the Mon Gracia decision.

I called my sister Vicki, to whom I turned when I needed advice, support, or a good pickup line. Each of those fears of going home that I could not address with Hailee came up in conversation with Vicki, and we laughed over the accuracy of each of them. She pointed out that I had not given due consideration or fear to the fact that were I to bring home a date some night, I could at any time find my mentally retarded sister walking down the stairs in her pajamas. While Nancy, in her own mind, was being subtle and sneaky by peering down at her younger brother, the miscellaneous bodily noises that could be expected to come from upstairs would be more than enough to alert us all to her presence.

We laughed about the absurdity and reality of each scenario. But the pressure to make a decision soon was overwhelming, and we concluded the conversation knowing that I would be staying in California. The San Francisco expedition came up briefly as I told her that I planned to use her as an alibi if questioned on my whereabouts. As always, Vicki agreed without reservation, wanted to hear about all the details of the trip, and supported me despite any moral dilemma she may have been hiding so well.

The Friday morning sun rose as I got myself assembled for the day with Hailee. Jim was asleep, or at least trying to sleep, as I showered, shuffled, and dried my hair in the bathroom that adjoined our rooms. I shoved pants from left to right across the closet rack, trying to find the one that said something other than "most important interview ever" or "least important philosophy lecture ever." I threw shirt upon sweater across the bed to find the one that said, "This is not a date, but I have been looking forward to it all week anyway." This whole endeavor was complicated by the fact that my wardrobe was as sophisticated as a seven-year-old boy who could belch the alphabet to Q.

How did I get this far in life without a $500 shirt like I've seen on the cover of GQ? I wondered. Never mind that the closest I had come to the magazine was while walking through an airport. I had never actually bought one.

The final waft of my hand through my hair pulled a solitary lock down from the otherwise precisely groomed mane. The black sweater with the khaki slacks and the hairstyle with deliberately casual imperfection was the look du jour.

I arrived at our prearranged meeting spot, a small coffee shop in the middle of our small town, about fifteen minutes early. Hailee and

I had met here once before to study together. It was an evening session that I neglected to mention to Mina because of the likelihood that she would blow it out of proportion. For this Friday outing, I told Mina that I was going to visit my sister Vicki, near San Francisco, for the day. Although everything was harmless enough, I was still a bit invigorated by the risky side of the day's adventure.

Hailee's white Honda pulled up in front of me as I stood in the lot. I was never certain if she had gotten the car because it suited her taste or if David had bought it hoping to inspire the soccer mom in her.

"Hey!" she greeted me with a giggle as she rolled her window down and tilted her head out the driver's side. "You're not going to believe it. I think I aced my O-Chem test!" Her smile danced playfully between giggles. Her cheeks were soft and blushed over the beautifully tanned base. Her eyelashes were jet-black and framed her ocean-blue eyes that reflected her immense excitement.

"That's terrific!" I exclaimed. "You are such a stud. You'll have to tell me all about the test when we're driving. Do you want some coffee before we go?"

"Nah, I want to get going. You are going to love this place. I can't wait to show it to you."

"All right, sounds good to me." I was actually quite pleased that she didn't want the coffee. For starters, I was not a coffee drinker. I had never acquired a taste for the bitter flavor. As a small child visiting my mother's work, I drank it in the Styrofoam cups with exorbitant amounts of cream and sugar, perhaps to feel like an adult. But the cream and sugar trick would hardly present a manly image. Not only that, but I didn't want to worry about my breath for the day. "So where is this place you're taking me again?"

"Don't you worry about it. You're going to love it. I go there all the time to look at the little art shops and have tea by the bay. Let's just consider it a surprise—my way of thanking you for helping me study."

I didn't argue. We drove down the 101 toward "the City," as San Francisco is known in northern California. I understand that there are many places referred to as "the City" in America, but it has always seemed funny to me that with all the large cities in California, San Francisco is the only one referred to as "the City." L.A. is, of course, L.A. San Diego is as well known and expensive as S.F., but nowhere near "the City" status.

The 101 was a beautiful and scenic highway by morning light. The scene began as a small, four-lane road heading south with pastures on both sides and cows grazing in abundance for miles toward the horizon. Hailee opened the sunroof, offering a brisk morning breeze and highlighting her dark hair and the metal rim of her sunglasses. I could still smell the faint ocean salinity in the breeze, and the Sonoma aroma of cow manure did not seem as offensive an accent to the scene as one would expect.

We discussed her test from the day before, and to hear her speak of it now, it was hard to believe that she had ever been nervous over it. Apparently almost everything we had covered in our sessions was on the test. The conversation evolved, and she asked where I was in my med school decision.

I had completely forgotten to tell her in the midst of her elation over her test success. Society and propriety teach us not to interrupt each other and to wait our turn to talk. But when I sat with Hailee, this wasn't just another rule to follow. I wasn't simply waiting for my chance to speak. Her voice and smile were so cute and enchanting, like a three-year-old girl singing "Happy Birthday" to herself.

"Oh, my God, that's right. I haven't told you yet. I decided to go to Mon Gracia. I called them yesterday and accepted."

"Oh, Jeff, that's so exciting. How did they sound when you accepted?"

"They sounded very happy and welcoming—which is to say that they told me to make sure the check was filled out correctly and the decimal point was in the correct place. No, I'm kidding. They sounded great. I had no idea who I was talking to, but they made it sound like they remembered me."

"And did you talk to Mina?"

"Yeah, we sorta talked. I just told her I was going down south. I didn't sit down and make plans with her about what we were going to do or anything. We don't even really hang out anymore."

"Okay, don't worry about it at all. It will work out. You don't have to think about it any more today."

We talked casually about our hopes and dreams. Why to treat animals, why to care for sick people, it all seemed so natural to share with her. To this point, I had never spoken so freely with anyone besides Vicki. Yet there was no obligation to impress with anything either of us said; there was no judgment in the voice that would reply. We laughed together over radio morning jokes, we laughed over each other's celebrity impressions, and we laughed over simple roadside advertisements. There was amazing peace in our laughter that morning.

We turned off the freeway just before reaching the Golden Gate Bridge. The road seemed so isolated as it wound under the highway. The entire stream of traffic continued on into the City for the final workday of the week. The absence of cars created a Zen-like silence that I appreciated through the open sunroof. Even the wind, which had previously been quite harsh, now existed only in memory. The fog of the bay mingled with the hills obstructing San Francisco Bay and slid through the valley just above our car. The sunlight was just blocked by the hills, and the mist threatened a chill. Then, as we made the final left turn toward our destination, the solar-powered welcome sign arose from behind those hills. I could see almost nothing for those few minutes. The silhouette of the hills was obscured by the glare of the sun and its reflection off the water. Hailee's secret Garden of Eden was still behind the stage curtain, waiting for her cue.

We pulled into a small parking lot on the northern shore of the bay. Just one car, an exotic BMW, shared the lot with us. I gazed in adoration at the car as Hailee powerfully cranked her stick shift and engaged the emergency brake. She looked over at me, and, with a poetic breath and pause, she said, "Well, here we are. Are you ready to be charmed?"

"I couldn't be more ready," I said.

I can't say that I had ever "strolled" in all of my life before this day. But the setting and the mood made "stroll" the perfect word to describe us that morning. We strolled side by side on the path along the calm shoreline. The choppy waves were but white crests in the distance, and the deep blue that dominated this painting merely caressed the seaside as we walked past. Hailee grasped my shoulder and led me about-face. With her arm steadied on my shoulder, she pointed toward a different part of the bay. Not too far out, toward the mouth of the bay, I saw a few sailboats with their main sails cast.

"That looks wonderful out there," I said. "I would love to sail like that."

"I didn't know you knew how to sail."

"Actually, I don't. I know how to ride on a boat, and that's actually what I like. I'll leave the work of sailing to someone else. I much prefer

29

lying on the front edge of the boat as it glides up and down over the waves."

"That does sound incredible," she agreed, leading me back around toward this little town of Tibouron.

Tibouron was a series of small shops, cafés, and bistros along the bayside, housed in white cottages with gorgeous bay windows that allowed equally beautiful views in and out of the main rooms. The art shop was a tranquil museum of elegant pieces. I had had little exposure to art and culture prior to this, and so I found myself with few intelligent things to say about the paintings other than, "This one's nice." In retrospect, I think I was probably pointing to something the curator's son had painted for her in kindergarten. Afterward, we sat in white wire chairs and gazed over the houses perched atop the hills across the bay in Sausalito. We made a pact that we would each own a home up on that hill one day. Sitting together, in front of such a view, none of our plans seemed unreasonable or out of reach.

"Come on," Hailee said finally. "I have someplace else to show you." She led me back to the car and put a thin scarf over my eyes to obscure my view. "This is a really secret spot that my dad used to take me to when I was a little girl. I haven't been there in forever, but I think I can get there pretty easily."

My heart was racing a bit, but not because I was nervous or scared. The cute games that she was playing and the care that she had taken in planning this day were so romantic, even if we were not romantically involved. My emotions directed my heartbeat like a maestro. As the maestro raised his hands, the power of my cardiac symphony swelled, and the tempo raced. How could I be feeling this when we had shown no romantic interest toward each other? How could the lack of such feelings have gone unnoticed in my relationship with Mina for the past few months? These thoughts seemed destructive, and I buried them for the time in the back of my mind.

A professor would explain that the coast of California had been formed by a cooperative of earthquakes and millennia of waves and rocks crashing against the shore. Earthquakes and waves alone, however, did not seem nearly magical enough to create such a place as Hailee brought me to. She let me gaze off the coast without speaking to me. The car came to rest in front of a quarter-mile stretch of fine sand. "Come on," she said with a quiet giggle.

The sun was touching the horizon. The water lay silently on the bed of sand that had been neatly made for it. The occasional gull swooped down from a distance, plucking some unseen meal from the glassy lagoon. Our bare feet softly trod through the sand on the beach, moving so smoothly that not a single grain flew from our feet as we walked side by side. Whether to blame her or myself, or offer credit to either of us, is ultimately unclear. But in a prolonged period of silence, each of our hands raised ever so slightly to meet. Our fingers interlaced with the subtlest of movements. There was no grappling over position to see who would get the dominant hand position; our hands just met with silent affection. Though I am sure we must have talked about our dreams, about our fears, about whatever, I can only remember the silence that evening when we first held hands.

After reaching the end of the beach, we paused to turn back. Again, I cannot remember if words were interrupted, or just the most intimate thoughts I'd had in years. But in the midst of our turn, our hands released, and our lips joined. *My God, what am I doing?* I thought. No sooner did this thought finish than I realized, *My God, why have I waited so long?*

I opened my eyes just in time to see that hers were still closed and just opening. The sapphire highlights in her eyes and the jet-black cashmere lashes asked questions that her innocent smile answered. Still in silence, our arms wrapped around each other's bodies. She backed herself onto a sandy hill so that her face would be level with my own. We kissed again.

We made our way back to the car with our hands remaining softly grasped. I thought back to many of the conversations that we'd had in the past: the fears of failure we had shared when walking in the rose garden at the university; the concern of losing those close to us that we had shared with one another; and even serving as the cheering section for the other when interviews or final exams neared. They had once been just fleeting thoughts among friends, and now, in retrospect, they were a framework that had been laid within our relationship without our realizing it. Somehow this had been created overnight while we slept. Or maybe these were just excuses for my wanting to take her clothes off right there on the beach. My feelings for her had both immediacy and profundity.

After opening her door for her, I skipped around the back of the car to my side. The clock on the dash read 7:30. We each took a brief cell-phone break. I called my sister to let her know how the day was going and alert her to keep covering for me.

"Hey, Vic," I said as she picked up. "Just wanted to call and say hi and let you know the day went well."

"I'm glad, bro, but Bleshu called about two hours ago and was looking for you."

I thought, *Oh, fuck.* "Bleshu" was Vicki's nickname for Mina. It was an inside joke referring to how long it had taken for Vic to pronounce her last name, and in the interim, it had always sounded like a sneeze. My high school friends had simply called her "Dot" because they couldn't believe I had gone to so much trouble to date an Indian girl. The nicknames never bothered me; they were in good fun and spirit.

"She said your phone must be turned off or something," Vicki explained. "She had been trying to get you on it for a couple of hours to see if you were going to be home for dinner."

"For dinner? Why the hell would she think I was coming back from your place to have dinner up at school?"

"Anyway, I told her you forgot to charge your phone last night and it ran out of batteries while we were at coffee this morning. I also said you had just left a half hour before she called, but that was two hours ago."

"Okay. I'll have to get home pretty soon then, I guess."

"But your day was fun?"

"Amazing," I whispered, shielding the phone from Hailee.

"And she is right there?"

"Yep."

"Well, I want to hear all about it first chance you get to call me," she said. "Love you. Talk to you later."

I looked over at Hailee, but the look of semi-innocent fantasy had disappeared. She was staring at her cell phone as if the voice mail had made some sort of mistake.

"I've had my phone off all day because I didn't want to hear from Dave today," she said. "He left a message around noon saying, 'Hey,' no big deal. But he called back at four asking if I knew where you were. Apparently Mina called him looking for you and made it seem like she thought something was going on between us. She told him that she had followed us once when we took a walk around the duck pond."

"But we didn't do anything at the pond!" I exclaimed, as though it mattered.

Hailee was becoming visibly tense. Her brows furrowed, and then their center lifted in distress. My heart was breaking for her. "He called three more times, saying things like he was coming looking for us, calling me all sorts of names, like slut and whore. Then, in the last one, he just said he was leaving me."

What had I done? She was not like me. Not just a young college student in a relationship that I was bored with. She was in an actual marriage. It seemed so much different from the "steady boyfriend/girlfriend" relationships that come and go.

We were both in shock.

"I have to call him back," she said. "Yes, that's what I have to do. I have to explain." She was rattled. She could barely keep her thoughts coherent.

I was quiet. I considered how much I had already fucked things up for her.

"Wait, Hailee. What are you going to tell him, first?"

"I have to tell him…I, just, um, I have to…I don't know. What do I do, Jeff?" She broke down into long, deep breaths. Her crying words stuttered in an agonizing rhythm.

"Let's just start driving," I said. "We can think on the way." I was already taking for granted that my relationship with Mina was over. That thought wasn't troubling me. Even the despicable nature of my own disloyalty did not bother me as it should have. Hailee was in trouble, and she needed help. She needed someone to step in and help her solve her problem. She needed a hero.

Chapter 3

"Hey, Jeff, it's me, Vic. I just wanted to see how you were settling into your new apartment."

"I'm doing good," I answered. "I picked the place out last week, moved in over the weekend, and now I'm just chilling. It's a great place, just one bedroom and one bath, but the living room is huge. The landlady is this cute old thing who goes to church at Mon Gracia, so she likes to give cheap rent to students there."

"So how did you persuade Dad to let you get the place?"

"I convinced him that this kind of isolation was what I needed in order to study and be successful in medical school."

"Did you mention the part about getting laid?"

"Oh, shit. You know what? I forgot. Do you think I should call him up and mention that?"

"Yeah, right, turkey," she came back. "Speaking of getting laid, whatever happened to Hailee? You told me about the breakup with Bleshu. It sounds like you handled that as best as could be expected. But last I heard of Hailee, she was driving back to Marin after your day together. Did her husband kill her? Come to think of it, did he kill you?"

I heaved a sigh. "So, that was three weeks ago. She went home and found a bunch of her stuff just piled in the entryway of their house. Her husband had gone. He left a note saying they were finished. I was afraid to call her because I might get her in more trouble, but she finally called me two days later. She was obviously really sad when she was talking to me. She just repeated over and over again that she didn't know what she was going to do."

"Oh, that poor girl."

"I had been thinking about how to fix things, so I mentioned that she could come and stay with me in So-Cal. She could finish college nearby and then go up to vet school after she graduated."

"I'm sorry—when did you start smoking crack, and isn't Mon Gracia going to test your piss?"

"I had to help her!" I said. "Then she said it. Over the phone. She said she loved me."

"You didn't say it back, did you?"

"What was I going to say, 'Yeah, most girls do'?"

"Well *do* you love her?" Vicki persisted.

"I might. I'm sure I could. She's a great person! She's beautiful and smart and sweet."

"And married?"

I relented. "I suppose there is that. But we saw each other a couple times in that last week of school. Her husband had left town and hadn't come back yet. We had planned for her to pack up some stuff and come down after I got an apartment set up. She said she would call me."

"Have you heard from her yet?"

"No, not yet. But it took me this long to talk to the admissions people over at U.C. and find out how to get her transferred."

"Okay. I'm sure she's just trying to get things sorted out up here. What about Bleshu? Have you heard from her at all?"

"She graduated with the class like she was scheduled to. She hadn't taken the MCAT, so she couldn't apply to med school yet. We acted polite to each other at graduation, but it was pretty awkward. She said she was going to go down and live with her aunt and uncle in Orange County."

"What is she going to do down there?"

"I couldn't tell ya."

"Well, congratulations again on your graduation, and good luck with med school soon."

"Thanks. There's a Friday night social gathering for our class coming up in a couple weeks. Sort of a chance to meet everyone."

"I know you'll make a great impression. Take care."

We hung up, and I sat there on the couch for a while. I thought about Hailee and the huge conflict we had both faced up in Sonoma and how the struggle had vanished when I moved back down to Southern California. Granted, the peace was just an illusion, because at any moment she could call and say she was coming down. I would have to get her set up in school, get her a job. All these things would have to be done. But she hadn't even called yet. What the fuck was keeping her?

It was midsummer in the Inland Empire, a place second only to perhaps the Sahara Desert in stagnant, dry heat. I soon realized that the apartment's surprising affordability was closely linked to its lack of air-conditioning. Every door and window was open, but I couldn't capture even the slightest breeze. One bright side to the dry heat was that it deterred flies and mosquitoes that would have been abundant in one of the East Coast Ivy League schools. Here, if the flies wandered out of the shade to pester anyone, the heat would most likely zap their little bodies like popcorn in a microwave, leaving only a smoking *Diptera* carcass on the sidewalk. Now, the sidewalk was occupied by the occasional lizard ignoring all recommendations to wear SPF 15, directly leading to the rise in reptilian melanoma.

As I pitied myself in all my sweaty glory, I looked toward the front door. Peering into the relatively cool shade of my living room was a short-haired cat with patchy black and white coloring. She had blue eyes and a tentative yet curious personality. I made all the silly noises one makes to attract kittens, the same sounds construction workers make to attract women on the street, now that I think of it. She humored me briefly, then turned around and left the apartment. I was surprised that a cat would come as close as she did; I had always thought of cats as timid creatures. I never owned one growing up because of my propensity to sneeze around them, but I had not sneezed in the solitary minute that she was here.

Having this longstanding relationship of sixty seconds, I decided I had earned the right to name her. I settled on Lois—Lois Lane, to be specific. But we were on a first-name basis. Lois Lane (the original one, not the furry one) had always possessed a sophisticated beauty that I couldn't resist, and her habit of getting abducted by the nastiest of villains gave Superman ample opportunities to feel needed. A Superman T-shirt had become my good luck charm. I had worn it for my MCAT. When I saw the influence it had exerted over my score, I began wearing it for other tests, and even gave the Oakland Raiders the little edge they needed to win an occasional game. It never came down to it, but I'm sure the president would have felt comforted to know that I had the shirt handy in case he needed some luck in a particularly sticky conundrum. Deep down, I realized that the superpowers were merely fringe benefits of a role that I wanted in order to hook up with Lois (again, the human one). But now that the cat had been dubbed Lois, I had my very own damsel in distress.

The phone rang again. This time, when I picked up the line, the voice on the other end whispered and sobbed, "Jeff?"

"Yeah?" I replied. I couldn't make out the voice because it was so muffled.

"It's Hailee."

"Hailee! I'm so glad to hear your voice. I was getting worried about you, but I didn't want to make things worse by calling you at home."

"How have you been? Did your move go okay?"

"It went fine. But forget about that! Tell me what's been going on," I frantically inquired. "When are you coming down here?"

"Um…that's just it. I've been nervous to call you because I didn't want to hurt you. And Dave…he's been keeping my cell phone from me and checking my email."

"Dave? I thought he was out of the picture!" I shouted. I saw where this was going.

"He came back a couple days after I saw you last, and we talked things through a little. I explained to him why I was so unhappy and why I felt unsupported."

She continued on, and I pictured the dreadful conversation that had taken place. I figured there was a fifty percent chance that he had cheated on her before she and I ever saw each other, and there was a ninety-five percent chance that he cheated before he ever went back to talk to her. I was on the edge of my seat to hear whether he had physically hurt her.

"He told me how bad it made him feel that I could see things in you that I didn't see in him. He said it made him feel angry. Angry, but guilty, too."

This sounded like some crappy ending to a movie that I would have walked out on long before it ended.

"He decided that he would give me another chance if I would never see or talk to you again," she said. "I told him that I wouldn't ever see you, but I didn't think it was fair to leave you completely in the dark by not talking to you ever again."

"I see."

There was no use arguing. This was a marriage, as I once understood it, and I knew that it should be given a chance.

"I still love you, you know," she sobbed.

"Be happy," I whispered. I couldn't prolong the romantic drama that was bringing so much pain to everyone involved. I wanted to say it, but I kept silent. My chest rose and fell deeply, but I held the receiver away from my head.

"Good-bye," I said, and heard her voice softly reply as I lay the phone on its cradle.

I wasn't certain whether I was hurt, angry, or relieved. This would mean I was not starting off med school with a huge dilemma to solve. Sure, I was still an asshole for cheating on my last girlfriend, but I soon convinced myself to let that guilt go. I was not going to be a better person by dwelling on it. I simply resolved to *try* not to cheat on a girlfriend again. But for the time being, I did not have a girlfriend, per se. I did have an opportunity, though—an opportunity to stick my toes in the water without getting completely wet, an opportunity to test-drive the sports car without placing the deposit. I now had an opportunity to meet and date more than one woman. I hadn't had the freedom to do that in years without the associated stigma of being a no-good, two-timing bastard who should do everyone a favor by smashing his balls in the car door, if I have quoted Mina correctly.

All this introspection about my love life was rather awkward. The last time I had been single, I was a sixteen-year-old boy jittering before he passed a note to a girl at the desk next to him. I needed to improve my confidence. I also wanted to improve my look, maybe look like one of those models who overdress for the beach and are always gazing into the distance at something slightly above the horizon. This seemed like the perfect time to make that kind of a change. It had always bugged me the way people would react to slight changes in anyone's appearance. I could see it almost certainly bringing out my insecurities. These insecurities had meant the end for any short-lived fashion statements I had tried to make in the past. I had noticed how rare it was that people might comment, "Hey, you look good with that new goatee." The more likely remark was, "Are you trying to grow a goatee?" People felt more comfortable with the status quo.

One week before the medical class gathering, I decided to venture out into town as the new me. "Med student Jeff" began the evening by walking down the Thursday-night street market that the "old Jeff" had last walked four years earlier. The valley heat had subsided for the evening as the sun dropped down over the mall to the west. I started at one end, walking slowly and noticing how different I felt.

I wore faded jeans, a black shirt buttoned well below the collar to show the color of the shirt beneath, and new boots. The boots weren't very comfortable, but the smooth black leather and the precise lines of the shoe complimented the jeans the way a bit of eye-liner can make the average lady stunning. The salesman promised me that I looked nothing like a cowboy, and that the boots were the latest thing in "urban sophisticate," whatever that was.

The small town usually allowed one or two bands per week to set up and play for the passersby. Tonight two guys were playing acoustic guitars and singing various songs by Journey and Phil Collins. The strumming melodies offered a refreshing trip back to the '80s, but each time the short, balding singer stepped to the microphone to sing, the speakers would screech. The Humane Society had brought out dogs for adoption that were each sitting in a cage to pet. As the feedback reverberated from the stage, the dogs began to howl in harmony about ten yards away. The mongrel and the basset hound were more in tune than the stage musicians, but with the next chorus, I turned my head away, quickly covering up my ears. I almost bumped heads with a girl making the same getaway.

"I think I would stick to the guitar if I were baldy up there," she said, looking up.

Within a second, a string on one of the guitars broke, leaving the twang reverberating in the speakers.

"Or maybe take up the tuba," I said, smiling and winking at her.

Our conversation started there, with introductions and such. Her name was Brooke, and she was a student at the local university and had been in town for about three years from San Diego. We had both come to the market with only a scant game plan. One has to wonder whether girls go to such events to gaze at everything or to be gazed at. In a black tank top and skin-tight jeans, this girl had to be aware that she was the object of attention for many.

"Hey, let's grab a drink," she said.

"You're not suggesting I steal the water from this cute puppy, are you?" I said with a smirk.

"No, there's a bar around the corner, and you're going to buy me a beer."

"Did I just get picked up by a strange girl on the street?" I asked rhetorically.

"Be careful that I don't slip something into your drink..."

The bar was actually a local brewery with huge vats, presumably full of beer, decorating the dining area. We sat on an upper level looking out the window over the street crowd we had just escaped. Modern jazz music played over speakers, a bit more loudly than was comfortable for conversation. Most of the clientele consisted of college frat boys who seemed to ignore it without missing a beat.

Brooke had naturally dark hair with a light streak woven into the left side. She would pull her hair to the side before she took each drink, never sipping. It was ironic that I was so amused by her style of drinking the beer, because I had never been a beer aficionado. But she was novel and gorgeous but unpolished. How someone as thin as Brooke could drink so unabatedly was beyond my comprehension. She drank with a seductive style. Leaning back ever so slightly, she extended her neck as the ale flowed between her lips. With her last drink, the foam lining the rim of her glass dropped to her chest, just above her cleavage. She giggled.

"So are you going to show me where you live, or not?" she asked with another giggle.

"You want to see my apartment?" I said in about the least cool voice I could have planned.

"I've never seen a real doctor's apartment before."

"No, I told you I'm a medical student. Not a doctor yet."

"I know. But you should let a girl have her fantasies."

Who was I to argue?

We walked over to my car and drove to the apartment. I feared that the sight of my low-budget apartment would scare her off, but I decided to play up the struggling student role. I opened the door to let her in, and she brushed past me while grabbing me by the arm. She pulled me inside and stared at me. "Yeah, this looks like a doctor's apartment."

God, I hope not, I thought. But she hadn't looked at anything. She was just staring at me. By now, the trendy stripe through her hair was driving me wild, to say nothing about the tank top. She pressed against me with her breasts bulging up from her shirt.

"What kinds of stuff do doctors know about how to turn a woman on?" she whispered.

I was floored. I wondered how I could have missed opportunities like this all these past years.

"I'll let you in on a little secret of the profession," I whispered as I leaned around to her ear. "We have skills that the average human does not possess. Talents and moves. The textbooks warn us to use them with discretion. But I never studied that section on discretion too hard."

She turned her head and kissed my cheek, leaving it subtly wet. She slowly unbuttoned the top three buttons of her jeans, revealing her tanned midriff. "Then here is your first anatomy lesson, Doctor," she said in a breathy voice followed by a giggle.

I imagined a soft-core pornographic scene, where she might do a complete striptease. But instead she pounced on me, pushing me to the couch. Her knees straddled me as she bent over, kissing me. She grasped the hairs on the back of my scalp and placed her lips before me, silently demanding that I kiss her. That moment, and the entire evening, for that matter, was completely surreal. It twice occurred to me that I was making out with a girl I had just met, but we were being far more passionate than I had been with Mina in over a year. Those were quickly fleeting thoughts, though. I focused on the present.

Brooke stood back up and took off her shirt. I couldn't believe it; the girl in the black tank top was no longer in her tank top. Underneath, she wore a sheer satin bra, without all that padding that so many girls wore. The contour of her nipples was evident when she turned toward the kitchen and the light struck just so. "Is your room back here?"

Her jeans were still undone, but the back clung to her buttocks as though the material had the same relentless lust for her that I felt. She showed herself through the apartment, kicking her black sandals off in the kitchen as she passed. "Don't keep me waiting, Doctor," she said. "You don't want an impatient patient."

I hopped to my feet and ran to catch up to her. I quickly ripped my shirt over my head and wrapped her in my arms and the shirt. She turned, bound by my shirt only, and removed her bra. While her breasts had looked amazing in her top, they were the image of perfection exposed. The muscle tone of her chest created exquisite lines that her amber skin followed. Her nipples were no longer subtle, and my forehead brushed briskly against one as I dropped to my knees. I held her butt firmly below the pockets while kissing her abdomen down between her opened zipper. And then, by those same pockets, I pulled her jeans down to her ankles. It was surprisingly easy, considering how tightly they had clung earlier.

She fell to her knees to meet me as we kissed each other on whatever parts presented themselves. To stand would have been too great an interruption, so we crawled over ourselves to reach the bed. I was flat on my back, staring at her straddling me again. Either I had inadvertently pulled her panties off with her jeans, or she hadn't been wearing any to begin with. I know it seems moot that she was bare beneath the denim, now that she was completely nude on top of me, but thinking of our earlier moments in the new context made this moment all the more erotic.

Her moaning and screaming were incredible turn-ons. Most girls I knew were too embarrassed to verbalize their feelings during sex, but she was above any shyness. I initially wondered if the neighbors, the Adventist grandchildren of my landlord, could hear us. After a few minutes, I made myself ignore the obvious fact that they could certainly hear us.

We collapsed with a collective sigh.

I awoke around 3:30 a.m. to find her in a slight panic. "Shit," she exclaimed. "I was supposed to finish a paper for class tomorrow. I was going to do that after the market. But I got…distracted, I guess."

"Yeah, I guess you could say that's what we got tonight."

"That was fucking incredible," she said. "But I need you to get me back to my car so I can go finish my paper before morning."

At the parking lot, we stopped next to her Honda Civic. She opened the door and wrote her number down as she got out. She bent back down into the car and kissed me. "You'll call me, won't you?"

"Of course. How about this weekend?"

"Perfect."

She walked around to my door and kissed my lips, sucking my bottom lip slightly, like only those few girls know how to do. She got into her car and drove away.

On my way home, I thought about how strange it was that we had done all that after meeting only a few hours before. Actually, I didn't even know what she was studying in school. There was a sense of loss when I realized that I had just entered another relationship that I would likely be committed to for at least a little while. But she was stunningly beautiful, and funny and…

Wait, I thought, *I didn't get her number.*

"She wrote it down," I argued with myself aloud. "I saw her! She wrote it down. You must be fucking joking! It blew out the window?" I half-laughed, banging my head against the steering wheel.

It had been a dreamlike evening, and I knew when I didn't call her, she would take it as a brush-off. A girl like that wouldn't come checking up on me at the apartment to make sure I hadn't forgotten her. I had gone out tonight a single man, and I slipped back into bed a single man again.

In the world of science, researchers observe what happens and make conclusions about the way things are or how they work. They can't be completely certain that it wasn't a fluke observation that is not likely to happen again for a million years. Of course, scientists try to avoid this problem by repeating the experiment or observation many times. The number of observations is called the N of the study.

My observation was that the new Jeff image was magical in its influence on the ladies. Unfortunately, my N was 1. Such a small N is often the reason for the erroneous findings of some research studies that make the 6:00 news. "Passing gas thirty times or more daily found to decrease risk of colon cancer—story after this..." It is extremely easy to believe the results of such an N when *you* are the N.

So, whether substantiated or not, I adopted my new style more or less permanently. I began to focus more on fashion than on merely spelling it correctly, if ever forced. I went so far as to begin reading men's fashion magazines, like *GQ*, even when no woman was exposing her seductive grin on the cover.

Friday, a week later, I wound my Camaro up the hills of the suburb, driving with the printed directions in my hand. This was the geographic/geologic feature that had separated the rich kids from the poor kids when I had attended elementary school there so many years ago. I had some friends who lived up the hill, whose parents were doctors, ironically enough. I always wanted to spend the night at one particular friend's house because his father drove a Porsche 928. It was a unique automobile of beauty and power, whose rear bumper, with its graceful curvature, resembled a lady's rump. Tom Cruise took one such car for a joy ride in *Risky Business*. This guy's father was an "oto-rino-larin-gologist" as he loved to repeatedly point out to me. As a fourth grader, I grew tired of hearing about how much his dad made as this mysterious specialist. After many years, I would come to find out that it was actually spelled otorhinolaryngologist. And that no one actually said otorhinolaryngologist, but rather "ENT"—or just ear, nose, and throat doctor, for God's sake, which is what they fucking are. That bastard kid on the hill could have just said ear, nose, and throat doc. But he refused to say anything other than oto-whatever-the-fuck. He probably did it just so his dad wouldn't sound like he picked boogers for a living.

I'll admit, even after fifteen years, the trees seemed just a bit more lush on the hill than they did near my home. Through some of the orange groves, now in full bloom, I could make out one of the historic landmarks of the town, an extravagant mansion owned by the founder of the town over a hundred years earlier. The house, with its Victorian motif and multiple windows in each tower, was named after him, as was the elementary school up the hill. I have always been fascinated by houses with proper names like his. But more interesting about this house was that it had been featured in several horror movies in the '80s, when the genre was so popular. Tonight, the turret of the guest bedroom peeked over the orange trees, and I could barely make out the Victorian trim in the dim moonlight.

Although the directions made no specific reference to it, as I pulled up the street and saw the cars lined up for blocks, it became apparent that the Deans' house sat directly across the street from the playground where I had once played dodge ball.

I was at least five minutes early, as was my obsession, but in this case it looked like half my new class shared the same habit. Seeing the trail of cars extending off farther than I cared to walk, I doubled back and parked in the school lot. I stepped out of the car and decided to undo one extra button on my outer shirt, revealing a tight gray T-shirt underneath. The pants were a charcoal shade, which complemented the T-shirt and created what I thought was a modern tone for the outfit.

I took a deep breath and headed toward the house. Just as I stepped around the back of my car, another car, a white Honda, pulled up next to me. Out of it came quite a surprise—an old friend of mine, a teammate from my soccer days in high school.

"Mike!" I blurted. "How the fuck are you?"

"Jeff? Are you coming to the dinner over here?" He sounded as puzzled as excited.

"Yeah, man," I said, sidling up next to him with a manly hug.

"I didn't hear you were going to be in the class."

"Yeah. Comin' back home to So-Cal. It feels good, let me tell you. How about you? I didn't even know you were going premed. Where did you do your undergrad? Did you play soccer?" I rattled off.

Mike had been one of the star players on the soccer team that had comprised the pinnacle of my athletic career. He had been as fast as an eagle when he ran up and down the field with the ball. I had been the goalie for this team for as long as I could remember, and as such, speed was never my forte. But Mike's speed and agility on the field had taken us to several tournaments around the world.

"Yeah, premed up at Northwestern. Didn't play any soccer, though. You know what the academic schedule is like."

I wasn't certain where Northwestern was, specifically. But I had heard of it from sports on TV and thought they had a pretty good academic reputation. Not wanting to sound foolish, I withheld any other questions I had about his alma mater.

"You know who else is going to be in our class?" he quizzed me. "Ronny."

"Really? Wow, this is amazing. I never expected so many people from our high school would be coming back for medical school. It's almost weird."

We walked up to the house. The path was lined with paper bags illuminated by candles. The mood was a quaint medley of Chinese Feng Shui and preadolescent lunches. Inside the house, the stereo softly played some Top 40 hit, and voices could be heard easily above the tune. The door was wide open as we stepped onto the porch. A large portion of the fifty or so people were congregated in the entryway.

"Jeff! I'm glad to see you here tonight, and we're glad to have you in the class." A man in a blazer made his way through the clutter of jeans-and-T-shirt students. Initially I didn't recognize him, but as I reflected on the nice welcome he had given me, I had a flash of recollection.

"Dr. Johnson. Thank you. I'm happy to be here, too, sir." I thought back to the crinkle he'd had in his left brow when he'd asked me to explain myself in that interview months ago. Everyone I had told the story to afterward was horrified by the fact that anyone would ask such a question, but I saw the interaction as a personal victory in the game of B.S.

He walked toward me and turned as he came close, shaking my hand and putting his arm around me. "Let me show you around. I'll introduce you to everyone." His hand fell in the center of my back between my shoulder blades, and he led me in this fashion around the house, introducing me to another student here and there. "I'm truly excited about this year's class. We have 160 students, one of our largest classes ever. I personally interviewed most of them, and I know that we have the top students from each of our Adventist universities. I think this will be one of our strongest groups ever, and I think you'll like everyone."

The enthusiasm in his voice was so intense that I actually abandoned the idea that they had just accepted me under the presumption that I would choose somewhere else or that God would cause the Earth to swallow me up before the first day of class.

"This is my wife, Jill," he said. "She is responsible for the wonderful dinner tonight. Jill, this is Jeff Triton. He grew up here in Redlands and is going to be in our freshman class this year."

His wife was the quintessential June Cleaver of the house. Dressed in a white lace apron and a light blue skirt down to her ankles, she mingled with the guests only to the extent that they lingered around the kitchen and buffet table. "How nice it is to meet you, Jeff," she said. "I hope you like dinner tonight; we're having haystacks."

I had no idea what a haystack was in a culinary context. It didn't sound like a delicacy, but I didn't want to be too quick to judge, either. Maybe I had misheard her. Of course, none of the other enunciations I could come up with, gay snacks or stray cats, sounded very appetizing, either. Then the predicament of a vegetarian medical school crossed my mind again. *Jesus, this could be some sort of initiation rite into a vegetarian religion where they actually feed me grass.* I kept both my ignorance and fear to myself.

"That sounds great, Mrs. Johnson."

By now, the masses were huddling around the front of the food table. I wiggled into a small group of students that I recognized from a weeklong medical orientation I had attended a few weeks prior.

"So when are they bringing the food out?" one of the five in our huddle asked.

"I heard pretty soon," another answered.

"I think we're having haystacks," the first said.

"Cool," a third added.

I was certain that I had heard them correctly this time. *Haystacks.* Even if the name was just a quirky eponym referring to the way it looked,

I did not see anything appealing likely being served with such an alias. "Oh, you guys have heard of haystacks?" I asked unapologetically.

"Yeah. You haven't heard of haystacks?" said the first guy, whom I later remembered was named Bill.

"No. Where would I have heard of it before?"

"I just thought everyone ate them. They serve 'em all the time at Vespers or Sabbath lunch."

I ignored the fact that I didn't know what Vespers was, or even what he meant by "Sabbath lunch." By this point, I didn't know whether I seemed naïve or illiterate. "So what are they?"

"They're like nachos," Bill said, "but they're Fritos with beans and cheese and salsa. They're awesome. You'll love 'em."

One of the other guys piped up with great fervor. "And sometimes they serve it with chili or guacamole."

"Oh," I replied, "so it's not like a real meal. It's more like an appetizer, then, huh?"

Bill looked puzzled and hesitated for a few seconds. "No, it's a whole meal."

I began contemplating an In-N-Out burger trip after the gathering.

June, or Jill, I guess her name actually was, walked in with her arms barely able to reach around the enormous bowl of Fritos she carried. Dr. Johnson followed her in with a slightly less impressive bowl of chili. In their finest China bowls next to the chips were mounds of lettuce, cheese, and sour cream, all with much more pride in their image than they deserved.

After serving ourselves, we funneled outside onto the patio, where chairs were arranged in a large circle. The patio lights were on, but some lunch-bag candles had also been scattered around the pool. My paper plate had sparse dollops of chili and bean dip, with some Fritos strewn haphazardly about. I had already sat down with my pathetic serving as all the Fritophiles reached over one another like animals crowding around the same watering hole, albeit rather polite animals. Unlike my own, their plates sagged in the middle or at least to one side, as they accumulated mountainous piles of chili and beans and avocado and cheese overflowing their concoctions. Their Frito portions were no less ample, but decorated the mountains as though the entire plate was a fourth-grade art project. They clearly couldn't wait to get this bonanza of junk food into their stomachs, chomping all the way as they sat down next to me.

I casually watched as my new colleagues made their way toward the poolside dining area. Most everyone appeared to be an average generation-*X*er. The sight of any of us on the street would not bring to mind the title MD or even MD2B. But each of us had that special gleam in our eye that suggested this would be a pleasant year. Admittedly, my attention was centered primarily on the female members of our class, who seemed to make up at least seventy percent of the crew. Who knew what to expect? Would they fit the paradigm of hypereducated, homely girls who would rather flirt with a textbook than with a guy? Or would they emulate their soap-opera role models from childhood, tempting surgeons and patients alike? At first glance, they seemed a modest compromise of the two. *Damn it.* I was instantly attracted to the girl-next-door quality many of them had. These were the kinds of girls you could take home to Mama, but deep down, you wanted to ask, "Who's your daddy?"

Bill sat down next to me. "Dude, is that all you're going to eat?"

I shrugged. "Yeah, I guess I had a late lunch or something."

"I don't know. It looks like you eat like a chick."

"Okay, everyone!" Dr. Johnson announced, standing in the center of the circle. "My family and I would like to welcome you to our home. This is our favorite part of every year as we get a chance to personally meet the students who are going to be such a big part of our lives for the next four years. I like to start off such an occasion by thanking the Lord for such amazing blessings. So if you would join me in a quick prayer…"

He made the request with such a matter-of-fact tone that I was stunned. My last pre-meal prayer had been said four years earlier as a habitual recitation by my mentally retarded sister. It was always succinct: "God is great, God is good, now we thank him for our food. Amen." The prayer served as more of a gesture of including Nancy in the mealtime ceremony than it was a ritual of devout faith. In fact, Nancy's style of speech made the entire blessing sound more like Louis Armstrong scat-singing the blues: "Dah-du-Daa Du-dah Duh-du…Aaahhh men." Thinking back on those quirky family moments still brings a smile to my face years later.

The solemn way Dr. Johnson bowed his head and the immediate silence that fell among us all was a stark contrast to the Dr. Seuss prayers I was used to.

"Lord…" He paused for effect, or possibly waiting for God to tune in to the correct station. "We want to thank you for our many blessings. Most importantly, I want to thank you for bringing together such a tremendous group of young people, and gathering them with the ambition to do your work. I sense, as I know you do, Lord, that these students have the spirit within them, and possess both the mind and heart to work miracles. Please bless these young people as they set about on a new journey, a new journey into the world of healing, a new journey that they take in your shadow. Please guide me to help them with their journey through medical school, and please bless their journey as you bless this food. In Jesus' name we pray. Amen."

I was completely aghast. I felt like the poor schmuck who thinks he was invited to a party but finds out once he arrives that it's a funeral.

"Amen," the circle echoed in unison, and then went on about the business of eating as though everything had been according to protocol. The rest of the evening was normal to the casual observer: conversation, laughter, and innocent cake and ice-cream desserts. After a not-so-quick closing prayer with a tone similar to the first, we went our separate directions.

Despite my feeling underdressed and over-blessed in light of the mood, I was excited about the class I was in and saw good things to come. The charbroiled burger that I had contemplated earlier was to come first, but there would be more intellectual achievements to come in the days following.

Chapter 4

There is a ritual in America. Many complain that this ritual is commercialized by corporations trying to make a buck off children about to begin the new school year. For at least a week before they actually trod into their tiny classrooms with the alphabet strewn across the front wall, every child actively pulls his mom into the local market to buy the latest Trapper Keeper or the biggest box of Crayolas his backpack can hold. What boy ever actually used the organizational qualities and subdivisions of his state-of-the-art Trapper Keeper, I will never know. But everyone got their "necessities" before school. But while corporate America is somewhat to blame now, the initial act of deviousness that turned this into a national shopping week was almost certainly committed by parents hundreds of years ago in the colonial days, I speculated. While deceptive, it was truly a stroke of genius to create this annual tradition that would make kids actually want to go to school. These poor kids get excited about the impending torture they will endure for the academic year.

And I fell victim again, becoming as excited and optimistic about the school year as I could be. It was Monday morning, and I was dressed and ready to go an hour early.

The classroom was a daunting amphitheater, able to house approximately 300 people. Chalkboards, whiteboards, and projector screens adorned the front of the room. My phobia of being late put me in a position to watch everyone come in. They still looked quite ordinary in the face of this promotion to professional-medical-student status.

I was surprised to find that jeans and a T-shirt was still the uniform of choice, as opposed to the shirt, tie, and white coat the movies portrayed. As at the party a few nights before, multiple huddles formed and reformed as everyone mingled.

Eavesdropping on the conversations was far more interesting than simply people-watching. The names of four or five schools kept being uttered amongst the chit-chat. These were the main Adventist colleges that fed into Mon Gracia.

One girl I noticed particularly, talking to four other girls about their respective alma maters. "You went to Southern Union? I had a friend who went there! Do you know Christina Friedman?"

"Yeah, she was in my O-Chem class. Did you know she was dating Jim Sheppard?"

"Yep. And that was after she broke up with…who was over at… Union College." And so the chatter went for fifteen minutes or so.

As 8:00 approached, groups disbanded and people dispersed more or less evenly throughout the room. The girl I had noticed sat down next to me and whispered, "Do you think they'll go easy on us the first day?"

"If they don't, I'll probably start crying before lunch," I said over my shoulder. "I'm Jeff, by the way."

"Oh, nice to meet you. I'm Jess. Are you from around here?"

"Actually, yes. I grew up ten minutes from here."

"Wow. That's awesome. I just got an apartment out there. It seems like a great town."

"It got the job done. How about you? Where are you from?" I asked. We were still whispering at the time.

The professor stood at the front of the lecture hall, apparently collecting his paperwork for class. He hadn't spoken a word, but class was in session as far as the nervous audience was concerned.

"I'm from Ohio," she said. "I went to school up at PUC."

I played this off as though I knew where this was. When someone says they went to USC, John Q. Public has the general idea that it's in L.A., even if he doesn't realize that it's in the ghetto section of Watts.

"Where did you go to school?" she asked.

"Oh, I was up in Sonoma."

"Really? You went to PUC, too?"

"No, I went to Sonoma State."

"Oh, that's right. I guess I heard that there was another college nearby. PUC is right there in Sonoma," she explained, trying to convince me. But it was ironic. We had each attended a school for the past four years trying to broaden our minds, and the idea of another campus of students with a moderately different outlook was almost treated as mythology.

I felt smitten with Jess soon after I met her. She had a confident demeanor, yet a subtle way of making herself noticed. The beauty of her face, her satin cheeks, her sage-green eyes, and her playful smile needed no makeup to accentuate them. I would later learn the fortuity of this fact, as the Adventist Church does not allow its members to wear any. She was as naïve about my heathen ways as I was about the extent of her piety.

"Sonoma State...what religion is that?" she inquired.

"Mmm...it's pretty much just regular," I answered tentatively.

"Yeah, just a regular Christian school. That would be kinda weird, to have two SDA universities that close to each other."

By now I knew that "SDA" was shorthand for Seventh Day Adventist. I let her subtle misinterpretation slip by without a comment.

"Do you know what the ratio of Adventist to non-Adventists is in our class?" she asked.

"No, I haven't heard," I said. I hadn't imagined they would calculate, let alone publish, such numbers. But she continued on with brazen certainty.

"I heard that it's just 45% SDA and fifty-something percent non-SDA. And someone said that there's actually an atheist in the class."

"Really?" I said, with all the feigned surprise I could muster. "Like an actual atheist? Who doesn't believe in *any* God?"

"I know. Can you believe it?" she said with her eyes wide and her brows raised in disbelief. "I don't know who it is, but I'm dying to find out."

"Well, let me know when you find him," I said. "Or her," I tacked on for the added anonymity.

By this time, the professor stood intently in front of us all. His papers were finally in order. Teaching the anatomy course seemed like a last-minute idea for him. He tapped his podium microphone as an awkward first-time politician might and welcomed us.

"Before the morning's lectures begin," he spoke in a monotone voice, "a student in our class has offered to give the opening prayer."

I would have been a fool not to expect an opening prayer, considering the previous acts of nacho blessing. But I had expected the professors to be more single-minded toward the coursework than to worry about a pre-lecture prayer.

Down the left aisle walked a guy who seemed the complete antithesis of either a medical student or a minister. He wore a hot-pink T-shirt and khaki shorts. His most prominent feature was the long blonde hair dangling halfway down his back, slight curls just waiting for an '80s rock song to flail to. He had a goatee and a tan, which fit more with Maui than Mon Gracia. He so epitomized the rocker image over the sacred image that I would remember him only as Slash for years to come. Slash stepped up behind the podium and introduced himself.

"Hi, everyone. I wanted to talk to you all this morning to let you know how grateful I am to be with you here today, to let you know what path I've taken to get here so that maybe you could come to the same understanding of God's power and workings as I have."

What is it that they say about a book and its cover?

"About five years ago, I wasn't thinking about medicine. I wasn't thinking about God. Man, I wasn't even thinking about me. I was a guitarist in a rock band that was traveling around, playing in small bars night after night. We were pretty good. I was having a great time. I would play the gig, then get drunk backstage or party in the hotel room. Sometimes I wouldn't even wait to get off stage to get hammered. There would be women and drugs in the hotel waiting for me. Every night I would give in to one vice or another, whether it was the beer or the cocaine. Half the time, I wouldn't remember the night before. The other half, I wished I couldn't."

His voice was peaceful as he recounted his adventures. "Then one night, which wasn't that much different from any of the other nights, whatever combination of sex, drugs, and alcohol I had hit me particularly hard. I just remember opening my eyes, probably hours after the party had ended. The morning sun was bright behind the black curtains. I had preemptively drawn them to keep out any light I could. And I swear…as I woke, I thought I was dead. I remember this distinct feeling that I had no distinct feeling. I didn't feel like I was there…and maybe I wasn't. I remember thinking, *How empty and worthless this life is. If I'm not dead, I wish someone would just let me die now*."

I was surprised by the casual way he spoke in front of us all. He was essentially admitting to acts that I had never met anyone guilty of. I had never known anyone who would know where to get cocaine, even if they wanted it. But the peace behind his voice and the confidence and necessity of his words were calming. The rest of the class seemed as enthralled by his speech as I was. Looks of sympathy rather than abhorrence crossed most faces.

"I lay there frustrated over the misery I was feeling at that moment," he continued. "I cursed everyone for the unfair life I'd had before then: a mom who was an alcoholic who didn't care about me, and a father who had left us both. This misery inspired apathy, and I just said, 'Screw it! If this is what my life is, then I don't even care.' I could barely move—just enough to look around and see that my head was next to a large puddle of vomit. I couldn't even be sure it was mine. But apathy soon turned to desperation. I asked myself, 'What have I become? What is this? What am I doing to myself?' I just wanted out of this emptiness as I hoped for death, the only salvation likely to take me at that moment."

The room was so silent, I thought I could hear someone blink in the back row during his pause.

"Just then, I turned my head away from the puke and saw this book lying underneath the table." He raised a Gideon Bible in his hand. "At this point, I felt completely hopeless. Almost from nowhere, I decided to give the book one chance to speak to me. I know I must have had a Bible in my house growing up, but in all those years, I never picked one up. I had never picked one up and just started reading it. And that's what I did that night on that motel floor. I opened it up and just started reading."

He could have easily been a televangelist or one of those *Five Steps to Change Your Life* motivational speakers, considering his presence and inflections.

"With each passage, I found myself having just a little more hope. I found words of a God who cares about me so much that he would give his own son in sacrifice. A God who loved me, even as I lay there in my own puke. I read that Bible for hours that morning. I knew from that moment that I needed to do something more. I knew that I needed to further my understandings of this man, Jesus. And in learning of him, I've come to believe in my calling as a healer, too."

Several responded with nods in the front rows.

"So I stand here, alive, because of *this* book. This has been my inspiration to be a healer, as I know it's been an inspiration for many of you. But I wanted to share my story and thank God in front of you all for the many blessings He has given me. And to ask His blessings for us all as we try to accomplish His mission and carry on His teachings. This I ask in Jesus' name. Amen."

Slash walked up the aisle toward a seat near the back, where his backpack lay on the floor. Almost every head was bowed, apparently in prayer, as he passed. The physical resemblance of Slash to Jesus himself, with his scraggly image, was uncanny, considering I hadn't noticed it before. His nickname would remain Slash, as not even I was so heretical as to nickname a classmate Jesus.

Before long, the professor replaced Slash at the podium, and we were jumping right into the subject of anatomy. No more pomp and circumstance, no "welcome to your calling," not even a quick reference to the Hippocratic oath.

The lectures were filled with innumerable references to proper names for vessels and nerves depicted by lines on the diagram that were indistinguishable from one another. I felt comforted by the idea that they couldn't possibly expect us to remember those names for the test, and I abstained from taking a single note.

After an hour of red and blue lines, we were dismissed to the anatomy lab. The first day in the lab was a wake-up call. The bodies lay on aluminum tables, four feet apart. The skulls had been cut open, the brains removed, and the faces neatly covered with a moist cloth. The smell of such a laboratory is far more traumatic to the unfamiliar than the sight of the dead bodies. The formaldehyde used to preserve the bodies possesses an odor that would be easily recognized even by those who have only wafted it once. It has a sour, bitter essence that sticks to the mucosa inside the nose. The smell entrenched itself into my nose and clothing long after I left the lab, like the rank stench of old tobacco on a smoking jacket.

Bill, from the previous Friday, was next to me in the alphabet. We bonded well within our group of four lab partners. Of our group, Mike clearly had the most talent in the realm of academia. He had attended a Christian college a few hours away in Southern California, but had a competitive drive to match his Christian compassion. The three of us divvied up the responsibilities of dissection, each hesitating as he attempted to follow the step-by-step instructions of the instructor. The fourth member of our group was a shy Asian girl who soon decided that medicine was not for her and dropped out.

The most sophisticated dissection I had performed prior to this was on a cat in college. The cat had been injected with red and blue latex, leaving his arteries and veins colorful and obvious, bearing a little more resemblance to the cartoonish illustrations I had seen. Such luxuries were long past. Arteries, veins, and nerves all looked like randomly dispersed dental floss.

Each of the cadavers had an interesting history of some sort. They had been donated to the school, often after dying in the adjoining hospital. Our cadaver, affectionately named Jesse the Body, had died of melanoma, a malignant skin cancer. His disease led to many interesting discoveries as we dissected different parts of Jesse's anatomy throughout the year. The cancer had spread to different parts of his body and seemingly consumed it. Pea-sized nodules speckled his lungs and liver like tapioca pudding. Even more unique to our virgin eyes was the fact that the cancer had impaired Jesse's ability to get an erection. Before the days of Viagra, Jesse had done what any man would do and opted for a surgical implant. The complicated-sounding machinery appeared to be nothing more than a flexi-straw attached to the bulb of a turkey baster. But after the hours that we spent with Jesse, we gained a sort of appreciation and familiarity with him. His imperfections weren't flaws but rather unique traits that we all had. All except for the flexi-straw in the schlong.

The first unofficial study session was Wednesday, 5:00 sharp, and we each showed up with our backpacks in tow. We agreed to base the night's practice session on Jesse's body. I hadn't realized that the roommate Mike had mentioned bringing was Slash, who showed up in his same California surfer garb. The two pulled out their textbooks and folders of handwritten notes, which had already grown to enormous proportions. I pulled the cloth from Jesse, and the quizzing began. It started out harmlessly enough. I correctly named some of the obvious structures, like the internal and external carotid arteries. The vagus nerve, which runs down the neck and supplies most of the body, runs conspicuously next to it, and I was thankfully able to identify it when they read it from the list.

That's when my dismay began. They began reading further down their independently constructed list, and I found myself able to do little more than watch with my eyebrows furrowed as each of them challenged the other with anatomical obscurities.

"What's this?" Mike said, looking up at me directly.

I stared back at him blankly, like a Saint Bernard competing on *Jeopardy*. "I don't know, man," I said with frustration.

He turned his head toward Slash. "What do you think?"

"Thoracodorsal nerve," Slash said simply.

"Right."

I shrugged my shoulders.

"What about this one?" Mike quizzed.

"Umm. Anterior scalene?" I offered tentatively.

"Nah, that's the sternocleidomastoid," Slash piped in.

"Fuck! I knew that." I sighed. Their ability to identify these obscure pieces seemed like overkill. Why would the professors ask us about such trivia? Surely they just wanted us to know the basics, the things we might see every day in practice. But these guys kept asking a barrage of questions, and I couldn't answer more than a few. To my credit, though, I did remember that the human head weighs eight pounds.

It was becoming clear that, at least among this "elite" crowd, I was a loser. I hung in there.

"How about this?" Slash asked.

I shook my head. "I haven't got a clue. Are you sure we're supposed to know that?" I was starting to wonder if I had been mistaken in throwing away what I thought was dental floss earlier. It was probably some vital organ that was going to be on the final exam.

"Yeah, man, that's the intercostovertebral artery," Slash came back.

I vaguely remembered hearing such a name before. That realization brought fear and frustration rapidly to my heart. "Goddamn it!" I exclaimed. "I can't remember any of this crap."

Mike and Slash stepped back from the cadaver, as though they expected lightning to strike me down right there, regardless of who else it might take. They looked at me as though I had spoken another language. And in some views, I had.

"You don't have to swear, man," Mike said.

"Yeah, it's not that big a deal," Slash echoed.

"Huh?" I asked, not even considering my language to have a PG rating.

"Why are you swearing?" Mike asked.

I was in another world. Deep down, I knew they were right. It wasn't *that* big a deal. But then again, neither was a *shit, fuck,* or *damn it*. I apologized, and we continued for a while longer, but still on the same course. They continued to pull out the minutiae from the text, but I had an understanding of the big picture, what I would need to truly grasp medical school. I left them for the evening to continue my studying at home and get an early night's sleep.

The next morning, I migrated toward the front of the class to interact a little more with the professors and make a good impression. I continued to watch the cute females in the class, of which there were many. I always had a chance to mingle between lectures, but I wanted to learn by any means possible. And if one is to truly utilize the powers of osmosis, one has to decrease the distance between the source of the information and the receiver.

In this setting, I found myself sitting within a smaller group of students, who seemed a bit more parochial even than my previous acquaintances. One girl within the group was particularly intelligent. Her notes were as pristine and organized as the Library of Congress, which was ironic because she never needed to reference them. In class, her head remained buried in the folder as the professor talked, and often her notes preceded his lecture. The only time she raised her head was to answer a question, sometimes even the rhetorical ones. When she did this, she anxiously raised her hand, and when she was called on, she batted her eyelashes feverishly before answering. I had heard that some method actors flirt with the camera to create a mood for specific scenes. Her subconscious eye flutter almost seemed to set the stage for her Bette Davis–like performance as she displayed her brilliance.

Another chap sitting in that left front corner of the room was a lanky Asian boy named Jim. While it was perhaps unfair to call him a boy if he'd made it this far academically, his demeanor and personality were so naïve and innocent that it seemed fitting. He reminded me of a six-year-old boy who sticks his head out the back window of a car, unbeknownst to his parents—those kids who always signal to passing eighteen-wheelers with a tug of the imaginary rope. I was never sure whether his classmates were humoring him with a snicker behind his back, as the truck drivers do the child. It was possible that considering their religious background, Jim's hair-trigger smile and prayer were genuinely welcomed. He, more than anyone, was convinced that it was his mission to convert everyone to Adventism with his smile and prayer. And, of any male in the class, he was the only one I would believe if he had told me he had never masturbated. Jim would sooner cut his hand off than befoul the hand that must do God's work.

So, with this small group and a couple others, I sat through lectures then joined my group for anatomy lab. It had been settled that Thursday night we would conclude our study time with a gathering to eat pizza and watch *ER* on television. Finally excited to be a social center after my somewhat monogamous college life, I offered my apartment as the meeting spot. Before I knew it, offers were coming in from several people to bring drinks, dessert, snacks, etc.

My studying went much like it had for the previous few nights. I plowed through the material just to say I had finished, then evacuated to get away from the smell. Jesse was tolerant when I placed the shroud back over him thirty minutes early and did not take my rushing too personally. At home, people started showing up an hour early as *Seinfeld* was on. I couldn't be certain who would show up, but people from all of the social circles were invited: the nerds, the babes, the dudes, as none of these lines had been clearly drawn, at least in my mind. With rumors flying so quickly and reputations preceding most people to the campus, one could never be certain if he had already been typecast.

The mood was sublime once everyone had arrived. We all knew we had a quiz in anatomy the following day, but elected to forget about it for the time being. And though we were not all planning on becoming ER docs, this show was the one declaration to America that our profession—medicine—was not only important, but also interesting. My new friends filled the couches and chairs around the living room. I knew some names— Bill was there, Mike and Slash, and Jim had come along with Flutter. Flutter had grown up in the religious schoolyards like all the others, but somehow she had developed the peculiar habit of fluttering about rooms with her head in the clouds and her eyelashes fluttering periodically, even without the professors asking questions.

The show ended at 11:00, and people made their way to the door as soon as the credits rolled. The looming threat of failing a quiz got everyone to their feet rather quickly. The sound of good-byes and good nights was supplanted by good lucks as they took to the streets, thinking ahead to the quiz.

Flutter straggled behind; she mentioned that she liked something in my house. I don't remember whether it was my whiteboard, my computer, or my refrigerator, but she mentioned something. Not many ladies before or since have liked my refrigerator as much as she did, nor has anyone displayed as much affection for *any* of my appliances. But as she told me about her approval, she stepped close. This is the point in most conversations or relationships when the sexual tension builds, as each person wonders what the other is thinking. There is usually a moment when they stare at each other or fumble over a word. We skipped the sexual tension and proceeded straight to the sex that night.

Before seconds had lapsed in the pause, our hands were wrapped around each other. We began kissing in soap-opera fashion, missing lips every fourth kiss, only to hit the other's cheek or neck. She grabbed my hair and pulled lightly toward her. I melted briefly into a submissive position, as my hair was my *other* erogenous zone. Having my neck exposed in front of her, she pulled me closer and kissed my neck more vigorously. My erection transiently waned when she interrupted the kissing to plant a bite on me. Don't confuse this with a colloquialism for pecking, nibbling, or leaving a hickey—she opened her mouth like she was chomping a Granny Smith and bit me!

First, I wondered if this was what they did in the Midwest, but I kept my mouth shut. Thankfully, she didn't chow down again. I have not, to this day, figured out from what section of the *Kama Sutra* she learned that one.

Soon she started taking off her blouse, even without my suggesting it. She pointed to the back room, which she hadn't seen yet. "Want to take me back there?" she suggested.

"Sure. C'mon." We fumbled back through the kitchen. There wasn't any mention of the refrigerator at that time.

THUNK. She pushed me down onto the bed. She leaned over and removed my shirt, then straddled my hips as I lay there. Her aggressiveness was a turn-on. I wondered what had happened to the quiet bookworm with glasses I had been sitting next to in class.

"Do you want to see me naked, or what?" she said. The confidence in her acting was impressive and got me heated up despite her atrocious scriptwriter.

"Fuck, yeah. Get those pants off!" I replied, meanwhile wondering if she would get pissed off by my profanity. I rolled her over, popped the buttons on her jeans one by one, and pulled them down her legs.

"Get 'em off and fuck me."

Profanity was clearly not going to be an issue. The raw lust in the atmosphere moved us to do and say things we were probably both surprised to hear. Her head tilted forward, and she peered at me with a mischievous look. I had been trying to foster the sexual tension between us by keeping my eyes locked on hers as we circled each other like predatory tigers. The tension was momentarily broken when I glanced down to see her in her underwear.

While mothers routinely advise their children never to leave the house with dirty underpants, they sometimes fail to mention that you shouldn't leave wearing your grandmother's underwear. I was surprised to look down and see her entire midsection wrapped in a pair of oversized mint-green cotton bloomers. Not too well obscured by the underwear was an enormous tuft of pubic hair.

While my initial reaction was less than amorous toward the presentation, I ultimately fell into the usual male pattern of chasing that which has a pulse.

After our somewhat romantic encounter, we lay there in the bed, her head wedged into my armpit. In these situations, we men are expected to endure any lack of circulation that ensues for the sake of romance. I lived up to these expectations until the moment that men truly hate: the post-sex conversation.

"Isn't it great that we found each other so early in the year?" Flutter cooed into my ear. "We don't have to spend all that time finding a boyfriend and girlfriend. Here we are—this perfect match. We can sit together in class, and study together, and..."

The saliva in my mouth dried up instantly. Somehow, this chance rendezvous, which had about as much foundation as democracy in the Middle East, was being promoted to an everlasting bond. I was speechless. I felt myself gasping a bit for air. I looked down to see if she had moved her head from my shoulder to my throat, but she remained still. She was stealing my oxygen through some other unseen force. *How would a political leader temper an uprising against his sovereignty?* I wondered. Many a leader has fallen with my same silence.

~~~

At 8:00 the next morning, I reluctantly found myself obligated to sit in the front corner of the lecture hall.

Jim approached in his pin-striped white shirt with short sleeves. "Good morning, Jeff," he said, enunciating each syllable as though it were etched in marble. "That certainly was a fun event at your apartment last night. I prayed last night that we might find the time to fellowship like that often this year."

With the care he seemed to put into his words, I surmised that his usage of "fellowship" wasn't a mistake. I figured that Jim spoke like that because he honestly believed that Jesus had spoken like that and that we should, as his followers, accept his teachings of grammar as well as morality. Which is to say, "Love thy neighbor and address him using proper sentence structure, never ending a sentence with a preposition."

Flutter had gone home the night before, but when she walked into the class, she sat down next to me, saying hello with a peculiar hint of a melody behind it. She did not exactly put her arms around me or give me a kiss in front of everyone, as I had feared she might, but just the way she looked at me had me perspiring through my shirt. She seemed to sway her body side to side, tilting her head as she spoke. The movement was like an interpretive dance declaring how much she looked forward to studying with me. Her eyelashes beat at an ever-fiercer tempo as she spoke.

Never had a lecture come as such a relief as that morning, when it served to halt Flutter's unending chatter. While some professors tended to drone over the material with nothing more than a monochromatic diagram and outline, this particular professor habitually posed questions to the students. Some of the questions tested our attention, while others transitioned to the next topic. With every bit as much enthusiasm as when she had attacked me the night before—minus the expletives—Flutter would thrust her hand up in the air to answer each question. Not limited by the difficulty of any question or even the rhetorical nature of the question, she bounced up as though her seat were electrified.

In the midst of trying to subtly hide my association with her, I occasionally glanced up to see that she was making the same frantic blinking gesture as she answered the questions. Furthermore, her head and neck were undulating in the same silly, coy manner as when she was flirting with me the night before. I slowly began to realize that this girl was *not* the most God-awful flirter in the world. This fluttering was a bizarre nervous twitch. And with each tilt of her head toward me, the thought of continuing a relationship with her became more and more frightening. I tried to put the problem out of my mind as the professor passed out the first quiz I would take in medical school.

I jumped from one state of panic to another as I looked over the questions: *What are the five muscles supplied by the whatindahellidis nerve?*

Shit! echoed through my mind, my rib cage, and maybe even the room. I knew instantly that I had screwed myself and was completely unprepared for the quiz in front of me. The strategy of skipping tough questions, which we had all been taught in elementary school, did not serve me well this time. I looked back over the test and realized I had answered only three of the ten questions.

What are the branches of the innominate artery? It may seem like a harmless question now, but when one is trying to filter out the less important information he is studying, an artery whose name literally means "artery without a name" hardly seems worth the effort.

I would advise all those aspiring physicians out there not to be fooled by the booby traps set by the original anatomists and clinicians. Anatomical descriptors such as "cervical" can be used to describe locations as distant as a woman's neck or something in her vagina, depending on the pronunciation. Other clever people would decide it was important to reassign numbers to the fingers of the hand beginning with the thumb, despite everyone's twenty-plus years of experience pointing with their "first" finger. Undoubtedly, this movement had been initiated by some manly orthopedic hand surgeon who could not bring himself to describe, in a medical note, his procedure involving a patient's "pinky."

I was devastated when we graded our own tests. Each answer he called out was like a jab in my side. I had missed more than I had gotten right. This had gone beyond failing, which I had never done before. I could justifiably be labeled "special needs" for this performance. I was in no mood to mingle with other students while they talked about how they had missed one or two. After the morning's assignments, I went home and adjusted my perspective on studying in medical school. Never again did I try to filter out the "unimportant" details I studied. I had come to the conclusion that I was a horrible judge of what was, in fact, important.

Not much can inspire a person to study more than panic over his complete and utter failure. I rushed home and began studying as though the next test were a day away. My adrenaline was so high that I didn't even think about women, making this moment fairly unique in my life thus far. I kept reading as my inspiration drove my study from subject to subject.

Across the room, a sound broke my concentration. The phone rang again, and I realized how out of tune with the world I was. Springing from the couch, I knocked the anatomy text to the floor with a thump that shook the ground and rattled lamps on the other side of the living room.

"Hello?" I said with the receiver not halfway to my ear.

"Hi, sweetheart!" Flutter heralded on the other end. My ears ached even before the phone had made contact with them. While I had been gladly ignoring her all morning and afternoon, it quickly rushed to my mind that she was in this for much more than I was.

"I was just relaxing a little this afternoon and reading my Bible," she said, "and I was thinking of you. I wondered if maybe you would like to get together tonight, or maybe you wanted to come to Sabbath school with me tomorrow. Wouldn't that be fun, honey?"

I swear that I felt my pounding heart trapped within my stomach. Now knowing a little bit of medical science, I realized that this feeling was not precisely consistent with the body's anatomical arrangement. But I could tell that my heart was not happy with either its imprisonment or this date proposal, because it raced all the faster. It felt as though it were climbing out of my stomach using some sort of spiked climbing gear. All the while, my stomach was growling, trying to wrestle this pounding heart back into the gastric cage.

I listened to her words, like "sweetheart" and "honey." To me, these weren't words that young lovers would use. They were words parents called their children, or perhaps each other, if they were seventy years old. And I didn't want a consistent role as lover, young or old. Regardless, going to church as though it were a date did not appeal to me, and neither did the company.

"Hmmm. You know, I think we need to talk about some things," I said in my softest voice. "I had a wonderful time last night, but I'm afraid that we may have gotten a different idea about what this relationship was going to become."

Silence came over the line. I hoped for a break in the tension, where she might reassure me that she had seen this merely as a booty call or something to shake out the cobwebs.

Instead, I broke the silence myself. "I hope I didn't mislead you," I said, then hurried through an explanation, hoping to avoid her wrath. "But I'm not ready to get into a new relationship right now. I just separated from a long-term relationship, and even though I really like you, I just can't get into something too serious right now..." I paused for a quick breath. "I'm sorry. I hope I haven't hurt your feelings too badly."

"Oh...no, I understand. I'll be okay." She paused. "I guess I'll go now, then. Bye," she concluded matter-of-factly and hung up before I could return the good-bye. Her voice carried a soft tone that somewhat reassured me about the "breakup," as it were. I returned to the couch with a Dr. Pepper and began my reading again.

Thirty minutes later, the screen door flung open. "How dare you fuck me and then dump me! I thought you loved me!"

I was stunned. My mouth gaped. I could hardly believe what she was saying. How could I possibly love her after one night?

As I thought back, I remembered that she had shouted "I love you!" just before she climaxed the night before. What I originally wrote off as awkward pillow talk now looked like the red flag I had ignored.

Lois crept behind the open screen and looked around, as if to make sure everything was all right. I couldn't be sure that things weren't going to get out of hand with Flutter ranting at the door, but I figured it best that Lois not become the hostage this villain would hold against me. I nodded to Lois, hoping she would understand and move on her way, but she just stood there, periodically licking herself. Neither comic book heroines nor cats are the smartest characters when it comes to getting out of harm's way.

My disgruntled counterpart assumed I was nodding to her and continued her shouting before I could say anything to calm her. "And you had the nerve to say you're sorry? Of course you misled me. I wouldn't have slept with you if I had thought you didn't love me! You completely lied to me. I don't ever want to talk to you again! You're a jerk!"

She whipped around and slammed the screen door shut.

Usually, silence is only awkward when more than one person is involved. But as I sat there alone, I wasn't sure what to do for the moment. Perhaps it was just the peculiar idea that I had convinced someone that I loved her by having a cool refrigerator or whiteboard, whichever. Perhaps it was the uncertainty of whether she would come back in holding a knife, or even a bouquet, for that matter. I resigned myself to never fully understanding the mind or intentions of a crazy woman. I also figured this didn't bode well for a specialty career in psychiatry. The end result was, no Sabbath anything. I slept in on Saturday.

Chapter 5

Fishermen are often given credit for being the most superstitious of all professionals, but those with advanced degrees are not above turning to superstition to get them through fearful times. In the early 1900s, any unfortunate crew member deemed bad luck was simply thrown overboard. In the late twentieth century, I personally turned to several rituals to bring fortune. It was clear that spending countless hours in front of mind-numbing books wasn't enough to get the job done.

It was mid-December, and the last of the semester finals was about to begin. The extra-large coffee cup rattled the metal trashcan as I tossed it over my shoulder while leaving the Starbucks in the next town over. My blood ran mocha, as it would for any test I took. My eyelids were open about a half-inch above my eyebrow as my car stereo blasted the latest heavy metal music. Legend suggested that the best way to avoid a mind blank was with caffeine and adrenaline. The sheer momentum of speeding through a test would make the answers jump into my head.

I also wore the Superman shirt that I had donned for the medical school entrance test. Now I sat at the lab table with a giant *S* on my chest for that extra confidence boost. I had put it on along with my game face that morning. There was no simple pass or fail. We were ranked from 1 to 160 by absolute score, so there was no way to hide the competitive side of these tests. And just like any competition, one had to have a uniform.

Despite the competitive aspect to the academics in our medical school, I never had the sense that others were out to get me or that anyone would sabotage my efforts, as I had heard of in other medical schools. There was a little nervousness in the smiles as we greeted each other on our way in. Not quite sure which seat would be good luck, some walked tentatively around the room and sat down as if to test the seat's aura. Jess sat down next to me. Her smile was comfortable and disarming, unlike many others, who could barely muster a nervous twitch of the lips before a test. She explained to me that she had been studying most of the week and was a bit nervous, but she had gone to Bible study the night before, and it had calmed her down.

Jess and I had studied together a couple of times during the semester. She was an extremely intellectual girl who had charmed me with her innocence. She was always able to find the bright side or a glimmer of hope in any situation. That, along with her short blonde hair and soft, girl-next-door features, made her a difficult distraction to avoid. I had followed my standard protocol of flirting with her, first smiling and winking when we met. I never missed a chance to compliment her, and her mildly embarrassed smile and blush were a welcomed reward. More than once, I had convinced myself that she was the perfect girl to be with forever. But the few times I had attempted to arrange a proper date with any resemblance to a romantic relationship, her shock was quickly followed by a semi-apologetic explanation of why she couldn't date a non-Adventist.

The shock was something I had seen in many of the Adventist girls, and had come to find humorous. You see, most of the Adventist men had grown up in an environment that fostered their shyness. They wore solid ties with plaid short-sleeved shirts to class and church. Their social events were not spur-of-the-moment impulses to party—with music, dancing, and drinking—but were prearranged religious gatherings on Friday nights, where Kool-Aid was a bold gesture. Male-female relationships were not established by traditional means of a man telling a woman how beautiful she is and then asking her out. Rather, if a male and a female were seen at three consecutive Vespers, they were considered by the rest of the religious community to be dating, especially if they spoke to each other at any of the three gatherings. After this relationship was presumed by their fellow Adventists, if all went well, they could go on dates—double and triple dates, that is. I'm not exactly sure how long it takes for Adventist men and women to actually feel comfortable alone with each other. However, this passive courtship ritual made the SDA women feel extremely glamorous when men actually approached them.

I sensed from Jess's blushing that she felt something for me, but there was an unwritten rule, or even written, for all I knew. Adventists should only get involved with Adventists, and Jess was far too proper to break such commandments. I thought back to our study-break walks, where we would talk about the possibility and impossibility of "us."

Before I knew it, everyone had funneled in and sat for the test. I was bitter over the buzzkill when I realized that the earlier Metallica songs that had fueled my test momentum had made way for sappy Kenny G love songs in the background of my daydreams of Jess.

Over the speakers in the three rooms came the announcement. Jim, who had been the only one to run for class pastor, announced that he was going to lead the prayer before the exam. This was always an awkward moment for me, as everyone solemnly bowed their heads, eyes gently closed. I did not believe in a being that could hear what was being said, let alone read all our minds. Did I want to conform? Did I want to reform? Every morning before class and on Wednesdays in Chapel—to which I had a marvelous attendance record, I must say—I closed my eyes and listened passively. I often questioned my own hypocrisy, but such contentions were not my greatest priority in the face of this pathology final.

After the pathology final came the anatomy practical exam. One hundred sixty medical students stood silently in front of forty cadavers with little stickers that resembled price tags. The professors had spent the morning finding some portion of each cadaver which had not been too horribly destroyed in the process of our amateur dissection so that something of importance could be identified. Both the silence and the stench of formaldehyde were so thick that you could cut through them with a scalpel. In the corners of the room hovered the professors, looking for anyone who might be tempted by Satan's thoughts of cheating. After four months of dissection and drying, the cadavers looked a lot like beef jerky. The arteries and veins would sometimes tear mid-test, leaving them attached only to the chest. The only strategy was to guess whether it led from the neck to the head or to the shoulder.

Afterward, my phone rang. I knew it was my father before I had even picked up the receiver.

"How did the test go?" he asked. "Was it hard? I mean, I know you studied enough that you did fine, but did everyone else find it hard?"

My father was under the misimpression that I was a genius with a photographic memory and that I studied twenty-three hours a day. I always thought of asking him what he thought I did for that other hour each day. "I bet all that studying you did on actual diseases, helping those people online, really helped, huh?"

I had told him some time ago about a hobby I used to break up the monotony of hours of textbook studying. When I studied, with stacks of notes and books on my desk, periodically jumping up to my whiteboard to write something I thought was testable trivia, I sometimes got on the Internet. As my alias, GQMD2B, I would place myself in a chat room with a title such as "Medical Speak." My personal profile, which could be viewed by any who happened into the room, gave personal information such as the general area I lived, that I was a medical student, and that I liked to answer any medical questions. The profile listed favorite quotes; mine was nothing from Hippocrates or William Osler, but rather, *"Sometimes you just gotta say, what the fuck!" —Tom Cruise,* Risky Business.

In the first years of medical education, the closest one actually comes to a disease is a slide containing an infinitesimally small piece of some organ, from some poor schmuck who happened to get this equally rare disease. It is painfully obvious to the young student who desperately wants to help people in their time of need, that an actual patient is at least two years away, and the only need is the student's own need to pass all the tests he is given. This little "Doc in the Box" enterprise I had set up was perfect for that. It was anonymous, so my lack of confidence was not prohibitive. Nobody cared that the medical student had to look something up when they were getting free advice over the Internet. It was convenient, and I could do it from the same desk I studied at, simply glancing up when the computer speaker chimed. But the most interesting benefit came in a form I had not predicted.

Three types of questions were most prevalent among the web surfers. First were the simple questions about basic medical problems and treatments. Second were from those who knew someone who knew someone with a rare disease, and had I heard of that disease. The last question often followed much like this: "You're in medical school? I am premed at XXX University. How do you suggest I get into med school? And what do you look like? ;-) " Everyone with a decent grade in biology in college considered themselves premed, but getting into medical school was an intimidating task. Everyone wanted to know the secret path. On more than one occasion, conversations with the female students had led to an exchange of physical descriptions. I was always surprised at how eager even the more beautiful girls were to spend an evening getting to know a medical student. I cannot say that any long-term relationships bloomed from this form of supplemental education, but who looks for everlasting love on AOL? And just a tip for any of you thinking of picking up women like this: it helps your image to use quotes from Tom Cruise over ones from Booger in *Revenge of the Nerds.*

"So how about we go to Spunky Steer to celebrate?" The words seem, on paper, like a question. Yet when transposed into my father's voice, they were somewhat more imperative. "Nan! Get on the phone! It's your brother. Come here and tell him to go to Spunky Steer with us!" This was one of my father's favorite games and/or coercive tools. If he felt there was any resistance to his plan of getting together, he would employ my mentally retarded sister to inspire a little guilt.

"Hi, Dickens!" Nancy's voice always bounced with jovial energy. In every day there was something to celebrate or laugh about in her mind. We should all be so lucky, I suppose. "When are you coming over?" she asked. A simple question, yes. However, despite her ability to understand my words, she could never understand why I was sometimes unable to come over to see her.

"I don't know, Nan."

"Tell him to go to dinner with us," said my dad. Speakerphones are the greatest evil of modern technology, I decided, as my dad sat with my sister in a wrestling hold, trying to get her to talk to me. "Tell him he's a cwee-owah-yair if he doesn't go," my father shouted as he tickled her. I have alluded previously to my father's fondness for using nicknames and teasing his children. In fact, from this propensity, a whole new vocabulary and language has evolved. With many years of study, etymologists have traced the origin of most of these words he uses to an ancient dialect from old-world Germany and an eloquent use of these words by a mentally retarded sister. And thus words like "cwee-owah-yair" would stick, referring to the "creep over there" who was abstaining from a night of fun and frivolity at Spunky Steer for one reason or another. Also from this all-but-extinct dialect come some classic words like "don-dons," "Mumer-dumer," and "Geeky." Of course, these refer to donuts, mother, and my sister Vicky (whose inclusion in this public list will surely not be forgiven). I have never figured out exactly what the fuck a hunkle-head is, for those of you who have been wondering for a few chapters what I meant. The truly funny thing is that I have not personally heard my sister butcher any of the words of origin like this, but I cite her as the reason for the word evolution because it is the least disturbing of all going theories.

"I don't know, Dad," I said. "I was thinking of going by the ER now that I'm a med student."

"Oh, you can go to the ER after dinner," he replied, then shifted his efforts toward Nancy. "Tell him he is going to worsa [hurt] my feelings if he doesn't come."

"Okay, okay. I'll come."

"So we'll pick you up at the usual time?"

"Sure, Dad, 4:30. See you when you get here."

Something peculiar seems to be genetically programmed into humans; as we get older, our circadian rhythm is kept by a miniature white man inside our brains, and therefore tends to be off beat most of the time. Thus it comes in early compared to the music around. And that little white man in all our parents' brains is absolutely convinced that he is in the groove and dancing like he were Fred Astaire. I spent most of my life eating the "early bird specials" at restaurants like Spunky Steer.

After dinner, I drove over to the hospital, which was about two blocks from the medical school. As I pulled into the patient parking lot, the sun had already set. The building stood singly as the only tall building in the area. The letters atop were lit for the night and accented by Christmas lights for the holiday season, which had largely slipped my mind because of my schoolwork. A pearlescent lighted cross stood on the roof next to the helipad. These were the same images I had seen growing up. Tonight, I felt a new sense of ownership. I felt like it belonged to me, and I belonged to it, quite honestly.

I recalled standing beside the hospital when I was ten, and my mother asked me if I wanted to be a doctor or a veterinarian. I told her that I liked the outside of dogs, not the inside. Tonight, going into the ER, I hoped to see a bit of people's insides. The excitement of the emergency room drew me to it.

During college, I had spent at least a thousand hours volunteering in the emergency department, or ED. My actual value in the department was quite miniscule, as I folded blankets, stapled papers, and performed other menial tasks. But as I became a familiar face night after night, the nurses and doctors had asked me to take patients to CAT scanners and x-rays. I was sometimes allowed to hand doctors tools as they stitched people back together. It seems a minor reward or responsibility, but with the laws that have evolved since, it would be unheard of for someone without training to be allowed around patients in this fashion. But this interaction with people, talking to them and finding out what they had been through, was great inspiration to keep going in my work.

As I walked through the hospital doors, I nodded to the security guard near the door. I showed him my badge, which identified me as a medical student as opposed to a volunteer. I was subtly warmed by pride as I held the blue plastic ID and clipped it to my waist-length white coat. He nodded back to me, waving me in and thinking he was sending in another poor sap to a night of work. But I was excited about the night ahead.

As a young college student, I had walked down these same halls three years earlier on my first night volunteering in the ED. I had been told to meet a nurse there named Mary. As the electric double doors opened, I had sheepishly walked in, looking as out of place as a snowball in Arizona.

"Can I help you?" a soft soprano voice had asked me those years before.

Being a new volunteer at the time, I quickly jumped back and apologetically explained my presence. "Hi. I'm the new volunteer, and I'm supposed to meet Mary."

"Great!" she said. "I'm Mary, and I'll be showing you around. Hmmm, where shall we start? I know. Have you ever seen a dead body?"

"No," I replied. I was actually surprised, as I thought about it. I had been alive nearly twenty years and had never seen a dead body. I wondered how many other people in the world had not seen a dead body other than on TV.

"Okay. Well, do you want to see one now?"

"Sure," I said, trying to sound like I was doing it to live up to my volunteer responsibility. Meanwhile, inside I was bursting with curiosity about the body. Would I be scared or creeped out? Would I feel nauseous?

Mary led me into a private room, where a black vinyl bag lay on the ground next to an ominously raised blanket. "This guy was found on the streets dead. When the paramedics find them, they bring them in here so the docs can pronounce them dead and send them to the morgue, so we have to bag them. And that's where you come in. This is a real pain in the ass when you do it alone, but with a strong guy like you helping…" She smirked.

I helped her with the body, placing it in and zipping up the bag. My feelings didn't go beyond the curiosity I had initially felt. I continued to be curious about what it had been like for this man to die in the streets. What were his final thoughts as he died alone and homeless? Mary explained to me that he likely had AIDS. I thought about how he might have gotten it. I wondered what he regretted in life. I wondered what he was proud of. And I wondered who might miss him.

I reflected on these thoughts as I walked through the same double doors as a medical student.

"Oh, my gosh! Jeff, it's been ages since I've seen you. What are you doing here?"

Mary had just walked out of a patient's room and almost ran into me. She was the same Mary that I remembered. She had a cute round face and dark hair flowing down her back. I had only seen her in the ER, so the outfit I always associated with her was a bright blue scrub uniform with an elastic band around the waist. She had never been without a smile in the years that I had known her. In moments of stress, when life and death were on the line, she had a casual purposefulness that got things done efficiently. Then she would come out with a smile that would comfort the room.

"I'm in medical school here now," I replied. "I figured I would come down and see what was going on in the ER and maybe work like a volunteer tonight. You know, see if things make more sense now that I have six months of medical training under my belt."

"That's awesome," she said. "We'll have to sit down and catch up later. I have to take this patient to the unit now, though."

"Okay, I'll catch you later," I said as she rolled the patient's bed down the hall.

The department seemed smaller than I remembered it. For a Friday, there was very little movement. Usually there would be sick or injured people lining the hallways. That night, only one or two rooms contained patients. I walked slowly through the hall, trying to appear as if my badge and coat afforded me some purpose there. Most of the doctors there did not seem to remember me from years before, and I didn't have the nerve to approach them that night.

On the stool at the nurse's desk sat a girl collating papers. She wore khaki pants, along with a dark blue, short-sleeved volunteer shirt. The shirts seemed much more elegant now than when I was a volunteer. I approached her from behind and sat down next to her.

"Has it been this busy in here all night?" I asked her jokingly.

"I just got here an hour ago, and it has been pretty quiet," she replied.

"My name's Jeff. I'm one of the students here."

"Hi. I'm Kathleen. I'm a volunteer. Are you a third-year?" she inquired, apparently realizing that only med students of a certain status got to take care of patients.

"No, actually, I'm a first-year. I used to be a volunteer when I was in college, and after I finished my exams today, I thought it might be fun to come down and see what action was going on."

"The only action around here is putting in and removing staples. But there was a thrilling moment when I punched holes in some papers and put them in a notebook earlier," she said with one eyebrow raised.

"That sounds pretty traumatizing for you. Should I get one of the counselors over here to help you through it?"

"Shit, don't they teach you guys to do anything yourself, like counseling people, in medical school?"

"I can fill in bubbles on an answer sheet. That's about it. Hey, if it's this slow in here, do you want to take off early and hang out?"

"Tell you what. You staple these papers when I hand them to you, and I'll let you take me out for a drink when we're done."

Everything seemed normal for a second. I began stapling her papers—a mildly flirtatious effort to stand next to her until I could come up with something clever to say. Then it occurred to me that she had shaken my world with two sentences. This girl had cussed and asked me out for a drink within seconds of meeting me. It took me a second to orient myself and figure out whether I was appalled or in love. I hadn't heard profanity or a positive response from a Mon Gracia affiliate in what seemed like forever.

Kathleen was a short girl, about 5'4" tall. She had long, straight brunette hair with an essence of brilliant red shining from it. She wore her volunteer polo shirt with each of the buttons conspicuously undone, showing off her well-endowed figure. Her skin color was naturally beautiful, and she wore striking red lipstick and stark mascara. These details, coupled with her tight jeans (without panty lines) were not often found around the hospital, which expounded the religious practices of the medical school and Adventist church. Her body type was not what I was typically drawn to, but she was beautiful, and I was immediately attracted to her confidence and charm.

We walked each other to our cars, which were strangely parked next to each other's, both illegally. Our criminal intent was just one more thing we had in common and discussed most of the night. We started at a bar in the next town over, because the city of Mon Gracia does not allow bars. The influence of the religion has reached deep enough that Starbucks cannot even get a permit to open up a coffee shop in the city, because Adventism discourages coffee consumption. The absence of a Starbucks makes the city unique in yet another aspect, and thus my café commute earlier that morning.

After leaving the bar, not too inebriated, we ventured back to my place to continue our conversation. It was exciting talking with a girl who was both enthusiastic about her goals and living a normal life in the meantime. Kathleen wanted to go to medical school ultimately, which explained her volunteering as well as her interest in me. But she also held an office job for a successful local company, which treated her very well and allowed her to take time out of her schedule for classes. She had a serious but serene disposition. I had a sense that if a problem ever needed to be solved, I would call her whether we ended up dating or not. But it also gave me a great sense of confidence and comfort with her.

It could not have been earlier than 2:00 in the morning when the movie finished in my apartment. It was not a romantic comedy, as I would have recommended to aspiring playboys out there, but rather an action movie—that *she* had chosen. We sat next to each other on the couch and intermittently scooted closer together. Not a word was said during the movie, but there was a silent sense of comfort in the room. It may have even been during a chase scene that she laid her head in my lap. I tried to restrain any inadvertent natural responses, which might be obvious considering her position, but after a few minutes I decided it was a losing battle from the beginning. She never mentioned noticing, but she did chuckle a few minutes after I first noticed a greater sense of fullness in my pants.

As the credits began rolling, her eyes looked up at me with the mascara appearing ever more striking by the light of the television. The look between us drew our faces closer, and we kissed. Her kiss was so unlike the girls I had previously dated. She was so deliberate in her touch and kiss. Often it feels as though women are allowing the man to lead the kiss, and the woman simply follows. When Kathleen's lips pressed against mine, there was no uncertainty in our movements. Her hands across my back were perfectly in sync as I leaned over to kiss her. Her lips pressed against mine firmly, but they were so full and soft that it did not seem in any way aggressive. Her breasts rested completely on my chest. As I kissed her, I glanced down at her cleavage and felt myself begin to perspire, hoping that she wouldn't notice.

With more coordinated movements, kisses led to caresses, which led to uncontrolled touching and disrobing. I felt her hands spread across my chest. First they were grasping me, then they shoved me through the kitchen toward the bedroom. Not once did our lips part, either to breathe or to catch our balance as we danced back to the room. Sensing the direction the evening was going, I moved to lead her into the room. But she grasped me by the back of the neck. I was stunned yet still locked in a kiss with her.

"Did I say you could let go?" she asked with one of her lips touching mine at each moment.

"No, ma'am," I said jokingly, but playing the submissive role to this girl was incredibly erotic.

"Then get over here and do just what I tell you."

She softened me up with her strokes then plowed me over onto the bed. The innocence of her volunteer shirt had been thrown to the side, and only her bra shone in the light from the window. She leaned over, pinning me to the bed as I watched her breasts swing from side to side. Kathleen's eyes peered over my face. I stared back, and her brilliant turquoise irises, with the dark brown ring surrounding them, were fantastic. Da Vinci would have spent years just to get the eyes this precise.

"Do you want me?" she whispered.

"Yes," I whispered back.

She undid her bra in the front. I was surprised to see the clasps in the front, remembering when front clasps were invented in eighth grade. In Kathleen's case, I considered it likely that gargantuan knockers like these would require some sort of extra support that maybe could be provided by the frontal steel. Anyway, she dropped the bra to the side, and her amazing beauty hung down above me. Both of them.

"How bad did you say you want me?" she demanded.

I wasn't tired of playing the passive lover, but she had simply gotten me too aroused, and I couldn't restrain myself. I pounced on her, rolling the two of us toward the wall. We slammed against the plaster with a thud but kept kissing as though nothing had happened. By now, our clothes had managed to find their way off. We stopped making love only for an alarm clock that went off at 5:30 in the morning, which we then proceeded to throw across the room against the wall.

"Nobody stops fucking at 5:30 on Saturday morning!" she shouted. "Get back here. You have another hour, at least. And don't think I'm going to let you quit using your tongue!"

~~~

So I had a girlfriend now. I know you couldn't predict that, considering the relatively short-term relationships I had been having prior to Kathleen. But I actually liked her. She was normal at a time in my life when most people I knew were just a little different. I had a girlfriend to keep me company when I came home. I had a real person to cuss for me when I started using words like "Gosh!" too frequently. She kept me grounded. She had goals to become what I was, but in the meantime I was pleased with what she was. But none of this changed the fact that I had to go to religion class twice per week, along with Chapel once a week.

Actually, Chapel was not so bad. Held in a large church with all the graduate students attending service, it was fairly anonymous. I could usually study biochemistry without being noticed. It was even feasible to have someone fill out an attendance card for you and never have the faculty be any wiser. Somewhere between the first and second year, though, the faculty caught on and forced us to turn them in to actual people instead of placing them into boxes.

Religion class, on the other hand, was not so easy to evade. Approximately thirty people attended each class, and they encouraged participation. I had the distinct fortune of being in a class with many of those zealous individuals I have already mentioned. Jim and Flutter both attended my class, so I found myself frequently annoyed by their pious expressions and their questions, "When does life begin?" and "Why is God the way he is?" Although my participation was encouraged as well, Jess also attended the class, and I couldn't bring myself to burn that bridge by expressing my point of view. As a result, religion class became a parody of itself. A simple question would be asked, and someone would give an answer either missing large pieces of logic or requiring large efforts of imagination. There would be a five-second pause of silence that seemed premeditated. Then someone, often Jim, would offer the conclusion, "And God is so great!" Then myriad other people would echo, "Yeah, God is good. I mean, great! God is great!" And this would repeat itself.

Meanwhile, I struggled inside with my understanding of religion and Christianity. I wanted to understand it if it was true, but I didn't feel I needed it simply for the sake of having it. I just wanted to know what was right. Notice, I only capitalized the first letter in each sentence of this paragraph, whereas my classmates would have capitalized several others, thinking that their truth is True, and that their rights are Right.

At night, when I was alone, sometimes I would have conversations with God. It may seem odd for an atheist to converse with a being he doesn't believe in. But you can imagine a burglar waving a bone in front of the guard dog's house, even though he thinks the dog is gone. He does this just in case.

I would bargain with God, my goal being to find out whether he existed. I refused to be frightened into believing in a god, bargaining for my life—to believe in Him or else. There might have even been an occasion that I challenged God to do something like that to me. I was a healthy guy without any medical problems; it would take "a god" to swoop in and take that kind of health away. Those challenges notwithstanding, I just wanted to be shown something that I wouldn't be able to explain otherwise. Then I would have to believe in God, right? I rationalized that if I knew there was a god making this world work, I would likely have to dedicate my life to such a cause. It occurred to me that such a vow might entail celibacy for some, but I never offered up any such point for negotiation. I never saw any bright ray of light from the heavens. I was never visited by an angel. In truth, and in Truth, I don't know if I have ever been shown a piece of God, but I am fairly certain it didn't happen on one of those nights, because I was looking pretty hard.

~~~

As the second semester arrived, I had put much of the medical education into perspective. While the anatomy was grueling and the pathology was tedious, I could survive it all, and I would soon be a second-year medical student. I had performed fairly well on all my exams thus far. The scores on the midterms and finals put me in the top portion of the class, and I wondered how I would have ranked at a place like Harvard, Yale, or Hopkins.

Kathleen and I were doing pretty well. We had been together four months by the end of the term. In the spring, we took a weekend jaunt to Las Vegas. After arriving in her car, we stopped first at one of the late-night dance clubs. Kathleen was dressed in her tightest spandex skirt and a pink leather bustier that offered her cleavage to any interested party. I tried to disguise my discomfort in the dance club. It is a well-known fact that no white male enjoys being in a dance club for the sake of being in a dance club. He may approve of it after he picks up a female at the club, but his feelings for the dance floor will be mixed at best from then on.

I was on the floor. Dressed in black, I moved subtly across from her. The theme for the room was sensual, and her style fit in perfectly. She moved erotically, touching her thighs and winking at me. Her lips were again glossed in the bright, rose-colored shimmer. Occasionally she would venture closer to me in a seductive manner, then she would turn away from me and ignore me for a minute or two. She would dance in small groups of strangers, sometimes girls, sometimes guys, too. I was enraged at first, then I found myself the voyeur peering into their dance circle as she rocked her hips, lifting her arms above her head so that her cleavage bounced. Then she would turn and pay me some more attention.

I was now turned on by a sight that I would never have fathomed. I was tolerating my girlfriend within feet of another man; I was letting her dance with a man, for fuck's sake! A smile came to my face. Was I maturing? I couldn't be sure, but I wasn't pissed off, at least for the moment, and I thought that was a good thing. I continued dancing, finding the situation somewhat humorous in that I hated dancing out there. But I turned a bit and found myself in a group of young girls celebrating a bachelorette party. They were giggling above the music, and I found it much easier to keep the beat with them playing. From here,

I could try to tempt Kathleen like she was taunting me with the guys. I turned and danced with a slow groove and sexy posture.

When Kathleen looked over at me, she instantly came out of her dance character and stomped over to me. "What the fuck are you doing?" she screamed at me. I could barely hear her words over the music, but her face showed her anger. She stormed past me, off the dance floor, and up to the bar. I had no idea what she could be so furious about. I lost sight of her, so I figured the best way to ensure I could find her was to stay put. I continued dancing with the bachelorettes, having a relatively good time despite my not feeling comfortable on the dance floor. Fifteen minutes had passed and Kathleen had not returned, so I figured I had no choice but to go find her. After searching the bar, I ventured into the entryway of the casino and sat there for a few minutes.

"What the fuck are you doing out here?" Her voice pierced the sound of clanging coins in the background. She approached from down the hall with her arms firmly folded.

"What do you mean? You were the one who walked off the floor!"

"But everyone knows you don't leave a building. That's just fucking stupid."   "Look, I couldn't find you. I thought you might be out here. It's in the same casino. You found me. Why do you have to be such a bitch?"

"What the hell were you doing dancing with those bitches?"

"Same thing you were doing dancing with those guys. Just trying to turn you on."

"Turn me on?" she screamed. "How is that going to turn me on?"

"I don't know," I mumbled. By now, I had forgotten what my argument was. For one brief moment I was focused on the important fact that I had matured in those few minutes. After that moment, I was focused on what a bitch Kathleen was.

~~~

We struggled to make the relationship work for a couple of months into the summer. During that time, I was working in a biotech lab for a friend. He was an older fellow who had been in my anatomy class. He already had an advanced PhD in biology from Duke and was studying cancer cells from various body parts. He was merely taking the class because he wanted familiarity with the anatomy if he was going to be using actual tumor specimens. Gus was a burly man with red hair and a red beard. His personality was as outspoken as his appearance. In this way, he was far more normal than the rest of us in this religious medical class. Gus would sit in the back of the class with some of the younger guys, myself included, and snicker while pointing out the particularly attractive females in the class.

"I'd sure like to get Maximus into her gluteus," he would say.

"Yeah, Gus, she's good from afar, but far from good. Who you need is someone like that..."

By the end of the year, our conversations continued throughout most of anatomy lecture. I was sure that no one could hear us, because my language would not have made me popular with the Christians, or the ladies, or the Christian ladies, for that matter. Actually, Gus was an Adventist like the rest of the Mon Gracia students, but instead of attending one of the Adventist colleges like the others, he had gone to Duke. It was there that he had broken from his shell and turned into the lovely, crass perv that he was. That was also why he liked me, I suppose; I was the closest thing to his Duke drinking buddies. For this, he invited me to work for pay in his lab at the local children's cancer research center for the summer.

I pursued this, like so many of my previous extracurricular activities, only for its spot on my résumé. For as long as I could remember, I had been either volunteering for organizations or gaining membership in groups I cared about only half-heartedly. Ironic that none of the groups that I cared about, like the Organization of Playboy Bunnies, really impressed medical schools or residencies. Mysteriously, people trying to break into those businesses never seemed to need as much volunteer work on their résumés.

Day after day, I commuted to the lab, where I ran experiments to sequence DNA from cancer cells to find a faster method. As interested as I had previously been in the mechanics of DNA, and as magnificent as it all seemed, when it's in a test tube in front of you, DNA just looks like snot. It was my job to siphon snot from one tube into another, then bake the respective snot tubes in the oven. As you can imagine, there is a great deal of downtime in between siphoning and baking the snot. During this time, I often emailed one of my buddies from high school, currently in graduate school as a physicist. Steve and I were always comparing notes on how, after all our years of education, we hadn't learned much in school except how to go to school.

Steve wasn't enjoying research any more than I was. We discussed anything but academics. Women, sports, and the stock market were our favorite topics. Sometimes we combined them. It was baseball season, and that year, two players were competing for the all-time home-run record. On a nightly basis, one, two, and three home runs were being slugged out of the park. And so we passed emails to each other regarding the last night's game. We each also had girlfriends who occasionally rubbed us the wrong way, as women sometimes do. This also garnered our attention as we built a parody combining the World Series and relationships. The fight was for which quality would be victorious as the reason I would leave Kathleen.

Steve, we are out here on this lovely afternoon, and it seems that we have a fantastic game in store for us. Each of these teams has brought their big guns tonight. The American League has brought their old stand-by. He is reputed to be quite a nuisance to the teams of the National League because of his ability to pick apart 'every little thing they do.' He's their ringer from Japan; his name is Nomo Nagimi. <CHEER>

But Jeff, don't get ahead of yourself, because the National League has brought their pepper tonight, too. You know, it's said that this player is so effective at pissing off the other team because of the flirting with other players. In fact, some have even accused this player of some personal indiscretions. But he is a stellar contender and he is here tonight! Please welcome, B.J. Zabound! <CHEER!!>

Now, this year there is an interesting conundrum in the league.

I thought we kicked them out of baseball and stuck them all in hockey. And I never found one I thought was interesting, Jeff!

I said conundrum, Steve. A predicament. That is, we have two brothers on opposite teams tonight, both in contention for the reason to break up. They are the Bro's Italianos. On the side of the American League: the chain smoker, Shearika.

And on the National League: disproportionately large DeSizah. In unison, VASS!!! <CHEEEERRRR!!!>

Jeff, never before have I seen so many powerhouse players in one stadium. It is getting so close that I think it's going to come down to the back-up players. And this is where I have to give it to the National League. They have gone out of their way to look high and low for the best. And they have found this fine specimen. It's said the he can talk for hours and not say one important or interesting thing.

I've also heard that he talks almost as much during movies, Steve.

That's right. That's why I think he is going to pull this one out for the National League tonight. Let's put our hands together for the only Arab contender tonight. Wisheed Shuddufuggup!!! <CHEER, APPLAUSE, ROAR!!!>

Needless to say, my relationship with Kathleen ended before the summer did. I cannot remember exactly which reason won out. In the end, maintaining relationships with nonmedical people was a Herculean task. The more immersed I became in medicine, the less time I had to spend with those outside of it, and the less insight I had into how they thought and felt.

Chapter 6

Surely this was the third time I had reviewed the study material. My mind now had the retention of a toilet bowl. I would occasionally get stopped up, and all the knowledge would sit in my head for a short while. But ultimately the outcome was always the same: time and some sort of mental plunger would clear the drain, and *whooosh*, it would be gone. Everyone had a different method of studying; some read the textbooks and took notes and others read simplified review books that boiled the material down to the essential information. These were extremely popular, as they would often be written in a comic-book style to keep those of us with short attention spans interested. The most popular technique of all was the use of pneumonic devices to remember lists of facts. Even those who were smart enough not to require the review books would annotate their textbooks with pneumonics they would acquire from other students.

MUDPILES. Scared Lovers Try Positions That They Can't Handle. Hot as a hare, mad as a hatter, dry as a bone. The patient can't see, can't pee, can't climb a tree. Some say marry money, but my brother says bad business marry money. This collection of pneumonic devices essentially summarizes my medical education from the first year of medical school. Somehow, each of these phrases was supposed to help the aspiring physician to remember the intricate inner workings of the human body and the diseases that might strike. The problem was that by early in the second year of medical school, one had approximately 243 pornographic phrases, quirky rhymes, and important capitalized words swimming around in one's mind, and it was almost impossible to remember which corresponded to what disease or body part. Nevertheless, I sat battling the gods of amnesia, preparing for the first pathophysiology midterm of the second year.

Periodically I glanced up a the computer screen to see that "Gynomyte" was hitting on "Nurse321" again in the chat room, and that no one had written any medical questions for me. I acted the voyeur for a minute until I was interrupted by the pone ringing.

"Hey, Jeff, how's it going?" said a perky female voice on the other end.

"Hey!" I said. "It's going great. Just studying. You know how it is." My words came out slowly as I pondered who it might be on the line. Truth be told, I didn't know whether she knew 'how it was' or not.

"I was watching TV tonight, and I noticed an actor that looks so much like you."

I couldn't for the life of me think of who would be calling just to giggle and chat.

"Anyway, you totally look like this guy, Dawson, on Dawson's Creek."

"Really? Hum. I haven't seen it, but I'll have to look out for him."

"Yeah, I was at work in the ER the other day, and…"

That's it! Mary, the nurse from the ER. First dead body and all that excitement.

"…and I told her that I knew this really great guy that I thought she should meet." Mary had continued on as I had my epiphany about her identity. "I wasn't sure if you had a girlfriend, so I thought I should call you to find out."

"Nah, I don't have a girlfriend." I didn't mention that I had only recently broken up with Kathleen; I found it a good practice to avoid mentioning women to other women, whether they were past, present, or nonexistent.

"That's excellent! You are going to love Elisabeth. She is the nicest girl you will ever meet. She is a nursing student over at the state college, and she works at the county hospital. She has traveled everywhere, and…"

As Mary was making the sale, I considered that this might be a great opportunity. My relationship with Kathleen had failed because our daily lives were so different and we couldn't relate in terms of our medical interest. I did love that Kathleen had been relatively normal, when many of the people I was around on a daily basis would not even *date* on a first date, let alone kiss on a first date. This Elisabeth was from outside the Adventist system, and Mary assured me that she was beautiful. I figured that I had nothing to lose, so we arranged to go on a double date at the end of the week.

Friday came, and I had only to complete the day's activities before the date. This was a somewhat special event for the second year of medical school. We were to be indoctrinated into the world of clinical medicine. In small groups, the same groups that shared an anatomy cadaver, we would be taken into the hospital and taught to interview patients. This seemed like it would be a largely self-explanatory process, but I was to learn that there are a few intricacies to it.

From the classroom, the four of us were led toward the patient wards by our doctor, a cardiologist from the nearby veterans hospital, We had been assigned to the veterans hospital, where we would be instructed on what questions to ask. Then each week, one of us would take the medical history and serve as a teaching example for the rest of the group. Our instructor was a docile man, small and balding. Many pens and pocketbooks hung from the pockets of his white coat. Unlike many of the cardiologists I had encountered before, he was calm when he spoke to us. Nothing seemed to be a life-or-death matter, which seemed ironic, considering his field proportionally involved more life-or-death matters than most other fields combined. Perhaps this helped him put his other responsibilities into perspective and not take himself so seriously. Regardless of how he had reached his current state of mind, I approved. I felt very comfortable around him—comfortable, that is, until I found out that I would be the first one to perform my newly acquired medical history-taking skills.

Mr. Ranger was to be my first patient. His name wasn't actually Mr. Ranger, but he had been a member of the Army Rangers in more than one war. Veteran buddies are incredibly respectful of their military heritage and one's past, but they are also fond of nicknames. Ranger had stuck with this codger. The cardiologist warned me that he could be a little bit "frisky" sometimes, but that he had some good stories and some interesting disease processes, too.

"Don't worry," the cardiologist said. "This guy has got more stuff going on in his body than most people in the other hospitals combined. I don't expect you to get it all on your first time. Just ask the questions you know to ask, let him talk, and we'll see what comes out."

The cardiologist led us down the hall, offering little bits of history and trivia about the veterans hospital. I couldn't focus on a word he was saying at that point; I was reciting the questions I wanted to ask this patient. It felt as if a bowling ball was rolling around in my intestines as my guts churned.

The halls were relatively dark compared to the bright lighting one expects to find in a hospital. The walls were painted a dark tan color, which accentuated the lack of light. Each corner where a computer sat, a white uniformed individual sat at the desk. With the mood so nerve-racking and the atmosphere so ominous, I pictured their devious gazes following us around as our group passed.

We approached the ranger's room, CCU 244, at the end of the hall. The cardiologist opened the double doors and led us in.

"Hey, Ranger! How goes the fight?" the cardiologist bellowed as we all entered. "I told you I was going to bring by the student physicians, and they're here now."

"Okay, Doc. I been waitin' for ya," said the little man in the bed across the room. "Say, Doc, when am I getting the hell outta here?"

"Oh, we talked about that, chief. We need to get your heart pumping with just a little more steam. But we can go over that again later if you want. Let's just work with the med students first. I'm excited to have you help them. You've taught almost half the doctors to come out of this school."

"That's right! I've been here a helluva long time. I could almost get a degree myself."

Ranger's room was not like I pictured most hospital rooms. His contained furniture he appeared to have purchased himself. Every tabletop had at least three pictures of his grandkids and his old army buddies. The window behind his bed gave the room a warm tone, much different from the dark hallway. Ranger himself was a thin, graying, wrinkled man lying in the bed with the sheets pulled up halfway. He was dressed in thin blue pajamas that had been brought from home. Next to the bed was a bedpan that had not recently been emptied. And while I was inclined to avoid it, the rest of the group positioned themselves on the opposite side of the bed so that I was left to stand next to the urine-filled bowl.

"Mr. Ranger, is it?" I asked.

"Ranger, you can call me," he said, and quickly clammed up.

"I'm Jeff Triton, the medical student. I'd like to ask you a few questions, if I could."

"Yeah, sure."

I fought off the palpitations I was feeling. As I asked him my "open-ended questions," hoping he would elaborate, he repeatedly ended the conversation abruptly.

"So tell me, sir, what brought you into the hospital this time?"

"An ambulance, same as last time."

Real fucking funny, man, I thought. "I mean, what made you decide to call the ambulance?"

"I couldn't fucking breathe, that's what made me decide to call. You woulda fucking decided to call, too!"

"I'm sure I would, sir. I just wanted to get a sense of the events that led up to your admission." I slowly pried each little bit of information out of him, apologizing over and over again for not being clear about this or that. It turned out that he was in the hospital because his congestive heart failure was acting up, and the cardiologists were debating whether to do a coronary bypass. He also had severe emphysema from his years of smoking. When I asked him about his smoking habits, he quickly interrupted my question.

"I used to be addicted to those damn things," he shouted. "Two packs a day for thirty years. But I kicked that damn habit."

"That's excellent, sir."

"Don't interrupt me! I used to smoke two packs a day. Now I only smoke one pack per day."

I paused, waiting for anything else he might say. Nothing followed for thirty seconds or so, so I thought it safe to continue my questioning.

After I gained a sense of the entire course of this three-week hospital stay, I had an understanding of why he had brought so many pictures of family members and friends. Ranger seemed like a lonely man, and these pictures gave him at least some strength when he had little control over the things around him. I wrapped up the interview by summarizing my understanding of his disease and tried to give him a positive spin on the treatment plan for him.

"Thank you, Mr. Ranger," I said. "I appreciate your time in helping me."

"Okay, Ranger," said the cardiologist. "I'm going to take these guys out and discuss how Dr. Triton did. Do you have anything you want to say?"

"Yes, I do," he bellowed. "And all of you guys listen to this, too. I'm the patient! And because I am the patient, I am the only one in this room that matters. None of you matter! So whatever happens, what I say goes. You got that?" Ranger pointed at the medical students around the room.

I looked over to the cardiologist to see if his face suggested that I had done something to piss this guy off. His face was quiet and expressionless as he looked back at Ranger.

"And another thing. You're not God, and you never will be!" This time he was pointing directly at me.

Holy shit! I thought to myself in silent, stunned amazement. I couldn't remember the last time I'd had any self-esteem in medical school, and this guy had just accused me of having a God complex.

"And because you're not God, you don't know what I'm feeling. And because you don't know what I'm feeling, you have to ask me…" Ranger continued with his rant. In summary, it seemed that doctors, with me as their leader, were a bunch of arrogant quacks interested only in making themselves look good. Perhaps they occasionally healed someone along the way. Ranger was happy, however, to thwart my rise to God-complex status and humble me.

When Ranger finally fell silent, the cardiologist turned around and opened the double doors behind us. We all filed out behind him, and I shut the doors once I was out. Sweat had accumulated on my brow and cheek within the final minutes of the confrontation. I closed my eyes and sighed, convinced that I had given a terrible performance.

"Well done, Triton. Strong work," the cardiologist said, a smile finally coming to his face. "You got a good history out of him. I know Ranger can be a pain in the butt sometimes. He didn't give you much info there at the beginning, but you got it out of him."

"What about all that stuff he said about me there at the end?" I asked.

"Oh, never mind that. He has been admitted here so many times and done this with so many medical students. He was just taking his frustration out on you. You didn't do anything wrong in there."

With my tail still tucked firmly between my legs, I drove home to get ready for the double date with Mary and Elisabeth. On the answering machine I found a message from one of my professors.

"Jeff, you mentioned that you would li-ike to tutor some sob-jects." Dr. Escobar was a tiny woman from South America with a strong accent. "I hob a student who would li-ike a some haelp. Her name es Tera Esheridan and her number es…"

I had actually wanted to do some tutoring to look good on my résumé as well as just to grab a little cash for studying with someone from the class below me. I picked up the phone and dialed the number.

"Hello?" answered the voice on the other end in a meek voice.

"Hello, is Tera there, please?" I asked.

Immediately, the meekness in the voice disappeared. "It's Tah-ra!" she said, emphasizing the correct pronunciation

My heart puttered away for a second. "Okay…" I paused to contemplate whether I had said something really offensive in my few words. "I, um, I got a message from Dr. Escobar that you might want a tutor for something."

"Yeah, I was looking for an anatomy tutor."

Anatomy was the only subject that I had not volunteered to tutor. I had scored only average in that class and didn't see how I could offer any help to someone in that field. "Oh, actually, I didn't sign on to tutor that subject," I said, trying to back out. "I don't know if I would do well for you in that one. I had planned on tutoring biochem or path."

"Don't worry. I'm sure you'll be fine. That is, if you want to."

"Um, yeah, I guess if you're willing to risk it with me, I can give it a try. Maybe I'll have a few tricks to teach you. When did you want to get together?"

"How about next Wednesday? 5:30 sound okay?"

"That sounds great." I gave her directions to the apartment and wrote her name and number on my whiteboard. I made certain to mark her name so that I would pronounce it correctly when she showed up next week.

Mary showed up at the screen door, opening it without a knock just as I finished buttoning up my jeans. "That looks great!" she said. "Turn around and let's get a look at that ass."

It sounded a bit funny coming out of this girl I knew as the chief of the nurses in the ER, but I played along. We closed up the apartment, and she led me to her car, where her boyfriend and my date were waiting. I got into the car before introducing myself, then took a second to look at the date I had been set up with.

I suppose, by definition, one has no right to have expectations of a blind date. But this girl was phenomenal—the mirror image of Catherine Zeta Jones. Though her name, Elisabeth, was spelled with an *S*, "Zeta" does her beauty justice, so I think back on her by that name. I shall, however, spell Zeta with an *S* to do her that courtesy. Seta was about 5'10", very thin, with long, dark hair. Her denim jeans were bland and straight, not contouring her legs at all. Despite her effort to hide her butt, my keen eye later picked it out from beneath the loose denim and recognized it for the work of art it was. Her hair was a perfect raven black and stretched down farther than I was used to seeing in professional women. It lay down her back, tickling the top of her jeans, which were accessorized by a studded black belt. Her skin was flawless, its softness implied by the natural shadowing in the dim light. I suppose she had what is referred to as olive skin, although I had never quite understood the term. I had never seen an actual olive that wasn't either black or some mucky green. But her skin was neither of these; it was a creamy tanned color, shaded perfectly at her cheeks, as I would learn was characteristic of Greek women.

Conversation that night was fluent as I found out that Seta was well traveled. She and her mother had traveled throughout Europe and Asia. She told of all those countries that she had not been and discussed her dreams of going. We each joked of our "work" and told how we passed our days. I shared my story of Mr. Ranger, and everyone got a chuckle out of a doctor's first patient experience. Before the night was over, Seta and I had set up our next date for the following night.

A first date—or first date alone, as this would be—can take on many shapes and forms. There is always the dinner and a movie when you have that fear of resorting to conversation somewhere in the evening. I didn't have that fear with Seta. She was beautiful in every way one could list. Anyone passing on the street would eye her and comment on her "bone structure," but her skin was so soft and glossy that you could not imagine something so hard and course as a bone beneath it. Her cheeks invited kisses all night as we sat across from one another. Her figure was on loan from a supermodel, tall and slender. Her hips presented themselves only enough to dangle the jeans she wore tauntingly. And those jeans. This girl, who was so beautiful that she could be a member of Hollywood or Broadway's nobility, was so down-to-Earth that she didn't feel comfortable wearing any outfit that did not include faded denim jeans. I could read everything about Seta in her jeans: a faded comfortable pair of pants that looked incredible with anything. So the words "dress code" could not enter into the itinerary for the evening.

Dinner and a movie is what I would recommend as a backup plan for a high school senior who has no desire to impress his female accompaniment. But then, if you had no desire to impress her, why bother taking her out to begin with? I clearly had a girl who appreciated the simple things in life, so I was not looking to Spago as the winning field goal. Rather, I turned to a trick that I had discovered in the previous year to impress ladies of any social class, any taste, and any level of commitment. After bringing her to one of my favorite Italian restaurants, we went to a nearby standup comedy club. The winning potential of this date was so vast because first, so few people have actually been to an actual comedy club, while having seen them on television. Second, everyone judges their date by how well they were entertained by the conversation; when you see a standup comic, you automatically get credit for half the jokes that the comic tells.

Just as I had planned, dinner was tasty enough to enthrall heaven's culinary critics, yet casual enough for Levi Strauss himself. And as I had suspected, she had never been to a comedy club. The extra twenty I passed to the doorman got us a seat near the stage, and her glowing brown eyes were wide all night. She laughed almost continuously during the show, until one of the comics commented on how beautiful she looked. I had been certain that one of them would draw attention to her looks; she blushed and tucked her grinning face into my shoulder. That Saturday night was her first night to be truly spoiled by a man.

The first half of the drive home, we relived the jokes which had had us rolling in the club. Her laugh was free and innocent, like a twelve-year-old girl who hasn't figured out to be embarrassed if she snorts. We shared jokes that we had heard at work and made up our own on the spot.

"It's 10:00," I said with slight hesitation in my voice. "I hope it's not too late for you. You see, I made you a dessert, and I was hoping you might come over for some pie."

"You made pie?"

"I know it seems stupid to make you dessert if we were going to the comedy club, but I hadn't decided on what we were doing tonight, so I started with dessert when I was planning to cook you dinner."

"I didn't mean it sounded stupid. I just thought it seemed wild that you know how to cook."

"Oh, yeah. I like to cook. I was hoping to impress you with dinner tonight, but then the comedy club idea came to me, and I just had to. But I made this pecan pie, so you have to come over to try it." In truth, I'd had the start, finish, and middle of this date planned before I had planned on Seta being the date. Baking a dessert for a woman was the perfect way, I had learned, to spoil her and dazzle her with my domestic skills.

"Oh my God, I have never had a guy cook for me. I would totally love to go by your place to try it."

"You mean your last guy didn't cook for you?" I had heard from Mary that the last guy was a real asshole and barely paid any attention to Seta at all. But I was not above making the differences between us two guys readily apparent to her.

"Cook? Shit, I was lucky if he would get me a beer from the fridge if he was in the kitchen."

"Man, that sucks. Then we'll just have fun tonight." I parked the Camaro in front of the house and led her behind it to my apartment. I had long since gotten over the embarrassment of living in such a humble castle behind a house. "Excuse the mess. It's just because I've been studying for finals." My apartment had the organization of a beaver dam, in which sticks, twigs, and leaves are jumbled into a somewhat cohesive structure by an animal you would otherwise presume to be no more intelligent than a common rat. Similarly, several textbooks adorned my bookshelves and desktops; my whiteboard had every biochemical pathway achieved by the human body diagrammed in a color scheme that implied some rationale. A woman would look at my notes scattered about and assume that I had them "organized that way," because a medical student must be organized, just as a beaver must be intelligent to throw all those sticks together. The apartment was actually cleaner than it had been in a long time. I had known that I would bring Seta back for pie and a little music.

"Have a seat here on the couch while I go start the pie warming," I said.

"Can I use your bathroom first?"

"Of course you can. It's just through here." I had even cleaned the bathroom. Don't get me wrong; I had not resorted to adopting the concept of guest towels or other girly things, but I was at least fairly certain that there was something clean to dry her hands on. I placed my fingertips on her hip and led her through the kitchen toward the back of the apartment where the bedroom and bath were located. "Let me get this light for you," I said as I slipped by her, nose-to-nose.

"Thanks. That's sweet of you," she said as the light clicked on and we passed each other again on opposite sides of the hall.

I flicked the oven on and ran over to the stereo, turning on the light hits, which were already cued. The sound softly filled the room with humble guitar and a romantic voice. The mood was complete with a few candles lit about the edges of the room. I made my way back to the kitchen, where there was but a hint of light making its way from the living room candles. I opened the oven, where the pie had been awaiting our return. The scent of nutmeg and maple filled the room, and Seta entered the room from the bathroom hall. She had taken her suede coat off, revealing a dark blue satin blouse which came down just to the waist of her jeans.

"That smells fantastic," she remarked. "And you cooked that from scratch?"

"Let's just say you walking in here tonight was not the first test this smoke detector has had today." The pan slid out from the oven simply into one hand. On my way to the counter, I detoured slightly to waft the freshly roasted pecans her way. The aroma was warm and inviting, and her eyes closed as she drew in the fragrance. Her head followed the scent as the steam, tinted with an essence of sweetness, danced from the tiny pores in the crust. I stood close to her. Her hand was perfectly contoured to my shoulder blade and pulled me closer. The minutes that our faces had been locked in gaze, along with the seconds they had crossed paths in my hallway, had taunted my passionate desires. Our bodies were as close as they could be without touching. Her breaths became deeper by the moment, and I could feel her breasts stroke my chest. Then her deep breathing brought her abdomen flush with mine. My breath seized instinctively to maintain this intimate second for three or four more.

Her chin lifted and her eyes closed as she placed a silent kiss on my cheek. The satin appearance of her skin had not betrayed me, as the sides of our faces rested comfortably upon each other. I peeked through my half-closed eyelids to watch this beautiful creature. Her hands walked down my sides to my hips as she rose to her tiptoes. She was tall enough that this was not at all necessary, but she used this positional advantage to expose my neck and proceeded to trail the kisses down to my collar.

"Can we go back there?" she whispered without pointing.

I refused to break away from our grasp, and with the lightest of touches on her back, I guided her toward my room. Her fingers slid through my hair as I traversed the kitchen in reverse. Perhaps watching a few more Michael Jackson videos in the '80s would have proven useful. When we reached the bedroom, the lights from the yard lit the room ever so slightly. I removed my shirt, trying as hard as I could to subtly imitate my perception of a male stripper. I pulled the shirt off with both hands, reaching between my two scapulas and then sliding it slowly and smoothly over my back. I was thinking over and over that I hoped my workout from earlier that day had left some evidence in my chest.

She muttered a tiny sound of approval then stepped back, reclining on the bed. She began unbuttoning her shirt, uncovering a black bra. I turned to light the few candles I had placed in the room earlier. They were an assortment of various beach-and-ocean-themed scents that I liked for a pseudo-escape from my daily study reality. When I turned back around to face her, she had completely removed her shirt. The bed creaked as she leaned back, her eyes wide, looking back at me with an unexpected element of shyness.

"I'm a little bit nervous," she meekly declared.

What I remember most about the rest of the night was the intimacy and adoration with which she touched me. Even as we simply lay there and talked hours later, her voice expressed such gratitude—an emotion I thought somewhat peculiar after sex. But the more I listened to the nuances in her voice, the more I sensed that she truly believed that I was the first one to care about her pleasure.

So she continued speaking, her head on my chest. "I was with my last boyfriend for three years, and he didn't care at all what I felt in bed. By the end, he didn't even care if we slept together at all. You were the first person to ever make me feel the way I just did. I think I'm falling in love with you." Her voice was choked up, almost as if she was going to break into tears there in bed.

Feeling a little awkward about her frankness, I began to feel similarly choked up as well. I was needed again. I felt much like the hero I had tried to be for Mena and Hailee, and probably many of the other girls I had been with. Seta appreciated me for being that hero. She had me convinced. "I think I'm love, too," I whispered back, thinking what a mess my agreement may have just caused. Despite my feeling so strongly about her before and especially after her confession, it was reflex to agree with her feelings of love.

It was like ending a conversation with your mother on the phone. When she says, "I love you," you cannot simply say, "Catch ya later."

Chapter 7

The end of the semester was approaching more rapidly than anticipated, along with finals. As December approached, the pace of studying picked up, and the tension in the back of everyone's minds increased. The first challenge I faced was a practical exam testing my history-taking skills. The system had been designed to assess the lessons that I was supposed to have learned in my encounter with the Ranger. Each of the second-year medical students was assigned a day and time to venture into the hospital and pick out a patient to interview in front of a video camera. The tape of that interview would be reviewed and graded by a faculty member, and then it would be watched and critiqued in front of small groups of students to help us improve. My assigned day was Friday, which meant that I had a week to prepare as well as talk to my classmates, who were doing this ridiculous test all week long. The thought itself made me a little damp across the forehead, considering the ridicule I had received from Ranger during my last experience. But I put off worrying as long as I could; there was little more I could do than study for it.

The early morning pharmacology class wrapped up at 9:00 a.m. My fellow students and I poured out of various amphitheater doors in each direction. *Religion class*, I thought suddenly. *Shit, it must be Tuesday.* Tuesdays and Thursdays at Mon Gracia were a slight deviation from the normal rut of cramming as much scientific information into our heads hour after hour, only to have it leach into our blood and then filter out into the toilet at the next restroom break.

I have heard it said once that we only retain ten percent of what we are taught. Perhaps the other ninety percent could be detected on something like a urine drug test as it filters out of our bodies. Someday, we might see our high school teachers equipped with urine knowledge tests. When Mrs. Webb catches little Lisa screwing around in class, she could send her to the restroom and have her pee in a cup. Then, with an eyedropper and a plastic test strip much like a home pregnancy test, Mrs. Webb could see how much knowledge Lisa had pissed away. Then, with a small calculation ($P=.90xH$, for all the algebra aficionados, where P is the knowledge quantified in the urine and H is the total information heard in class) the teacher can determine that Lisa was staring at Tommy rather than listening to her for approximately 1.3 hours.

As mentioned, Tuesday was a departure from routine, as we had an hour of religion class to break up the monotony. Religion class brought some relief in that it was not graded and there was no pressure to pay more than glancing attention. But it was not without its frustrations. The first year of this endeavor revolved around reading passages in the Bible and interpreting them as a small group of twenty students. Regardless of the passages being read, the interpretations would be strikingly similar. Whether it was Matthew, Mark, or Luke, 3:16, 6:24, or somewhere around noon, the discussion would follow a general pattern.

"...and the Lord gave them a son. And He was named Jesus." The pastor would pause and look about the room with a glad sigh, as though he had just smelled his mother's freshly baked apple pie. "Who would like to tell me what this passage means?"

Hands invariably shot up around the room, like those of eager children hoping to open their birthday gifts. "Well, God sent Jesus to us because He loved us soooo much. And Jesus was to come to Earth and show us that our god is a loving god. And it is just sooo beautiful that God was sooo loving."

Or the pastor might ask, "So, can anyone explain why Jesus, the son of God, was a carpenter?"

Again, the hands would shoot up. "Well, it was to show that we don't need to be of high social status to be close to God, because God is such a loving god. And it doesn't matter how common we feel. God still loves us, as long as we are loving. And even if we are not loving, God still has love for us. We just have to ask for His love and accept

Him." (This was where most of the eyes in the room would drift over toward me.) "Because God is so loving and godly."

Nods and whispers passed around the room. "Yeah. God is a good god." "Yes. He is such a loving god."

"Tiresome" is the word I would use to describe my experience during that first year of religion class. None of my questions were being answered in a way that brought evidence or rationale to the truth behind the Truth. I honestly thought the discussions were going to degenerate into pep rallies, where the pastor would merely ask, "Okay, who would like to compliment God?" Presumably the hands would raise just as before. "God is good." "Yeah, God is a loving god."

In this second year of religion classes, the depth of discussion improved somewhat. Often, the conversation would diverge into theories of how suffering could be permitted on Earth if God was so loving, or what the role of a physician should be in promoting faith in the ill. Even as an atheist, I enjoyed the conversation and often played the devil's advocate—pardon the pun—just because I liked the amount of thought that went into these topics in contrast to the previous year's team-spirit gatherings at 9:00 in the morning twice a week.

I never argued with my classmates over these issues. In fact, in most circumstances my philosophy was very much in line with theirs. If I had a patient whom I thought would be comforted by my praying with them, I felt certain that I would improvise some encouraging pep talk in the name of the Lord to get them through the hard times. I believed I would do this despite my general belief that there was no God. Some might call this hypocritical, for an atheist to pray to God. But I was not 100 percent certain there was no God or god. I was a scientifically minded person who felt that science was slowly developing the answers to the questions of the universe, and the explanations did not require the instigation of an all-powerful god to exist. To that extent, I felt that any scientific atheist who did not have some degree of agnosticism in him was too closed-minded and not indeed a scientist. Similarly, I felt anyone who strictly called themself an agnostic was either too cowardly or apathetic to fall on one side of the theistic fence.

After close to a year and a half, my pious classmates had stopped being suspicious of "Jeff the atheist." They no longer spoke of me in the third person in my presence. Many of them still probably referred to me as "the heathen" when I was not around. And since I had dated a half dozen of them within the first weeks of medical school, I am sure several of them were still calling me far worse names. But I think they actually enjoyed having me to spice up the classes as well. I always tried to leave them with the sense that they had won the debate. My goal, however, was to make them leave the conversation with more questions about their faith than they had entered with. In any case, there was no mistaking the fact that the students and faculty saw me as a project. Hell, perhaps they had only accepted me to the medical school because they had seen me as a conversion project from the start.

The official day ended around noon as we trekked into the hospital to find a patient and interview them on camera. I stopped at the university gym for a quick workout and a game of racquetball before I hit the books again. The weight room was fairly expansive, with a good selection of free weights, isometric machines, and cardiovascular equipment. During medical school, I had developed the habit of working out for an hour a few times a week. This included the obligatory breaks to look at the fine selection of spandex models that routinely partook in the Stairmasters on the north side of the gymnasium. Mon Gracia, being so in tune with God's desire for us to be healthy, was teaming with young women practicing what was preached at them. The school of physical therapy was particularly "blessed" with regard to attractively healthy and healthily attractive female students who frequented the cardio room. Today, there was relatively little going on in the gym. Perhaps it was the early hour or just too close to finals. A few older physicians and professors had decided to call it an early day or take their lunch break and jog a few miles on the treadmill.

I left the light stench of sweat and blaring Christian rock of the weight room for a quick game of racquetball, then went home to study. Once I got home, I fell easily into the routine of studying. I filled a trashcan-sized glass with Mountain Dew and reclined on the couch with an assortment of textbooks and a folder with the semester's notes. It is difficult to recall what time it was when she called, because I tended to lose all temporal perspective when I studied. But the phone rang somewhere between ulcerative colitis and diverticulitis.

"Hey, sweetie. It's me," Seta said in her smooth and perky voice. "I just got off work from the hospital, and I was dying to talk to you."

"Did you have a hard day or something?" I asked.

"Nah, I guess it was fine. It was just another one of those days where the doctors and the patients are hitting on you. It totally gets annoying and old. I mean, I have to be nice to the doctor because he said he was going to try to get me a full-time job here after I finish all my classes, but he just flirts all the time."

"Sounds like a real dick. But you're almost finished, and then you can forget about him," I said. While I was not delirious with jealousy or rage over someone coming on to my girlfriend, as I would have been a few years back, I felt slight insecurity about competing with someone who had already finished medical school. "How was the rest of the day?"

"It was good. I spent a lot of it daydreaming about what we did over the weekend."

"The concert was pretty cool, huh? I had a great time with you out on the lawn."

"I was talking about afterward." She giggled. "So what were you doing when I called?"

"Oh, I suppose it's just the same old thing. Studying for finals." I groaned. "I was reading about Crohn's disease a little while ago. It actually seems pretty cool. Did you know that sometimes people with this disease actually get tracts that form between their intestines and their skin or their bladder? It's freaky! So one day they're normal, and then the next day they're standing next to some guy at the urinal, dropping a log out of their weenie."

"I've taken care of a patient with that. Those Crohn's patients have really smelly crap."

There was a pause in the conversation as I contemplated what she had said and wondered which patients did not have smelly crap. That she had seen an actual patient, a real live patient, with this disease gave it a new tint of reality that it hadn't had before. I had never heard of the disease before pathology class, and it had such a mysterious sound to it that I could not imagine ever seeing someone with this bizarre condition—much like I would never expect to see someone with plague. But while bringing reality to my studies gave it some importance, to sum up the complex disease process that I had studied for thirty minutes by saying that their shit stank, also gave the condition a sense of triviality.

"Can I see you tonight?" she asked.

"I'm sorry, angel, I have to do the tutoring thing tonight. Can we do it tomorrow?"

"Sure, I get off work at six tomorrow."

"Perfect. You gonna come straight here?"

"As fast as I can," she said. "Love you, honey."

"Love you, too," I said as we hung up. I leaned over the side of the couch to pick up the book again. Just then, a shadow appeared through the screen door.

"Hello? I hope I'm not too early," Tara called into the room.

"No, you're fine. I was just studying." I assumed she couldn't see well through the screen as I scrambled to put on my shirt. "Come on in," I said. The living room was less than presentable; I had left books and notes in each spot I had occupied while studying over the past three days. Physiology notes filled the leather recliner by the window. My desk was layered with multiple books pulled down from their shelves, along with an empty milk glass and a plate with residual crumbs from the microwaved cookie dough I had eaten the night before. My socks and tennis shoes were still piled on the floor next to me, and the couch was covered by the pathology notes I had been writing.

"Wait here for a second," I said as I sprinted out of the room with the footgear, still moist from the afternoon's activities.

Once back in the living room, I found Tara sitting on the couch, leaning over to pull her books out of her backpack. We had been holding the tutoring sessions since the beginning of the school year. I was under no false impression that I was a fantastic or even decent tutor of anatomy. Our first few sessions, I struggled to remember any of the kooky phrases my friends and I had devised to memorize some of the nerves, muscles, and so on. As the year progressed, we had deviated into some of the other subjects that I felt more comfortable tutoring, and my confidence had gone up tremendously.

Tara was an extremely bright girl, an English major in college at UCLA who had traveled to London to study abroad. She had studied for some time at Ivy League schools and had done research at Harvard. It was not difficult to be impressed with her résumé, but I was particularly impressed because I had wanted so badly to go to the Ivy League for medical school. I often asked her why she would come back to Mon Gracia after going to Harvard. She always spoke of her family. The idea was charming, but I knew my family would think I was insane if I left Harvard to come to Mon Gracia.

She was a tall girl with a slender, athletic figure that looked good in the summer shorts of California. I was always careful to be subtle, sneaking a peek at her firm abdomen when she reached across me wearing her half-shirts. California weather is truly remarkable, allowing summer clothing to be worn well into the fall and winter. She had straight blonde hair that ran halfway down her back, just the kind of hair one would expect in a California girl. However, she was not a California girl at all. In fact, she was originally from Ireland, which was where her name, Tara, had come from. Apparently, any true Irish Tara would have taken similar offense at my egregious mispronunciation.

Most striking about her were her soft cheeks, which didn't appear to have changed since she was an infant. They looked as if some adoring grandmother had made some googling noises and pinched her cheeks, leaving two voluptuous dimples. The cheeks turned bright red like a forest set ablaze with even the slightest emotional response. Demonstrating the attachments of the biceps muscle on her arm would have lit the room with her blushing.

Ethically, I supposed it would be inappropriate to date her, since she was technically a student of mine—although I would have had a difficult time convincing anyone at that time that I seriously considered ethics when it came to relationships. I tossed around the idea of dating her at times. Like every guy, I was under the presumption that girls have some clandestine infatuation with me. However, in the context of some conversation, she had mentioned that she had a boyfriend studying law at UCLA. Besides, I was actually happy with Seta and had no intention of cheating for perhaps the first time in my life. My last few girlfriends had gotten me used to the temporary nature of most relationships, and I truly saw them as filling a very simple role in my life. That role was to take me away from the mundane lifestyle of a medical student briefly, although regularly.

"So, how hard do you think the test is going to be this week?" she asked. I was caught off guard, daydreaming like a teenage boy, about Seta, Tara, and perhaps even Lois Lane, each playing the adoring girlfriend role in their own special ways—but all at the same time, of course.

"Huh? Oh, it's gonna be tough, but you'll do fine. Everybody goes into the test pretty scared and comes out kinda shaking their head like they got hit by a boulder. But you know this stuff. I've been listening to you week after week, and every time you're a little more confident. And that's what it's going to take to get through this thing." I had noticed that when I tried to be encouraging, I got into a zone where my speech took on a mind and personality of its own. In this case, I saw myself as Mickey motivating the Italian Stallion as he went into the big fight. It would not be stretching the truth too far to say that I heard trumpets playing the *Rocky* theme song as I gave Tara the pep talk. Meanwhile, she simply looked back at me with her wide blue eyes, as though I was revealing the wisdom of the universe rather than ranting like I was under the influence of a little alcohol and a lot of caffeine. "Just go in there and trust your first instinct when you're not sure. You are going to kick everybody's ass on this test."

"Wow. Okay, I'm ready then. I'm just going to polish up some of the rough edges over some coffee."

It was interesting how many students at Mon Gracia were closet coffee drinkers. The local coffee shops substituted for both nightclub and library in the local suburbs.

The screen shut behind her with a slam, and she walked out toward her car. Behind the screen, I saw Lois come from the opposite direction. She glanced in at me and then stared down the walkway as Tara departed. She did not hiss or purr in any particular way, but the duration and intensity of her gaze made her disapproval of the situation clear. I recognized that this must have been where the term "catty" originated. I quickly tried to smooth things over by inviting Lois in for a bowl of milk. Thankfully, she was an understanding feline.

That night, I found it particularly difficult to fall asleep. The sheep I was counting seemed high on cocaine, jumping over the freaking fence at light speed. Once they got over the fence, they would dash off in different directions. Obviously, it was my mind's responsibility to follow them wherever they went as sheep number one ran toward the section of my brain where my physiology final was stored. Sheep number two seemed interested in the interview at the end of the week. Sheep number three was initially drawn to the late-night comedy show that I had started to watch earlier before deviating toward the Howard Stern bikini-model contest on cable. What could I do? They were sheep. Clearly, they had minds of their own.

I recognized the futility of minding these sheep whose trough was apparently sponsored by Starbucks, so I took a breath and reflected on the religion class I had attended that day, hoping to slow down my mind. I wondered if each of my classmates prayed that night in bed. And if so, what did they pray for? Our public prayers were always benevolent, but did even the purest of Christians pray for an *A* on the final exam when they were alone? After more than a year with these people, I honestly could not imagine them praying for anything more than "to do our best." Or, if they were to ask for a good score, I was sure that they would add the caveat, "if that is what you want for me, God."

I figured that I would try to be a little more persuasive with God if I were the praying type. My prayer would sound something like, "God, realizing of course that you probably have some big plan for me and all, I thought maybe you would reconsider and bump me up a little higher on the curve." It sounded respectful enough to me, while merely offering my input on how things should play out. But I just could not grasp what prayer meant to my friends without believing in a god. And I was in this frame of mind when I did what I thought I would never do. A year before, I had been bombarded by friends stressing to me that God just wanted me to have faith and believe. I considered it a matter of integrity that I would not be forced to "believe" and pray even on my deathbed just because I was afraid to die. But that night I spoke to God.

My monologue would not quite merit the status of prayer, because it didn't offer all that faith stuff that my Mon Gracia peers were demanding. "God," I said aloud, just so He couldn't later defend himself by claiming that nowhere in the Bible does it say he is a mind reader. "I know most people say that you just want me to have faith that you are out there, in control of everything. But I just can't believe that you would give humans these scientific minds, then ask us to ignore our desire to have proof. I'm not saying you're not out there, I am just saying you should be willing to toss me something a little more convincing than some tears coming from a statue or an image of Jesus ingrained in a cloth reputed to have been his burial shroud…although that is a pretty cool trick. And that parting of the Red Sea—that was impressive. But you have to understand my skepticism here. We humans have a tendency to exaggerate stories and even mess with each other's minds from time to time. How about we make a deal? You just make a quick appearance tonight, or even some other night, and I would immediately become a Christian, or whatever you tell me I'm supposed to be. I would totally not sin. Oooh, except for that promiscuity thing. I might have a hard time giving that one up. But all the others—I could give those up without a doubt. So, meet me halfway on this one, and I think we will both be happy in the end. Just think about it and let me know."

It wasn't the miracle I had in mind, but to those who want to give the Big Guy the benefit of the doubt, I fell asleep shortly after my "dialogue" with God.

The next few days flew by without much to speak of. All my friends were performing their interviews, each still swearing that it was nothing to worry about. Then my turn came. Friday afternoon was a day like any other Friday. The university, and even the city of Mon Gracia, were slowly shutting down, preparing for the total lack of business and almost lack of visible life that was Sabbath in Mon Gracia. I had come to class that morning already wearing my pleated slacks, the white shirt, and the cute tie with the dolphins forming a subtle mosaic pattern. I had to return to my car to get the white coat that would allow me to migrate from the classroom side of the campus to the hospital side. Approaching the automatic doors, I placed the white coat over one arm and then the other. It did not have the luxurious feel that I had always expected a professional's coat to have. It didn't have my name embroidered on it, and it felt very empty, even with me in it. It did have a plastic nametag with my name on it, along with the words "medical student" conspicuously larger than the name.

Once the coat was on, the doors opened knowingly. I entered the hospital with simple instructions: find the head nurse on one of several floors and ask her if she had a patient who would be a good test patient. They would do the rest, I had been assured by my instructors.

It had been recommended to me to start with the seventh floor because they seemed to have the friendliest nurses as well as a large number of patients to choose from. When I got to the floor, I realized that identifying the charge nurse would be more difficult than I had first thought. I approached the secretary's desk and asked her how I might find the nurse in charge. An older, obese lady with graying, curly hair, she looked much like the secretaries I remembered from elementary school. She wore such thick glasses that it was difficult to see how light made it through them at all. Her head was down, busy reading either a list of doctors' orders or a *Glamour* magazine.

"The charge nurse?" she asked even before I spoke to her. "I'll get her," she said as she dialed the number on the desk phone. Her glasses made her eyes look like fish eyes, bulging out of her head. "Yeah, you got another one here. No, I didn't get his name. Okay, see you in a second."

Within a few minutes, one of the nurses came up to greet me. Her expression as she approached was less than elated.

"Hi, I'm Jean. I'm the nurse in charge on this floor. I imagine you're looking for a patient to interview for your examination."

I nodded. "Yes."

"I've got to tell you, our supply of patients has been pretty picked over for the past week. I guess that's one of the downsides of testing on Friday. Most of them have already done it at least once."

As she explained all this to me, my first thought was that maybe they would let me out of the test, perhaps just give me a courtesy "pass." Then I realized that would never happen and quickly dropped the idea before I set myself up for more disappointment.

She continued, "The other problem we're up against is that it's Friday afternoon, and most of the doctors have been scurrying around the hospital to get their patients out of here before the weekend so they don't have to come in on Saturday. So the place is pretty bare, too."

"Well, I'll take whatever you can give me. I'm not picky or anything."

"You know, I may have someone, if she's still here. Hold on, I'm not sure." She turned around and left me in a small room, staring at a vision-testing chart with the *E*s pointing in every direction. She returned after approximately five minutes. By then, I had memorized the chart and felt confident that I could pass a vision screen while blindfolded.

"I found one," she said. "I know it's not the ideal patient for your interview test, but really, this is all I could find."

"Don't worry," I said. "I'm happy to take any patient you have."

"Ms. Smith is one of our postpartum patients. Usually they would be gone by the second day, but her baby had a fever. So we let her stay an extra day on our floor while they checked out the baby. Everything was fine, and they have been discharged to go home. But I asked her just before I came in here if she would help us, and she agreed to be interviewed."

"That's great. Thank you," I said as she walked out to get Ms. Smith. I wanted to make sure I sounded grateful, but inside I was stricken with a slight sense of panic. I didn't know what the hell to ask a woman who had come to the hospital because she was going to have a baby. I had prepared to talk to someone who had a complaint or a medical problem. For that, I knew to ask them when they first noticed the problem and if they'd had any other symptoms with it. I knew to ask them if anything made it better or worse. I didn't think it would be useful to ask Ms. Smith when she had first noticed she was pregnant, but that was what I had been taught to do for my history. I decided that for the purpose of being graded, I would look better if I asked the questions they told me to ask while in this extraneous context, as opposed to appearing to have forgotten the questions they had specifically told me to ask.

I quickly scanned my memory for any education I might have gleaned somewhere along my academic path pertaining to obstetrics. Alas, there was very little. I recalled some of the pictures from embryology, which was the study of fetal development in the context of never seeing a patient or a baby. Oh, and half the embryos were from creatures other than humans. I remembered how some of the frightening chemicals in things like fertilizer could cause severe birth defects. But none of those chemicals had been put in fertilizers after the '70s, when they had discovered the harm.

"Okay, Ms. Smith. Come on in here. This is Jeff. He's one of our medical students here. Jeff, this is Ms. Smith."

"Hi, Ms. Smith. Congratulations on the new baby. Was it a boy or a girl?"

She smiled. "Thank you. He's a boy."

"Excellent," I said. "So I'm going to be asking you questions about your entire pregnancy, as well as your overall health."

"That's fine," she said. Her antsy fidgeting and her frequent attention to the wall clock conveyed her real feelings about the interview. She did not want to be kept any later on a Friday than I did.

"Shall we get started, then?"

"Sure."

"Tell me…" My deepest instincts told me, just before I spoke, that I needed to make this the most professional and distant question of the interview. In order to accentuate the professional tone of the question, I sat up straighter in the chair and straightened my coat. I furrowed my brows a little bit instinctively, just to prove that knowing this was not for my own satisfaction. "How old are you, ma'am?"

"Twenty-nine."

"And is this your first baby?"

"No, he's my second. My daughter is three."

"And when did you first realize that you were pregnant?"

She stared at me for a couple seconds and then answered, "About nine months ago, I guess."

"No, I'm sorry. I meant, what were your first clues? Were you having problems with nausea, or did you just miss your period?"

"I just missed a period."

"And so you took a pregnancy test then, or you went to see your doctor?"

"I went to see the doctor, and she told me I was pregnant."

"Did you have any problems with this pregnancy, ma'am?"

"No."

Reflecting back on the lessons we had been given on taking a patient's medical history, I remembered that if the patient said "No" or couldn't think of any answers to our questions, we were supposed to prompt them with answers I was most concerned about. The problem was that I didn't have the foggiest idea what kinds of symptoms to look out for during a pregnancy.

"Did you have any problems like nausea or vomiting?" I pressed her. "Maybe some abdominal cramping?"

"No, I was fine," she reiterated. "Although, wait. I did have a little spotting."

Spotting, I thought to myself. I didn't know if that was dangerous or not. I was impressed with myself for recognizing "spotting" as a term describing bleeding from the vagina. It seemed like a term chosen because it sounded deceptively harmless. I didn't see how blood coming from the vagina during pregnancy could be harmless. But I didn't know what else to ask. What kinds of things might make bleeding seem more dangerous? Pain, I guessed.

"And you did not have any pain during this time, too?"

"No."

The other thing that seemed "fishy" was I did not know how much someone could bleed from their vagina and still be considered "spotting." The thought of this woman bleeding and bleeding at home with no one there watching her because they thought she was fine scared me a bit. I decided that I needed to further elucidate exactly how much blood we were talking about. Of course, I didn't really know how much blood to consider too much. I would just get the amount now and save the evaluation until after the interview.

I thought about how to measure blood and couldn't think of how to ask the question. The first methods of measuring liquid that came to mind were the graduated cylinders that I had used in college chemistry class. It seemed ideal, because there had been three different sizes of about five milliliters, ten milliliters, and 100 milliliters. *Shit.* One of the first lessons in interviewing patients was to be sure to use language that they understand. We were in America; I couldn't ask someone to use the metric system to measure anything. I tried desperately to think of some common form of measurement that this lady might know off the top of her head.

"And how much blood would you say that you had?" I asked her.

"How *much*?" she asked incredulously.

I admit I had to expect this. How would a patient know how to measure her own bleeding if I didn't?

I went with the American forms of measurement I could think of. "Would you say that your bleeding was about a teaspoon?"

She didn't respond with more than a puzzled look on her face.

"Or perhaps a shot glass?" I had not intended to be crass, but when my analogy came out, I realized what I had done.

Her eyebrows quickly raised in the center, and the lines on her forehead implied both disgust and pity. Her voice creaked with hesitancy as she answered. "I would say it was about a *pad.*"

A pad! I thought to myself. *Damn it! Why didn't I think of that?* I consoled myself briefly that no guy knows any of these things on his own. I was lucky to have known she was talking about bleeding in the first place.

After that, I finished the rest of the interview relatively uneventfully and unproductively.

~~~

During finals week, the coffee shop in the neighboring town was the nidus of excitement. Knowing full well that God was frowning on my every sip, I sat with my pathophysiology notes and a grande mocha. Students from each of the medical school classes, and even students from the nearby colleges, were there. The last of the tests had come and gone by the following Friday morning. The routine seemed vastly calmer than it had on the first round of finals. As we walked from the last test, scores from the first test were being posted. Crowds gathered to see the ranks from top to bottom; they praised one another all the while, wondering if they would beat the other next time.

Back in the hospital one last time before Christmas vacation, we gathered in small groups to review our performances in interview skills. The room was sterile, cramped, and entirely not worth the effort, but we sat in front of a 1970s television set with videotapes of ourselves and our patients. By now, any errors I had made during my interview had sunk into the depths of a hopeless memory.

"The first interview we are going to watch is by Jess," said the instructor, her voice accentuated by the clunk of the videotape. "This was a masterful performance that you can all take something home from."

"Good morning, Mrs. Stanford," Jess said on the videotape. "I first just want to thank you for joining me here today."

The camera took a position just behind Jess, looking at the patient. *Christ!* I thought. *What is this, a PBS special?*

The patient nodded and smiled. "My pleasure."

"Can you first tell me, Mrs. Stanford, why you were in the hospital this week?"

"Well, I was diagnosed with pancreatitis." This went on for approximately forty-five minutes, despite the presence of five other people who had interviewed patients.

"I'm terribly sorry for using up the entire class with one video," the instructor said finally, "but I thought it had so many good things to offer. But in the last few minutes, there is one other segment that I wanted to play for you." She turned her back to us and popped in another tape.

"Did you have any problems with this pregnancy, ma'am?"

Shit. That was my head on the screen. I didn't seem nearly so confident as I had hoped I would in a soap opera.

"No." The silence in between sentences seemed quite a bit longer than I recalled during the actual interview.

"Did you have any problems like nausea or vomiting? Maybe some abdominal cramping?"

As a spectator, I was rocking back and forth in my seat, wishing I would just hurry up and ask the next fucking question.

"No, I was fine," she reiterated. "Although, wait. I did have a little spotting."

I looked around the room to see if there was puzzlement on anyone's face, but the women were experienced and the men were apathetic.

"And you did not have any pain during this time, too?" By this time, I felt truly frustrated with my inability to coach this interviewer from the sidelines.

"No." Come to think of it, she sounded more frustrated this second time around, as well.

"And how much blood would you say that you had?" I asked her.

"How *much*?" she asked.

"Would you say that your bleeding was about a teaspoon? Or perhaps a shot glass?"

The room erupted in laughter. The instructor paused the tape with the image of my face as solemn as a face has ever looked.

"A shot glass, Jeff?" the instructor said.

She pressed pause again, and the very next image was of Ms. Smith's horrified face. There it sat while she tried to determine the best way to respond. "I would say it was about a *pad*."

That night, after an evening with Seta, we returned to my apartment. On the porch I found five shot glasses and a small box. Dangling from the box was a small note that read, *From Jess*. Within the box was an elegant shot glass in the shape of a German beer stein. A metal nameplate was affixed to the front of the glass. Two horizontal lines had been drawn on the plate, one above the other. Beneath the bottom line was the word *Mini*, and above the top was the word *Maxi*.

"Who is Jess?" asked Seta.

"She's one of the girls in my class. You remember her."

"Is she making fun of you?"

"She is not making fun of me. She's just having fun. Besides, she did a good job. Someone with pancreatitis."

"Oh, my God! I had this one patient with pancreatitis. I had to clean him up so many times. He smelled like a freaking sewer." Seta blurted like Paris Hilton in a proctology reality show.

I lowered my voice. Her immature straw had broken my med student camel's back. "We need to talk," I said quietly. "I'm not sure we have as much in common as we should. I don't think it's working out between us."

She stared at me in shock. "What do you mean, it's not working out?" she shouted. "How can you say that?"

"I've just been noticing we don't have as much to talk about as we used to, or as much as I would like."

"You are such an asshole. I can't believe you're doing this to me."

"I'm not trying to do anything to you. I just—"

"Fuck off! I don't care what you're trying to do. That's fine. I'm history." She slammed the screen behind her.

I stumbled over my words dozens of times again in my head, wondering if there was some poetry that would have allowed that breakup to go more smoothly. None came to mind. I resolved not to dwell on it and went to bed. Surprisingly, I slept well.

~~~

I woke Saturday morning and made my way to the bathroom mirror to find my hair flailing in a starburst pattern as usual.

Just as I pulled the moist towel over my face, I heard a loud rap at the door. I wasn't expecting anyone, and I didn't know of any old friends who might be in town to surprise me. But not being a particularly shy person, I answered the door in my Superman T-shirt and underwear from the day before.

It was Seta. "I couldn't go home last night," she said, stumbling over her words. It was clear that she had been drinking the remainder of the night. "I stopped at a bar and then went to a liquor store and got stuff to drink in the car the rest of the night. I've been trying to figure out what went wrong."

"You've been drinking all night? Are you fucking nuts?"

"I just had to think."

"And how well have you been fucking thinking, plastered like this?" I shouted at her.

"Look, I'm not going to beg you to get back together. I'm not even going to try to talk you into it." Her arms were dancing between wild gestures and keeping her balance.

"Does your mom know where you are?" I asked in a panicked voice. "She is gonna be freaking out, wondering what I did with you."

"I called her last night and told her I was at a friend's house because I had too much to drink. Just listen...I don't want to get back together. I just want one more time."

"One more time?"

"Yes. One more time in bed. You know, that thing you do. With your tongue."

I was speechless. First, I couldn't believe that she had been drinking all night. While I knew it was a common practice, I had never actually known someone who had tried to drink away their problems. More importantly, I could not believe the request I was hearing. It seemed I really had not been giving this alcohol a fair shake, if it was this strong of an aphrodisiac.

"Beth, you're drunk. You don't know what you're saying. Let's just get you home and let you sleep it off."

"No! I've been thinking about this, and this is what I want."

I wanted to think that this was a natural reaction that any woman would have to me; but not even I could convince myself that that was the motivation. I got that nervous feeling in the pit of my stomach again as I traced out her potential devious plans. Maybe she was trying to make it seem like I had gotten her drunk in order to rape her. Or maybe she was trying to get pregnant so she could hold that over me forever. All this to get me back for breaking up with her. What the fuck had this world come to?

I thought about how crazy the scenario had to be to force me to do what I was about to do. But it *was* that crazy, and I had to. I turned down sex with a beautiful girl.

"Why don't you lie down and sleep off the booze?" I asked her.

"No. I'm fine. It's all worn off by now."

"I don't think that it has. You still seem kinda swervy."

"Leave me alone! You had your chance. Now I can decide things for myself." Again, the door slammed behind her.

Chapter 8

Pathology is the study of how disease attacks the human body, breaking it down by various mechanisms and making it look like an oatmeal-chocolate-chip cookie under a microscope. The difficulty in studying pathology is figuring out which disease baked the oatmeal-chocolate-chip cookie you are looking at, as all the diseases are baking with the same ingredients. This is why medical school included a pathology lab in the curriculum: to spend three hours, twice a week, looking at slides of various oatmeal-chocolate-chip cookies so that we could later pretend that one cookie looked different from another.

To facilitate an interactive environment in pathology lab, the entire class was divided into smaller groups of about forty students. This being the first day back after the winter vacation, I sat next to Jess to tell her of my tragic breakup with Seta and perhaps gain some sympathy points toward a date with her. For the year and a half that I had known her, she had always seemed the perfect girl for me, or possibly just the perfectly unattainable girl for me. My adventures into relationships with random girls who promised adventure had only led to boredom. I would never have anticipated getting bored with a relationship with a beautiful or well-endowed woman who lacked a little in intellectual prowess, but it had happened over and over. I couldn't compromise in my next relationship; I needed someone like Jess who was both smart and beautiful. Our conversations always began the same way, with her long, dark eyelashes dancing about her winking eyes and persuading me to trust her. But they would always end with her explanation that we could not date because I was not Adventist, and therefore we could not get married.

The lights were dimmed and the first oatmeal-chocolate-chip cookie of the semester flashed up on the screen.

"How was your Christmas?" I asked Jess.

"It was great," she whispered back to me. "Dave went home with me to meet my family."

What the fuck? I was stunned. I had heard rumors about them being at a Vespers before the holidays, but they needed two more religious gatherings before they were allowed to date. What the fuck was this? They had completely jumped the gun. Dave was a thin guy in the class, known for his dorky laugh and his perpetual bad jokes. The thought of him with her brought me silently to a rage. I had the slight vindication of knowing that he was not getting any premarital sex, by virtue of Jess's virtue. But still, I could not be completely consoled.

"…yours?" I heard her say.

"What?"

"I just asked how your vacation was. Did you go anywhere or do anything with Seta?"

"Actually, Seta and I broke up. It just wasn't working out between us. But I went on a snowboarding trip to Idaho over the break. That was awesome."

"That's too bad you broke up. She was gorgeous. Who are you dating now?"

"What makes you think I'm dating someone already?"

"You're always dating someone."

"That's not true. I'm usually trying to date you," I said, my voice rising a little louder than I intended.

"Whatever. I've counted, like, seven girlfriends in the last year. And they were all hot, that I saw." Jess had a way of dismissing my advances so that my ego was never shattered after getting turned down. But the other consequence was that I never took the hint.

"I want to find someone who has something in common with me. I was thinking about asking out the path teacher." In truth, I had briefly entertained the fantasy of asking out the pathology instructor during the past semester, but the blind date with Seta had come up and developed into a three-month-long relationship. Linda was the instructor's name, and she was a pathology resident at Mon Gracia hospital. She had graduated from medical school two years before and begun looking at oatmeal-chocolate-chip cookies from actual people for a living. She was of average height, with medium-long blonde hair. Her looks were above average, but plain. She was slightly overweight, but not at all insecure. Her plain appearance was perfectly complemented by an innocent lisp. She always smiled at me when she called on me to name the cookie on the screen, then smiled again when I guessed it right. I had thought about what it might be like to date an actual doctor; it seemed like a true step up in sophistication. I had just mentioned asking Linda out because I wanted to see if it would get a rise out of Jess. I had not realistically considered asking her out at that time.

"You would not ask her out," Jess shot back.

"Of course I would. I'll bet you I do." As the idea sank in, asking out the teacher became more and more attractive. First, there was the idea of graduating to dating a doctor, which was pretty sexy in and of itself. Second, even if she was plain, the questionable nature of dating one's teacher brought a sense of adventure to the otherwise bland sport of dating Seventh Day Adventists. I realized that such a bet was more like dropping down to fifth grade than graduating to a doctor, but sometimes we need to create our own motivation.

"All right. You're on. I bet you that you don't ask her out before next class is over."

"It's a bet." I contemplated quietly how I would ask her out. Would I ask her some pathology question after class? Should I just follow her out of the class and ask her as we went outside? Maybe compliment her skirt, her hair? *Fuck!* It all seemed so overused. Granted, it was mostly used in cheesy, *B*-movie pornographic plots that she probably had not been exposed to, but maybe she had heard of them anyhow.

Before I knew it, the class had ended and it was lunchtime. I bent down to pick up my texts and wandered over toward Linda to make up a spontaneous-sounding conversation. But as I stood, at least thirty-eight of the other thirty-nine people in the class rushed her desk to ask pathology-related questions. The only one still sitting was Jess, who watched me with a smirk. Damn, it was a beautiful smirk. I wandered up to the desk, realizing that I couldn't ask her out in front of all the other students, but I listened in to see what excuses they used to talk to her.

Their discussions did not prove useful, as I had no intention of asking her to elaborate on uterine fibroids and then ask her out. One of the girls had approached the instructor not to ask a question, but rather to boast of her performance on the final exam a couple of weeks prior. I spent much of the lunch resenting the other students in the class, and the rest of it calling myself variations on the theme of "wimp" until I convinced myself that I needed to go into the hospital and ask her out on the spot.

My heart was racing, and I knew that I was taking several risks, but the euphoria had set in. I parked my car in the patient parking lot and walked again through the entrance of the hospital. The last time I had walked in this way, I had wound up fumbling over my words and asking some woman about a shot glass. I had to be confident this time, and speak clearly and concisely.

The first dilemma was finding the pathology lab in the hospital. Inasmuch as patients are never expected to find a pathology lab, hospital designers never put it in obvious or well-demarcated areas. After taking more than one wrong turn, I made my way to the basement. I identified myself to the secretary as a medical student looking for Dr. Linda Reed, and I was taken back without question. Linda was sitting on a stool with another attractive girl, both of them fiddling with globs of mush from some poor guy's surgery. Undoubtedly that glob was to become an oatmeal-chocolate-chip cookie that would make or break someone's life. The two raised their heads toward me and interrupted the giggling.

"Hey, Jeff. What's going on?" Linda asked without making reference to how odd it was for me to be all the way in the hospital as a second-year medical student.

"Not much. Hey, I wanted to thank you for going over that stuff from the kidney last month. I totally recognized it on the test when it came up."

"Awesome. I'm glad it helped."

"I was also wondering if maybe you would like to go grab something to eat this weekend." I tried to sound as casual as I could. I realized that every word I had to think about was a word that I was likely to fuck up, especially in front of an audience. The other girl just sat there smiling; I didn't recognize her.

"Um, sure. That sounds great."

"How about I get your number, and I'll give you a call tonight or tomorrow, and we can work out the details."

"Yeah. Here you go." She wrote down her number on a sheet that had originally been printed for the purpose of informing a doctor that his patient had cancer. I grabbed the slip and gave the two girls a wink as I turned and walked out of the basement. Before I was out of the hospital, my cell phone had speed-dialed Jess to let her know that I was going out with Linda that weekend.

Weeks passed, and it was now February. Linda and I had been dating for over a month at that time. Her residency kept her busy, but I didn't mind. Dating her was my first look into the actual working world. At 6:00, she got off work and invited me over to her apartment for dinner. When I arrived, her three cats swarmed around me, apparently realizing I was allergic to them. On this particular night near the end of February, Linda accompanied me to my intramural soccer match. My class had formed a team early in the first year and had played consistently throughout medical school. Every Tuesday night on the field outside the university gymnasium, we would battle with teams from other classes and other departments, such as dentistry.

That night's match was against the physical therapists from the hospital. We had beaten them soundly the year before, and the anger had not been lost since then. Their team was known for being somewhat dirty out on the field, often tripping other players if it helped them get to the ball first. Growing up, I had never possessed the speed or the foot dexterity, so I had learned to play goalie at a young age. I continued to love the position and sport into adulthood. It was probably a mistake to play that night, since I had a midterm exam the following morning and should have been studying. My performance on previous exams left me teetering at around the ninetieth percentile of the class, and it was still my hope to become a neurosurgeon at Harvard or Johns Hopkins after I finished medical school. The only way I could see myself achieving that was to finish at least in the top ten percent of the class; otherwise, I would never be accepted into such an elite program as number one or number two in the country. But my devotion to my team prevailed, and I went out onto the field in my uniform, complete with Superman T-shirt.

I wish I could elaborate on the details of the game, perhaps describe some fantastic saves I made or some amazing plays that led to our scoring. I wish all of that was possible, but the first and only event I remember from that night was waking up on my back in front of the goal. My teammate had forced his fingers inside my mouth, and the taste of mud and sweat was a harsh awakening. Finding myself like this was a peculiar surprise. I had no question of where I was or when it was, but I had no clues as to why I was on my back.

"Jeff! Jeff! Are you okay?" Bill shouted four inches from my face. "Do you know where you are?"

"Yeah, I'm okay. What the fuck are you shouting at me for? And what am I doing on the ground?"

"You got a knee to the head. You've been out for five minutes."

"Did I stop the goal?"

"Yeah, you stopped it. The ball went way the heck over there. But while you were out, you started clenching your teeth and shaking. Some of the guys thought you might be seizuring."

"I think it's called seizing, dude." I propped my arms behind my back and was surprised to feel pain in both my shoulders as I lifted myself up. It was at that point that the throbbing in my forehead became pronounced. My eyebrows felt like they weighed fifteen pounds apiece. I shook my head briskly to disrupt the throbbing sensation. That was a decision I would regret for the next two to three minutes, as it felt like my brain continued to swirl in my skull like water down a toilet bowl.

"Can you see straight?" Linda had come from the sideline and supported my arm as I rose to my feet.

"Actually, it's quite odd. I'm not seeing straight—instead, I'm seeing around corners. Bill, I wish you could see the legs on this chick around that building."

Linda rolled her eyes. "Smart aleck."

"Unless I close one eye, then I see straight. Except I see straight out of my ear."

"He's fine," Linda said, reassuring the referee. "This is normal for him, if you can believe that."

"Okay, that's good," the ref said. "We've called the paramedics to take him over to the emergency room."

"That's all right," I protested. "I'm fine. I don't need an ambulance."

"You should get checked out at the ER," Linda repeated.

"Well, you're a doctor. You can take me over there." I said this, realizing that I did not want my injury to fall anywhere near her specialty of pathology.

After coaxing, pleading, and persuading, I finally convinced Linda, the referee, and the paramedics who had shown up to let us drive to the ER ourselves. We drove the quarter of a mile to the ER and parked in the emergency patient lot. We walked in through the employee entrance and mingled through the crowd of patients, nurses, and doctors. I tried to gain the attention of anyone I knew, but they seemed oblivious. Finally, I spotted a resident I knew from my days volunteering in the ER.

"Brad!" I tried to subtly shout through the crowd. "Hey, I was wondering if you could help me out for a second."

"Jeff, what's going on, man? What brings you down here tonight?"

"I was playing in an intramural soccer game, and I got the crap kicked out of me. I got knocked out for a little bit."

"How long were you out for?" he asked.

Without hesitation, Linda piped up, "He was out about five minutes. He had some lip smacking, and then his arms and legs shook for a few seconds."

"Do you remember any of this?" he asked.

"No, I don't remember much of the game at all."

"Do you remember what you had for breakfast?"

"Are you kidding? I'm in med school. I don't eat breakfast, unless you count the double espresso I have before my midterms."

"We should probably get a CAT scan of your head to make sure you aren't bleeding in there. But it's pretty crowded tonight. There were, like, three car accidents with five people waiting to get CAT scans. It's gonna take at least two hours before we can get you in there." He looked over his shoulder at the line of stretchers sitting outside the radiology door.

"Two hours? Really? How important do you think it is? Do you really think I have a bleed, or are you just covering your ass? You know I'm not going to sue you. I need to get home and review for this midterm tomorrow and get some sleep. If I don't get home to sleep, I am going to completely suck on the exam."

"You probably don't have a bleed, but you can't tell for sure. I can get Dr. Green, the attending. He might let you go."

Dr. Green was not only the attending—which made him the boss and instructor over all the residents in the department—he was also the director of the entire emergency program. He had also written a little drug reference that every doctor in the world carried in their coat pocket to check the dose of that drug they just couldn't remember and inform them of that obscure drug they had never heard of. I had volunteered more hours in this very emergency room and had never met this famous and powerful man. It was somewhat embarrassing to meet him looking like I had just gotten my ass kicked.

A man in a white-collared shirt and a beard last groomed in the '70s hustled over to me as I sat in the middle of the room. He asked many of the same questions but seemed impatient and distracted by the noises in the department.

"I don't think it's wise that you leave. And you will have to sign out against medical advice. We can't just pretend that you didn't show up here tonight. Will anyone be around to observe you tonight? To make sure that you don't get drowsy out of the blue or start losing your balance?"

"Yeah, I can stick around and watch him for a while," Linda said.

"And you are?" Dr. Green asked.

"I'm his girlfriend. I'm one of the residents here."

I was astonished. Such a declaration of relationships in Adventist public places, let alone the implication that we were having sex, was almost unheard of...especially since we weren't. I could just see the scarlet letter being drawn on her scrubs as she spoke.

I felt slighted by this director's complete obliviousness to the fact that I had volunteered for so many hours in his department. I had a certificate of gratitude on some wall with his signature that had probably been placed with a stamp. *Oh well, fuck it.* I had a test in the morning. Linda drove me home and watched me study for a couple hours. She convinced herself that I wasn't going to hemorrhage in the middle of the night, or at least that her cats weren't going to get fed even if I did. So she left me home for an uneventful sleep.

~~~

Some weeks passed, and I found myself back at the coffee shop, sitting outside and sipping my mocha as usual. I had a textbook of some sort on my table, but the focus of the evening was the sweet caffeinated beverage sitting in front of me. Somehow, the flavor was deeper and richer when the coffee was not merely being used as a means to energize one's study efforts. The sun had fallen at least an hour earlier, and the outdoor tables were lit by lanterns strategically placed to provide perfect romantic mood lighting and keep lovers there to sip their drinks together all night. Alternatively, they could have been placed to provide just too little light for med students to study all night, likely nursing a single coffee the entire time. Either way, my needs were met. I nursed the book more than the drink, reading a few lines, taking a sip, and watching the activity at the tables around me, then reading the same lines again.

It was midweek and yet another busy night at the café. High school teens gathered around their custom purple and orange Hondas in the parking lot. They grasped their large coffee drinks that rested on the hoods of the cars and patted each other on the back for one foul joke or crass reference to the same girls I was watching that night. Their brash laughter begged for attention in the parking lot, just as their thundering exhaust and amplified stereos would beg when they drove away.

Families, as well as single parents, brought in children from age four to fourteen. A four-year-old begged his mother for a "mochaccino" that left ice cream and whipped cream covering his face as he sat at the counter. He proudly wore his green shirt and jeans, periodically threatening to pinch the stranger sitting next to him who had forgotten it was St. Patrick's Day, just as I had. (To clarify, I had forgotten to wear green and did not pinch the guy next to me.) The smile as the parents conversed with apparent relaxation was pleasing even from my distance. Their son was completely immersed mentally and physically in his fashionable milkshake, almost surely according to plan.

A fourteen-year-old came in soon afterward, with her mother, I assumed. Unlike the joy I saw in the boy's face, the freshly dubbed teenager seemed like she tolerated her mother's company in order to get her fix. The brand name on her shirt was faded, most likely from the time of purchase. Yet it was that name that surely brought with it the $60 price tag and entitled her to her friends' acceptance. I wondered if the four-year-old would be wearing the same brand next year when he went to kindergarten, probably still with whipped cream on his nose.

A tall blonde figure appeared before me. "Hey, how have you been?" Tara was out in her tan safari shorts with a couple notebooks in her hand and a tea bag visibly hanging from her paper cup. "I haven't talked to you in ages."

"I know. I've been doing great. All the tests are done, at least for now. Just sorta reading at a slow pace while I relax. How did your tests go?"

"They went fine, I guess. Your tips really helped me."

"Oh, excellent. I was thinking of you, hoping you did well."

"I was thinking of you, too, the other day," she said. "I saw you out in the quad area kicking the soccer ball around with your buddies between your classes, and my friend told me that you got knocked out or something during a soccer game recently." Her voice rose in disbelief.

"Yeah, I guess I got whacked a little."

"Did you really go unconscious?" She sounded amazed that anyone she knew would put themself in a situation to be knocked out.

"Yeah. I was out. I don't even actually remember what happened. But I'm okay now."

"Mind if I study with you?" she asked as her notebook flopped on the table.

"Only if that doesn't imply that I have to study." I smirked back.

Her discipline to study was clearly much greater than mine. Her head hovered over her notes, and her pencil retraced the diagrams she had drawn earlier. I was disciplined to the extent that I did not spy on all the other mochaholics in front of Tara—at least, not in an obvious manner. This wasn't a date, but I still didn't want to leer over other women in front of her.

Once again, the thought of dating Tara crossed my mind. I then thought about the dilemma I was facing with Linda and our relationship. We had been dating for a while and had become somewhat intimate. But the dynamics of a sexual relationship with a woman whose religion stated that going all the way was tantamount to going to hell was less than fulfilling. I might compare it to an eternal rundown between third base and home plate, with the catcher and third baseman repeatedly closing in and throwing the ball to each other. I had not been thrown out yet, but ultimately, when it comes to a crucial point, the runner usually knocks down the catcher when scoring. And that did not seem like an option for me. Anyway, Linda was preparing for a lecture she was to give soon, and I didn't expect to hear from her that night.

"It looks like they're closing the place down," Tara remarked. The analog clock face next to the lantern near us read 10:00. "Do you want to grab a drink at one of the bars nearby?" she asked. "It's St. Patrick's Day, and I'm Irish. It's almost criminal if I don't at least have a drink before the day ends."

I considered feeling guilty when I agreed to go, but the thing with Linda really wasn't going anywhere, I wasn't going to do anything with

Tara, and I was really just trying to stop a crime. Not to mention the fact that I had not quite mastered the feeling of guilt yet. That was an elective I had skipped in college.

The bar was dark and small, located just outside the limits of Mon Gracia. We played pool and drank the obligatory green shot and green beer. Not being much of a drinker, I thought that this might have been the first shot glass I had ever held for the purpose of drinking. I looked at the empty glass and chuckled.

"You're not drunk already, are you?" she asked.

The following is probably evidence that I was, but I said, "No, I was just thinking of a story." I continued to tell her the story of my obstetric interview experience.

"That has to be about the dorkiest interview I have ever heard of," she said when I finished. "Didn't you have sisters or something?"

"I had sisters, but under what conditions should I, an eight-year-old boy, have asked them to measure their bleeding before they moved out to college?"

"I guess I see. But didn't you see pads in the trash?"

"Well, I sure as hell had no intention of measuring anything like that. Besides, the whole question—actually, the whole interview—just caught me off guard."

"Okay, okay. You're off the hook. But it is pretty funny."

"I know. That's the only reason I bothered mentioning it. I don't see it as a great clinical success, worth bragging over my interviewing prowess." I had not begun to stutter with intoxication, but I was sure it would follow shortly. My academic goals and lack of drinking experience in college had left me with the alcohol tolerance of a hummingbird. I hovered over the green, frothy sedative to delay any embarrassment it might bring about. "So, how did you know about this place? It's kind of out of the way."

"A friend of my dad's used to own it. He ended up losing it to his wife in the divorce."

"I'm sure a bunch of guys wish they could get away with just giving their ex-wife a pig's ear. Although I think they are imagining something more in the spirit of *The Godfather* rather than a pub named the Pig's Ear."

"Actually, the guy is going to open up a new bar in the town nearby. I think it's going to be called the Falconer. It should be open this summer. You wanna go when it opens?"

By now, the two drinks I had consumed had already devoured any memory I had of that emotion I had been considering an hour before. "Yeah, just let me know when you want to go. Give me a call or something." I looked at my watch. "We should get going soon, though. I have class tomorrow morning."

"Okay, me too. But I bet most of your class comes in late with a hangover tomorrow."

"Oh, Christ! Do you mean that these Adventists get hangovers from Nestle's Quick now?" I joked.

Arriving home, I opened the door to my apartment, and my attention to my path was interrupted by the flickering light coming from my desk. The answering-machine strobe ticked away as if to the beat of a Sousa march. I stumbled over the empty plate of mac and cheese I'd had for dinner. It's a little-known fact that a generic version of the macaroni supplemented with a gluttony of butter can give Kraft a run for its money on any cooking show. The glorious yellow noodles were always quick to vanish from its plate around me. The plate, however, was not so agile. I kicked the spoon across the room but managed to regain my footing. With no one else to blame, I directed my profanity at the spoon, then pressed the play button on the machine.

"Hey, Jeff, it's Linda. I just got some news that I have to tell you about. Call me when you get in, even if it's late."

I contemplated the news for a moment. It couldn't be that she wanted to break up, although that wouldn't be the worst thing in the world. We had been dating for months, and it was clear that this Christian guilt complex was truly going to rain on any romantic parade. Her rules were not absolute because, she told me, "God's rules are not absolute." We had been quite intimate on several occasions but had never done anything so official that anyone would be forced to admit that their parents had performed the same act.

"Hi, honey," Linda answered as she picked up. "I'm glad you called. I need to come over. There's something I need to tell you."

"Okay...come on over." She had already hung up. I picked up the kicked spoon and the macaroni dish. Her news did not sound like a breakup proposal. She was too perky. She wouldn't seem so happy about being pregnant, either, and besides, the only women I'd had a chance to impregnate in the past couple months were mental images of Victoria's Secret models.

I heard a timid knock at the door—certainly not a knock to complement the glee I heard on the phone. She didn't typically knock when she knew I was home.

I opened the door, and Linda stood outside in her pink flannel pajamas.

"Come in, come in," I said. "So what's going on that you wanted to tell me this before tomorrow? And in person, no less."

"Thanks," she said as she manually placed herself in my grasp and spun around me. "I got the spot!"

I had no idea what she was talking about. I quickly scanned my memory for any plays, sports teams, and even dinner reservations, but nothing came to mind. "You mean that spot your cat left on the comforter?" I said in my confusion. "It's about fucking time. That thing was grossing the crap outta me."

"No, a couple weeks ago, I applied to transfer programs to Texas, and I just got news that they want me, and want me to move out before the weekend is over."

"Move?" I was more shocked than saddened. She had a job! Why would anyone leave this place? And she wasn't transferring to Harvard or the like. This was some place in Texas. "Why would you move programs?"

"Oh, I'm sorry, honey. I know you're disappointed. I didn't want to leave you."

I stumbled over my next words as I thought about her concern for my poor breaking heart. "But what made you want to leave?" I asked.

"There's too much fighting going on in the department. The director doesn't like me. It looks like the only way I'm going to get ahead is to get out of here."

I was dumbfounded. This was the resident they had chosen to teach the medical students. How could they not like her and think she was the best? And fighting? What the hell was there to fight about in pathology?

"Anyway, I wanted you to be the first to know. I'm giving my resignation tomorrow and leaving on Saturday."

"Wow," I said with a profound expression. "I guess this means that we won't be seeing much of each other from now on."

"That was another thing I wanted to talk to you about. Seeing each other."

"What do you mean?"

"Well, I just wanted to say good-bye," she said with an impish voice.

We lay there in relative innocence, periodically kissing and holding each other. I said nothing. As we lay on the carpet of the living room, ignoring the less-than-ergonomic features of the thin carpet for the sake of one last impromptu fling, I secretly agonized over her decision to leave the residency. My feelings were not of grief and loss but fear for her. Hell, I had concluded long ago that she would have to get rid of at least three to four cats before I would consider staying with her on a semipermanent basis. But I understood how important it was to get accepted to good institutions, then work hard to achieve admiration at those institutions so that we could get accepted to another good institution when we were finished. Such is the pyramid scam of medical training. Linda had been asked to teach medical students about pathology and so was obviously respected by her superiors. Linda was giving up the two years that she had done here to go somewhere else, where she would have to construct her reputation from scratch. But the decision was made, and I didn't want to be the wet blanket that ruined the occasion.

It was nice to lie with her there, but a picture of us would not live up to the Hollywood standards of beautifully decorated living rooms with perfect lingerie left in pristine condition after a romantic encounter. There were no bearskin rugs but a crumpled towel on the couch that I had left there after showering that morning. There was no soft candlelight in the room, and I had not even turned on the blue mood lights. But she lay there, half across me, with her hand cupping my chest and her head cradled beneath my chin. Normally I would have fallen asleep next to her by this point in the night, but I was fervently thinking of any way she could recover from this setback and accomplish all of her pathology dreams.

Then it occurred to me. This had just been the smoothest breakup of my life. Tragically, sending girlfriends to Texas is not always a convenient solution to relationship troubles.

~~~

With the end of the second year approaching, competing attitudes swirled in each of us. While the tests that we faced were possibly the most important of our medical education, lifting a book to study for any of them was like dragging the iron ball we had been carrying for two years. We all felt tired, and so much of what we had learned seemed only remotely related to the patients we had babbled so much about in our essays to get into medical school. So we studied half-heartedly. The pages were read, the sentences were highlighted, often in multiple colors—each color bearing some significance, in the case of the females of our class. But in each of us there was a profound sense of relief to be done with the portion of our education that so distinctly resembled education. How many years can one spend in a classroom? I cannot answer exactly how many he would survive, but I can tell you how many he would be sentenced to without parole if he were to pursue a career in medicine. I can also tell you that the two would approximate each other.

The class titles became more clinically related in the final semester, perhaps because the university knew its students would be impatient by this point. "Human behavior" morphed into "psychology." "Pathophysiology" evolved into "physical diagnosis and disease." The pictures presented in class started to resemble people instead of alien creatures repeatedly threatening to infect our future patients. In this way, the material we were being tested on in the coming June seemed more relevant than the previous final exams.

Our last religion class was a momentous occasion, in my view. Over the months of teachings and discussions, I had vacillated on my view. No, I had not flip-flopped from an atheist to a God-fearing Christian, but I had changed my position repeatedly on whether to argue with my classmates' outlandish claims or whether to remain silent and save an argument. At this point, I was in a quiet time in my religious life, which is to say I was not calling everyone around me nutballs. But my position was well known, and I remained somewhat of a novelty to the members of the Adventist church. I was even asked to speak at a conference/debate on the existence of a god.

I was told that it would be a small gathering of church members who simply wanted to understand my perspective on topics like the creation of man and the universe. I showed up making no claims of being an expert on the subject but happy to discuss differing opinions among friends. What I found was something slightly different. Two concepts come to mind when I recall that night. While this was billed as a discussion, the terms "exhibit" and "intervention" more accurately convey the tone of the evening. Approximately 500 people had gathered in the cathedral, which had been opened up only two years prior. A friend and classmate of mine stood at the podium, asking how I could believe that the world was created without the loving guidance of a god such as Ours. (I realize that "Ours" is an odd word to capitalize, but such unconventional proper nouns are one of the benefits of hardcore Christianity.)

The many faces, most my age, stared up from the audience as I answered in plain English, not advocating Satanism or evil of any sort. I simply told them that I believed that God was too easy an answer. I thought that the Egyptians, Greeks, Romans, Incas, and Mayans all felt that they had found a different answer to the eternal questions of "Why?" and "How?" As Christians, "we" were no more sophisticated than the previous cultures if we did not require proof from our higher powers.

My statement was not perceived as the eye-opening, thought-provoking idea that I had hoped. I had inadvertently insulted 500 people, calling their belief system prehistoric—an insult which was somewhat paradoxical, since I didn't think the Adventists actually believed there *was* a prehistory. A large portion of them subscribed to the notion that the world had been created in seven days, all of this occurring 6,000 years ago.

The meeting concluded after several questions from the audience regarding the mechanics of creating a universe. While this was a topic in which I'd had an interest since attending medical school at a Christian university, I had no more qualification to explain the intricacies of the Big Bang than did the host of *Wheel of Fortune*. Probably a little more than Vanna White, but that was where my credentials as an evolutionary theorist ended.

After the discussion, as we huddled outside in the seventy-five-degree darkness, I was approached by multiple individuals and groups offering to provide me counsel and guidance in my journey to find the Truth. I thanked them for their kind offer with the same sincerity I would offer a telemarketer, explaining that I had work to finish at home.

I was not preparing for any tests. Thankfully, they were all behind me. Another drawback of the type-*A* personalities who go into medicine is that they possess the indelible need to prepare for everything. In my case, I was preparing for my date with Tara. I was aware that between my two parents' genetic lines, there had likely been no more than three incidents of alcohol consumption, and it is not certain to this day whether the third incident—the occasion of my great-great-grandfather's communion—involved wine or grape juice. Given that strong inherited alcohol tolerance and my not-so-rowdy youth as a band geek, my greatest exploits of booze had consisted of that time I really felt ill and decided to take two shots of some night-time, sniffling, sneezing, coughing, aching, stuffy-head, fever, so-I-could-rest medicine.

Needless to say, I had the liver of a chihuahua, and I knew that a first date with Tara at a drinking establishment meant trouble for me. So I spent the two weeks prior to the date "practicing" my drinking to avoid making a fool of myself. I'm sure there have been triathletes with less planning in their training regimen, but I kept to the letter of my plan. By the night before the date, I was able to drink three bottles of beer and still be able to recite the Presidents of the United States as well as the states and capitals. It did not occur to me until the last night that I might be establishing bad habits. While I was, in all honesty, drunk off my ass, I was able to demonstrate impressive fourth-grade academic prowess. I spent much of that Thursday night in bed reminding myself not to be a dork on the date and hoping I would not accidentally blurt out the capital of Louisiana to test my own intoxication.

The following night, we walked from the quaint little Thai restaurant to the newly opened pub. The sweet essence of coconut lingered in my mouth, while the more subtle spices of ginger, garlic, and pepper floated somewhere between my nose and my imagination. During my twenty-plus years in this very town, and I had never noticed this restaurant; my tastes had never been described as eclectic. But the sweet curry we shared and the delicate noodles that contoured to the tongue like an erotic centerfold stayed on my mind.

Though no street is ever completely free of traffic noise in Southern California, the sounds seemed distant and negligible as we walked and talked. This beautiful girl, who had previously blushed if conversation required her to speak, told me entire stories that night. Though born in Ireland, she had spent her early years in Tanzania, where her parents had worked as doctors in the undeveloped lands of Africa. These bright blue eyes and voluptuous cheeks could read and speak Swahili, and on this particular night, it seemed they could do so without blushing. Her tribal name was Twiga, which in Swahili means *giraffe*. Her height even as a child had gained her acclaim even in Africa, as she always stood head and shoulders taller than the Tanzanian children her age. She had dreams of going back to Africa periodically to provide care to a people who have few to care for them. I found myself being comforted in a time when I didn't realize I was in need. This slim figure offered a diamond of levity when I was satisfied with my gold of intensity. She had given to these children with whom she shared so little and spoke to me only of the happiness that those moments had given her. She was truly the first example of benevolence that did not seem misguided to me.

The edifice of the pub melded into the local clothier and the quaint little shoe-repair shop that never seemed to have a customer. Were it not for the moon directly behind the buildings, the brick would have similarly blended into the darkness of the sky behind them. The entrance hardly heralded the grand opening of this bar I had envisioned as too tumultuous for the conservative tastes of this small, Mayberry-esque town.

As we entered, the music marked time with our steps with a deep, bellowing beat. The happening feel of this new college hangout was far from that of the owner's divorce casualty, the Pig's Ear. We scuttled by various small groups of socialites, avoiding the cigarettes they had snuck inside against California law and ducking under the beers they lifted like torches of liberty. The small pub seemed to hold more people than I was aware even populated the small city, and each person was in their own subtle way vying for the next seat to become vacant.

"Taraaaahhh!" a voice bellowed, like a grandfather seeing his grandchild at the annual Thanksgiving reunion. "If I had known you were coming, I would have told your father! He was here last night, you know." Rich was a man of medium build and mediocre features, who would have blended into any crowd were it not for his lopsided European accent, which seemed to weigh heavily on some syllables and limp away from others, favoring them like an injured foot.

"Rich!" she replied. "This is Jeff. We have been dying to come here together for the first time. But we haven't been able to get down here because of finals."

"Oh, yeah. Your dad is always talking about you being in medical school. He goes from being proud as a peacock to shitting his bloody pants, afraid for you. It depends how much his job pisses him off that particular week. Jeff, how the hell are you, man? You take good care of this girl. I've known her since she was twelve."

"You and I both know better than to piss off an Irish woman, Rich." I had no idea what the fuck I meant by the statement, but it was the kind of thing that any divorced Irishman was able to find some humor in, especially in Rich's state of intoxication.

"Don' I fuh'en know it!" he said as his drawl came out more prominently. "Anyway, you guys have you first roun' on the house, eh. I'll have my man set you up with a couple of pints. Just relax and forget abou' all that medicoh shit you guys fuss over all the time. Tim! Set 'em up over here." He spun around into the background chatter and flirting of the pub nightlife.

The ale inched downward in the pint glass as we talked and chuckled to ourselves. Tara's stories offered a glimpse of what I had missed in the Ivy League, as she had followed her literary degree with science training and research in Boston. She spoke of these famous researchers as friends, like I would have spoken of a high school classmate. She spoke of her degrees, research, and publications as though they were simple assignments completed by a generous deadline. Her experiences offered so much to envy, but her perspective brought me into her world with no jealousy.

Sipping the last of my first pint of ale, I failed to remember any of the preceding gulps which had led to the empty glass before me on the oak bar. I asked for a second glass and confirmed that Tara wanted another of the same. Already, my reach for my wallet revealed my declining dexterity as I fumbled with the button securing my pocket. Excusing myself from the stool with a wink, I moved in and out of the crowd to get to the restroom. I counted the steps that I took down the stairs as absurdly erroneous proof of my sobriety. When I returned, I found that she had gone to the restroom and come back all in the time I was gone. Her next glass was actually half gone (or half full, if you're an optimist). I could only hope the jokes I undoubtedly told as the night went on were as funny as she allowed me to believe. But I was even skeptical at the time. At that time, my humor was all I wished for, to keep her smile upon me for the rest of the night.

Later that night, when I lay alone in my bed thinking of her, I repeated my wish asking for her to read some kind of passion or profundity into my wit that would make me worth another call.

Who do we imagine is listening when we make wishes about love? If it is God, what is a fair offering in exchange for something so pivotal? I was still not ready to seek His counsel and assistance in winning the heart of this maiden, especially since at least half of my plans for our relationship did not fit into the biblically depicted chronology of relationships. I drifted into sleep, thinking of the kiss we had ended the night with. It was the first kiss we had shared in the ten months we had known each other, the first exchange of intimacy other than the imagined ones months before, the first erotic moment other than the ones I had stolen when her half-shirt had permitted a glimpse of her abs during our tutoring sessions. It was also the first time since junior high that I had contemplated a first kiss as a monumental event.

I left my wakefulness with that thought.

~~~

Weeks passed, and it was finally time for our Hospital Floor Training course. Officially, each day of medical school, including those of the first two years, are supposed to train us for working in a hospital. However, the apt title of this particular course seemed an acknowledgement of the fact that the first two years had prepared us only for the tests soon to follow and had little to do with the actual care of patients. In a subgroup of approximately twenty people, we sat with our eyes fixed on the chalkboard, which would give us the information needed to take us to the promised land—the land of actual patient contact.

As it turned out, the approach to the third and fourth years of medical school would be an awful lot like the approach to the first and second years. The list of items to be included in a complete history and physical of an ill patient could be remembered by a simple pneumonic device. Similarly, the list of orders to place when admitting said ill patient to the hospital could be remembered by another simple pneumonic. In fact, it seemed that any of the potentially millions of diseases for any specific complaint could be listed using some "simple" pneumonic. The problem, of course, was that after a while, one needs pneumonics to keep track of his pneumonic devices.

We plugged away, jotting down notes and learning our *ADCVANDIMLs*. These serve as the equivalent to the *ABCs* for the intern, helping us to admit a patient to the hospital, but they do not come with a similarly catchy jingle. We learned to write our SOAP notes, a quick way to remember what to say about our patients when we documented our daily visits. All this alphabet soup went on for several hours.

(It is natural to wonder whether they taught us, in this secret conference, to write prescriptions in an absolutely illegible font. I wondered if they would, myself. Sorry to disappoint, though. They taught us to abbreviate various words correctly so they would never be misinterpreted, but they did not teach us to read the incoherent scribblings of other doctors.)

"I would like to close with a prayer," the dean of religion bellowed as we began to pack our bags. Bags dropped instantaneously as silence fell over the room. "Jesus..."

I always hated it when people began prayers with "Jesus," as though they were writing an email or making a cell-phone prayer. But who was I to criticize? I had been in this religious medical school for two years, and I still had not "been saved."

"Jesus, I come to you today with many students, students not only of the medical arts, but of your healing arts. Lord, these individuals are about to embark on their lives' journey to offer compassion in your image. Help them to achieve this. Help them to find their healing spirit. And give them strength when they need healing, too. In your name we pray, amen."

Chapter 9

I got out of the car just as the familiar voices of my favorite Los Angeles morning DJs were interrupting the not-quite-hits of the '90s that routinely played in the off-peak hours of the night. I grumbled almost as much about leaving their antics as I had when I woke thirty minutes prior as the digital clock harkened 5:30. It was late July, and the sun had not yet made a habit of rising this early for the year. You may ask yourself why I bothered to wake at such a nonsensical hour during a month when I should have obviously been on summer vacation. Or perhaps you are simply questioning my memory of the dates or times—something for which I could never fault anyone. Tragically, my days of enjoying a summer break had passed. Despite the seemingly endless years I had left of training, I would never be granted the central entitlement of a student, namely a seasonal escape from the torture of academia. In fact, I had been acting as a third-year medical student for the past two weeks, just enough time to get over the fear of getting lost in the hospital.

The parking lot for third- and fourth-year medical students was far removed from that of the freshmen and sophomores, to think of it in educational terms we are used to. It was more than a brisk walk even from the hospital itself. The uncovered parking lot two blocks from the building was nearly empty, save for the unfortunate students who got stuck being on call over the weekend so that their cars sat alone in the distant darkness overnight. I would have liked to further explain this somewhat vague term and obligation of call, but to this point I had not been forced to do this as part of any rotation. The mystery would hold both excitement and intimidation as I walked past the four lonely cars in the lot.

Currently, I was rotating through neurosurgery, one of the more intense and precise branches of surgery. The demand for such precision rendered my contribution as a medical student near nothing. I was not required to stay overnight during this distinctly hands-off block. General surgery would follow two weeks later, and despite my actual contribution being similarly little, the general surgeons would squeeze every minute out of me that they could. The goal was to make us suffer just as the resident surgeons did in order to truly understand the profession.

The suffering of a neurosurgeon was evidenced by the perpetual expression of despair on the face of the neurosurgical intern, my immediate superior. Trent, a tall and stalwart man, looked like the one kid in every elementary class who was just a little bit older than the rest of the class. You always thought that kid should be good at basketball, considering his height, but that kid inevitably had the grace and dexterity of a Saint Bernard. Trent's size and rugged disposition commanded some respect, as did just about anything in the eyes of a virgin medical student. But despite the respect I had for Trent, following him throughout the day, seeing patient after patient with him, I found him meeting nothing but resistance.

He had worked all night in the hospital and would remain for hours after I left that day. He also told me that he had set foot in the operating room only once in the three months that he had been working in neurosurgery. His responsibilities were limited to the mundane task of checking peoples' wounds after surgery and making sure they weren't having hallucinations of purple dinosaurs. (Everyone knew that purple dinosaurs were not allowed to venture over from the south wing, which held the pediatric ward.) I felt bad for the guy. I had wanted to be a neurosurgeon for some time, cutting out brain tumors, which had probably been the greatest health fear in anyone's mind before AIDS appeared on the scene. I felt sure that he must have shared this dream, although he didn't speak much of hopes and dreams in his frantic rush from room to room. But he must have wanted these same things I had, and he was being deprived of the awesome impact of this field he had chosen. I supposed the hopes and dreams could wait; at this point, Trent just needed some sleep.

After we had quickly visited every patient on the neurosurgery service just to see that everything had gone smoothly overnight, it was time for rounds. Rounding is a traditional part of medical education, whereby residents and medical students are barraged by an endless line of questions from their supervising physician, "the attending," as he is known.

Sometimes the questions were as simple as, "Is the patient awake yet?" or "Did the patient spike a fever last night?" Often, the pointed questions required the retrieval of a factoid dubiously situated deep in the brain. Not uncommonly, the question would have no obvious pertinence to the patient's disease. Nothing blindsides you like a question about the patient's lifelong fiber intake while you're rounding on someone with an inoperable cancer spread to the brain. Granted, the cancer might have spread from the colon. But it seemed to me that this knowledge would only allow us as physicians to say woefully to the patient, "If only you had eaten more Frosted Mini-Wheats..."

The rounding process was also ceremonial. The team was all gowned in our shirts and ties, with the appropriate coats. The medical students wore a short white coat whose back reached only to the waist. The residents and attendings had earned a tail, which typically reached to their knees, these two being distinguished primarily by the many miniature books, pens, notecards, and pagers adorning the former. Even with the advent of hand-held computing devices that had brought on the extinction of pocket-sized reference books, the frazzled hair and persistent look of anxiety on their faces always heralded the resident's title.

In addition to the formality of the regalia, there was a regimented method of presenting a patient, whereby the intern detailed the patient's whole life leading up to this point, medically, surgically, socially, and so on. The intern must recount the entire physical exam performed on the patient, documenting details as fine as each drop of pee expelled during the night. Only after explaining each of these, as well as the results of lab tests and x-rays, was the intern allowed to fill the role of the MD degree he had already received. He then got to succinctly lay out his diagnosis and plan for treatment.

This script was usually performed in a monotone voice cruising as fast as possible, stopping only when the intern found he had forgotten to write down a specific detail. Any deviation from the expected structure triggered a stern scolding by the attending, like writing outside the margins or uncrossed *T*s would bring in red ink from a third-grade teacher.

From this description, you can see that this formalized rounding process was somewhat like a cross between elementary school and the ritualized human sacrifice practiced by the ancient Aztec civilizations. One couldn't easily ignore the influence of the Spanish inquisition, though, in the unspoken messages of many of the attendings' questions: "Why the hell did you admit this patient to my service?" or "What the hell did you do to screw up this patient I did such a marvelous job of saving in the operating room yesterday?"

After these presentations, there was typically a redirection of the plan based on the attending's experience, or idiosyncrasies, in some cases. This would go on outside the patients' rooms, and then the group would file into the room, where the attending would do a cursory physical exam on the patient, essentially for show, relying on the presentation of the intern for all his clinical decisions. Once every couple of days, an attending actually focused on one specific portion of the physical that he personally thought was more important than anything else, all the while pointing out everyone else's incompetence for neglecting the creases in a patient's earlobes, for example, and its relevance to all aspects of his health. Contrary to popular television depiction, very seldom do rounding conversations take place in the room, discussing a disease, treatment, or prognosis in front of the patient, as though he were a fly on the wall. This is partly because of the uncompassionate frankness of the discourse that takes place on rounds. But it's also because of the degrading and insulting language used by some attendings to critique residents' and students' plans, which would make a drill sergeant cringe.

After rounds, I, as a medical student, was scooted off to the operating room, where I was to observe the actual neurosurgical operations I had been salivating over for several years. Aneurisms bulging from a once-normal brain blood vessel now were on the brink of bursting, and only I—or we, or, actually, only the neurosurgeon—could stop it from bleeding. I imagined tumors growing out of control, giving patients voracious headaches, seizures, or making them randomly flip people off, and only the neurosurgeon could stop this horrible process.

I made my way to the elevators as Trent scurried off in his trance-like state, scribbling orders in various charts as he passed patients' rooms. Despite the sterile white lights in the ceiling, the hallways had a mildly warm glow, thanks to the slightly pink shade of paint on the walls and the artificially peaceful paintings hung intermittently.

On and off again, two floors down, the elevator doors opened. I stepped onto the surgical floor. This was like a completely different world from everything else in the hospital. The walls, floors, and ceiling were all a light blue color, for which I do not have a specific name. One shade lighter, and it might have been baby blue, a color that might comfort a small boy in his bedroom alone at night. One shade darker, and it might have been sky blue, a color that takes one's breath away as it spans the horizon, interrupted by the occasional cloud or mountaintop. But the shade of blue on the surgical floor only sent shivers down my spine for years to come.

I had been instructed to go to operating room 4. That was, however, the limit of my directions. The rooms were supposedly numbered, but those numbers were hidden behind boxes of surgical sponges and latex gloves. I walked at a slow pace to search for any reference numbers on the walls around me, unable to hide my disorientation as my head shifted from left to right, searching for the room. Nevertheless, I tried to make each slow step seem confident and directed.

"You!" came an androgynous shout from down the vile blue hallway. I couldn't make out anyone who might have been speaking to me; I saw only an employee pushing a bed away without looking back.

"Hey! You!" This time, a pudgy face peeked out of a window I had not seen along the corridor about twenty yards down. "What are you doing in here?"

"I'm a medical student, ma'am," I replied in a robust voice as I walked toward her, trying to avoid drawing too much attention to myself. "I'm supposed to be in room 4 for neurosurgery."

"Well, don't come walkin' over here—you don't have a hat on!" she blurted out with disgust at my approach. "Besides, OR 4 is that way, behind you and around that corner to the left. You can get your bonnet where you came in."

I did not know whether I was more humiliated at being thought an idiot for being lost already and not having a hat on, or by the paper cap that could probably help a woman subdue any stray hairs. On me, it puffed up like a big blue marshmallow—in the same toxic blue as the OR walls, no less.

At the entrance to the OR sat a giant steel sink where I was to sanitize my skin before entering the room. I placed the face mask on and began to scrub my fingers with the iodine-soaked sponges: forty strokes for each finger, making sure to approach from every angle, just as we had been taught. Then proceeding back to the hand, with ten strokes on each side and similarly up the arm. To add to the pressure, there was always an OR nurse not officially spying on everyone, but distinctly and discretely watching us from three of the four corners of her eyes. Readers who are naïve to the process of "scrubbing in," as it is known, may not understand or appreciate the tedium of the ritual, but they should realize that it has taken them more time to read my description than they likely spend washing their hands before a meal. And I have not yet described the scrubbing of the opposite hand. I will spare you the painstaking description and assure you that it is quite similar to the first side, now making this a five-minute description and a ten-minute activity.

While the lack of coordination in my left hand left me fumbling over the brush as I cleaned my right, it was coordinated enough to respond instantaneously to the tickle on the tip of my nose under the surgeon's mask. Not even aware of the reflex action, my head snapped 180 degrees around as I heard her voice.

"Now what do you think you're doing?" It was nurse pudgy-face turning the corner.

"I told you, I'm supposed to be in OR 4. They're removing a brain tumor today."

"I don't care if they're baptizing Christ himself," she said. Her cheek pudge, chin pudge, and neck pudge all tightened as she gave me her sternest look. "You're not going in there while I'm in charge. You've contaminated yourself!"

Unaware of any problem, I wondered if she was accusing me of breaking wind, or worse. Had I pissed myself?

"No, I didn't," I said, hoping that the argument would end there and I would go into the brain surgery.

"You did, and I saw you. You cleaned one hand, and then you touched yourself."

Man! What was she accusing me of now?

"Why don't you look in the mirror, Rudolph?" she said, walking by with a snicker.

I glanced up and saw a prominent red spot on my mask covering my nose, obviously left by the iodine when I got the tickle. I threw the sponge in the trash in frustration and reached for another. From down the hall, I heard Pudgy bellow, "Don't forget to get a new mask, too."

Once I had repeated the entire procedure, I entered the surgical suite, where the operation was already three hours underway. Their backs all faced me as they hovered over the patient whom I couldn't see. Only one nurse turned her head, noticing my entrance. Then her attention swung back to the monitor in front of her. I slowly made my way toward the screen she and everyone in the room seemed to be watching. It was a modest-sized screen, hardly worthy of having the football game on during an unexpected Sunday surgery. Several lines ran horizontally across the screen in a seemingly random squiggly pattern of static. Even I, the amateur, could tell that it was not monitoring his heart, as that screen sat behind the patient with the anesthesiologist and gave the reassuring rhythmic beep with each beat. These lines in and of themselves were valuable for neither informational nor entertainment value, from my viewpoint.

The patient remained shielded by the people dressed in blue, but everything I had been waiting for was behind that wall of scrubs. After three hours of the surgery, I figured they had half the tumor cut out and were just cleaning up the last little bits of cancer. I expected to hear the neurosurgeon shout, "Get this specimen off to pathology. I need a read on it, *stat!*" I didn't know if the specimen would be in a small jar of yellow liquid or if it would just be a piece of brain slopped on the nurse's gloved hand. Nor did I know what a read would consist of, but it seemed a reasonable thing to anticipate. Just as physicians make up ridiculously specific hyper-syllabic words of little relevance, they also take small, vague words and make them sound remarkably scientific and important.

The command never came. I shifted about the room, trying to catch a glimpse of the cutting, but the best I could see through the blue barricade was the blue sheets draped over the patient.

This continued for about an hour as I continued to go largely unnoticed. Then the silence, which in the operating room still retains at least three asynchronous beeps and buzzers, was broken.

"There we go. I think that got it," the surgeon said as he tilted his head back and shrugged his shoulders to stretch out those muscles in his neck that were, no doubt, nagging him with tightness at each slice of the patient's tumor.

I looked up at the monitor again and saw absolutely no difference in the amorphous lines running across the screen. This must have been the monitor guarding the normal brain tissue, making sure that nothing important was removed. And how amazing that these immaculately precise hands of the neurosurgeon could cut out the entire tumor without making any noticeable tweak in the brainwaves! I was crawling out of my skin to see the tumor lying on the table in front of the doctor.

"So, how are you doing, Mr. Cedar?" the surgeon asked.

Wow, this was phenomenal. I had heard of the brain surgeries that took place with the patient awake. The brain itself doesn't have any of pain receptors, so throughout history, doctors have conducted experiments, poking different parts of the brain while a person was awake, then mapping the parts that made him see flashes or made his arm bend. But this was going on right in front of me. The adrenaline level in my blood was high enough that it was probably detectable in my sweat. There was no doubt that this was what I wanted to do. Despite the misery of the residents doing this, I would work my ass off, excel on my boards, whatever it took. I would go to Harvard for my neurosurgical residency, because that was what it took to become famous in these types of fields. Maybe it would be better to be from Yale, since Harvard was so cliché. But something of that caliber of reputation was necessary. Then I would discover a new tumor, or better yet, a new treatment for some tumor. This would be a pivotal moment in the solidification of my career dreams.

The patient cleared his throat. "I'm doing fine," he uttered.

This was excellent. The patient was doing well, to boot. The doctor stepped back from the table, and my eyes widened with horror and disgust. The patient's head was completely intact. Not a single cut had been made on this patient. The left side of his head had been shaved below his part, and there were tiny pins stuck in his scalp, not just in the bald areas but over the entire skull.

"Great. Now we can take a few readings, people," the surgeon said with nowhere near the drama of my speculated phrase. We were four hours into the surgery, and we hadn't even cut the guy. My back was already aching from the erect posture I had maintained up to this point. I had struggled to keep my mind from wandering several times, and all for this anticlimactic moment. At least I had managed not to lock my knees during the "operation" thus far, a mistake that many young medical students make. That error causes blood to pool in one's legs and prevents it from pumping up to the brain, leading to many a macho medical man fainting. You might expect such a traumatic experience to be treated with sympathy, but the closest to sympathy I have seen was a female surgeon who responded, "Get that pansy out of here before he contaminates my surgical field!"

The technicians and nurses stepped away from the table as the doctor adjusted several dials on a computer panel next to him. One of the technicians, a plump man with his 5:00 shadow peeking above his surgical mask well before noon, moved next to me in order to write down some data that evaded my perception.

He looked like a youngish guy who might relate to my impatience, so I spoke to him. "What are all these wires for?"

"Oh, they're mapping out his brainwave pattern so they can just go for the section of the brain that isn't making any electrical noise."

"Perfect!" I said. "That makes sense. How long does it usually take?"

"Well, this part usually takes five hours with the placement and the mapping. But the whole surgery can take upwards of twelve hours."

My heart sank back into the recesses of my stomach, and I was nauseated either by its presence in one place or its absence from the other. The adrenaline had been filtered completely from my blood, or enzymatically chewed up, or whatever it is that happens to adrenaline when watching something like *Sleepless in Seattle*. The sweat that I had barely noticed during those intense moments earlier was now cold and slimy around my collar and down my ribs. I probably couldn't even pay attention to a supermodel for twelve hours straight, let alone a surgery that was much less exciting than I had envisioned. With no more attention on me than when I had entered, I moped silently out of the operating room.

With but a hint of guilt, I bid farewell to the blue halls of the OR and immediately stuffed the bonnet in the red wastebasket outside the automatic double doors as I passed through. I slid the short white coat on again and took a deep breath, aware of both the security and the humility it bestowed upon me. While the conscience of most would prevent them from simply leaving the assigned surgical room, I reasoned that if the purpose of the neurosurgery rotation was to give me a taste of the specialty and see if it was right for me, I had seen enough to meet that requirement. There was no way that my self-diagnosed attention deficit disorder would allow me to perform twelve to eighteen-hour surgeries. I knew I would find myself going straight from the blue walls of the OR to the green padded walls of the psych ward.

I walked down the two flights of stairs to the lobby and then passed the receptionist at the desk in the entryway. As one of several older ladies who volunteered to greet people and answer questions as they came into the hospital, she always wore a genuinely friendly smile.

"Have a nice day, Doctor," she said to me as I passed by her at her stately desk in the front atrium. The image of importance that the desk and chair presented was not a misrepresentation of her role. Her job was to make people feel comfortable and welcome in a place that was not inherently comforting or welcoming. Rather, it held you hostage for undue periods of time in very uncomfortable circumstances. This applied to both patients and medical staff, and she softened the blow for each of us.

"You too, Ima. I'll see you tomorrow," I answered with a wink as I walked by. I never corrected Ima, or anyone else who called me doctor before I graduated. Most people were simply unaware of the differences between med students and residents and weren't sure if any of us had finished medical school. To correct the patients would require a time-consuming, painful clarification, much like trying to explain to your grandmother for the fifth time the difference between a live-in girlfriend and a wife. Allowing them the small error of title allowed me to get some respect, get straight answers, and get work done more efficiently.

Ima was not making such a mistake, though. She had seen twenty years of medical students walk through those doors and could tell how far along someone was in their training without the coat size and academic spillage from the pockets I mentioned earlier. She just knew that these little ego boosts and the smiles they brought were exactly what we medical students needed to keep going when life got stressful, as it often did. But if we are to ponder alongside Shakespeare, perhaps a rose by any other name has just not graduated "aromatical" school yet.

The Mustang growled as I turned the key, and the stereo quickly followed with hard rock playing on my station from the morning. I pulled out of the parking lot a mere seven hours after pulling in. This was hardly worth the sub-minimum wage earnings that I would be getting in a couple years as a resident, but it seemed more than ample for the tens of thousands I was paying to be put through this. I parked in the driveway at home and walked around to the door of my apartment.

Lois was reclining in the shade of the porch. When I unlocked the door, she hopped up onto all fours and stared at me expectantly. This, I think, is as close as cats come to speaking. If she could, I think she would have said, "You don't expect me to get that for myself, do you?"

A few hours later, as I was browsing through my surgical *Cliff's Notes*, preparing for the inevitable exam at the end of the rotation and the more eminent pimping sessions, the phone rang. I lifted Lois from her sprawl on my lap to answer it.

"Hey, Sweetie," Tara said. The sounds of Southern California traffic indicated she was on her cell phone. "I didn't expect to get you, but I thought I would call to see if you got out early."

"Yeah, I got out of there pretty early."

"Do you want to meet me at Grounds for Enjoyment to study together?"

"Sure, the weather is nice, let's sit outside."

By now, Lois had already wandered outside. Closing my phone, I picked up my keys and hopped in the Mustang. I drove with the windows down along the back roads to the coffee shop. The red clay that made up the soil in this section of the state reflected the afternoon sun, making sunglasses a necessity.

When I pulled up, Tara was already sitting at the table we had shared so many times over the past couple of months.

"What are you studying today?" she asked as I situated myself in the chair.

"*Surgical Recall*," I said. "It's apparently what everyone uses to study for the tests. It just has a bunch of surgical trivia questions and the answers."

"What kind of questions does it have?"

"Like, what are the signs of compartment syndrome?"

"Compartment syndrome?"

"Yeah, where your leg swells up so much inside that it cuts off its own circulation."

"Oh, so what's the answer?"

"There's some pneumonic," I tried explaining without the book open to remind me of the answer. "I think it's the five *P*s of compartment syndrome. Four or five, I can never remember. Hell, maybe even six. Basically, I just keep spitting out words that start with *P* until I can't think of any more. But they're things like pain, pallor, pulselessness, parasthesia…Hmm, I guess there are only four signs today. Maybe there will be more tomorrow."

"What's parasthesia?" she asked.

"It's that tingly feeling you get when your leg falls asleep."

"So do you cut off the leg when that happens?"

"When your leg falls asleep?"

"No, with that department syndrome, or whatever," she replied, only slightly amused and equally frustrated with my need to make little sarcastic jokes every now and then.

"Department syndrome? It's not a disease you get from chronic frequenting of Nordstrom and Saks Fifth Avenue. That disease is called terminal MasterCard debt."

She rolled her eyes. "Ha ha."

"I think they try to cut into the leg to relieve the pressure before the foot turns blue, but I'm only on neurosurgery. We haven't learned any of that stuff yet."

"So how was your day?"

"It was all right," I answered. "Actually, it was kinda lame. I went into a case that I thought was going to be really exciting—a brain tumor removal. But it was four hours into it, and they hadn't even cut into the guy yet. I was so bored, I decided it just wasn't for me. So I left."

"Did you see any other cases?" she asked, looking discouraged.

Still embittered by the hustle of the morning with the letdown in the OR, I came back, "No, I just rounded with the resident in the morning before I went into the operating room." I was about to stop there when I remembered Seta and how her stories were so cynical. I didn't want my stories from the hospital, the place to which Tara was aspiring, merely to be ones of different fecal stink. "But there were a couple of interesting cases on the floor. They had me do a neuro exam on this guy who had just had a stroke. He was paralyzed on one side, and his tongue was flopping to the other side. He could barely talk because he couldn't move his tongue at all."

"Wow! Could you tell where the stroke was from that?" she asked with the intrigue that I remembered feeling.

"Yeah. You remember that part of the brain where all the nerves controlling your muscles cross over from one side to the other?"

"Uh-huh."

"Well, the part of the brain that controls the tongue sits right above that. So this guy had a stroke right there in that tongue center. So it messed up one half of his tongue, and also knocked out the nerves that were going to the opposite side of his body."

"That's got to be so weird. I mean, I know I've read about all that in class, but I can't imagine actually seeing it in a person."

The excitement that bloomed from that conversation reminded me of the curiosity that had inspired me to persevere. There were so many things that did interest me in many of the fields, including neurosurgery. I resolved at that moment to reflect periodically on the aspects of each that meant something to me: the patients, the science, the excitement and mysteries.

"You shouldn't be studying. You're on vacation," I said as it occurred to me that our schedules were no longer in sync.

"I'm not studying. I'm just reading this book I bought. It's about this murder of a businessman in England—"

I interrupted her with half-feigned dismay. "You mean you're reading a book for fun, after all the books they make you read for school?"

"Yes, I like reading. I just haven't had time to read novels in a while, and this is the perfect place to do it."

"I think the last book I read for fun was about a nosey monkey who had a propensity for getting into mischief. And, come to think of it, I think my mom finished that one for me." I was joking, but I honestly admired Tara's intelligence and sophistication, qualities that had been missing in some recent girlfriends. These were the qualities I had seen in Jess that had made her unavailability so painful. Perhaps they were qualities that I wished I had, myself.

~~~

I was standing in my room. I was standing on my bed, actually. A man I didn't recognize stood in the doorway to the bedroom. What the fuck was I doing standing? I was asleep a second ago. I felt slightly dizzy; the room shifted leftward and rightward. Where the fuck was I? Oh yes, it was my room. But there was something wrong. Right! There was a man in my room.

"Just stay right there," I shouted at the man across the room. "Don't come any closer. Don't move!" I took on a fighting posture, ready to strike him with all my might. I glanced down and realized that I was also completely naked.

"Jeff, calm down," came Tara's voice. She stood to the side of the bed. "Calm down and just stop for a minute."

"What?" I exclaimed. What was she doing here? I figured she had slept over. But I couldn't remember specifically. Whatever. She was wearing a long nightshirt and some sweatpants. They looked like a pair of sweats I had. I looked at the clock, but whatever time it said did not register in my mind.

"Take a deep breath, Jeff," she said, trying to get me under control.

"What are you talking about? What the fuck is going on here?"

"Jeff, it's me, Tara." Her arm extended toward me from a few feet away.

"I know who you are," I snapped. "What the fuck is going on here?"

"Mr. Triton." The man across the room drew my attention away from her. He was dressed all in blue. Was he trying to rob me? Was he trying to kill me? Whatever it was, I had caught him! Now I had to figure out what to do next. He started to take a step toward the bed.

"Stop!" I blurted. "You stay the fuck over there where I can see you!" I noticed once again that I was standing on the bed and my footing was not too stable. I wanted to get off the bed, but I couldn't give up this advantageous position.

"You can still see me, sir," said the man in blue. "I am just coming forward to help."

"I don't need your fucking help," I shouted with my fists raised. "I should be in bed sleeping. What the fuck do you want here?"

"Jeff, you had a seizure," said Tara.

"What? What are you talking about? I'm fine. I'm standing right here."

She was breathing heavily. "You had a seizure about twenty minutes ago, while you were asleep."

I stared at her. "That's ridiculous."

"No, it's not." she said, calming down slightly. "You had a grand mal seizure in your sleep. I called 911, and these paramedics came to help you."

I quickly remembered the man in blue and snapped my head back to the right, where he had inched closer to the bed.

149

"Get back!" I screamed at him. I took a few breaths, shaking my head. I didn't have that dizziness anymore. I just felt so sleepy. It sure would be a good time to take a nap. *But wait. A seizure?* "Just give me a minute," I said, no longer shouting.

"Mr. Triton, I'm Andy. I'm with the paramedics. This is Jack." He pointed to the shorter man in blue, who had apparently gone outside. "We need to get you to a hospital."

"Wait a second. I need to think," I said, trying to put two thoughts together consecutively.

"Jeff, why don't you lie down?" Tara said softly. "They need to get an IV in you so they can put you in the ambulance."

I was finally able to concentrate enough to follow the simple instructions. I lay down on the bed. The pillow felt so good cradling my head. I had that wonderful euphoria that comes on right before you fall asleep. This must have simply been a dream.

"Okay, Mr. Triton, I am going to put this IV in your left arm," said one of the men in blue.

By now I was feeling extremely sleepy, as though half my brain was asleep and the other half was getting a massage. I cannot say I have experienced a brain massage, but the concept seemed feasible at the time. Light subtly went dim within my view. The raucous sounds of someone, or something, moving about the room were almost hypnotic as I rolled onto my side to get some sleep.

"One, two, three," I heard.

When I opened my eyes next, it was dark. Thank goodness they had turned the lights off. Now I could get some sleep. But I was cold. And I was on my back; I never sleep on my back. I started to roll onto my side to get comfortable, but a soft hand stopped me with some firm pressure on my shoulder.

"Stay there, sweetie," said Tara. "You're on a gurney, and the paramedics are going to put you in the ambulance. I will follow you down to the hospital in the car."

I closed my eyes again briefly. With a light nudge in the back, I opened my eyes to see the starry night sky yield to the closing door of the ambulance. I felt somewhat more conscious. The thought crossed my mind of being brought into an emergency room where everyone would know me. I worried that I might look too vulnerable, possibly even unfit for medical school.

"What time is it?" I asked the paramedic in the rear of the ambulance with me, trying to get a sense of who might be in the ER at this time.

"It's 12:30," he replied.

"And it's Thursday, right?"

"Yep. So what were you doing last night?" he asked.

I thought back. It was starting to form a picture. I did remember going to sleep the night before. It was a normal night like any other. I hadn't stayed up extraordinarily late or drank too much. It was December, I finally remembered. And I was on pediatrics.

"Nothing, really. Fuck! What is going to happen when I don't show up to peds tomorrow?"

"They'll understand. Let's just get you taken care of." He calmed me down. "Are you on outpatient or inpatient peds?"

"Outpatient," I said. I thought again about being seen by everyone in the ER. I certainly didn't want other medical students to see me. And since finishing my surgery rotations a month before and essentially ruling it out as a career, emergency medicine had quickly become my objective. So I certainly did not want the people I might be working for to see me in such a precarious position.

"Is there any chance you could take me to a hospital besides Mon Gracia?" I asked.

"Sorry, none of the other nearby hospitals has a twenty-four-hour ER with a CAT scanner. It would be fifteen minutes out of the way to go to another one."

"I suppose you will consider this experience when you choose how close your next home will be to your work," I mused with the paramedics.

They laughed. "Don't worry. We'll talk to them in the ED and make sure it's just the attending who sees you in there."

"Thanks. I really appreciate it."

I overheard some talk on the paramedic's radio, and then the vehicle came to a halt. They moved around very efficiently, and within seconds I was being wheeled into the emergency department. The lights were blinding as I rolled in through the back emergency entrance.

"Room 6," someone said almost immediately after we had come into the thankfully warm building.

The fluorescent white lights along the ceiling seemed to speed by me the way the lines of the freeway did during those precious few hours when the term *rush hour* did not apply. At the same time as I was perceiving this speed, I looked up at the paramedic steering me, and he seemed to be strolling in at a casual stride, waving to the nurses who would throw him a smile and wink. The wheels of my chariot locked as I pulled into the emergency bay and the medic pulled the curtain behind him.

"All right, you think you can slide yourself over, or shall we get someone to come in here and help me lift you?"

"You think you can get that nurse to come in here and help?" I asked.

"Ah. So your level of consciousness has improved, I see. That's good. But I think you can do it on your own if you're back to thinking about the chicks."

I raised my butt off the mobile bed that did not seem anywhere near as stable as the metallic clang of the wheel lock had suggested. I shoved with my feet still on the gurney and supported only by one shoulder blade and managed to achieve one cheek on the stone-like bed. Trying not to put much weight on the arm with the IV, I flailed around like a beached mackerel. The medic gave me a final boost and then pulled the rail up behind me as though I were in a six-foot-long crib.

"Good luck, man," he said, leaving me there in my sweatpants.

Tara ducked in shortly after that, lifting the curtain away. "Hey, how are you feeling?"

"Not too bad, considering what happened. Actually, come to think of it, I can't consider what happened, because I don't know what the hell happened."

"You had a seizure."

"Like, a full-on seizure?"

She nodded. "Yes, a grand mal seizure. I woke up because you were sort of grunting. I thought you were just snoring, so I was going to move you around a little. But then you started clenching your teeth really, really tight. You were breathing through your mouth, even with your teeth closed, so you were making this loud hissing noise."

"Jesus, how long was that going on?"

"It was about thirty seconds for each of those parts. I realized what was happening, so I turned on the lights and tried to shake you to get you to wake up. But even though I was shouting and rolling you around, you didn't react at all, you just kept on hissing. And by this time, you were starting to foam at the mouth and your lips were turning blue. So I called 911 and got them to come out as fast as possible."

"Fuck. That's pretty horrible."

"That's not even half of it," she said, sitting down on the seat beside the bed. "Then your lips started smacking, making all sorts of noise, and your head started rocking back and forth, but I could see that all the muscles in your neck were super tight. And then it was as though the seizure was marching down your body. Your shoulders tightened up and went up by your ears. Your arms started bending and straightening at the elbows while your hands were in these tight fists. You started flailing at the hips and legs. Then you sorta finished by stretching into this big, rigid mass on the bed."

"I did all that? The first thing I remember is when the paramedic walked into the room and I was standing on the bed."

"Well, you were starting to wake up even before that. While you were lying there, you were breathing through your teeth again. The paramedics got there about three minutes after I called them, and you had just stopped shaking. I opened the door for them, but they weren't able to wheel the bed in because the door was too narrow. So I brought the three of them back. The first one came to the bed and started talking to you. You were still out of it at the time, so they were going to try to carry you out to the bed. When the first one grabbed your arm to put it across your body, you woke up and went wild. You started cursing and thrashing around with your arms. You even whacked the guy in the side of the head."

"Oh, shit. Really?"

"Yeah. Then you were still pretty delirious, but when I talked to you to try to calm you down, you at least seemed to recognize me. You didn't make any sense except when you were swearing. You started coming around, and then it looked like you noticed the paramedics all over again and jumped up from the bed to shout at them. They must have thought we were white trash from that show *Cops*, with you there naked, yelling at the camera, and me standing there in your sweats and a T-shirt."

"I guess so," I said in a soft voice. "Man, I don't remember much of that at all. I remember talking to them and getting put on the gurney and rolling out."

"Umm, you didn't get on the gurney in the room. Remember, they couldn't fit it in the apartment. So instead of them trying to fight you again, I convinced them to let me help you get dressed and walk out to the ambulance. By then you were following simple instructions, and I was able to get your sweatpants on. You were able to walk out, but every now and then you would stop and yell at us to give you a minute. Then you would walk some more. It was fairly cold out, but you didn't seem to mind too much. They put you on the bed by the ambulance and put you inside."

"Were you going to ride in the ambulance?"

"No, I knew you would need clothes. And I knew I would have to get you home. So I brought the clothes and followed you in the car. I was right behind the ambulance when we were driving, and I could see you sitting up in the back. Your blonde hair was sticking straight up in every direction. You looked like a Q-tip back there."

We chuckled briefly just as the doctor walked in. He was not a doctor I had worked with previously, and by the end of the night, I had forgotten his name.

"So, can you tell me what happened?" he asked the two of us.

I rotated my head to Tara, trying to show how lost I felt.

She quickly came to the rescue and answered for me, telling the entire story, minus the assault.

"Hmmm. Has anything like this ever happened before?"

"No. Never," I answered desperately.

"Have you had any head trauma recently?"

I answered no, forgetting the concussion that had happened the previous semester.

"Any alcohol, caffeine, or drugs?"

"No, we were just studying for exams." Tara piped up. "We're medical students here, and we were just studying late tonight. We went to bed, and all this happened."

"Okay, well, this stuff can happen sometimes to young people, and it doesn't necessarily mean something bad. But we should get some blood tests and a CAT scan."

The wait for the test did not seem long, although in my experience these tests never got done as quickly as the patients thought they should. While waiting, we heard the moaning of an elderly woman sharing the room, which was divided by another curtain. She groaned in pain, but did not shout anything to reveal where her pain was. Tara heard something drop from her bed, so she dipped behind the curtain to see if she could help.

A small handbag had dropped to the floor. Tara picked it up and placed it on the bed with the woman.

"Oh, thank you, my child," the woman said. "You are so kind. Are you married?"

"No. I'm not."

"Oh. You're so pretty, my dear. You should be married."

Tara's face wore a smirk as she returned from behind the curtain. Neither of us had a chance to comment on the incident before I was rolled off to the CAT scanner.

After the CAT scan and another wait, the doctor returned and told us that there was nothing on the CAT scan to be worried about. He explained we would still have to get an MRI within the next month to make sure that nothing had slipped by, but he expected everything would be fine. This was probably just exhaustion. In the meantime, I was to take Dilantin, a medicine to prevent any more seizures, until I could be seen by a neurologist.

I slept well for the remaining three hours of the night and then woke to go to my outpatient pediatric clinic, where I was under the supervision of Dr. Ramos. Dr. Ramos was a gentle man with a small frame and a thick brown beard. He and I had a great bond that had been strengthened a week before when we discovered that Tara's mother had been his intern when he was a resident at Mon Gracia so many years before.

I walked into his office feeling like my chest had been crushed overnight by a boa constrictor, and the muscles under my arms and in my legs felt as though I had just competed in a triathlon. My step had a distinct hobble to it, and my hair was pressed back with gel to avoid styling time. Dr. Ramos could see that something was up. He asked if I was ill, and without thinking much of it, I told him the entire story. I told him of the medicine I had been started on. We calculated together and determined that I would have enough only to last me through the weekend, so he prescribed me a month's worth to last until I could see a neurologist. He insisted that I take the day off, a request that I heeded without remorse.

Chapter 10

Tara and I sat next to each other in the ergonomically basic chairs of the neurologist's office. We took turns laughing over the personas and teaching styles of some of our common professors. Thirty minutes had ticked by, and we were still staring at an open cranium with a Cabbage Patch Kid brain inside. I was still anxious to get back to work as soon as possible, but I had grown accustomed to the hurry-up-and-wait process of the medical system, the greatest offenders being the HMOs. As a patient, I was a member of Empire Medical, one of the local health maintenance organizations. I had been born in an Empire hospital, the very one we were sitting in, to be precise. My parents had maintained their insurance through their careers and kept it even after retirement. My name was kept on their insurance plan as a matter of convenience, even though I had not been to a doctor in fifteen years—until now.

The inertia of the medical system is immense. Just to reach the chair I sat in now, I had made several calls to neurology, only to be told I needed a referral from a primary care doctor. I, of course, took the soonest appointment I could get with any doctor who would see me. After the week of waiting, I had a less-than-informative appointment with a physician who prescribed an MRI and a neurology visit, both of which I had known I needed to begin with. The MRI was two weeks after the initial visit, and the neurology visit three weeks after that. By now, I had mastered the waiting process and simply sat, balancing the chair on its hind legs.

The lighthearted mood in the room was not a false one, at least on my part. I had little doubt that the seizure had been a fluke, an incidental occurrence that would never happen again and meant nothing. Maybe it was due to the stress of exams approaching, fatigue from the work hours, or one too many concussions on the soccer field. But I was a healthy guy, at the peak of my life, going to medical school and dating beautiful women. My thoughts usually ended there. The first time I had stopped to contemplate the remote possibility that something might be wrong was when I had gotten the MRI of my brain three weeks earlier.

~~~

The concept of an MRI is fascinating; high magnetic fields are used to make water molecules in your body shine for the camera to show amazingly high-definition pictures of things that are normal and those that are out of place. An analogy might be having a classroom with dark-haired boys and girls divided in half by gender. To a fly on the ceiling, they would all look the same. But if that fly had a special magic power to get all boys to look up and girls to look down, the contrast of light faces and dark hair would be resounding. This is what an MRI does with water, making those spots with water shine and those with less water dark. However, I had learned that this technology requires a substantial amount of time to produce such images.

The MRI office was quiet when I arrived early one January morning. The four patients in the waiting room had little to discuss with the secretary when they arrived. A simple flash of the insurance card, and we each sat down to pick up our six-month-old edition of *Home and Garden*. A television hung in the upper left corner of the room, but the volume was turned down to an inaudible level. Regis would not be allowed to brighten our day, it seemed.

A nurse in scrubs came from behind a door under the television. "Mr. Triton?"

"Yes." I stood quickly, as if to avoid being overlooked in a room of four patients.

"Come on back." She was a petite redheaded woman with a nice smile and curly hair. "Did you fill out your questionnaire?"

"Yes." I handed her the form. "Do you think that if I had a bullet in me, like the form asked, the MRI would shoot it out of me?"

157

"No, it would probably just mess up the magnets. You can get undressed behind those curtains. Take off all watches, jewelry, et cetera."

The gown fit awkwardly over my arms and tied around the neck in the back. The material was remarkably soft, but about as durable as a generic paper towel. I was not overcome by embarrassment as I walked down the white hall with my underwear hanging out the back of this gown. It almost seemed a just recourse for all the patients I would one day put in these same gowns.

Upon entering the room, I immediately saw the incubation chamber which would be my dwelling for the next two hours. It was an enormous box with an opening and a tunnel the size of a torpedo bay. They quickly surveyed my body to make sure no watches had slipped by; I still laughed at the idea that someone's hand might fly off if it were to happen. Then I was placed in the torpedo rack.

As I rolled into the tube, I noticed the surreal feeling it evoked. The tube created a true sensation of being buried alive, and if I weren't able to simply close my eyes and forget about things, panic would not be that far out of the question.

Shortly after I had rolled inside, a voice sounding like mission control asked, "Are you ready?"

I acknowledged with a directed wiggle of the toes, which I assumed he could see. Within seconds, the MRI scanner began emitting rhythmic clicks and honks at volumes that would deafen a rock star. The patterns changed at approximately thirty-second intervals, and for some time, it was mildly entertaining to try to predict the next click-honk-beep pattern. But after a while, this became tedious, and I tried instead to plan the activities for the remainder of the day. The ticking and ticking and ticking prevented any directed thought or attention, until I finally aborted my efforts. The only mildly restful activity was to let my mind wander on its own. In this daydreaming state, I considered the notion that the MRI might actually find something dangerous. Although I wouldn't say I worried about it, I had more time to reflect on the possibility in this tube than I would have devoted otherwise.

~~~

I emerged from my reminiscent daydream when the neurologist entered the room. Tara and I sobered up and portrayed the serious concern that a patient presenting with my problem should. The doctor walked from the door at the far side of the room to stand behind his desk and behind the Cabbage Patch brain. He was a short man with curly gray hair waving back behind his ear. His robust jawline and moderately wrinkled face, along with his serious demeanor, gave him the appearance of a Hollywood senator or cabinet member. He wore a shirt and tie, with his white coat buttoned all the way up to the knot of his tie.

"Hello, I'm Dr. Morton," he said in a posture that would impress a rusted tin woodsman. "It's nice to meet you. You're Mr. Triton, and you are...?"

"This is my girlfriend, Tara. She saw the seizure that night."

"Yes, ultimately I would like you to discuss the seizure you had, but first I want to talk about options." He paused with his hand fisted in front of his mouth and a concerned furrow in his brow.

Tara and I were each puzzled by the statement but waited for him to explain. The seconds stretched on, and nothing was said. It was as if he wanted us to offer him the options. The options for what, I didn't know.

The tension of the silence became intolerable. "Options for what, sir?" I asked.

"You mean, you don't know?" he asked almost with a gasp.

Reflexively, I blurted the question, "Know what?"

"Haven't you gone over the MRI with someone yet?" He looked at me with the same furrowed brow, but one cheek was raised slightly. Every crease that became accentuated beside that eye implied I was crazy or incompetent.

"No. You're the first person we have seen since it was done," I said. "What did it show?" My heart was racing as the dramatic mood swing in the room came to a climax.

"Well, it's...it's not normal."

The racing heart abruptly halted. It stopped completely. I couldn't hear it. I couldn't feel it. My fingers became numb the instant he uttered those words. I would remember those words for the rest of my life. I would remember them better than the lyrics to my favorite poem. I would remember the tone better than the chords of my favorite song. There was no sarcasm, but surely no compassion. There was surprise in his voice, but no familiarity in his approach. He was distant, separated from us in the room, separated from his words. *It's not normal.*

That simple sentence was all he said. And again there was silence. There was silence to the ear, but also to the heart. Tara and I looked at each other in shock.

I swallowed deeply and turned back to Dr. Morton. Unlike the several hours compressed in my mind during the seizure, I spent but one minute agonizing over the possible diseases I had. That one minute dragged on for years in my mind, as time moves slowly when it carries the weight of our emotions on its back. Despite my education, I struggled to think of any diagnosis but one. GBM, the textbooks called it. It is such a benign-sounding disease for a brain tumor that grows so fast it surpasses its own blood supply, leaving a pit of detritus at its core. Textbooks showed CAT scans with gaping holes in the brain where the cancer had essentially eaten out the rest of the normal brain. Color autopsy pictures showed brains just removed that had deteriorating edges and looked like pieces of meat left to rot in the woods. In my skull. This is what I imagined.

"So, what do you think is wrong?" I asked.

"I'm not sure." Again, he answered in the most politically savvy way.

"Then what is 'not normal' about the MRI?" I asked, exuding my frustration as I exhaled.

"Here, let me just show you," he said without motioning for us to join him. He stood up with the large envelope he had entered with and turned to the special light box behind his desk. Having seen MRIs in the past, I knew generally how to examine one. It was difficult, however, to get a sense of orientation with twenty slices of my brain depicted on each sheet of film. His finger circled a small area in one of the images. "This is it, right here." He continued to demarcate the imaginary boundary with his index finger. It was just a gray space, not much different from the rest of the gray that made up my brain on the MRI. The shades were only minutely different, the size unimpressive, and the border almost nonexistent. But it was not normal.

"So, how long do you think it's been there, doctor?" I asked.

"It's impossible to say at this point. We don't know what it is or how quickly it grows. It could have been there for years and not grown much, or it could have started months ago and be growing rapidly. It is in your hippocampus, so I wouldn't be surprised if you were having some memory dysfunction."

"You mean you can't tell us anything about the mass itself?" Tara interjected, her voice raised. She had been silent up until now. My eyes had been on the MRI films since he placed them on the light box. But when she shouted at the neurologist, my head swung toward her. Her eyes were swollen and red. The tears had not fallen yet but rather rested on her lower lid and leaned against her eye. "You went to medical school and did a neurology residency, and *all* you can tell us is that it's not normal?" She sobbed slightly, and the first drop ran down her cheek. I hadn't seen her cheeks this red since the day we met and she had blushed during the tutoring session.

I stood closer to her for comfort. "It's okay, dear," I whispered. "Just give it a minute. We'll figure it out. We need to stay calm."

"I'll say it looks like an astrocytoma, but we can't be sure without a biopsy," the doctor said, trying to offer at least *some* information.

"A biopsy?" I asked. "Is that the next step?"

"Possibly. But first you need to see our neurosurgeon. I have one that I can send you to. But he's not in this office. He's out in Los Angeles."

"How soon can we get the appointment?" Tara asked.

"I'll talk to my assistant, and we can see how soon he will be available." And with that, and no further questions or answers, he walked out the door through which he had entered.

Tara buried her head in my shoulder and cried. I'm not sure if I found strength at that moment or was simply in shock, but I stood there quietly stroking her hair.

A woman in a teal-green skirt and a long white coat walked through the doorway. "Mr. and Mrs. Triton, I'm Terry. I just spoke with the secretary at the Los Angeles office, and they can fit you in next Friday at nine, if that's okay."

"Yes. Thank you," I said.

"If you'll come to the checkout desk, we'll give you all the information."

We had not been in the car two minutes before Tara was on her cell phone with her mother. I, however, would wait until that evening to call my parents to tell them. I didn't have the courage, and I didn't have the words to tell them yet.

The first of a new breed of sunsets appeared that night. It was not different in any way from the previous thousands I had seen. It just wasn't normal.

161

I sequestered myself in the bedroom of my apartment while Tara called her father in the living room.

The phone rang three times as I pictured my mother putting the last of the dishes in the dishwasher before picking up the telephone.

"Hello?" The familiar voice of my mother on the line was more soothing than I remembered.

"Hey, Mom. It's me."

"Ooh. How are you?" she asked as though it were a casual greeting among relatives.

"I'm okay. But I wanted to call and tell you guys about the doctor's visit today."

"Oh, well, wait. Let's get your dad on the speakerphone."

I heard the rustling of the phone against her side as she called my dad to the phone. That familiar hollow sound clicked into my receiver as I heard my father's voice. "All right, we have it on speaker now. How did the appointment go?"

"It's not as bad as it could be, but it's not great. They found a mass pretty deep in my brain. They are not sure what it is or how dangerous it is, but they have me scheduled to see a neurosurgeon next week."

When I was a child and got hurt, my mother was always the picture of encouragement, sending me back in to play when I got anything but the most severe of injuries. Her silence tonight was the best encouragement she could muster. That silence tore at my heart, because I knew how much pain it would take to choke the words of strength and love from her lips. Through the silence, I could hear the fear in their hearts.

"Does this mean they're going to operate?" my father asked, clearing his throat slightly to speak.

"No one knows for sure. The neurologist today seemed a little bit out of his league with this problem. He wouldn't commit to anything. He couldn't offer us any solid information or prognosis. I'm just hoping that the neurosurgeon is better."

"And gives us better news," he said.

"I'm sure he will, Dad. Okay, I'm going to go. I need to do some studying for tomorrow. Try not to worry about this. I think everything is going to be fine."

"I know it will," my mom said. "We'll be praying for you."

The closing comment as we hung up struck me powerfully. My parents almost never spoke to me about religion, knowing how I felt about the subject. But the principles that allowed her to remain silent when her son took on philosophies different from her own were of little priority when the safety of her child was in question. Every source of hope had to be exhausted.

"Thank you, Mom. Good night."

That night, I lay in bed with Tara's head on my chest. The feeling of her there brought a sense of safety, if only for now. I thought about my mother, a few miles away, praying for me tonight. I thought back on the nights past when I used to think, or pray even, that God might come down or send some evidence that he was there. I had wanted to believe. I never got that evidence from Him. Now I lay awake wondering if this could be a form of punishment for my disbelief. Could God be imposing a death sentence for my heresy? Or, perhaps worse yet, could God be trying to coerce me into believing in Him or praying to Him by threatening my life in this way?

The thought festered in me that night, the way the tumor had been festering in me for however long. That a god could think I was so weak of heart that I could be swayed by the threat of harm…the insulting thought sickened me. I thought of all the people who subscribe to a religion out of fear of a mythical hell. I refused to kneel before a cross to save my life. I challenged God to call my bluff and deliver this plague of cancer upon me. There, in that bed, I threw down the gauntlet before God. If he was a god that would do such heinous things to the beings he created and supposedly loved, I wanted no association with him. I would place no faith in Him, even if absolute evidence of Him was offered to me on my deathbed.

~~~

I looked down at the name "Rose" on my cell phone's caller ID as it rang. I was on the road home from the neurosurgical appointment in Los Angeles just before lunch, and traffic on the freeway was beginning to get heavy.

"Hello."

"Hi, Jeff," Tara's mother said in her usual perky voice. "How did the appointment with the neurosurgeon go?"

"It went pretty well. He seemed pretty sure that it was a low-grade astrocytoma, although he agreed that he would not be able to tell without a biopsy for sure."

"So he is recommending a biopsy?"

"Well, he gave us two options, essentially. We could choose to get a biopsy, where they would try to go in with a thick needle and get a sample through the skull. The alternative would be to watch it with an MRI in six months and see what it does."

"Which one are you thinking about?" she asked.

"I really don't know. I hate the idea of not knowing and having this thing growing inside me."

"Yes, it is pretty awful, all right," she said, confirming my sentiment. "Listen, I took the MRI copies that you gave me to Dr. Aster, the pediatric neurologist I work with here at Mon Gracia. I talked to him about what has been happening and what has been said. I asked him what he thought of the neurosurgeons with Empire, and he said you should avoid them at all costs. He said he wouldn't let them cut on his dog."

"Wow. So what does he think it is?"

"Well, he isn't sure, either. He said it looks like an astrocytoma too, but he couldn't tell how aggressive it might be. He called the person he employed to write the chapter on temporal lobe brain tumors for his textbook and asked her who she would recommend on the West Coast as the best in the field. She apparently recommended a Dr. Edwards, up in Sacramento. Aster called personally and got you an appointment for Monday, so I think we should fly up there together and get a second opinion from him."

As slowly as my first tests and appointments had progressed, my appointment with Dr. Edwards came quickly. A half-hour flight landed me in the Sacramento airport with Tara and her mom. I was eager with anticipation, as the information could only get more promising.

When we arrived at his office in the rental car, I was struck by the ordinariness of the building. It did not have the fanfare that I would have expected of one of the greatest neurosurgeons in the country. Inside, the waiting room was decorated with children's toys and furniture. The paintings on the wall were brightly colored and playfully drawn. Two children played in the playhouse in the corner, casually mingling with each other. Both were about four years old, but the girl had a shaved head and a triangular pattern of stitches arranged above her ear. I smiled at her with an undertone of pity in my mind. She smiled back with nothing but the careless elation of a princess sitting down for afternoon tea in her palace.

The three of us were soon led back to the personal office of Dr. Edwards, where he sat behind his desk. He immediately rose to greet us when we entered. "You must be Jeff, and Rose. And that makes you Tara, right?"

Tara smiled. "That's right."

He was a short, thin man whose hairline had reached well behind his ears. His white coat hung on the back of his chair, while he was clad in a simple outfit with monkeys dancing on his tie. He did not protect his hands as though they were the breadwinners. Instead, he offered them to shake each of our hands, as though he thought that was where the treatment and healing might begin.

"I'm sorry to hear about all that you've been through. I got the story from Dr. Aster over the phone last Friday. He sent the films to me overnight, and I had yesterday to look them over. There were some interesting things about the scans."

"What do you mean 'interesting,' sir?" I asked.

"I'll get to that in just a minute. I think you'll like it. But I want to ask you a few questions first, so I can gain a complete picture. Do you have problems with forgetfulness?"

"Yeah, I do."

"And when did these problems arise?" he asked as his chin wrinkled upward.

"I guess around the time I began medical school. I had a pretty good memory in college."

"Now, I don't just mean forgetting some component of some biochemical pathway or the third artery to branch off of the aorta. I don't even mean forgetting where your keys are. Everybody in medical school is forgetting those facts, and they are all losing their keys because of the stress of med school. I mean things like forgetting the names of people you just met, forgetting if you saw a particular movie. Have you had problems with any of those types of things?"

"Since you mention it, I suppose I have always had a little trouble remembering names. I always thought it was because I was being lazy and not paying attention when they told me."

"That may be the case, but you may have had some help. Or been lacking some help, however you want to think of it. And if this has been a longstanding problem, that would be very interesting to me. Are there any neurological problems that run in your family?"

"I have a sister who is mentally retarded. They never figured out why she was retarded."

"Hmm, it's probably not related but good to know. And you have never had any other seizures or blackouts?"

"Not that I know of."

"Okay. It was probably just fatigue and the stress of your rotations that made you susceptible."

"You mean it was not the tumor?" Tara asked.

"No, it was the tumor. But Jeff became more sensitive to its effects because he was tired and probably stressed. If he had things like alcohol, caffeine, or any drugs in his system, they could make him more likely to have a seizure, too. But in this case, I think it was fatigue on top of the tumor. But this brings me to the interesting part that I have been anxious to tell you."

"What's that?" I asked.

"I don't think you have the same thing that you've been told that you have by others."

"What do you mean? You mean it's not a tumor?"

"I'm sorry, no. It *is* a tumor, of sorts. I don't think it's an astrocytoma, like you've been told. I think it's what is called a dysembryoplastic neuroepithelial tumor, or DNET."

"I haven't heard of that," said Tara's mom. "Is it not as dangerous as the astrocytoma?"

"It's a relatively new discovery. I did a fair number of studies on them when I was working for the university system. It's found mostly in children, who tend to get their brain tumors in the same area that you did. And it's less dangerous than the astrocytoma because it didn't spring up from a single cell like cancer would. Rather, you were likely born with this funky hamartoma. You see, instead of growing and growing without turning into any specific kind of cell, as a cancer behaves, a hamartoma is just made up of a bunch of cells that got confused early in development and turned into the wrong kind of cells."

"So this DNET is a certain kind of hamartoma? And it's not going to grow and kill me? Are you sure?"

"Yes, it is a certain kind of hamartoma that usually grows in children and is almost always found in the temporal lobe—in your case, the hippocampal section of the temporal lobe. And no, they generally don't grow. But of course I can't be 100 percent sure; I'm just looking at the appearance and the position, which look very much like a

DNET. And you have had problems remembering names for a long time, which means that this probably isn't new and growing fast. So I am optimistic."

"Well, why didn't the neurosurgeon at Empire mention this?" Tara asked.

"It's not the kind of thing that every neurosurgeon is going to follow when he is out of the academic medicine world. Besides, I mentioned also that it is usually a kids' thing."

"Do we need to get a biopsy to be sure, then?" I asked.

"We could do that. But if this is a DNET, we would have poked through your brain for nothing. I would recommend that we just watch it with frequent MRIs to make sure it doesn't start growing on us. If it does, then we can decide to biopsy or operate, or whatever."

The three of us looked at each other, and I turned to Dr. Edwards in agreement. "That sounds good," I said.

We exchanged farewells and established six months as the time for my next MRI and appointment.

That night, I felt an amazing difference in my outlook. I thought back to the appointment with Dr. Edwards and realized that we had spent no more time in his office than with Dr. Morton or the Empire neurosurgeon. But in that same short time, we had been offered answers, explanations, and hope. Hope! I looked up articles on DNETs and found several published with Dr. Edwards' name as an author. I couldn't help but have a new sense of confidence, which I shared with my parents and my sister on the phone.

I could never be sure whether it was my tone or the conversations she'd had with my father since our last discussion, but my mother responded quickly with, "I am so relieved. I know you'll be okay now." And with that vote of confidence, I was the young soccer player sent back onto the field to finish out the game. I went in to work the next day as if I had nothing on my mind, or in it.

Being sent back into the game on a medicine like Dilantin is not without its difficulties. The medicine was one of the first to be invented for seizure treatment. The purpose of the medicine is to numb the brain just enough so that the seizure-prone areas go to sleep, while hopefully leaving the rest of the brain awake. The latter goal is apparently more difficult to achieve.

I had been on the medicine now for over a month, initially getting quick little covert prescriptions from Tara's mom, which I filled at local pharmacies. The medicine leeched me of every drop of energy and motivation. Each step I took on the pediatric floor, I was carrying the ten extra pounds of medicine that saturated my blood. When I attended lectures on subjects like congenital illnesses, my eyelids became unbearably heavy. Even my forehead felt heavy. Without constant, concentrated effort, I thought even my browbone might fall down, closing my eyes. I had no desire to treat the children, interact with my friends, or even spend time with Tara.

Despite my fatigue, I kept on working. I even continued to take call, staying in the hospital overnight to help care for the patients. To begin the day fatigued almost ensured that I would end the day semiconscious. One night, the exhaustion cradled me so well that a one-hour nap extended into a night's sleep in one of the hospital bunks provided for residents. Fortunately, the fevers of local children magically vanished that night, and no one had to be admitted. I slept soundly on the squeaking stone slab with sheets. I had forgotten my evening dose of the medicine and forgot it again in the morning, when I rushed to get caught up on the work I had put off. When the morning was over, I dragged myself home for an immediate nap on the couch.

The door opening that evening woke me as Tara walked through the door. I was disoriented, but not like I had been after the seizure in January. She stood me up and walked me to my room to change clothes into something more comfortable and less grungy.

"I'll cook you some dinner," she said. "What would you like?"

"I dunno."

"I'll just make us some soup. How 'bout that?"

"Sure." I couldn't muster the motivation to help her, or even to offer decent conversation. After putting on some sweatpants, I returned to the living room and sat in the leather desk chair. The recline of it was perfect as I listened to the air hissing from the cushions. I relaxed a little more and lifted my feet onto the ottoman. I found myself in that semi-awake state where dreams come so freely. I had gone through a traumatic struggle at work, but now I was unencumbered of my need to stay awake. Nevertheless, I remained awake and simply enjoyed the euphoria.

I drifted into a dream that I had had before. I didn't know when, but it had a sense of familiarity. It had other senses, too. Voices spoke to me personally and not around me, as they do in movies. I could actually hear them in my ear. It was Holly, from *Land of the Lost* again.

No matter how many times I had the dream, or how plotless the dream was, it was always comforting. I got a warm feeling in my stomach as she spoke to me; it was a feeling of simultaneous desire and satisfaction. It wasn't erotic or romantic—more like craving ice cream and taking the first bite. But that sensation would last for the entire dream. She just kept repeating a few words, but the ice-cream sensation was so intense that I didn't want to wake.

"Jeff!" Tara shouted.

"Yeah?" I said.

"Snap out of it!"

"In a minute. I'm just thinking," I said in a low voice. I could have snapped out of it, but the craving for more was so great I did not have the willpower to do so. I ignored Tara for a few seconds and just relished the warm sensation that was welling inside my stomach, inside my chest, inside my throat.

"Jeff! Wake up!" she shouted again, now grabbing my shoulders and forcing her face before my eyes.

The sensation in my stomach was gone now, as were the voices from my dream. In fact, the entire euphoria of that semi-sleep was blown. "I was coming to the table. I just needed a second. I was thinking."

"You weren't thinking. You were seizing."

"I wasn't having a seizure. I was completely awake. I was just daydreaming."

"You were sitting in that chair and your lips were smacking like you had peanut butter in your teeth. I was talking to you, and it took you ten seconds to answer. And even then, you talked really slow, like you were drunk."

"I'm just tired. And I was daydreaming. I didn't hear you very well."

"You weren't daydreaming. Look at you. You are totally pale. You shouldn't look like a ghost after a daydream."

I was reluctant to buy the seizure explanation. I was aware that there are certain types of seizures called partial seizures where you don't actually shake. Sometimes just certain parts of the body move, or you exhibit weird repetitive behaviors. But you are supposed to get an aura or a warning sign before such a seizure. I didn't have that—no smell, no sound. I just had my daydream. A simple daydream.

~~~

Soon after the visit with Dr. Edwards and a couple days after the daydream incident, Tara, her mother, and I decided that Dr. Aster should be my neurologist. There was the great advantage of convenience with him being at Mon Gracia, but he was also next to Rose's office, so my occasional visits were not conspicuous to the faculty. I went to his office to discuss the side effects of the medicine, and after weeks of sleepwalking though the hospital, Dr. Aster offered me a new medicine, recently released. The medicine had not been used much outside of trials, but it had done wonders for children with seizures similar to mine. The beauty of it was that it did not leave patients feeling so withered as I felt. They had much more energy. He called it Keppra. I had never heard of it, but there were many drugs that I hadn't heard of at this point.

"How have you been doing otherwise?" he asked. "No more seizures, I take it."

"Otherwise, I've been fine," I said. "You know, there was something recently. I was really tired one night post-call. I was sitting in my chair just sorta zoning out. I was having this daydream, and then all of a sudden Tara was trying hard to wake me up, saying that I was smacking my lips."

"Smacking your lips?"

"Right. But I swear I didn't realize I was smacking my lips. I was just zoning."

"Did you have any strange sensations during the dream? Like smelling burnt rubber or garbage? Maybe a taste in your mouth? Hear any funny sounds?"

"No, none of those," I answered. "But wait…now that you mention it, I had a strange feeling in my stomach when it happened."

"In your stomach? You mean, like pain?"

"No, it wasn't painful. I don't know how to describe it. But it didn't hurt."

"Well, that could be your aura. It isn't the typical one, but it is possible. And all things considered, it's not a bad one to have. Have you ever had this dream before?"

"Here and there, a couple times. But it is usually short. I have always tried to keep it going longer because it felt so good, but it always quit on its own after a few seconds."

"All right, well, we can try this new medicine and see how it works for you. You let me know how it makes you feel, and make sure that you tell me about any new seizures."

"You got it, Doc."

~~~

A similar one-centimeter pill a couple times a day, yet the difference was delightfully profound. Rooms were immediately brighter, voices more animated, days did not seem as long. The weights mysteriously lifted off my eyebrows. I could hardly believe the medicine could be doing anything for me if I wasn't suffering from the brutal side effects, but if no one complained about me thrashing about in my sleep and whacking them on the head, I certainly wasn't going to be the one to suggest that this godsend of a medication wasn't working.

By now I had moved to the next rotation, which was psychiatry. Mon Gracia, being a particularly child-friendly hospital, had one of the most renowned children's psychiatry departments in the nation. I, of course, had the distinct displeasure of serving in this frustrating subspecialty of a specialty that I had little interest in to begin with. Actually, to say that I had no interest in it is a misstatement. Rather, I could not step out of myself to understand how an otherwise normal person could not realize that the things he was saying and doing were absolutely ludicrous. Furthermore, I couldn't see why we were calling kids crazy now, when they were identical to the kids who had once kicked my butt in elementary school. Back then, we simply called them assholes. Nevertheless, the rotation offered a great deal more relaxation time than did the previous rotations, and I encountered a few clinical novelties every now and then.

It was Friday, March 17, the big day: I was on call. I suppose there is always a sense of dread when you go into a call day. Psychiatry is not the worst specialty to take a call in; after all, the number of people killing themselves rarely approaches the number of people having heart attacks. And if you factor out the number of those who are successful in their attempts (which reasonably takes them out of the psychiatrist's jurisdiction), the duty becomes much less burdensome from a medical student's perspective. But I knew today would be a long day from the start.

Tara knew that I was on call, so we exchanged our extended good-byes on the chance that I might not get time to call her from work. Her mood had improved, and we were generally both optimistic about my brain and my likelihood of being all right in the end. We had reached the deep nadir of our depression during that period where we thought our options were brain surgery and/or death. But we had found a diagnosis and a doctor who could give us hope, whether correct or not, and that was the springboard our outlook needed. Tara also found strength in slapping my wrist for missing any doses of medicine, so perhaps that role was doubly beneficial. Despite the fact that she had been with me for several months, longer than any of my other med school relationships, and had seen me spend many nights on call in the hospital, she always seemed sad to see the extra day pass between our meetings. Today, her mother had invited her to a champagne cocktail hour in the afternoon at an elegant restaurant with a balcony overlooking the valley, while I tended to the troubled tykes.

One aspect of Fridays in the child psych ward that amused me was the "question hour." Every day at the inpatient children's center, sessions were devoted to each of the age groups: elementary, junior high, and high school children. Anger-management sessions allowed one violent teen to counsel other equally violent teens on expressing themselves without a machete. Depression and coping skills were provided for thirteen-year-old girls whose hospital pajamas seemed exuberantly upbeat compared to their usual monochromatic black accoutrement. However, the bright colors clashed tragically with their jet-black dyed hair and similarly gothic fingernails. The short sleeves of these gowns revealed the disturbing image of scars along their wrists. Where had these kids lost hope?

But Fridays brought more amusing morning sessions with the question hour. This was an hour devoted to children eight years and younger, as all others were excused back to their rooms or various other group activities. There were usually about fifteen children in the group at a time, considering the influx and efflux of these emotionally disturbed squirts. Occasional cases of depression showed up in this age group, but for the vast majority, behavior was the issue. Most had a propensity for mouthing off constantly, some even for violence. There was one in the group who had stabbed another child in his class with a No. 2 pencil. Needless to say, the Center offered only Crayolas.

The purpose of the question hour was to allow the children to ask any question they wanted of the pediatric psychiatrist, who would then answer honestly and objectively. The idea had been developed by one of the foremost researchers in pediatric psychiatry. He believed that by demystifying many of the words and ideas that these kids were exposed to, he could make them less appealing. For example, on occasion, when there were several new kids in the group, one would ask, "What's cock?"

A few giggles would erupt from the group. The psychiatrist, with a face straight as a board, would answer, "Well, a cock is a slang word for a penis. Do you know what a penis is?"

"Oh...yeah," the child would inevitably reply, somewhat disappointed by the dull response he had obtained.

"Well, what does motherfucker mean?" the next child would inquire.

"Let's break it down. You all know what a mother is..." He always paused as he broke down the compound obscenities. "And 'fuck' is another word for sexual intercourse. So a motherfucker is someone who has sex with someone who is a mother."

Within three questions, the goal would cease to be upsetting the psychiatrist. Instead, each child would try to outdo the other in terms of profanity, crassness, and pure disgust value. The concept seemed a little silly to me, since I had known what each of these things meant by the first grade, and I am sure these kids did too. So nothing was demystified. This outlet merely gave them a stage on which to perform their vulgar linguistic artistry. And these were masters of the fine art of profanity, words mixed and matched in such a way as to show an irreverent disregard for syntax and grammar in order to create the beautiful poetry that was, "What does bitchy ass dick suck mother cunt nigger shit mean?"

After the stunning performances and almost successfully maintaining a look of stern seriousness throughout the session, I exited the center to take care of some other pressing personal issues.

The Mustang sped up the highway, sparsely traveled by California's standards. I felt the pressure as I realized I was running a bit behind schedule. The morning psychiatry session had taken longer than expected, and my covert arrangement with the other medical student was to leave after that session. Indeed, the long day that I had planned was not to be confined to the boundaries of walls or pagers. Rather, I had pieced together a more elaborate scheme.

While most would agree that promptness is a worthy virtue, my phobia of tardiness had invaded areas of my life in ways that others would find pathetic. For example, the concept of being fashionably late, even at such parties as the term was coined, was terrifying to me. And even though fears of being perceived as irresponsible or worthless in those situations are clearly irrational, I knew it was important to meet with Mr. Wharton by our noon appointment, as he might be tending to other clients after that. I was nervous behind the wheel, as this was my first deal like this, and meeting with Wharton would start me down a path from which I could not return.

The trail to the remote cabin was narrow, and the sign that marked it discreet. The building was absolutely isolated from civilization, trees surrounding it for miles. As I approached the door, a man opened it. He was just as I imagined someone in this business would look.

"Mr. Wharton?" I asked.

"Yes? Mr. Triton?" he replied in a mellow, monotone voice.

I nodded.

"You can follow me. I don't have the stuff set out yet, but I trust you will like it when you see it later."

We walked up the steps carefully. They creaked. Would that be a problem for me? I wasn't sure. He left me in a small room alone to inspect what I was paying for before the large sum of money changed hands. It was fairly dark, no lights on, lit only by the natural light through the glass. I looked out the window. The view was acceptable, but more importantly was the lack of people for miles. A bed stood next to the wall, covered by a canopy. It was actually quite elegant. As I sat on the bed and stretched my neck, I was able to gaze under the bed, where I spotted an empty bottle of alcohol. I shook my head as I picked it up and threw it away. I wondered if some other poor schmuck had had to get drunk to do this. Was I doing the right thing? Hell, I might be dead in a year. But after all I had been through in the past year, after all we had been through together, this was the right ambience for what I needed to do.

Tonight I would propose to Tara, the girl who had stood by my side as I faced mortality. The plan to make this the greatest surprise of her life was coming together.

I walked down the stairs alone, my sunglasses on. I nodded again to Wharton as I went out the door to signify that it would be fine. *Just get me what I need.* I ducked my head into my coat, as the breeze in these parts was more piercing than down the road.

The drive back was much less stressful, as I had taken care of the most tenuous part of the deal. The few issues that required my attention on the way back were more easily disposed of. The man in the black suit greeted me at the door, expecting me from my cell-phone call. He escorted me in and pointed across a vastly empty room to the one man sitting near the window.

"That's the one," I said with satisfaction in my whisper as the man in the black suit escorted me out.

I stopped by *K*'s place, too. When he saw me, he simply went into the back of his store and got me an oversized black plastic bag. I looked inside to make sure everything was as we had discussed. I had been referred to him by a friend I knew who had done this kind of thing before. Everything seemed right. No money exchanged hands; everything, including payment, had been arranged beforehand to facilitate a smooth exchange. The exchange had to go flawlessly if this were to work.

I made it back to the Mustang without difficulty, then went directly home. The slap of the water against my face in the shower was a reminder that my day was as real as it was surreal. I lathered up and rinsed, wondering what my life would have been like tomorrow if I were not about to go through with this. I got out and got dressed. My radio played in the background, as it always did when I got ready. Stepping out the door at precisely the time I had planned, I started back up the hill.

I pulled over after approximately ten minutes up the hill and parked beside a small restaurant. The traffic below already seemed distant as I viewed the freeway through the canyon. Inside, the waitress led me down the hall, walled by an extensive wine rack. I noticed my familiar favorites from Northern California counties as well as some novel labels from Tuscany and Italy. I walked down the four steps to the patio, which overlooked the entire valley. Here, couples and small groups were enjoying their cocktails, musing over each other's humorous stories and the obvious hectic commotion that was the commuter's life in the valley.

The fire was subdued, surrounded by a wall of brick. The two ladies' glistening shoes perched on that brick as their dresses fell over
their slender legs and floated melodically in the wind. Tara sipped her
mimosa, gazing into the fire as her mother played the active conver-
sationalist. Rose reclined in her chair, her sparkling champagne and
nectar at the ready as she smiled with each word. This was possibly
the happiest I had seen her, just happy to be with her daughter. Tara,
however, stared more distantly through the fire. I couldn't make out
the words being exchanged, but it seemed rather pointless, because
Tara's mind was elsewhere. Was she processing all the stress of medical school? Was she reliving all the nightmares that had come upon us
in the recent months? Was she simply blue because I was relegated to
my hospital tasks tonight? I couldn't know.

I watched Tara sip the last drop from her glass, and with flawless
timing, I approached her from behind. Kneeling down with another
champagne beverage in my hand and adorned in my suit, I did not
look too out of place to the unwatchful eye. But as I took her glass and
handed her another, I spoke.

"Can I offer you another, angel?"

Her head turned in amazement and recognition.

"Oh, my God," she cried. "What are you doing here? You're supposed to be at work."

"Well, I made a little deal with someone at work and got the evening off. I thought I might take you to dinner."

"But my mother and I are supposed to meet some of her friends
from work here tonight," she said with an awkward hesitation in her
voice. "But I'm sure you could stay with us."

"Um, I think your mother might be all right with us taking off," I
said. "Would that be okay, Rose?"

Rose shooed her off with casual nonchalance. "Of course. Go and
have fun."

Tara rose from her chair, still stunned by my arrival, and walked by
my side up the stairs and through the restaurant.

"I don't know why Mom's friends were so late. We were just sitting
out there waiting for them," she said as we drove up the hill. "I guess
it was lucky, though. You might not have found us if they had gotten
here and we all left to eat somewhere else."

I was amused that she had not concluded that her date with her
mother had been arranged by me weeks in advance. I maintained the

story that I had been granted leave at the last moment and ascribed the fortune merely to good luck.

We parked the car in the small lot twenty minutes up the mountain. I opened the car door for her and helped her out as her sapphire-blue dress trailed behind, dangling just above the ground.

"This place looks crowded. Do you think we can get a table?" she asked as we approached the front door.

"I think we can probably get one. It's only a little crowded," I answered, opening the door.

"Ah, Mr. Triton," said the maitre d', dressed in black, as he removed Tara's shawl for her. "I am so glad you could join us this evening."

Tara looked equally confused and amazed. She didn't speak but simply followed as we were led down the hall. The maitre d' seated us at the table beside the window, the very seat I had seen earlier in the day with the single man in the restaurant. The view was breathtaking, and the city seemed hundreds of miles away. The lights no longer looked like headlights, streetlights, and building lights, which represented angst of daily living. They were silent, and moved slowly like the ebb and flow of a peaceful harbor. The conversation was light, mainly about the food, the wine, and the view. No word of tumors or seizures approached the table that night.

The meal was perfect, and the environment was beyond perfect. We were escorted to our car by the maitre d', who thanked us again for joining him. Tara was still taken aback by the amazing table we had gotten, but thankfully accepted the explanation that I had treated him recently in the hospital and had been invited. We turned right out of the parking lot, continuing up the mountain.

"I want to keep going," I explained after making the unexpected turn. "I think there's a side road up here where there is an even greater view. I'm not sure exactly how far it is, but it shouldn't be too long." We ventured on as the distant sea of lights gave way to the darkness of the night and the trees sleeping within it.

The next right turn into the woods was more foreboding in the night, lit only by our headlights, than it had been earlier in the day. I looked at my watch with some nervousness but was relieved to see that it was late enough. As we approached the dimly lit cabin, Tara was surprised by the lack of a hillside view.

"I guess we must have missed the turn I was looking for," I rationalized.

"What do you think this place is? It's kind of scary."

"I'm not sure. You wanna get out and take a look?"

"Do you think we should?" She shrugged. "Eh, sure. Why not?"

Astonished that she seemed to accept the events of this evening as coincidence or luck, including happening upon this building, I was also surprised that she would muster the courage to venture out into the woods under the circumstances.

We got out of the car, this time Tara on her own, holding her skirt close to her knees. We trekked up to the cabin, where there were no lights to suggest anyone was awake or expecting guests. The front door was unlocked, and I led Tara up the stairs of the front porch.

"Are you sure we should do this?" she asked.

"Don't worry, this is just for fun and adventure," I said, peering into the front entryway. A dining-room table to the right was set for several people. "Let's go check out what's upstairs."

"Now you're nuts," she said in a forced whisper.

"Just come on."

She followed me up the pitch-black staircase. The steps creaked as we lifted and placed each foot. We paused with each step, still feigning the covert operation, although I think she was finally realizing that this was not actually a spontaneous trespassing adventure as it originally appeared.

The wooden door at the top of the staircase looked no different than the ones next to it. There were no numbers, just a simple flickering light underneath the door to distinguish it. I opened it slowly and led Tara through.

The candle flame recoiled, then approached in a flirtatious manner as the door wafted the air in. Tara entered first and gazed around the room in amazement. A luxuriant king-sized bed with four posts stood beneath a canopy of lace. The white sheets appeared orange by the candlelight. We sat on the bed next to a silver stand, where a bottle of champagne was chilling on ice. I lifted the bottle from its resting place; it was the same elegant French label I had seen on the bottle I had found earlier in the room. The golden etching of the label glistened against the green glass of the bottle.

The cork popped off easily in my hand, and the microscopic bubbles effused over the edge of the bottle. After pouring the drinks, I teased Tara with their scent and led her onto the balcony. Completely hidden by the forest on our way in, now the beauty of the cabin's view was astounding. Tara stepped forward and leaned against the wooden railing, the satin of her gown pressing against the crystal in her hand.

I don't remember the exact words that followed as well as I remember the perfect backdrop of the full moon upon the still lake. I do remember getting down on one knee and presenting the ring I had picked weeks before and picked up earlier that day. I had not prepared a speech, but simply spoke from that portion of my heart that often gets me in trouble. It refuses to be restrained by my better sense, frequently leads me stumbling over my words, but sometimes unearths a lost eloquence that truly reveals how I feel.

I remember the internal struggle I had in deciding if this was for the best, considering my questionable health. How does one human being ask another to commit to a life with him when there is a distinct possibility that he might be dead or a drooling mass in a few years? Was it fair for me to offer her a diamond ring in exchange for the constant fear and concern that our family might not endure forever because of my health? These ideas and questions plagued me for some time before I proposed. I'd had some reservations even as I asked her mother for her permission and help in arranging the meeting that afternoon. But then the look in her mother's eyes told me how overjoyed she was for her daughter and that there was no reservation in her blessing, and I relinquished all doubt. I saw that I was not asking a person to join my family and commit to a life of risk and tragedy in order to love me. I was acknowledging a family that had long since adopted me and was deeply committed to my well-being. To propose to this woman I loved so much was the only way to show her that I owed my strength, and possibly my life, largely to her standing by me. And although I frequently try to no avail to remember exactly how I expressed myself, I am left only to hope that my words expressed how deeply I appreciated her love, on that St. Patrick's Day, one year after our first date.

Chapter 11

When I was a young boy, my sister Vicki—in addition to wrestling me down to the ground and tickling me helplessly as any older sister might, or sneaking me out to the horror movie that only our mature tastes could appreciate—used to sit me on the couch and force me to watch *The Wizard of Oz* any time it appeared on television. While she did not dress me up like a girl or even a munchkin to watch it, my talent of quoting the movie line-for-line does not ride alongside farting the tune to Ozzy Osbourne's "Iron Man" as my most manly of skills. Dorothy's struggle to find her way through Oz scarcely takes on more than a concrete meaning to a seven-year-old boy. It is especially hard to gain any insight into the allegory when focusing on the more eminent responsibility of appropriately portraying Glinda, the Witch of the North, on cue so that Vicki could find the necessary inspiration to play the role of Dorothy.

The innocent days of standing above my sister and saying, "I'll get you, my pretty, and your little dog too," had passed. Even the pressure of getting my lines right at the risk of a walloping from my big sister seemed miniscule compared to the pressure of performing well and making it into the specialty of my choice. But even determining the right path seemed a formidable task. Each field seemed to lack an essential feature or possess a crucial flaw as I rotated through.

My fantasy of massaging amazing genetic treatments into surgically exposed brain tumors to magically dissolve cancer had been shattered by the twelve-hour surgeries and twenty-four-hour days.

I looked at many other specialties with an open mind, but nothing brought that high of finding a problem that needed obvious and immediate treatment and solving that problem right before my eyes. Surgery actually allowed me to play such an active and immediate role in curing people, but the ritual sacrifice of the profession's young, and the long road of suffering that would await me like anal copulation awaiting a new prisoner to prison, quickly dashed any interest I had in the field. Furthermore, the worst part about surgery was dealing with surgeons, and I wasn't about to condemn myself to this ninth level of hell. I admired the internists who faithfully stuck by their patients' sides, attempting to solve the medical riddle that plagued them. The puzzles themselves interested me more than the patients. But, in the end, I could never find the patience to wait for the problems and solutions to unfold over the months and years that they would take.

Like Dorothy who found that to achieve the excitement and novelty that she desired, she never needed to go beyond her own backyard, I had come to a realization. My first experiences in medicine had been in the emergency department, where I watched people in their most dire hours, as emergency physicians stepped in with the greatest confidence and offered them at least a chance at survival. The technical skills of a surgeon and the intuitive clinical skills of an internist were at his disposal. I had been searching the past three years for the right field, following the yellow brick road through Oz. I don't remember exactly when I clicked my heels, but I found my way back to Kansas and knew that emergency medicine was the specialty for me. From that point on, I focused my education on learning and being accepted to the best emergency residency in the country. As for the *Wizard of Oz* analogy, it wouldn't be fair to ascribe any of my friends with the roles of scarecrow, tin man, and cowardly lion, but it is near impossible to avoid thinking of that OR nurse as the Wicked Witch of the West. To this day, I swear she had the characteristic wart on her nose, and inasmuch as my imagination is much better than my memory, she may have even had a slight greenish hue to her makeup.

~~~

By this time, television had glorified the role of ER doctors, allowing sexy heartthrobs to play the roles of sensitive pediatric emergency physicians and assholes to appropriately personify the ever-combative surgeons. Every child who ever saw himself as a superhero wanted to be an ER doc. Competition to be accepted into this specialty became as fierce, if not more so, than even to get into medical school three years before. Although my goals had changed somewhat, the rules still applied. I wanted to live in the trenches, saving the innocent bystander who happened to fall in. I wanted to see death merely as a less-than-formidable competitor that I toyed with as I sent electricity through the silent heart with my command. I wanted to be the one whom hospitals prayed would staff their emergency department and the one whom families prayed was on service the night tragedy struck. And it was clear again that this could only happen if I showed my worth and went to the most highly regarded residency in the country.

Unlike medical schools, however, which had been established hundreds of years prior and gained their reputation as the best through years of accomplishment and discipline, ER was a young field. For many years, emergency rooms had been staffed by surgeons and internists who had gotten bored, underpaid, or fired in their previous careers and had come to the emergency room as a last resort. As casualties from violence rose and general health care declined, it became apparent that specialized training needed to be offered to those who would meet this growing need. Interestingly, while the most prestigious medical schools were founded on the premise of elitism and academic superiority, some of the most important ER programs were founded in the pit of the most violent and dirty areas of the country. The education was subsidized by the gang warfare and the state of poor health of America's lower socioeconomic classes. Downtown Chicago at Cook County, the heart of Baltimore at the Shock/Trauma center, and south-central L.A. at L.A. County, along with several others of the like, comprised the Ivy League of gore. I knew if I could get into one of these programs, I could one day go on to work and maybe teach in such a program. I could work with people who wanted to learn the specialty as I did. I could feel their adrenaline rush and share mine with them like a bunch of guys around the television on Super Bowl Sunday.

I was obviously not without friends and mentors in the field, since I had volunteered in the Mon Gracia ER off and on for several years. Torrey was one of these mentors with whom I had developed a particularly close bond. He was the type of guy one couldn't help but be envious of, with the all-American athletic look. He had blonde hair

and blue eyes, as I did, but there was a proper quality to his bone structure, and his face had a youthful appearance even though he was years
older than I. However, no one would question his authority because
the confidence behind his kind voice would bring a mysterious peace to
the room even in crisis. I followed Torrey to Canyon County Hospital
one month early in my senior year of medical school on his advice. He
reasoned that everyone at Mon Gracia already knew me from my years
there, and if I wanted to get more letters of recommendation, I needed
to work at another hospital. He also convinced me that everyone interested in emergency medicine residencies would be rotating through
Mon Gracia's ER this month, and I would have to compete for any
attention whatsoever. All this made sense to me, so I began a month in
the midsized county emergency room.

The flow of patients at Canyon County was fairly constant. There
were rare crunches where all the workers were hustling about trying
to find the test tubes to send blood or other unspeakable samples. In
a county hospital, the patient population consisted of those who were
too poor to afford any other medical care, too naïve to know what
they were walking into, or so sick that they were unable to plead with
the paramedic to take them elsewhere. It's not that the care was poor,
but the presence of the first population tended to intimidate others
such that all but the latter two parties tended to go elsewhere for their
care. This made for some outrageous experiences for me as I followed
Torrey out to the helicopter pad for emergency cases flown in from
who-knows-where.

"Do you have 'em with you?" he would shout under the hum of
the propeller.

"I've got 'em right here," I shouted back, barely able to hear my
own voice beneath the roar.

We stayed off to the side of the pad until the chopper completely
landed. We hunched over as usual, as if the extra foot of height would
prevent our decapitation even at this distance from the helicopter.

"Now you remember, you always have to carry two large-bore needles with you when you go out to the chopper or any trauma. Do you
know why?"

"In case he has a tension pneumothorax."

"Right. Okay, let's go."

From the first day with Torrey, running out to the helicopter for
one car accident victim after another, I never had a patient with a lung

collapsing so severely that it prevented the heart from beating, forcing me to puncture the skin through the rib cage to immediately release the pressure. But for years to come, I would carry two large-bore IV needles with me at all times in the emergency department for that one patient who might be saved.

The attitude around the department was fairly relaxed. We were not above telling jokes, laughing at ourselves, and occasionally laughing at a patient behind closed doors. Clipboards would be placed into a pile, where they would be claimed by residents who would then manage patients' stays in the ER. As a medical student, I could take charts and manage the patients to some extent, but I was not allowed to take the complicated cases with the red stickers on the charts.

One case I will always remember came on a particularly slow afternoon. Torrey was the resident working above me, and the attending was a lighthearted, jovial guy trained in the more traditional specialties of medicine but settled down in the more liberated field of emergency medicine. The two stood above the triaged chart pile, looking contemplative and even concerned. Torrey accidentally let out a whisper of a chuckle as I approached.

"What's up, guys?" I asked as I set down my twelfth treated case of asthma for the day.

"Hmm. Er, nothing," the attending said, clearing his throat. "It seems we have a case that would be perfect for you. A real learning case." He handed me the chart. With my eyes still on his pondering brow, he added, "It's over in the lockup section."

Canyon County Hospital provided medical care for the largest maximum-security prison in Southern California. In doing so, sometimes patients coming into the ER would be being arrested as we saw them, fresh from a gang battle or from a high-speed chase leading to a high-velocity impact. Sometimes the patients were inmates of some time, with a toothbrush cleverly sharpened to a razor's edge shoved into their abdomen. These patients were always escorted by prison guards, in chains, to the locked quarters of the emergency department. This was the first case that I had seen in the lockdown unit, so my excitement level was high. I thought it was sure cool of them to invite me to take care of this patient, considering my interest in emergency medicine. That's what I thought until I looked at the chart that was handed to me.

The bold type at the top of the chart, next to the heading *Chief Complaint*, read: ***8" knife blade in vagina***.

I did an immediate about-face and looked back at the two of them. They looked up from the textbook they had been perusing together, as if oblivious to my perplexity.

"Is there really a patient in room 3?" I asked, thinking this must surely be a joke.

"I'm sure there is," the attending replied.

"And is this really their complaint?"

The attending shrugged his shoulders.

But how in the heck could anyone…"But—" I started.

Visibly working to restrain his laughter, but as calm as if the chief complaint was a broken nail, he pointed behind me to the lockdown area. "I don't know. You'll just have to ask her and find out."

I walked back to the prison lockdown unit of the ER, holding the chart in one hand and using my thumb and index finger of the other hand to estimate eight inches.

The halls of county hospital in general tend to be more bland and more poorly lit than private hospitals. Presumably this is because they have less funding, and, because many of the "clients" have no insurance or money, they have little incentive to cater to the more subtle aspects of a patient's experience. The casual absence of paintings on the walls of the rest of the hospital was outdone by the blatant omission of any comforting décor or artwork in the lockdown ward. The lighting was poor, supplied by a series of halogen bulbs dangling from the ceiling. They reminded me of the veterans hospitals I had rotated through, where I surmised the dark environment was intended to prevent flashbacks in the PTSD patients. Here, I couldn't fathom what such lighting would provide except to set the backdrop of a future horror or action film in which a convict escapes a hospital cell and goes on a rampage.

As I approached Room 3 the hospital security guard hoisted the mammoth ring of keys toward the door and turned one, evoking a *clunk* that echoed down the hall. The door itself was at least eight inches thick, which I was able to discern, having just referenced that length with my fingers. The burly guard used both hands to swing the door toward me and signaled me to enter. After I stepped into the eight-by-eight-foot room, the guard closed the door. Although it was no louder, the *clunk* of locking the door behind me left a far greater impression than the first one had, and I fought the reflex to reach for it.

Two guards, one man and one woman, stood in opposite corners of the room. The patient sat on the cheaply adorned cot in her orange jumpsuit. I was surprised to see a female prisoner, despite the obvious implication of the chief complaint. But there she sat. She looked moderately slender, although I couldn't see well. The standard prison uniform had not been designed with the goal of accentuating the feminine figure. Her hair was bleached blonde, with tight curls dangling down to her shoulders. Her skin was a shade of a crusted brown that is not achieved through birth and genetics, but by a lifetime in the desert sun. The crevasses that lined her face were highlighted by the tobacco pus that either precipitated from the smoke or was exuded by her skin after decades of two-packs-per-day smoking. The creases radiated from her mouth in every direction like a supernova of nicotinic expression.

I took a deep breath. "Ma'am, I'm Dr. Triton, one of the student physicians here, and I wanted to come in and talk to you about what brought you in here today."

Prior to her speaking, I was under the misguided impression that there was nothing uglier in the world than a woman with no teeth. To those who are still not in the know on such issues, I must tell you that such a woman would be a princess in comparison to the woman with three teeth. I would later learn that this was typical of the methamphetamine addicts or speed freaks so common to the desert areas surrounding the hospital. These users had developed a pretty sophisticated understanding of physiology and realized that injecting the drugs in certain places like the gums could allow the drugs to bypass the liver and increase the high. The downside was, of course, that their teeth developed the nasty habit of falling out of their mouths.

The patient opened her mouth and calmly replied, "Hi. Nice to meet you."

I was again surprised by her calm demeanor as she sat there. Were I in police custody, I wasn't sure I could remain so sublime. I noticed the multiple scars dotting her arms like craters on the moon. I was already aware that this was a sign of skin popping. Meth abusers would use the drug so much that the veins in their arms and legs would scar over and shrink. This left them with few alternatives to inject the drug into their bodies; therefore they shot the needle up in the nearest unoccupied square inch of skin they could find. Often, this left a bleb to turn into an ulcer and ultimately a scar, as I saw in this patient.

I wasn't quite sure how to break the ice, considering the issue at hand. Asking about any recent vaginal bleeding in the hopes of eliciting her story might have been a reasonable approach, but rarely have I used the word "vagina" in my opening sentence, right after introducing myself. Instead I simply tried the subtle, yet time-tested approach: "So, is anything bothering you today?"

"No," she answered simply and calmly, while looking back at me as though I were silly for even wondering.

I scanned her outfit and didn't see any obvious protrusions or blood around the groin area. I looked back to one of the guards, perplexed by her placidity in the face of this saber in her genitals. He shrugged his shoulders as if to say, *Whatever.*

"I was told by my nurse that you might have a problem," I meekly probed.

"Nope," she said, again replying in a quick, emotionless tone. "Oh, wait. I need an Ace bandage." Now she spoke a bit more quickly.

"An Ace bandage?" I asked. The number of ways an Ace bandage could be used in this setting sprinted through my mind as I tried to see what she was getting at.

That's when it happened. She began speaking in a rapid voice reminiscent of an auctioneer and a tommy gun. "Yeah, an Ace bandage. You see, I was minding my own business, gardening in my yard, when I saw my neighbor. He's always talking shit about me, and he was talking to this cop. And I knew that he was talking shit about me because he's always doing shit like that. Anyway, the cop starts walking over toward me, and I figured that it was because my neighbor was talking shit about me because that's what he does. So I ran in the other direction and climbed over a fence and jumped down on the other side and landed wrong. And I hurt my knee. And that's why I need an Ace bandage."

"I see. And that's all that you hurt?"

"Yep, just my knee," she sped on. "Because I jumped over that fence, because my neighbor was talking shit about me to the cops. He is always doing that shit. And I hurt my knee when I landed, so I need an Ace bandage."

"Hmm. I'm a little bit confused, ma'am. You see, my nurse told me you might have had a knife in your vagina."

"Oh." She paused, seeming to recall for a spilt second. "Yeah," she added with no fear.

"Do you want to explain that to me?"

"Oh. Well, I was gardening with the knife, minding my own business. That's when I saw my neighbor. And he is always talking shit about me. And I saw that he was talking to this cop, and I knew that he was talking shit about me. So I had to get away, right? But I knew that if they caught me with the knife they would bust me because my neighbor is always saying shit about me. So I had to hide it. And since I didn't have any place else to hide it, I put it in there."

I was stunned. My clinical interview script had been derailed completely by this. The silence in the room was deafening, making me painfully aware that I did not know what to say next.

"You mean, you put the knife…in your vagina?"

"Yeah. I had to, because they were gonna bust me because that asshole neighbor is always talking shit about me."

"The same knife you were gardening with?"

"Yeah. They were gonna bust me. So I got it in there and I ran over to the fence and then jumped over. But I landed wrong, and now my knee hurts. And so I just need an Ace bandage, and then I can go."

"Now, ma'am, you realize that you can get seriously cut and infected from that, right?"

"Well, I'm not *stupid*! I didn't put it in blade side up." She looked at me with the most sincere eyes, and clearly thought *I* was an idiot.

Ultimately, I clarified that the prison guards had removed the knife and she had just been brought down to the hospital as protocol. And if she refused a gynecologic exam, which she did, I did not need to do any more.

~~~

Much like the days in the emergency department, the fourth year of medical school was spent finding myself in a professional sense, choosing elective rotations to determine whether something like radiology or oncology might be the path for me. But every look into other lifestyles supported my idea that I was meant to be an emergency physician. I sent out applications to the nearby residency programs, trying to get into the most reputable. Because Tara was a year behind me in school, I couldn't simply apply all across the country and spend the first year of our marriage away from her. I made an exception for some programs, however. I still felt that I needed the feather in my cap of going to a big-name program so that I could get any job I wanted after training. So I applied to those prestigious institutions: Harvard, Yale, Johns Hopkins. Again, I knew that these schools were not known specifically for their emergency departments, but they couldn't be too deficient. And people don't know the specifics about such places. Hell, Yale has not put out a decent president in God knows how many years, yet we keep electing the schmucks. This was the name recognition that I wanted.

The interviews at each of these places seemed to go well. I found myself enjoying conversations with each of the program directors, speaking relatively little about medicine. During my interview with the director at Yale, we spent much of the time discussing a referee's call during a recent football game, which cost my favorite team a trip to the Super Bowl at the hands of the New England team. In a similarly informal setting, I interviewed with the director at L.A. County's ER program during a month I chose to work in their emergency department. I remember following his motorcycle to a nearby sports bar after a shift. He was a young and energetic guy, and his license plate was personalized to read *IN2BATE*, denoting his confident and aggressive style in saving lives and managing airways. In retrospect, interviewing over a beer and *Monday Night Football* might not have been the best way to make a serious impression on a prospective employer, unless he was extremely concerned with writing off pizza as a tax deduction.

By February, most of my class was in a frenzy. The rumors about who was applying to where and in what specialty were the hottest gossip. About half of the class went into primary care. There was a general sense that one could better care for the spiritual needs of a patient in a family practice office than in a surgical suite. Because there were so many programs to train people in these fields, the competition and the stress surrounding these applications were much less. However, a program on the beach in Orange County would have stiff competition even if it was in the field of midget proctology.

I recall having dinner with my family late that February. We had been discussing the interviews I had completed and verbally hoping for a spot in one of my top three picks. There was a general sense of optimism at the table as I recounted the four of us sitting at the same table when my father told me, "If you are the best one at any school, you will do well wherever you want to go." That statement had come to mind several times over the past four years as I was "only at Mon Gracia." But at this point, it seemed my license to overcome that setback and make it into the world of prestige had been granted.

"And what about that MRI you got last week?" my mother asked.

"Oh, I have an appointment with my neurologist this week, and we'll discuss it," I said. "I'm sure it's fine, though. I haven't had any problems recently."

"You're taking your medicine, right?"

"Yes. This medicine has been great. I don't feel tired or anything."

"Well, we will be praying for you when you go to the appointment," she said.

Once again, this sounded a little strange coming from my mother, who was not the type to bring up religion in casual conversation. I knew how religious she had been growing up and before we left our church, but she had mentioned little of it thereafter. The only exception was that anytime I mentioned I was an atheist, she would abruptly stop me and tell me I shouldn't say that. My mother had been strong and silent throughout this "illness," or whatever it was.

"You should pray, too," she said.

"You know I don't pray, Mom."

"Well, you will pray this time, anyway."

It was the only way she felt like she could play any role in protecting her son this time. She had always been there for me growing up—a kiss on a skinned knee, a word of encouragement for a low grade on a test. I don't know what she knew that night or what she feared. But she didn't believe her kiss could cover the wound, and she didn't think it was I who had failed the test. She needed to know that everyone was praying for me so that I could get better, and that included me.

"Okay, Mom. I'll do it this time."

It was the type of lie you tell when you are trying to hide a surprise birthday party from someone. It was the type of lie you tell when a female's jeans actually do make her ass look big. My mom's feelings were more important to me that night than any set of principles I had developed as part of my identity.

After dinner, I headed back home to meet Tara. We had planned to try to settle some of the wedding details over dessert. I sat at the computer desk in the living room as she cut into a pie.

"Do you want milk or tea with that?" she called. Why she even needed to ask was beyond me. And why Irish people felt the need to drink tea with every meal, snack, and biscuit (which means something different to you and me, incidentally) was beyond me as well. Of course I wanted milk. Who doesn't drink milk with pastries and desserts?

"Miiilk, dear."

After we picked out the official wedding colors and the restaurants for the rehearsal and reception dinners, we went to bed. I hadn't forgotten my promise to my mother about praying. I lay there in bed debating with myself as to whether I should actually go through with it. But ultimately, my mom was someone particularly hard to break a promise to.

God was not someone I had a difficult time taking a stern tone with. I pointed out to him that he still had not lived up to my expectations of omnipotence in proving his existence to me. And, as I had vowed, I still wasn't going to cave in and become the faithful subject just because he had threatened me with a brain tumor. I also pointed out that in doing this to me, he was fucking with people who had placed their trust in him: Tara and my mother. I drew his attention to how devout my mother was, and shamed him for doing this to such a wonderful woman. And while I asked to remain alive, I made it clear that I was asking on behalf of my mother. In conclusion, I mentioned that the least he could do was to give me a residency at Harvard or Yale, after all that I had been through.

~~~

On the second morning following my so-called prayer, I received an email from the dean of the medical school. The contents were no mystery. If you got one, you didn't want to know what was in it. It was standard practice to email all the medical students who did not match to a residency program two days prior to the day that all official announcements were made to allow two days to "scramble." That is, to allow the medical students who did not get into one of the programs they chose to pair up with one of the programs that did not fill with the medical students they chose. There is always hope that others will find value where the first did not. This email meant that I had been passed over. Passed over by Harvard, by Yale. Passed over even by the emergency department at Mon Gracia. I cursed myself for doing my

191

month of emergency medicine at the county hospital, where I couldn't impress the big wigs.

The following morning, I showed up at the dean's office as the email instructed me. The office, however, was almost unrecognizable. Tables and chairs had been brought in from lord-knows-where in the school. Thirty to forty chairs, along with phones and faxes, sat in lines horizontally across the room. No one else had arrived yet, and the empty seats left me feeling as hollow as their implication. Within thirty minutes, we were gathered in those seats. We, the medical students who had reached beyond our means, the students who had not sold themselves appropriately, the ones who had fucked up, were told how the day would proceed. We would be given a list of programs that hadn't filled in each specialty, along with phone numbers for their department. When the clock struck eight, we were permitted to begin calling and trying to get into whatever program we were able.

The list came. Emergency medicine had only four residency programs in the entire country that had positions available. Most of the openings were in areas such as internal medicine, family medicine, and pediatrics at the smaller hospitals, a daunting fact that kicked my optimism in the chin. As I wrung my hands, preparing for the endeavor before me, I saw Jim, the innocent little twig from my class, sitting at the table in front of me. He was scanning the emergency programs as well. I couldn't believe it! The naïve boy who had probably never heard someone swear before he met me, let alone seen someone who was shot, was going into ER? I was dumbfounded that this kid who was obsessed with approaching all his patients to pray with them, would go into the fast-paced and slightly less bonded field.

"Jeff," the dean called from his enclosed office space, "why don't you come in here for a second?"

I felt somewhat attached to the dean by this point in my career. I had been forced to come to him with the news of my tumor and the seizure pretty early on. He had encouraged me to take some time off but supported me when I couldn't bring myself to step out of school. I rose from behind the stack of phone numbers and went to his office.

"Jeff, I just got word that the internal medicine department here at Mon Gracia is looking for two people to fill preliminary internship spots. This means that you would only be committing to a year of internal medicine and could apply for the match again next year. They want to offer this to you now, before the scramble starts and the phones start ringing for the positions." He spoke rapidly and precisely. And although the words made perfect sense, my mind took a few seconds to catch up with my ears, which thankfully heard every word.

I sat silently at his desk for all of two minutes, considering the options. One: I could take the position and put off emergency medicine for a while, if not for good. But that would keep me here with Tara for the first year of our marriage. Two: I could turn down the offer and try to get one of the four ER spots elsewhere in the country. I had never heard of any of the ER programs listed. But they were ER. And Tara could do month-long rotations wherever I went. But what if I didn't get one of those spots? I might be condemned to some backwoods hospital, practicing veterinary medicine if that was all that was left.

"Thank you, Dean. I'll take it." I stood up and shook his hand. Despite feeling like an utter failure in my quest to become that famous ER doctor, there was some sense of relief that at least it was settled. I would spend the first year of married life with my wife in Southern California. Walking out of the hall, I picked up my backpack, which had copies of my curriculum vitae, board scores, and letters of recommendation. I was silent, knowing the tension in each of the students sitting at those fax machines. When I walked outside, I was somewhat startled by the sun sitting only slightly above the horizon. I had walked out of the hall with my tension piled high and massive like ballast weighing me down from deep within, yet the day would seem at its beginning to most.

Chapter 12

This wasn't the first day I had woken up as a doctor. Officially, I had graduated from medical school a month before. But the *MD* behind my name didn't mean terribly much without a patient in front of me. Today was the first day I would step into the hospital as a physician—a resident physician, but a physician. The embroidery on the white coat I was given read in brilliant red lettering, *Mon Gracia Hospital, Resident Physician, Internal Medicine*. The final line evoked a sensation of shame just behind my sternum, not too far from where the letters sat. The department was nothing to be ashamed of; in fact, many would have been ecstatic to have my position. But my friends had left, getting one step closer to their goals, several of them in emergency medicine where I had seen myself. Even though I had much to be thankful for, how does the minor-league baseball player feel when his best friend gets drafted to the majors? How does the small-town boy feel when his girl-friend leaves for college in the city? How does Ben Affleck feel every time he sees Matt Damon make a decent movie?

This wasn't my first day as a married man, either. The wedding had taken place two weeks before graduation and, while fairly small, had actually been considered a pretty big social event around the medical school. Although med school led to many marriages between students, at Mon Gracia only the rare wedding has an open bar at the reception. After the ceremony, we spent two weeks in the Caribbean, ignoring all that we had learned in med school and rejecting any sunscreen that required more than one hand to count the SPF. Today was the first day, however, that it seemed like a real marriage rather than an elaborate and extended date. I woke to the alarm in our bedroom, in our new apartment, to go to my new job. It sounded like something out of Ozzie and Harriett, aside from the fact that Ozzie didn't have to get up at five in the morning.

I arrived at the county hospital where I was to work that first month. My senior resident for the month, a soft-spoken Asian guy, gave me the abbreviated tour of the hospital in light of my previous experience there.

"You're gonna start out with three patients," he said, knowing that I had been exposed to the routine in med school. "You will take call every four days, where you will admit however many come in. You will get rid of however many you can in the meantime."

"That's fine," I said.

"Two of your patients are pretty straightforward and will probably go home soon. You can go meet them on your own. I want to take you up to the detention ward, where your third patient is. I can show you how to get in there. He's pretty complicated—been here forever."

We took the stairs up to the sixth floor. The staircase was enclosed by thick concrete that seemed to encroach on the stairs, squeezing them until they were as steep as they could go. The window at each floor presumably looked upon some desert landscape. But it was impossible to tell for certain, as they were each frosted and shatterproof. Once we reached the sixth and top floor, steel mesh covered the pointless windows to prevent an escape onto that unseen landscape. The corridor to the prison ward of the hospital was an even more foreboding interpretation of the detention hall in the emergency department. The halls were surprisingly dark, marked by an orange stripe on the tiled floor. Video cameras were staggered throughout the hall and fixed also on the first doorway.

My senior pushed a button beside an intercom, and a buzzer went off inside the door.

"Yeah?" a deep female voice shot from the box.

"We're here from medicine," my senior said, bending over to the intercom.

"Okay."

With that, a deep *clack* came from the door and echoed down the hall. I followed my senior as he pushed the heavy door open. A second door, equally formidable, was approximately thirty yards down another corridor. There were no side doors and no windows. The vents where the side walls met the ceiling may have been simply for air, but seemed conveniently placed to deliver tear gas in the midst of a riot or an escape.

"Have you ever cared for someone with Crohn's disease?"

"No, I haven't."

"Well, this guy has about the worst case of it you will ever see. He has had about forty-five surgeries to repair his bowel, but he keeps getting obstructions."

"That sounds pretty bad."

"That's only half of it. His body keeps forming fistulas from his intestine to his bladder and to his skin. It's terrible. Just as soon as they repair one, two new ones form."

"Jesus," I said, recalling the pictures I had seen in medical school but had never expected to witness in person.

We looked up at the closed-circuit camera when we reached the opposite door, and the *clack* sound once again echoed through the hall.

"So why is this guy in prison?" I asked.

He shrugged. "Who knows anymore. Probably drugs or something. Robbery. Who knows? Maybe he even killed someone. All I know is that at some point in time, this guy went freaking nuts. I mean, seriously wacko."

"Really?"

"Oh, yeah. Most of the prisoners are allowed to be unshackled in their cells and eat with plastic utensils. Not this guy. He attacked a nurse and guard after eating half of his mashed potatoes. Imagine that! Trying to take down a 300-pound guard with a freaking spork."

"So they keep him chained up all the time because he attacked someone?"

"Partially. But more than that, it was because he would sit in his cell pulling out all his hair one by one or picking at his skin until he had sores all over his body. That's the real reason they had to chain him up all the time. I'm telling you, man, this guy is about as big a nutball as you can get."

"I guess so."

"Now put on your protective covering and your eyewear. This guy has bugs you don't want to spread around to other patients."

We donned the thin plastic yellow overwear. The clear plastic goggles covered my eyes, my forehead, and even some of my hair, despite their inclination to slide down my nose. My senior put on gloves, and I followed him and the armed guard into the cell.

"Mr. Stanley, good morning. It's time to wake up. I wanted to come and introduce Dr. Triton, who is going to be working with you for the month."

"Another new one, huh?" Mr. Stanley rolled toward us to the extent he could with his hands bound to the bed. "This should be freakin' great," he said with sarcasm in his breathless voice, chuckling to himself.

The patient was not of the stature I expected, considering his reputation. He was a thin, frail white man with a shaved head, no doubt a response to his plucking habit. A stubbly beard covered his protruding chin. His unkempt appearance reminded me of the pictures I had seen of Charles Manson after he was arrested, even down to the orange hospital gown he was forced to wear as a prisoner and his psychotic gaze, which rapidly jumped from one person to another. Nevertheless, he remained relatively calm as my senior discussed the process of caring for his wounds.

"So we just need to take a look at the fistulas periodically and see if they are healing up, or if we need to get surgery to take another look." He leaned over Stanley as he lifted the orange gown. A large bandage that appeared to be made out of a pair of Pampers was taped to the patient's abdomen. "Sorry about this," he said as he peeled some of the tape from the patient's skin.

"Yeah, that's okay. Whatever," Mr. Stanley said, continuing to chuckle in that wispy tone. The chuckle had me fearing he was quietly planning our murders.

My senior peeled away the pad from Stanley's abdomen and leaned over to point to the fistulas. I had a perfect view of the pencil holes around his navel for all of one second. Then the patient strained to take an enormous breath, and, before either of us could worry about what was happening to him, he grimaced and contracted every muscle in his body. His face turned deep red, and his jugular vein distended and climbed up his neck. His hands grasped the side rail on his bed, and his head shot forward. Only after it was too late did it occur to us what was happening.

Like the sound of whipped cream propelled from a canister, there was a violent roar, with several eruptions of inefficient gas loss. No description can truly capture the image of several streams of molten, spinach-green and brown shit flying at my senior. The brunt of the flow hit the yellow gown, but the careless lacing left his collar and tie exposed, and both were slapped by errant feces. My senior managed to turn his head at the last moment, sustaining only superficial turd shrapnel to the neck.

Mr. Stanley howled with laughter as the rest of the room fell silent. I was stunned, while my senior seethed with anger. When the guard pulled us out of the room, I wasn't certain if it was to discipline the prisoner or prevent my senior from doing just that. My senior never returned to see that patient, although he supervised my care from a safe and hygienic distance. Whatever was said to Mr. Stanley in my absence appears to have worked, as he never pulled any stunts of that kind for the duration of the month.

I ended up becoming good friends with the guards and nurses up on the detention ward. It takes a certain kind of person with a certain type of humor to work in an intense environment like that. But it is easy to make lighthearted conversation with such people when you can always fall back on jokes about shitting on your senior through your stomach, like we did.

The following month, I was assigned to Mon Gracia hospital in the cardiac intensive-care unit, or CCU, as it is known. The routine was pretty simple to catch on to. The patients were all variations on either heart attacks or heart failure, both of which are paradoxically simple to care for, considering the ominous sound of the diagnoses. The challenge was not to figure out who had the heart attack or what to do after the diagnosis was made. All of that was largely rote. The challenge was always to block or prevent the admission of those patients who were unlikely to have a serious heart disease and thus comprised a significant body of fruitless busywork. I learned to quote postulates such as Occam's razor, which states that "common things occur commonly" and "if you are standing in a meadow and hear hoofbeats stampeding toward you, you should turn around to look for horses, not zebras." This is an internist's way of saying that the middle-aged man with a long history of heartburn that has chest pain after his chili dog, probably has heartburn again and not a heart attack.

The page came around 3:00 one afternoon two weeks into the CCU rotation. Any resident will tell you about the pagers they carry and how the sound evokes a Pavlovian reach for the phone and the pager simultaneously. This page was unusual because it came over the loudspeaker.

"Dr. Triton, please call two-two, two-two. Dr. Triton. Please call two-two, two-two."

I looked around the group of residents and medical students I was talking with. We had been discussing the appropriate medications to offer patients with chronic heart failure, and we were all somewhat puzzled by the announcement.

"Who did you piss off this time, Triton?" my co-intern asked.

"It's probably some hot young lady looking for a date who didn't get the news I was married," I joked as I walked to the phone at a nearby nurse's desk. I dialed the operator.

"Dr. Triton?" she said.

"Yes, this is Dr. Triton."

"I have your father on the line. He says he needs to speak with you."

"Okay…put him through, I guess," I said with confusion and reluctance. What would it be? Could I pick up my sister from work? Did I want to stop by the house for dinner? Did I tell you I ran into that kid from band you guys used to make fun of?

"Jeff?" His voice cracked and then he coughed, not altogether missing the receiver.

"Yeah, Dad, what do you need?"

"Your mother is sick here in the hospital. She was in so much pain I decided to bring her out here to Empire. Her sciatica was acting up, and they gave her some shots to try and kill the pain. They said since it wasn't working, they were going to admit her for physical therapy. But I think you should come out here and see what's going on."

"Sure, Dad," I said, stuttering slightly. "I'll try and get out there as soon as I can."

None of this made much sense to me. I knew my mother had recently had sciatica. It had kept her from walking up the stairs to the bedroom to sleep. The living-room sofa had been made up with sheets and pillows that were neatly folded on one of the chairs in the corner of the room every time I had come over for three months. But she had been walking around just fine for the last couple months. I wasn't aware of any problem. And inpatient physical therapy? That was for people getting over strokes or just out of serious car accidents. The pieces didn't quite fit together.

Surprisingly, it only took the mention of my mother in an emergency department to get excused from my afternoon duties. I drove out to Empire Hospital along the main freeway. The traffic was primarily going the opposite direction as people got off work at 3:00 in the afternoon.

I was not terribly worried. Sciatica is a condition that can cause excruciating and debilitating pain, but after the inflammation in the leg dies down, the pain almost completely resolves without leaving any disability. Actually, I was focused more on the people driving on the other side of the freeway, driving toward me and going home from work. I didn't resent them for their lazy expectations of getting off at a decent hour; I almost pitied them for not having important enough jobs to have shitty hours, too.

I parked near the emergency room and walked in. A bovine security guard with her hair pulled tightly back into a bun called me back to the waiting room with her mouth still dripping special sauce from her Whopper.

"I'm Dr. Triton," I said firmly. "I was called urgently to come see my mother, who is here in the ER."

"Okay. Go ahead right back."

She did not glance closely enough or care enough to see that the badge on my pants was from a completely different hospital. The doors opened automatically as I approached. The ER was all but deserted. I couldn't imagine getting the Mon Gracia emergency room this empty, even if the fire alarm went off. I had only to pass by the patient cupping his bloody nose to find my father and sister sitting next to my mother.

She was curled up in a fetal position on her left side underneath a single hospital sheet. Her upper body bobbed rhythmically toward her knees as she exhaled, moaning slightly with each breath. Her eyes were closed. The muscles in her shoulders and arms were clenched tightly.

My father's eyes and the pallor of his face showed every bit of fear that his voice had hinted at. "I'm glad you're here," he said. "The doctor just walked over there. He said they are going to bring one of the orthopedists down here to look at her. They don't have a spot at the physical therapy department tonight, so they're going to keep her in observation overnight instead. When we first came in, she was in so much pain she couldn't even talk. They gave her a shot of something

I think he called Demerol. That didn't seem to do much, so they gave her another dose about fifteen minutes ago. She's a little better now, I suppose."

"They gave her Demerol?" I asked.

"Yes. I think that's it."

Demerol was a narcotic medication that heroin addicts would come looking for when the dealers on the street started watering down the junk or upping the prices too much. It has several times more pain-relieving ability than morphine, and it has a little extra kick of euphoria that makes the difference between simple pain relief and, as we in the field would refer to it, being "high as the fucking Goodyear blimp." Most of the hospitals in the area stopped offering it to patients after people with chronic pain conditions learned to ask for it by name. The more savvy ones with conditions like sickle cell and similar diseases with frequent pain crises learned to ask specifically *not* by name, citing, "I remember something worked last time. I think it starts with a *D* or something."

They had given my mom, a woman who probably had the tolerance of a squirrel, two shots of this stuff, and she still couldn't speak in more than two-word sentences because the pain was so overwhelming.

"How is your pain, Mom?" I asked, leaning over her.

She simply groaned, then gasped. She finally got out a word, and I realized she was just repeating, "Pain."

"Can you tell me what happened today, Mom?"

Again she just winced, this time rolling onto her back. She didn't open her eyes. She said only, "My leg…" Then she rolled back onto her side.

I looked back to my father. "Did this start when she woke up today, or did she injure it sometime today?"

"She started feeling it pretty bad last night, so she took one of those pain pills her doctor gave her. Then, when she woke up this morning, she couldn't walk at all."

I was becoming decidedly concerned at this point. Beyond the shock of seeing my mother, someone I had grown to think of as invincible, in such pain, this actually seemed more serious than I had initially thought.

A doctor, or someone I thought was a doctor, approached. A moderately obese man, he wore a white coat and held a clipboard with a handful of papers wedged in it and several others attempting to fall off.

"Let's see," he said, shuffling through the paperwork. "Is this Mrs. Triton?"

My mother didn't speak. Her breathing continued every bit as deeply. I answered for her. "Yes. This is my mom."

"I'm Jerry. I am the nurse practitioner for physical medicine. I am just coming down to see her before we take her in to the observation ward. Now I understand she has had sciatic pain in the past?"

"Yes. She had it about four months ago," I spelled out. "It lasted two to three months. It took her a month to be able to walk at all."

"Okay. I'm just going to check out a few things here, before we go then."

He began by attempting to get her on her back, a task that required my father and me to help roll her with me actively looking away from her pained face. He raised her left leg at the hip and got it no more that three inches off the bed before she yelled out in pain. He bent her knee in a couple different directions. He felt for pulses in a few different spots. But ultimately his interview and physical examination were done in five minutes. He wrapped up just as a Hispanic man in pink scrubs arrived with a gurney. The two worked to slide my mother onto the gurney.

"Are they going to get a CAT scan?" I asked.

"She got one two months ago, I saw, when she had the sciatica before. So we don't need one now."

The explanation seemed logical to me, so I didn't put up much of a fight. I still felt helpless, though, seeing my mother wheeled away in a hospital. I walked around the ER, trying to find the emergency doctor I had seen earlier. He wasn't immediately visible, but I walked around comfortable with the similarities among all emergency rooms. A stack of patient charts bound in green plastic folders sat on the nurse's desk. I picked up the one marked *Triton* and glanced through it. Most of it was a shorthand account of my dad's explanation. There was documentation of the old CAT scan as well as the medications they gave her. No surprises until I looked at the lab work done on her blood. Her white blood cell count was 32,000. As a reference, yours and mine are probably on the order of 5,000, 8,000 when we have a cold. Someone with pneumonia likely has a WBC count in the 15,000 to 16,000 range.

And someone with a WBC count in the 30,000s is pretty damn sick, certainly not just having some nerve pain acting up.

I hustled around the ER more frantically, trying to find the doctor to clarify his thoughts on the matter. In his absence, I settled for a nurse that was around as I approached her with the chart.

"Can you please help me?" I begged. I was no longer showing or feeling any of the professional confidence I initially walked into the ER with. "My mother is being sent off to Obs for sciatica, but I noticed she had a white count of 32,000. I just wanted to make sure the ER doc had noticed it."

"I'm sure he noticed it, sir," she said in a breath of exasperation. "Now you should not have this chart. The information in there is confidential." She reached into my hands, took the folder, and abruptly turned away.

I stood with so many words and questions pinballing against the inside of my cranium. My mouth hung open, as I hoped one of the questions would spill out on the off-chance that someone might hear and answer it. Did I fear an aggressive response from the ER doctor? Did I fear him secretly thinking I was an idiot for making an asinine observation or claim? I was not sure exactly what I feared. But I didn't trust my understanding of sickness enough to challenge another doctor's authority, even when it pertained to my mom. When I finally found a doctor who admitted to having seen my mom, he simply blew off my concerns, pointing out that she didn't have a fever, implying that it couldn't be that serious.

The next evening, after my work in the CCU had finished at Mon Gracia, I drove over to Empire. I had called my father to find out where the physical therapy unit was, only to learn that she had not gone. She was in too much pain, so she was kept in the observation unit, getting pain medication. The drive down this night was much different. It was later in the day, and rush-hour traffic had somewhat dissipated. But more importantly, I wasn't focused on the cars and their directions or speeds. My thoughts were absolutely immersed in my mother's health situation. What the fuck was going on?

The observation unit, or obs, as it is called, was a smaller ward on the first floor of Empire, in the back section. Arriving on the unit after 7:00, I realized that "observation unit" is a misnomer. In fact, there was very little observation going on at all. There was one nurse assigned to the front desk, watching all the patients as closely as someone might watch their wardrobe in a closet overnight. Granted, such a person would be pretty irate if his Calvin Klein necktie was missing, but he probably wouldn't notice until he looked in the closet at the scheduled time the following morning.

My mother was lying on her bed with a large Tupperware pitcher of clear fluid on the table next to her with a straw in it. She seemed completely exhausted and perhaps a little bit delirious, still with her eyes shut. I recognized the signature Tupperware shape and went to the nurse's station and asked, "Is that contrast dye in there with my mom?"

"Yes, orthopedics decided to get a CAT scan on her since she wasn't feeling any better."

"Well, she hasn't drunk any of it. When is she scheduled to go?" I asked.

"In about an hour, but she has to get the contrast down first."

"Okay, I'll go help her," I said, turning, frustrated with the lack of effort around the hospital.

Mom was fast asleep when I reentered. "Mom. Mom, you have to wake up," I said, nudging her.

"Humm. What?" she asked in a groggy voice.

It was good to hear her speak at all. Yesterday had been quite frightening, seeing her in such a vulnerable position that she could not talk for herself.

"How are you feeling?"

"A little better," she whispered. Her mouth was dry and the words resisted coming out.

"I found out that you're going to get another CAT scan. This is good. Now we can figure out what is going on with you."

"Uh-huh," she answered lethargically.

"Here, let me help you drink this," I said, rubbing her back between her shoulders. "Let's sit you up a little." I pulled on her back just enough to get her on her side.

"I can't. I can't drink any more," she coughed out. "Need to throw up."

I reached quickly around for the tiny pink tub. She spit out only a few drops of clear fluid but hovered over the bucket.

"I know you don't feel good, Mom, but you need to drink more of the contrast. Otherwise, they won't see anything on the CAT. I'm going to get them to give you some medicine for the nausea." As I walked out of the room, it occurred to me that I didn't understand why they were making her drink the contrast. That type of CAT scan was usually reserved for something bad going on in the abdomen. Perhaps it had to do with her nausea. Nevertheless, the nurse gave a shot of Compazine, which helped superficially.

"Drink a little bit more, Mom. You're doing great." I was coaching my mother, as she had, no doubt, done for me when I needed to take one awful-tasting medicine or another as a child. Her lips pursed out toward the straw to minimize the work of her body in reaching it. She backed away from the Tupperware with a cup or so left in it. I decided it was all right to let her rest.

"You did excellent, Mom." I had begun to whisper, too. "I love you. And I'm sorry you're feeling so badly."

She just breathed deeply on her back, with her eyes gently shut. Then, with a sudden sense of urgency, her arms clenched and her hands grabbed the sheets and thrust into the bed. She pushed herself into a sitting position, and several cups of clear fluid erupted from her stomach and landed in and around the pink vestibule.

"Oh, Mom, are you okay?" I sat down next to her on the bed and leaned her back against me to take the burden of strength off of her. I subtly moved another bucket near the bed as I held her head close to my chest and shoulder.

You are probably never more human and vulnerable to your emotions than when you are cradling your own mother in pain. I felt that pressure building behind my eyebrows that was always the first sign heralding my emotions brewing to the point that I needed to cry. And while I was this emotional inside, I could only be silent. Even in this moment of sadness, my obsessive-compulsive side ripped me from my peaceful cradle of emotion and dragged my attention to logistics, as though it were on a leash. It was critical that we get at least some of the remaining contrast in her so the CAT scan would not be worthless. I held the Styrofoam cup with the remainder of the clear yet foul liquid to her face.

"We have to drink just a little more, Mom."

How stupid she must have thought I sounded, saying "we" when I was not nauseated, nor did I have to drink that piss.

At that moment, another hospital technician dressed in pink scrubs came through the door with a gurney.

"CAT scan?" he asked.

"Yes!" I blurted as though he might change his mind if I didn't show enthusiasm.

The shoddy joints of the gurney creaked as we slid her over the sheets onto it. I helped the tech wheel her out into the hall and offered my farewells and as I tried to get one last sip of the contrast dye into her mouth. And then she turned the corner down the dark hallway. My departure wasn't grand; the desk nurse said nothing, if she even noticed that my mother or I had left.

The next morning, I was on call in the CCU back at Mon Gracia. Even more than the average day, today my body belonged to Mon Gracia. I would work, eat, and sleep, or at least attempt to sleep, in that hospital. The only sunshine I would see would be depicted in the paintings in the lobby. Some would find themselves miserable on these days. I tended to feel very placid on the call days and spend the three days in between dreading that one day. Today I was more subdued than usual on a call day. My face and eyes looked at the nurses and the patients I talked to, but I did not see them. I was elsewhere, pondering the potential findings of the CAT scan. I was preparing. I planned to call my father after rounds at noon and see what they had found. I would be prepared.

My pager went off in the middle of rounds. The tune was simple yet obnoxious and sounded almost like an SOS Morse-code signal. Faster than Bill Hickock could draw, I reached down instinctively to stop the miserable tone. I didn't recognize the number; the prefix was not one I recognized for the hospital. *Damn it!* It was probably a fucking transfer from the VA hospital. If some homeless person walked into the ER at the VA, they were required by law to start treatment, but they would always transfer or dump the patient the next morning. Those patients typically had long-standing medical problems that had been ignored for years and years, not the least of which was the aged cheese that grew in on their feet as a paradigm.

"This is Dr. Triton, CCU. I was paged?" I said after the phone was answered.

"Is this Dr. Jeff Triton?" a voice said.

"Yes, this is Jeff Triton, CCU. Who am I speaking to?"

"Dr. Triton, my name is Jack Vincent. I'm the surgeon who is taking care of your mother."

Surgeon? I paused. What would they have found that would need a surgeon?

"Oh, thank you for paging me, Dr. Vincent. How is my mom doing? And what did you find on the CAT scan?"

"Well, that's why I'm calling you. You see, I'm calling you from the operating room. Your mother is being prepped for emergency surgery. The CAT scan showed that she had a psoas abscess, and we determined that we needed to take her to the OR as soon as possible."

I was not prepared. Despite my attempts to think of every potential diagnosis and prepare for it, psoas abscess was far too rare and remote. It was so obscure that it hadn't even been mentioned in medical school since my first year in gross anatomy. It was mentioned in the context of pointing out a muscle called the psoas that connects the butt to the leg and explained only enough to say that it was rare enough that we would probably never see one.

"I see," I said. "So what is the surgery going to entail?"

"That was something I wanted to talk to you about as well. I discussed everything with your father this morning, and he thinks that it would be best for you to assume the power of attorney for your mother."

"He did? Why the hell would he think that?"

"Well, there are going to be a series of medical decisions that are going to need to be made in the near future, the first of which is now. And he thought you would be more qualified to make those decisions. Would you be willing to assume power of attorney, Dr. Triton?"

"Yes, of course, if he would feel more comfortable. I'll do whatever you need."

"Okay, then. Let's get back to your previous question," he said. I noticed that his voice was much more calming than I would have expected from a surgeon. He spoke to me as a professional and as a family member. My own personal experiences with Empire had brought me in contact with physicians who showed about as much care for me as an automobile assembly-line worker has for that second left piston rod he is in charge of. Somehow, though I am not sure how, this surgeon's compassion was apparent. "The surgery that we are looking at depends on you to some extent."

"How is that?"

"The abscess in her psoas has tracked down her leg and gotten into part of her hamstring and into her calf muscle. So we have two options at this point."

"And what are the options?"

"We can perform a BKA. Or we can do a simple dissection of the muscles that we see are infected by the CAT scan."

BKA—the eponym for below-the-knee amputation. The severity of what was going on began to hit me. The blow was not conducive to any objective decision-making.

"Of course, if we do the latter procedure, there is a chance that we would have to go back and do the BKA anyway," he said, still in his soft and understanding voice. "And the BKA might give her a better chance."

"So, is that the one that you would recommend?"

"You know, I really couldn't say. I want to leave that up to you."

"How much time do I have to make the decision?"

"Your mother is in preop right now. So you have about twenty minutes before she gets down here. We can allow a little more than that and still have all the orthopedists on hand that we will need."

"Give me your pager number, and I will reach you as soon as I decide."

I hung up the phone and raced to the elevators. I was in way over my head, and I couldn't even see the surface, I was so deep. I had to find help, and I had to ask someone I knew only by reputation. The chief of orthopedics at Mon Gracia was known nationally for his skill, and I had known of him previously because he had performed a spine surgery on a high school friend of mine.

Opening the door to the orthopedics office, I was out of breath from running. I could feel the razor-sharp sting in my airway with each deep inhalation. "Is Dr. Bone in the office?" I asked.

His name was pronounced *Bah-nay*, despite the elegant irony of the more obvious pronunciation.

"He's in a meeting down the hall," the secretary said. "I can tell him you stopped in if you like."

Before she finished her sentence, I had left the office and gone down the hall, serially examining doors for a sign demarking a conference room of some sort. Thankfully, the door marked *Conference Room A* was unlocked. I swiftly opened the door, drawing the attention of the twenty or so people around the elongated table. I recognized Dr. Bone only from a freeway billboard depicting him with a child he had treated for spina bifida.

I knelt down next to him and whispered to him in the hopes that everyone else would continue on with their discussion. "Dr. Bone, I'm sorry to bother you like this, but it is crucial that I talk to you right now. Could you please give me a second in the hall?"

He followed me out silently with a look of understandable concern on his face.

"Again, I'm sorry for interrupting your meeting like this," I said. "My name is Jeff Triton. I'm one of the medicine residents here. I have a personal issue of a serious nature that I need some advice on."

"I'll see what I can do. What is the problem?"

"My mother is in a hospital nearby, and I just received a call that she has been diagnosed with a psoas abscess." I spoke at my hyper-caffeinated pace, listing off all the muscles Dr. Vincent had said were infiltrated by the infection. "They have asked me to decide between a dissection of the muscles and a BKA. My question for you is, if I choose the dissection, how much will that worsen her chances?"

"That's obviously a difficult question for me to answer, having not seen her case at all. But for the sake of helping you make this tough decision, let me simplify it this much. If they do the dissection and they have to go back in for another operation because the infection progressed like you are worried it will, they may have to amputate a little bit more of the leg than initially planned. Maybe even an AKA. But if the infection turns out to be that aggressive, the odds are that she would have required that second operation even if they did the original BKA."

"Okay. I think I understand." I closed my eyes as I responded. "Thank you again for doing this for me."

"Certainly. Good luck with your mother. And I'm sorry this happened to her."

I ran as quickly up to the CCU as I had run down and made the call. "Dr. Vincent," I said as someone picked up the phone on the other end of the line.

"Yes, Jeff. I'm glad you called back. Were you able to reach a conclusion?"

"Yes. I would like to try the dissection first. If you get in there and decide that there is too much affected muscle, you have my consent to do the BKA. But give it your best shot to leave the leg."

"You bet. I will give you a page when we get out of the OR."

"Thanks." I hung up gently. I sat there for a few minutes in silence, ruminating over the operation my mother was about to undergo.

By the time I got that anticipated page from the foreign prefix, it was nearing 5:00. The heart attacks of the patients I had admitted all day seemed trivial when I dialed Empire's operating room.

"Everything went perfectly," Vincent said before I even had a chance to identify myself. "Your mother did fantastic, Dr. Triton."

I sighed. "Thank God."

"She is in post-op now. But her pressures are stable, and everything seems to be fine. We're just going to watch her here for the night and see how things go."

We closed and hung up. I could have said that the hardest part was over now, but that would be bullshit. Maybe for the surgeon who had to do the cutting in some remotely precise fashion, or maybe for the anesthesiologist who had to make sure she had just the right amount and mixture of drugs to keep her asleep during the operation, the hard part was over. But I had to wait to see what the true outcome would be, and live with the results.

~~~

The next day, having spent the night in the CCU, I finished work shortly after noon. Of course, I went directly to Empire, where I was met with the startling surprise that she was in the operating room again. According to the nurse who had cared for my mother in the surgical ICU, or SICU, the night before, my mother had developed a severe fever, and her blood pressure had dropped early in the morning. They had performed another CAT scan that showed the abscess had recurred in a nearby muscle in the calf, and Dr. Vincent decided to go back in immediately and perform the BKA. They had been in the operating room for five hours at that point. Like calling the phone company to find out how long the service would be out or asking the airline agent when the late plane would arrive, the nurse couldn't tell me when they might be out of the operation. At least in restaurants, the waitress will say the food will be out shortly, albeit with little sincerity.

Finally, my mother was wheeled back into the ICU room. She was still attached to the ventilator by the plastic tube and hose, its components making their familiar whir and hiss. Her heart monitor blipped at a regular pace that gave me some peace. But even just seeing her face with that tube was horrendous. Her shoulder-length hair was molded back into the pillow from the past few days of gravity acting on residual hairspray. The skin of her face seemed dry and bland. She had never been one to wear rouge or makeup, but the paucity of color today was obvious even in her. Seeing her face so void of color, expression, and even life, the despair caused me to forget the specifics of the surgery she had just undergone, and it was at least thirty minutes before it occurred to me to look down at her leg.

The several sheets she was under concealed the results of the surgery, as a single linear mound extended down from her neck. After tracing down with my hand and then lifting the sheets, I was able to see the bandage and abundance of surgical tape wrapped around her leg just below the knee. It was much like an illusion done by one of those magicians in Vegas. Her leg simply ended below the knee. It was difficult to believe, and I actually had to put my hand on the bed where her ankle should have been to convince myself that it was, in fact, gone. If I turned my head back to look at her face, some deep portion of my brain would insert the missing appendage into my peripheral vision.

I sat with her for a while, just so she wouldn't be alone, then I decided to leave. I covered her up again and kissed her good-bye. On my way home, I got a call on my cell phone from Dr. Vincent, essentially reiterating what the nurse had told me.

I was awake for the rise and fall of the sun on each day that followed. A few weeks ago, these events had been nothing more than a checkpoint in the eternal schedule of the resident whose work forces him to think ahead, not to the seasonal change and crop rotation, not to the holidays and occasions that await in the next month, but to the three or four days ahead to see nothing more than when he is on call. Just casual markers in a calendar that held no day to be special, except for the rare day that held no clinical obligations. It had seemed infinite as Copernicus saw the universe and time. Archimedes was the first to really capture the essence of time as we see it. He was able to measure it because it was not infinite. He used water or sand to add weight to levers as time passed. His clocks had rotating gears that turned and levers that tipped as the seconds, minutes, and units lengthy as seasons passed. But eventually the sand in the urn or the water in the reservoir would run out. It would run out as my mother's time seemed to run out with the rising and setting of the sun. Daily phone calls brought news that she had either spiked a fever again, her blood pressure had dropped more, or she required another surgery.

I visited her every day that I could. But the infection had been too aggressive. That next Friday, when I was in her room in the intensive-care ward, she no longer even resembled my mother. The tube was still there, in her mouth, pumping at its same pace. It taunted me, making its mechanical gestures sitting there beside her bed. It didn't truly breathe as a person would if they had the means to by themselves. Instead, every breath was like a sigh that begged, "Okay, you've won. Just let this end." And that sigh was more haunting than my mother's words could ever be, even if she allowed herself to show any pain and say them.

Sepsis, they said it was. The concept was not beyond my understanding, even as a physician youngling. When an infection attacks the body and works its way past the body's defenses into the blood, the body responds by secreting all sorts of hormones which produce fever, increase the heart rate, and increase the blood pressure. But if the infection gets even more out of control, the toxins secreted by the infectious bacteria, and even some of the chemicals secreted by the body and become toxic, start to cause the opposite effect. The blood vessels that clamped down initially now dilate. The heart that has been pumping so hard and fast exhausts itself, and the blood pressure falls. Sometimes this can be so severe that there is not even enough pressure to coax the blood into the skull, where it can nourish the brain. Sometimes patient temperatures can reach 105 degrees. As for my mother, the fever was not so impressive, but present nevertheless. The diabetes she had, even as mild as it was, had left her unable to mount a fever early on to suppress infections even in such an onslaught.

Dopamine. Levophed. Neosynephrine. As a medical student and young doctor, I had always been frustrated that drugs sounded so much alike, and rarely sounded like what they were for. As the son of a patient lying in the ICU, I regretted that they didn't have more pleasant and inspiring names like "fluffy bunny sunshine juice" or "amazing save-the-world power medicine." But these intimidating vials hung next to the bed nevertheless, dripping constantly, keeping my mother's blood pressure from dropping to the floor.

Her face was no longer recognizable. It had swelled to twice its normal size, thereby losing all of her features. Of course she had the ventilator tube, which I had begun to recognize as *hers* after this week of hell.

What would she have done differently if she had known she was going to be in here for more than a week? Would she have put on more makeup? Less makeup? More comfortable clothes? I supposed that didn't matter, as I reflected back on her first night, when I helped her out of her clothes and into the hospital gown, still respecting a mother's privacy and dignity with my head turned.

By now, the toll of surgery had become massive. The asymmetry of the sheets reflected what I already knew from the phone conversations with Dr. Vincent. After six surgeries, two of which were emergent, they had amputated her left leg in its entirety, as well as several muscles of her abdomen and back. In moments like this, the thought crosses everyone's mind of how she will react when she wakes up to find her leg missing. I had the comfort or perhaps the misfortune of understanding her true prognosis. I had called my sisters two days before to urge them to come to California, as the end was likely approaching. She'd still had half of her thigh left at that time, and now only one of those menacing-sounding bottles hung above her bed, but the warning signs were there.

Tonight, only one of the sisters had arrived, and it was my emotional burden to be sure that Vicki got to see her mother one last time before she expired.

"A gathering," it was called. Dr. Vincent had asked that my father and I meet with him that Friday to discuss her code status. So many political implications to the public figure. So few to the physician. And I, the family member sitting across from my father, was forced to negotiate my knowledge and understanding with my pain and devastation.

"What do you think, Jeff?"

He called me Jeff. Not "Dickens." Not "Creep." Not any of the childhood names that had stuck to me like flypaper. Was his heart so lanced that he couldn't even find comfort in these names? Or had we each grown up together in this one solitary week? We saw each other's emotions as we talked in that quiet room on Friday. An onlooker might wonder how we could discuss such a decision with so little feeling, our elbows resting on both knees. But the emotion was in our distinct lack of emotionality. What would usually be an undue vote of optimism on either of our parts could not even be mustered. My father accepted my recommendation, whether professional or personal, as gospel, and never questioned it despite the pain. We hugged that night before we left Empire. We left, and no one even mentioned stopping at the Spunky Steer for dinner that night.

~~~

My pager rang early that morning. It was Saturday morning. *Fuck!* Was I supposed to be on call today? *Fuck, Fuck!* Wait, I had been on call the weekend before. *How dare those bastards page me when I'm off!*

The number was not one I recognized. I got an electrical sensation radiating from my stomach symmetrically through each of my limbs. I remembered the last time I was paged to an unfamiliar number and realized what was facing me.

"Dr. Triton?" the meek voice said as she answered the phone.

"Yes, this is Jeff Triton."

"Dr. Triton, this is Donna, your mother's nurse in the ICU at Empire Hospital."

"Yes?" The saliva mysteriously vanished from my mouth as I tried to speak, leaving me inarticulate.

"Sir, I'm sorry for bothering you this morning. Your mother is still alive, but she is going downhill. I have been working the ICU for several years, and I have come to recognize the signs. I think you should come down here as soon as possible. I have called your father, and he is on his way. "

"Yes, thank you. I certainly will." We hung up. I found that I suddenly could not move.

"Is everything okay, dear?" Tara said from the other side of the bed. She knew that things were anything but okay, much as they had been for the past week.

"They say my mother is going downhill. She doesn't have long."

"Oh, my God. How long? Did they say?"

"I didn't ask. But she said I should get down there as soon as I could."

"Let me just throw on some jeans. I don't want you driving."

When we arrived in the ICU, my father and youngest sister Nancy were standing by the bedside. The cardiac monitor was turned off and dead black. My father's glasses lay on my mother's bed as he wiped his tears repeatedly from his cheeks. His mouth was agape with his cries, but they were silent as they escaped. I had never seen him cry before. Nancy stood next to him with a concerned look, gazing over my mother. She was dressed surprisingly well for what had to be the work of my father dressing her in two minutes after having received the ICU call. Perhaps he thought the clothing should show her mother respect in her last minutes. Perhaps he wanted to instill the confidence that her daughter would be in capable hands in those last minutes. But Nancy showed no tears at that moment, merely holding my father's trembling hands.

The two looked up as I approached the bed.

"Oh, good," my father said. "You're here. The nurse told us she passed just ten minutes before we got here. She said that it was peaceful and that she didn't feel anything."

"That's good, Dad. I know she didn't feel anything." It was true. With the infection and surgeries she had undergone, it was imperative that she be treated with massive doses of morphine and sedatives over the past few days. It gave me peace and allowed me, in turn, to give it to my father.

"You should take some time with her by yourself," he said to me as he pulled Nancy toward the chairs in the hall. There was no more conversation at that moment. Tara had stopped to comfort my father and sister, and I was there alone with my mother.

"We'll just shut this curtain behind you so you can have some private time together," said a nurse whom I had not even noticed as she walked by, closing the glass door and curtain to the room.

The room was conspicuously quiet without the bleep of the heart monitor and the purring of the ventilator. The machine still sat there in the corner but remained motionless, with its accordion bag half-expanded. The gray of my mother's once-pink cheeks had faded even deeper into a dusky hue. The swelling that had made her face and chin taut only two days before was gone, leaving only limp skin to drape over the bed next to her. That goddamn tube was still in her mouth, although it had been disconnected from the ventilation machine next to her bed. There was no sound coming from the plastic, no condensation on its walls. It stood erect approximately five inches, taped to the side of her half-open mouth, showing her vulnerability even in death.

I refused to look at the hip where her leg had been removed. I wasn't afraid of gore, but there was no need to look. Yet again, I wanted to allow my mother to maintain the flawless dignity she had maintained throughout my life. She had never lost her temper. She had never cursed in pain. She had never told me or my sisters, or my father, for that matter, when we were acting as dumb as rocks. She was my mother.

It is said that there are no atheists in the army or the ICU. I contend that there may be atheists in those places, but I promise you that they hold no beliefs at those moments; they hold only hopes. I had only hopes. I hoped that she could hear me. I hoped that she was in a better place, maybe watching over us. I hoped that there was a god caring for her as she had cared for me. In essence, I hoped I was wrong about everything I had believed before I walked through the automatic glass doors of the intensive care unit. I spoke to her aloud, telling her I loved her. I vowed to make her proud with my work. I apologized repeatedly for allowing this illness to take her that first night in the ER. But none of these expressions held the valor and honor that they would in a movie. I didn't sound like a prince vowing to bring justice and make his king's death mean something. I felt like the crippled son, crushed by tragedy, begging for his mother to listen one last time.

However, despite my overwhelming emotions, I could not cry. I couldn't evoke a single tear. It wasn't even that the sadness was submitting to my anger at that point. I just couldn't release it. I tried for a brief moment to create the saddest thing I could think of in my mind, but then I withdrew from the thought immediately, disgusted with myself. My mother had just died! How much fucking sadder could things get? It was as though I was a third person watching myself, thinking what a despicable specimen of a son this boy was.

Chapter 13

"Did she have a favorite passage?"

"To be honest, I'm not sure," I told Pastor Bill. Tara and I had come to his office unannounced and broke the news to him. He had met my mother not four months before, when he had presided over the wedding. We were all so happy then. "I know she was very religious inside, although we didn't go to church."

"I think I can put together some verses that I think she would like. I spent some time talking to her at the rehearsal dinner. She was an amazing woman in her devotion to her children. She spent almost twenty minutes telling me how proud she was of you. She was smiling all night."

In many ways, happiness is a simple emotion. It is simple to identify in yourself and in others. Smiles. Laughter. Words. Even subtle little gestures or behaviors that we don't always perceive consciously make the emotion as apparent as a desert sunrise. Shit, even sadness would be fairly simple to identify by these means. I would have considered such a simple burden of sadness and loss to be a blessing: to cry for my mother and wish only that we could have had more time together.

The sentiment that oppressed me was vastly more ambiguous. In three dimensions, I was being pulled by feelings of anger and hatred for the emergency physician who had not noted the signs of infection as well as the pain of grief. Simultaneously, I was weighted down by the guilt of not fighting harder for what I had initially believed to be right for her. And this huge tug-of-war was being played out in absolute darkness, so I couldn't identify any of the singular forces that were at work at any one time. The confusion this brought me was a burden unto itself.

A week after our discussion with Pastor Bill, I stood now amongst our closest family members and my mother's friends. Most of them I had never met, or had only met at my mother's work while I was still in diapers. By no means had she been a socialite. She was bound to her family responsibilities as she saw them. But don't mistake this for being unsocial, as she was loved by all she worked for and with. Her nursing staff wept more freely than I could above the perfectly rectangular hole in the grass.

In the week that passed between our discussion with Pastor Bill and the funeral, so much had happened. First, I was approached by Empire as to whether I wanted an autopsy performed. The question seemed simple enough, but it reeked of a Mafia-like cover-up. So, as any man would do when his father-in-law is the county medical examiner—or ambassador of death—I called for a favor. Hopefully the dead would not hold a grudge as my mother was pushed to the front of the line, ahead of the forty or so murder victims that had accumulated more quickly than they could be examined over the summer.

My sisters crowded into the house where we had all grown up, each having traveled long distances to get there. My oldest sister had flown in from her home in Colorado, while Vicki had gotten a last-minute flight from New Zealand, where she and her family's forty-foot sailboat was docked. Vicki had set off on a sailing trip around the globe a year before. The issue had become contentious with my mother and father, who worried that the trip was too dangerous for their daughter to do alone with her husband and two children. In the midst of the silence that often settled in the house that week, I think we each wondered if, to some extent, my father resented Vicki for not being there when my mother died. We all felt guilt, and anger, and sadness. I suppose it is natural to project those feelings onto others. But awkward silence is much worse in a household than it is on a first date.

Unpleasant quiet spells notwithstanding, we caught up and talked. Much of the conversation revolved around my explanation of what had actually killed my mother, and the key question on everyone's mind was, *Did she go peacefully?*

A good friend, Torrey, happened to call and ask the same questions that everyone else had. But when I explained the medical details I was amazed at how he seemed genuinely devastated over the loss of this woman he had never met, even though he witnessed death on a daily basis. He expressed his sympathy and insisted that I take the next two weeks off of my ER rotation duties. "I'll cover most of your shifts," he said, "but there are all sorts of people down here who would help you if they heard what you're going through." I was touched by his offer and agreed after several minutes of persuading. Though I felt relieved of that responsibility, my strength, willpower, and any sense of optimism lay prostrate on the ground.

Of all the conversations that took place that week, the one I remember the most was the one I had with God on the night before the funeral. For an atheist, I would say my frequency of talking to God was ahead of the curve (excluding gamblers and people with frequent hangovers). I had negotiated deals trying to persuade him to offer me proof, and had disparaged what I saw as his attempt to convert me with fear in the face of my brain tumor. And on this night, I fully castigated him for taking my mother to spite me. I likened him to a petty teenage girl who seeks revenge at any cost. The thought of him completely disgusted me, and I made it audibly known when I was alone. With all I accused him of that night, nonexistence and a settlement of atheism would have been a respectable plea bargain on his part. But I would not let him off so easily. I wanted him to hear my hatred for taking this great woman. I wanted him to know that he had not won my allegiance through punishment or fear. And if there was no God to hear me, then I wished all my words of hatred to be cast on Empire Hospital and its emergency physicians.

~~~

Pastor Bill tossed the first few grains of dirt down on my mother's casket as he referenced God a few times. I wholly ignored the religious pretense around the ceremony as I looked down at the coffin and said good-bye. As lonely as I felt looking down on the pearl-white box with gold trim lying deep in the dirt, as insufficient as the brass grave marker with her name and earthly dates, I still could not cry. Perhaps this was the punishment God envisioned for me, and my mother was just necessary collateral damage. I offered him the opportunity to fuck himself.

That night in bed, I thought back to the events leading up to her hospitalization. I had not thought enough about her sciatica before. I had not trusted my instincts regarding her tests and the poor condition she was in. I could have changed so many things if I had believed in myself or taken things more seriously.

By now, this had turned into nightly speculation. Tonight, though, I thought about the night when it had been just she and I in the observation ward at Empire. Things had seemed a little more serious, but nothing was clear. I was thankful her pain was slightly better, but she was still writhing when she wasn't dozing off from the medication. I wondered how much of it she actually felt or heard, and how much she would have remembered today if she had not left us. I remembered the frantic rush to get her to drink the last of the contrast after she threw up what she had already drunk; it was a rush to be her advocate, to make sure she got the CAT scan that she needed.

What I couldn't remember was what would deeply haunt me. I couldn't remember if the last words I said to her were "I love you." Those were her last minutes awake on this Earth. I was the last person she spoke to. I had time with her alone to say anything. Time to tell her all I appreciated in her. Time to tell her what I would do to make her proud. Time to tell her, "I love you." While I surely said it at some point—it was almost a rote valediction—I couldn't be certain that it was the absolute last thing I said to her. How troubling it must have been, I thought, to be in unearthly pain and perhaps even have some insight into her imminent fate, only to be badgered by another clinician, this time sharing half her chromosomes. I feared that her memory of me would be that of a nagging doctor instead of the loving, apologetic, thankful son I wished I had been. That dread tormented me, even before I was aware.

That night in bed, after the funeral, remembering our last night together, my first tears were awakened. I begged my mother to hear me as I thought about how much she meant to me. Over and over again, I assured her that I truly thought she would get better, and I would always regret how wrong I had been. At first, only one or two tears surfaced. But more followed in a stream, and then refused to stop. My emotional collapse that night was actually invigorating, like the first exhalation after holding my breath for ten days. I had exhaled and was ready to breathe like a normal human. Let me never forget how again.

~~~

It did not take long for me to get back to work—two weeks or so. I put on a strong visage, and changing rotations placed me in a new environment where people had not heard the news. When I was on call every fourth night, I continued to wear the Superman shirt that had brought me luck over the years. It helped maintain the strong yet playful image that I wanted to portray, but it also helped me to see myself as something other than a victim. An errant attending would sometimes think to question whether it was professional to dress that way. But I felt like there were so many doctors in their white coats, some with shirt and tie, others in haggard scrubs, that the occasional smile I got out of a patient proved the need for at least one Superman in the hospital.

On the late nights, admitting somewhere between eight to ten patients during that call, it occurred to me how inappropriately fate strikes us. My mother, who had been a relatively healthy person, developed an obscure infection that traveled to her blood and killed her, despite her clean lifestyle. And nightly, without exception, I would admit homeless people who would trade the few dollars they got by panhandling or giving blowjobs to people who were not quite homeless for heroin. Often the same ones would return a few days after leaving the hospital, again high on vitamin H. "A failure of society to care for its needy," politicians would call it. It always seemed a great irony that society should be responsible for these people who not only couldn't care for themselves, but didn't care about themselves.

There were others who were lost, not to the medical system, but lost *in* the medical system—like the elderly with shopping lists of medical problems sent in from their nursing homes. Many times I was left to put my head in my hands as men nearing their centennial birthdays were sent in with what was believed to be a heart attack. The problem was never about diagnosing a heart attack, but rather what to do if I found one. In a man of such age and fragility, the treatment would likely kill him quicker than the heart attack itself. I always wondered why they didn't just let the patient continue to sit calmly in front of his reruns of *Murder, She Wrote*.

It had been just such a day as that. Three admissions since 10:00 p.m., and it was approaching midnight. I always attempted to get to sleep as early as I could, because the only sleep you could count on in residency was the sleep you had already gotten. Just as my senior resident and I were leaving the emergency room after the last admission, Dr. Chatholm, the ER attending, shouted to us across the room.

"Hey, guys. I think I have another one for you before you head upstairs."

Mike, my senior, looked at me with a suspicious eye, suggesting that I had broken the resident code of superstition and comments on the quiet pace of the ER.

"I didn't say shit," I replied before he had a chance to actually accuse me.

"All right, let's go get this done," he said.

"Chest pain. Rule out," Chatholm said. "He's over there."

I had always hated Chatholm, even when I was working in the ER. During slow shifts in the afternoon hours, by his design, he would sit on a bookshelf chatting with one of the middle-aged female nurses, laughing at his own jokes. He had a well-deserved reputation for simply eyeballing a patient and deciding to admit them to the hospital without determining what was wrong or even how serious it was. As medicine residents, we hated him because all the busywork was left to us, and we often had to wait hours for any clinical answers because we did not have the ability to get tests and x-rays as quickly as the ER did. As an emergency-medicine enthusiast, I found him discouraging because he saw no intrigue in the patients he treated, and he was bored as a result. And I was as bored as a seventy-year-old housewife before Viagra when I had to work in the ER with him.

The patient was in his early forties, a normal-looking guy. He had been out with his wife driving home after dinner. He had felt some chest pain that was bad enough to make him pull over to the side of the road. "He said it was just heartburn," his wife explained to Mike and me. "But then when we got home, it came on again and didn't go away."

The man was a pretty classic case of "someone who is not a classic case for a heart attack." He didn't smoke. He didn't have high cholesterol. He wasn't old. He didn't have any bizarre genetic predisposition. He was one of those guys we admitted every day with chest pain from something unrelated, usually heartburn or peptic ulcer disease, merely because the heart happens to be located in the same general area.

By the time we finished talking to him and listening to his various body parts with our stethoscopes, some of the lab tests had started to return and show up on our computer. Mike and I looked them over as the patient went to get a chest x-ray before he went upstairs.

"Nothing too impressive here," Mike said.

"I'll do the *H* and *P*," I suggested. "You write the orders."

"Don't forget to mention in your history that he had spicy pasta for dinner. And I didn't find anything special on his physical exam. Did you?"

"No, huh-uh."

The patient returned soon afterward. We instructed the nurse to give him some more morphine to try and get his pain down. We were starting to get concerned that this guy was going to keep us up all night wanting more pain medication. We had thrown everything for heartburn at him as well as the morphine, but nothing was touching his pain.

"You think he's a seeker?" Mike asked.

I shrugged. "He doesn't seem like one, except for all the narcs he needs. He seems clean otherwise."

"Okay, well, we'll get him on the monitor upstairs, then get some sleep before the next set of labs comes back on him." Mike stood up with the orders in his hand.

"Oh, shit. I almost forgot to check the chest x-ray. Maybe it's back by now."

Mike yawned. "You go ahead and check it. I'll get these orders in the chart."

I sat down to the computer that was kept in a small, dark cubby of a room next to the ER. The solitary computer was for looking at the x-rays and CAT scans transmitted there from radiology. Scrolling down the names of the few ER patients, I came to our gentleman. Nothing struck me initially, as I expected. There was no big pneumonia, and his heart was in the right place.

"Umm, Mike?" I said

He didn't bother turning his head as I called him. "Yeah?" he had already begun to walk toward the automatic double doors of the emergency department.

"You may want to come take a look at this."

"What do you have?" He turned around, expecting nothing more than the overactive imagination of a naïve intern.

"Does this aorta look abnormal to you?" I asked. The aorta is the firehose that lets the hydrant, or the heart, pump everything to the rest of the body. Usually it extends straight up from the top of the heart. "You see how it kind of arches out to the patient's right, like that monument in St. Louis?" I tend to lose the names of national landmarks around 11:30 at night.

"It's probably nothing," Mike said. "Just an artifact of the angle of the x-ray."

He was probably right. This kind of weird illusion can happen when you display three-dimensional objects in two dimensions.

"Do you want to get a CAT scan or something?" he asked.

I thought for a second. I considered my mother's situation, where one piece of information had not been taken seriously. "Yeah, I think we should. Just to be sure."

I approached Dr. Chatholm, who was back on his bookshelf reading some paperback novel. "Dr. Chatholm, we see something on the chest x-ray that has us concerned." We had already learned to use doctorspeak to persuade other doctors into doing what we needed. The word *concerned* is vague enough that it does not commit us to a particular diagnosis or even to any level of certainty. But it does force others to take some level of action, because if one is concerned enough to say he is concerned, then that should be concerning to other concerned parties. "We are concerned that he might have an aortic dissection, and we want to get a CAT scan."

An aortic dissection can best be described as the freak tearing of the inside of the large blood vessel. It starts just by some random chance. Then the pressure of the heartbeat causes it to tear more, causing excruciating tearing pain in the chest. All this happens until the aorta actually bursts, which occurs in almost 100 percent of cases of this type.

It is hard to say whether it was our persuasive nature, the empty emergency room, or his generalized apathy, but the attending did not resist our efforts to get the extra tests done in the ER. Mike and I were anxious to get upstairs and get to sleep, but we had also gotten ourselves slightly excited about this potential yet unlikely diagnosis, so we sat in the radiologist room as the scan was being done.

Through the glass, we saw the patient, now sedated with morphine and several other drugs, lying on the metal table with a single sheet covering him. His body lay motionless on the table as it moved notch by notch through the doughnut-shaped machine. We stared at the screen as the images began to appear.

Mike pointed to the center of the screen. "There's the trachea."

"Lungs look good," I said. "And here we are starting to see the aorta."

The images filtered through, slicing pictures of his viscera like a ham.

"Holy shit," Mike said as soon as the sixth or seventh image appeared.

"It's almost fifty percent dissected!" I said, unable to believe what I was seeing.

As the images kept appearing on the screen, each scanning farther down his chest and abdomen, we saw that the tear was not stopping, either. Straight from his heart, all the way down to the beginning of the legs, the pouch was as big as the open portion of the vessel.

Mike and I looked at each other, knowing that hope for this man was grim, and that was even on a minute-by-minute basis. We hurried out to Dr. Chatholm and explained what the CAT scan showed. His usual stoic look flinched for one second and showed an ounce of concern.

"Well, we don't have a vascular surgeon in-house here at county at night. The nearest one is at Mon Gracia. So we either have to drive him there by ambulance for forty-five minutes or get a helicopter here and get him there in about twenty. What do you want to do?"

Both Mike and Chatholm looked at me. It would have been peculiar for them to pimp me when seconds seemed to matter so much for this patient. But I actually got the sense that they were placing the decision in my hands, possibly because I had seen the problem first on the x-ray. The likelihood was that I would get ridiculed by my superiors for whichever decision I made, whether on the basis of cost, futility, or sufficiency. The decision was obvious to me, though. I called the helicopter company and escorted the wife and patient to the roof, where they were picked up. After all were strapped in and the doors shut, the helicopter lifted off and sped away. In the dark distance, I could see only the spotlight tracing a path over the trees and hills toward Mon Gracia as the rapid thump of the propeller faded.

I got to sleep after talking to the vascular surgeons at Mon Gracia to warn them what was coming in. The rest of the night was peaceful, probably because Chatholm considered Mike and me to have bad karma after the last patient. The rest of our sleep was uninterrupted.

The next morning, we actually received immense praise from our attending, who raved that we had probably saved that man's life. The doctor's reaction to saving a life is correlated with a few things, such as how well he knew the patient, how young the patient was, how acute or surprising the medical problem was, and how quickly one could see the results of his work. I can imagine that after some time, the act of saving a life becomes so commonplace that the emotion dwindles. The feeling was still young for me. But this was more to me, even. I had pursued the dangerous but unlikely cause of this man's pain, as they had failed to do for my mother. I endeavored to find meaning and justify my mother's death to teach me and save this man's life, and the thought brought me some peace.

Two days later, however, I spoke to a friend who was on a rotation back at Mon Gracia. He informed me that the patient had died on the operating table two hours into the operation.

~~~

I find it odd that death affects us so strongly. Obviously, death serves as quite a change for those who die, but the rest of us create these images of a heavenly destination. We convince ourselves that infantile winged angels are playing herald trumpets as we enter the gates and walk along the clouded path. Yet we cry for those who are doomed to this Eden. Our tears are greater when the death is unexpected, which leads me to believe that it is for ourselves that we cry, not our loved ones. I related to the wife of this young man with the chest pain. While she surely had the concern of any wife of a man with emergency chest pain, the diagnosis had quickly changed from "noncardiac chest pain" to "dissecting aortic aneurism." The former sounds rather harmless, and hearing this, his wife had stood next to his heart monitor and assured him that we would come with the pain medicine. I wonder what she thought after hearing the latter. Surgery sounds threatening by its very nature, but I had not told them that there was an eighty-five percent chance that he would not survive the night. What were their last words to each other? "Good luck" and "See you when you wake up" just didn't sound profound enough to me. Yet I suspect that these were likely the last words spoken that night.

I allowed myself to cry for a short time in private about the gentleman with the chest pain.

It's a misconception that doctors are discouraged from becoming emotionally attached and crying for their patients. Perhaps we are discouraged from crying in public. But this is more like a "don't ask, don't tell" policy. Those tears were followed by more tears for my mother. Tragedies became an homage to her, while successes became a tribute to what I learned from the events that August.

~~~

By December, the temporary nature of my position had become evident to me. I wasn't being encouraged to leave; in fact, I was being asked to continue on as an internal medicine resident the following year. The problem was that, while I felt gratified having seen the people I had and lifting them from sickness when I could, I yearned for the job that would allow me to lift them not from sickness but from death itself. I wanted my career soundtrack to feature Metallica rather than the London Philharmonic. It was then that Tara and I began applying for residency together.

While the process had been complicated for me the year before, finding places where we could both be happy was a real challenge. I did not repeat the mistake of applying to too few places. Between the two of us, we applied to approximately eighty programs and interviewed at about sixty. There was no doubt in my mind that Tara was the star of our joint application. Under these circumstances, I had to wonder which anesthesia programs were trying to persuade their emergency compatriots to accept me to gain her for themselves. While we both had exceptional test scores and grades, Tara had the personality that endeared her to everyone.

We interviewed at residencies across the country, considering the possibility of seeing the world before we settled down. I still had the dream of being an Ivy League giant in my field, encouraging her in each case. We interviewed at the major universities on the East Coast, making note of which ones had programs best for each of us. Several programs held excellent potential for us both, while others offered a fantasy position to one and an average option for the other. In some cases, we decided that competing programs across cities like Baltimore and Boston might give us the best programs.

I recall specifically when we interviewed at the Mayo Clinic in Minnesota. The facility holds great notoriety, yet most don't know where it is. And rightly so. Leaving Minneapolis, we drove at least forty-five minutes west into the middle of nowhere, through snow and wind, to get there. Only after this drive through the barren ice plains of the Midwest did we see the emerald city rising up out of the flat earth: several immense buildings surrounded by no cities or life-forms of any kind, as far as I could see. It was like the city of Las Vegas rising from the desert, although this was owned by a single hospital. We stayed at a towering local hotel, only to find that it would be destroyed in the coming summer. A wealthy Arab prince was coming to the hospital to have a minor prostate operation, and the accommodations of this twenty-story, four-star hotel were not sufficient. He had offered to donate the money to upgrade sufficiently.

Inside the hospital, instead of messengers to transport blood samples to the lab, robotic systems ran along the floor and ceiling like something out of a *Star Trek* episode. Four gymnasiums within the hospital proper allowed the residents to maintain a reasonable lifestyle while working there. I don't actually recall the chef they had imported for the cuisine, but my guess is that they likely flew in a new one for each day of the week.

Shortly afterward, we interviewed at Yale. On our first day in Connecticut, Tara was amazed by her experience. She had interviewed with one of the authors of the leading textbook in anesthesiology. The director of the program was a woman, which was almost unheard of in her field. The operating rooms looked good, although that might have had more to do with the shades of blue paint, for all I knew. My interview was a bit more awkward, not as much like a first date—more like a second date that was set up by a friend. A friend who did not realize you had already had a crummy first date.

Actually, neither the first date nor the second date were bad. I simply entered with the knowledge that they liked everyone in their intern class better than they liked me, since I had been interviewed and denied the year before. The director was a short, stocky, balding man with a prominent goatee. He was dressed in a suit for the interview that day, but he clearly was no more used to wearing a suit than I was.

He spent the first fifteen minutes expressing how surprised he had been the year before when I had not been accepted. "It is very rare that someone with your qualifications and ranked so highly does not get accepted," he said. "We simply matched very well this year." Of course, that could mean anything from my being ranked seventh, with six being accepted, to my being thirty-twelfth.

Nevertheless, after getting over the initial disappointment of my not being accepted previously, we discussed a football game between our respective favorite teams, and joked about the felonious calls of the referees against each of us. We each laughed most of the interview away and exchanged relatively little information of substance. The misstatements I remember from that interview day were how pleased everyone had been with me, and the Patriots deserving that absurd call.

Tara and I finally finished our interview tour—she to take Christmas vacation and I to take call at the VA hospital.

By now, the stress of my mother's death had largely resolved itself. I went through a long period of straightforward hatred toward everyone involved, including myself. After discussion with surgeons around Mon Gracia and Frank, who had done the autopsy, I decided to pursue a malpractice lawsuit against Empire. I was disgusted by the ER doc who had devalued my mother and missed such a severe diagnosis, and similarly I was disgusted by one who would make the field of emergency medicine look this bad. I convinced myself that he had trained in another field like family medicine or internal medicine and had been merely moonlighting to make ends meet. I struggled to figure out how to bring my wrath down upon the system as hard as it deserved.

My first step was to find an attorney. This is usually not a difficult step in California, but the task of suing Empire required someone with experience. I searched the web for articles about people who had successfully sued Empire and found one attorney. He became the one I turned to. Mark Simms had represented a woman whose lung cancer had been missed after years of smoking because her smoking had brought on a pneumonia that masked it on a chest x-ray. Not considering lung cancer in a thirty-year-old smoker who worked as a banker was malpractice, as the lawyer said.

After speaking to him initially, it was clear he knew a few medical words, but I was not certain whether it was my medical vocabulary or his that left him perplexed. However, we struggled on.

"I'll need $5,000 to get a professional witness for the case," he said. "Someone to review the evidence and speak for us."

"I have several professionals who would be willing to speak," I replied.

"No, we need them to be objective and not related to you. How soon do you think you could have the $5,000?"

"I suppose in a couple days. Is that okay?"

"That should be fine. I have someone in Orange County who I go to for these types of cases. I will let him know."

In that time, I got the money from savings accounts and collected the medical records of my mother's death. I was amazed by how difficult it was for me to get them, as a relative and advocate, especially considering how blasé I had treated patient notes as a resident, often losing them or ignoring the nine out of ten pages that didn't interest me. I was resisted at every step of the process in getting those records—supposedly on the basis of patient privacy, as opposed to protecting their asses. The folder they handed me after several days contained hundreds of pages, many of which were those last pages of a document that the printer prints, yet have nothing but the date. All of these cost me ten cents per sheet.

With each step of the lawsuit, I was encouraged by Simms to recognize that I wouldn't get much in the suit because my mother had retired already, and the bulk of settlements were from lost wages. But I didn't hear this, and with each roadblock I experienced, I wanted only to have the head of the doctor who had fucked up. I wanted him to lose his license. I wanted him ridiculed in front of me and his peers so all would know that he was the poor excuse for a doctor that I knew him to be. Who would make such a mistake as to miss such a white blood count? Not even I had missed it. I wanted to see him fall.

After a month of his specialist looking at the files, it became clear that this was not going to be the clear-cut case of "fucking up" that I saw it to be.

"It appears that the organisms that grew out in your mother's blood are normally found in the bowel," Simms said to me over the phone.

"So what does that imply?"

"So, the problem is that it suggests that her infection was caused by a natural process."

"So the fuck what?" I screamed over the phone. "I know it was a natural process, as you said. My problem is they didn't catch that fucking natural process and stop it in its goddamn tracks."

"Look, even if we prove that the ER doctor missed the diagnosis, we still have to prove four things to win the suit: relationship, cause, avoidability, and damages. And, unfortunately, the last point is measured only in earnings. Since your mother was retired, this really isn't going to be much."

My lungs ceased mid-breath. I realized that, for this lawyer, this wasn't about the case. Nor was it about right and wrong. I saw that I did not actually have anyone on my side. And what was it about to me? I began to question why I was pursuing the lawsuit so vigorously. I was not an advocate of malpractice suits in general. And I really wasn't thinking about the money. In truth, I just wanted the guy who fucked up to fry. I wanted him to pay. I wanted him to know the pain he had made me feel. I wanted him to think of my mother the next time he saw someone with something that seemed meaningless and take a second look, assuming he should be allowed to practice anymore. But I began to realize that this was not the goal of anyone else involved. The lawyers were only interested in monetary claims, which didn't do justice to my mother's death. Even my own desires would not bring her back, do her proud, or help anyone in the future. I saw my hatred for what it was—selfish. Not that I didn't have a right to that hatred. But I realized that it would not achieve the things I had deluded myself into thinking it would.

I decided to give up the suit and just avoid such mistakes when I was an emergency doctor. In the end, the resolution I attained for myself was more important than any court award that I could have gotten. Thankfully, my family was relatively unaware of my anger toward Empire. I don't think they would have been so easily appeased as I was if they had understood the mistakes made back in August.

~~~

With three months to go, Tara and I opened the letters showing our fate and what outback hospital might be housing us for the next four years. We had listed a total of forty-two combinations of her favorite choices along with mine, and every combination which allowed us to be within twenty miles of each other. Actually, Tara was the only one partaking in the ceremony, while I was two floors above, rounding on my patients. But as 9:00 came, I received a call on my cell phone alerting me that we were going to move to New Haven, Connecticut, because we had been accepted to Yale's residencies.

Yale was actually our third choice behind Duke and Mayo, but we were pleased, to say the least. I sighed within the first few seconds, realizing that I had achieved what I had been dreaming of for so many years. I was going to Yale. I had ached for so long to achieve more than I had been born into, and now it was mine. I saw doors that were once locked now opening up to me, and my key was engraved with the word *Yale*.

Now the events of our daily lives became background to the planning of our future. Tara and I would talk in the middle of the afternoon via cell phone to discuss the houses we had each seen advertised. The routine of staying up every fourth night to be on call at one of the hospitals was mildly tedious, but not too malignant. On the days between call, I would drive home, dictating the events of my patients' hospitalization over the cell phone to a very receptive and unquestioning voicemail, which would mark that chart as completed. As I would dictate, my language would sound very official and proper, with the background of rock music over the car stereo. Having taken care of the majority of my patients' needs, I would go home to the apartment on Orange Street and recline by the pool. To this day, I think my best doctoring was done in swim trunks and a tan. I would gladly answer nurses' pages, directing this test or that medication. It was almost impossible to trouble me with the comfort of the sun and the security that I was going to Yale the next year.

By year's close, we had bought a house after chasing Internet realty ads. We checked out a few and settled on one. The calculations done by the website suggested that it was in our financial interest to buy if we were planning on staying longer than three and a half years. Strangely, the website made this prediction only after we notified it that we were staying for four years. But we had a house waiting for us, and that was one less thing to worry about.

Chapter 14

If there were a way to quantify the difference between the East Coast and the West Coast, I am certain that it would tally greater than the geographic miles between them. I could tell you that the food on the East Coast, or at least in Connecticut, was far worse than I was used to in California. I could tell you that the nurses I worked with were far more combative and less attractive than the nurses in California. I could tell you that the attending physicians were far less helpful than I was used to in California. All of this would be true and important in painting the picture of Connecticut and Yale. But I would come to learn that the sum of these details fails to put it into perspective the way a single analogy by a comic did for me. He described a scenario first on the West Coast and then on the East Coast.

"A man walks down the street past another man in L.A. The first man says to the second, 'Hey, nice hair, man.' The second says, 'Thanks,' coifs his hair, and walks on. A man walks by, in the same way, in New York. The guy he passes says 'Hey, nice hair, man.' The second guy says, 'Fuck you. What's wrong with it?'"

~~~

My excitement to be at Yale, working in the emergency department, was like that of a young child who discovers how much he likes blue ice cream and realizes he has a whole life left to enjoy it. Every morning (or night), I drove in to work a shift with a smile on my face. The Mustang would growl as I left the off-ramp that declared my arrival each day at Yale New Haven Hospital, exit 1. With the windows open to the New England summer air and my bootlegged live recording of *Master of Puppets* blaring, I would flash my ID badge across the computerized gate master. The parking structure was six stories and crossed over the street beneath it, all of which dwarfed what I was used to at Mon Gracia. Shops on the ground level included a Dunkin Donuts, a Subway, and a convenience store. Every morning (or evening, depending on the shift I was working), I walked through a glass-covered bridge, avoiding the traffic and stoplights of the regular pedestrian to get to work, the thrashing of the heavy guitar chords and the tommy-gun bass-drumming of the music still in my head. I couldn't recite a single lyric perfectly, but the notes made a perfect melody as I walked to work, mentally role-playing the entire routine of medications to give someone coming into the ER in full cardiac arrest.

The differences were as evident within the hospital as without in the daylight. Yale's hospital was very much like the shark tank that small fish are thrown into to feed the inhabitants. The lucky ones are dead before they are thrown in, while the majority live long enough to see their predators and understand their fate. Yale featured an array of different species of shark. The obvious ones with the characteristic marking of sharks were the surgeons. They generally shied away from humans, lurking in their operating rooms and making their presences known only when the foolish summoned them. The tenuous relationship between surgeons and humans, namely emergency physicians, was ubiquitous. So it wasn't a great surprise to me when I arrived at Yale.

Other breeds of shark were more of a conundrum. The nurse shark in nature is a universally placid fish, feeding on the sludge at the bottom of the ocean. At Yale, this species is no benign creature. Like its Discovery Channel counterpart, the Yale nurse shark is a bottom-feeder. However, the docile exterior of the Yale nurse shark only masks the ferocious teeth from its would-be prey. The most common prey of this animal is the species Internis naivis, known more commonly as the scut monkey.

Another enigmatic breed of shark in the Yale aquarium is the attending shark. Members of this species are unique in the animal world, in that they are so sly in their attack methods, often the prey is unaware of the attack until they incidentally notice a limb or career opportunity missing. In the event that the attack was noticed, it will usually be obscured by a flurry of torn flesh and debris. And once the debris settles, there are usually several members of the pack nearby, all with dubious smiles in an effort to divert attention. Survival manuals would suggest that if one finds himself in this situation, he should check himself for more than one lost appendage. They also point out that the aroma permeating the water in such an attack is the shark defecating, also to obscure the attack. The manual warns that the distinctive smell can be misleading, but assures us that despite our misguided confidence, this shit is most certainly not from a bull, as all reason would suggest.

I wasn't initially daunted by the thought of swimming with the sharks. The PBS specials growing up had taught me that if they didn't smell blood in the water, they wouldn't attack. So I went into each shift with a confident smile and a joke. I discreetly watched how the older residents addressed the nurses and attendings and tried to mimic their behavior. It actually didn't feel like too much of a stretch to act confident in this new environment. The medical problems I encountered here were not *that* different from the ones I had seen on the West Coast. Sure, the patients were shooting up heroin instead of speed, but the medical issues were largely the same.

On this particular Thursday night, the emergency department was overflowing with patients. As an intern, I was responsible for seeing the less serious patients who were not likely to die within the next hour, and who also made up the bulk of the patient load. My nurse, Frankie, was a thirty-year-old girl with dark hair and an athletic shape. I assumed her name was not actually Frankie but something like Francis or Angela Franks. But the gruff nature of the name, Frankie, befit her persona much better. At thirty, she was younger than most of the nurses in the Yale emergency department, but she had been employed there for at least five years, giving her some authority. By virtue of this, she was able to mingle with both the older witches who had worked in the ED since ambulances were pulled in by horses, as well as with the twenty-something nurses who giggled about their boyfriends and celebrities.

On a night as busy as this, a resident absolutely fears a patient who requires a great deal of time and attention. Someone with a serious disease is not a problem, because these are often quickly identified and decisively dealt with—in other words, sent to the ICU or the morgue. But the patient who was placed in bed 7 was much more troubling.

The dry-erase board at the front of the department announced the woman's name and complaint. This system was designed to help the supervising attendings direct the care of a large number of patients. Next to her distinctly Hispanic name was a chief complaint of *Pain*. The issue sounded simple enough to address, but I had come to learn that the triage nurses tried to be as specific as possible without violating any confidentiality rights of the patients. So, to see a complaint as vague as *Pain* written on the board was tantamount to saying the pain would be my own.

In room 7 I found a portly, dark-skinned woman writhing in pain on the bed. Next to her sat her similarly robust husband, sitting with her purse on his lap. She could be heard throughout the department as she wailed out constantly, "Aye! Aye! Aye!"

I stood by the bed. "Ma'am? I'm Dr. Triton. I need to find out what brought you into the ER tonight."

She opened her eyes and lifted her head from the bed. "Que?" she answered, or asked, rather. "No habla ingles."

Her husband looked up at me, offering his own confirmation. "She no habla ingles."

It was clear that his ability to translate was going to be minimal, although he had offered me the courtesy of at least one word in English.

"Senora, que te problema?" I asked somewhat abruptly.

She looked up again with some surprise, then rested her head back to the pillow to explain from that position. "Ohhhh! Me dueleeee! Ayeeee!"

As you can imagine, her announcement that she was in pain was of little help in discerning the problem. "Where is your pain, ma'am? Donde es su dolor?"

"Ohhhh! Me duele!"

I was getting nowhere, stat. "Donde?" I shouted in frustration. "Aqui? O aqui?" I moved my fingers over her head, then chest, then stomach, trying to elicit some focus for her pain.

"Ayeee! Es todo!" she cried.

I probed her for about five minutes, completely in Spanish, and finally discerning that the pain was mostly in her abdomen and had begun the day before. It had been getting worse when she developed severe nausea and vomiting with profuse sweating. She had diabetes but had not seen her doctor since coming to America ten years before.

She had once been told by an emergency doctor that she had an infection in her stomach somewhere, but she did not know where. Although there were several questions I wanted to ask, I began to examine her while I asked to expedite the process. As soon as I laid my hands on her abdomen, just above her liver, she began to scream.

"Aye-yi-yi-yi-yi-yi!"

After that moment, she would answer no more questions. She just continued to roll on the bed and cry out. I left the room and gave the nurse the plan.

"I want to get CBC, chem seven, LFTs, UA, and blood and urine cultures. I will order the CT of the abdomen and pelvis."

"Blood cultures?" Frankie questioned. "She didn't even have a fever when she came in."

"I know." I reflected briefly on my mother, who hadn't had a fever, either. "But she has diabetes that hasn't been checked in years. I wouldn't be surprised if she can't even mount a fever. And she seems pretty sick to me."

"We can't get blood cultures unless they have a fever." She dug her heels into the ground.

"Look. Just get the cultures. I will explain it to Leonard."

She stormed off to gather the glass tubes for the blood samples. I watched to make sure the larger bottles used only for blood cultures were in her hands before I turned away to present the case to Dr. Leonard.

"So you got the Aye-aye-aye Syndrome case, huh?" Dr. Leonard asked me as I did an about-face.

Dr. Leonard, a petite woman who had grown up in New England, was the assistant director of the emergency residency at Yale. To see her, with her tiny spectacles and short blonde hair, one would assume she was a librarian or a junior high math teacher. Regardless of her image, she was an interesting person, able to share the excitement of a frightening moment in the ED or at least able to pretend she understood what activities might be entertaining to a young person. She did not have the reputation that some of the more vicious attendings had, but it was well known that she was not stupid, nor was she a pushover.

"Aye-aye-aye Syndrome?" I asked.

"Don't tell me you haven't heard of Aye-aye-aye Syndrome? Being from California?"

"I don't suppose I have."

She got closer and whispered, "You know...when the little Hispanic ladies come in complaining of everything under the sun, and all they will say is, 'Aye aye aye.'"

"I gotcha. Yeah. That was her. So she apparently has abdominal pain, there for a day. Maybe a history of uncontrolled diabetes and some abdominal infection she does not know much about. When I went to palpate her stomach—"

"Don't tell me," Leonard interrupted. "She went into Aye-tach."

"Aye-tach?"

"Of course. People with coronary syndromes go into ventricular tachycardia, or V-tach. People with Aye-aye-aye Syndrome go into Aye-tach. You're lucky if they stop to breathe. I once had to intubate a lady who was in Aye-tach for at least five minutes. She was taching so long she became cyanotic."

I raised my eyebrows. "Anyway, I'm gonna get labs on her and a CT," I said. "And I'd also like to get blood cultures on her."

"Why do you want to do that?"

"I just think she is pretty sick. And if she has early sepsis from some abdominal infection, I don't want to miss it. I've been burned before."

"All right, but you have to watch what all you order here. I know you are used to ruling out every possibility from your medicine training, but here you just want to rule out the most immediate possibilities. Let the hospital teams figure all that other stuff out."

"Okay, I understand," I said with a slight sense of failure.

"And another thing, you should be careful how you come across here. Some of the nurses think you are too cocky and that you don't take your job seriously."

"What? They don't think I take it seriously?" I asked, stunned. "How can they think I'm not taking this seriously? I am working my ass off."

"They see you smiling all the time, talking to the patients and the staff. You know, they already have a nickname for you. They are calling you Hollywood behind your back."

"Okay. I guess I'll have to watch it."

I gave in, but inside I was absolutely pissed off. The rage within me siphoned up to my mouth, where it perched, ready to tell that bitch of a nurse what I thought of her. But I withheld my words. My mouth remained closed, surely for the better. But with each moment I saw her and said nothing, the fury cranked my jaw muscles tighter and tighter. A name like Hollywood by itself would not be offensive to me at all. In fact, under most circumstances, I would have found it quite flattering. But the disdain I envisioned in the nurses' voices with their wrinkled smirks shriveled as much as their sun-dried, bleach-frayed hair, irritated my stomach like the grind of sandpaper.

Later, the CT scan showed that the patient had appendicitis with a possible perforation of the bowel. It was certainly dangerous, but I never got to see whether the blood culture came back positive.

Within a few hours, the sun was rising somewhere, although we would not be aware of such natural phenomena inside the ED, as no natural light or air made its way into our world. Our only cue that morning approached came around 4:00 a.m., when the drunks gradually stopped being brought in by the police after stumbling around the bars, which closed at 2:00. Near that time, the last of the truly sick patients who would need to stay in the hospital for at least a day would finally trickle from their emergency beds and be taken to the bed upstairs, only a mere five hours after it was determined that they were sick and needed to stay. And the flow of patients had slowed to a crawl, as it takes much more pain to get a person out of bed than it does to keep him from going to bed in the first place.

As 7:30 neared, the first of the morning patients showed up, realizing that a trip to the emergency department for their cold, diarrhea, or rash might be preferable to actually going to work. The evening's drunks who had been sequestered in the back to sleep off the "ALOC d/t ETOH" (an acronym for altered level of consciousness due to being shit-faced drunk) were slowly filing out the double doors. Each wondered aloud how he could have let himself drink so much and recited his mantra, swearing that he was never going to drink again. Thankfully, the police and EMTs had the courtesy to rotate which of the four ERs in the area they took the drunks to, or else the drunks had the good sense to drink in various parts of town. This allowed them to save face and claim that they had lasted a week or two before being brought back to the same gurney in the back. They, of course, thought ten years had passed while they pissed and vomited on themselves for anyone who was willing to watch.

Well before this change of shift, deep fatigue would set in. The minutes each dragged along as though burdened by a massive anchor as they passed into hours. I could feel my body fighting the natural physiology that evolution had developed when humanoids began hunting and gathering in the daylight hours. Had there been any patients left in the ER, sign out to the residents working the day shift might have taken as long as a half hour to discuss each of the patients in detail. But all had been sent home or to the hospital floor.

I squinted my eyes as I walked through the glass tunnel, passing over the traffic. The sun had broken through the clouds, which had apparently brought some showers overnight. Early in the year, I had learned to shield my eyes from the sun after a night shift, since one brief moment of exposure could reset that circadian rhythm I had worked so hard to fuck up with multiple night shifts. Then I wouldn't be able to get to sleep for hours when I got home. Exhaustion being such a strong motivator, I was happy to walk all the way to my car with my eyes entirely shut, my head lurched forward and my chin down into my chest.

As I pulled onto the freeway, the traffic was going the opposite direction, as the commuters headed toward New York City. The morning radio program with Howard Stern was not nearly so welcoming as the duo I had grown to love back home in California. I admit I chuckled at many of the jokes my wife would have been offended by, but it lacked the neighborly sense of greeting all of Southern California with jokes and laughter that seemed wholesome by comparison. The seagulls swarmed over the interchange, looking for currents of fish brought into the nearby sound by last night's rain.

As the Mustang curled under the overpass at thirty miles per hour, the centrifugal force fastened me to my overly reclined seat, as it always did. Before my mind had time to respond and my heart even to skip a beat, I was halfway through the leftward turn, and the car began to spin. I started to veer off the road. Remembering the public-service announcements from growing up, I avoided the impulse to slam on the brakes; there was no way I was going to steer into any fucking turn as I spun off the road, no matter what they said in driver's ed. My front left wheel had only nudged the mild embankment when the counterclockwise spin continued, pulling my tail before my head.

This was the only moment when I remember an actual thought with actual words going through my head in all of this. *Holy shit*, I calmly thought. *How am I going to get this turned around without anyone seeing me?* I was pleased to see in the fraction of a second that there was no one within sight behind me on the freeway. But the spin had not stopped. My body was cognizant of its general momentum going forward, or backward, as it was at the moment. The rotation of the car around my body seemed like an incidental observation.

When the spin had exceeded 180 degrees, it occurred to me again to turn into the spin. Within the next second, which seemed like minutes, I felt the tug of the seat beneath me. The body of the car rocked side to side over the chassis and wheels, which had finally gained a foothold on the pavement. The hood of the Mustang peered squarely down the lane with a perfectly symmetrical ten inches on each side. I gently lay my foot on the gas pedal again, almost wondering if there would be any response or if this was a dream and thus not abiding by rules of logic. Sure enough, the hum of the motor reliably came beneath the car, and the car slowly accelerated northward into the straightaway as I meekly depressed the pedal. It must have been a half mile before I took my first breath and reflected on how narrowly I had avoided disaster and possibly death. My total lack of panic and even lack of sensation through the entire event seemed, and still to this day seems, mysterious.

I arrived home and made my way through the house, finally letting gravity catch up with me as I flopped onto the bed. The curtains had been left completely closed to obstruct all light, and I fell asleep immediately as if it were midnight.

I awoke around 5:00 that evening before Tara got off work. I had the night off and began cooking dinner with the television on in the background. Grilling the steaks or mashing the potatoes was certainly not as simple as ordering pizza on our only night together in the past week. But cooking and other overlooked pastimes had become treasured moments, a chance to be creative, to actually make something without the stress of someone's life depending on it or, more likely, someone yelling at me for the effort.

The power garage door opened just as the potatoes finished cooking and just as the cable news parody was starting. Tara came in from the garage, haggard and in scrubs. We gave each other feeble hugs and exchanged hellos. After remarking on the dinner, she went back to change into her usual sweatpants-pajama medley.

Arriving home was not the obvious relief and joy for Tara or myself that one might expect, given such a stressful work environment. There was an unspoken rule in the house that we would not discuss the workday. The rule had evolved from trial and error—the errors being mostly mine, it seemed. Previously, when she had come home telling of her hospital worries, I had reflexively offered my opinion or advice. In turn, when I came home telling my stories from work, she soon became tired and bored by conversations about medicine after twelve hours of work. As a result, our routine now consisted of sitting down in front of a simple dinner and watching reruns of *Law and Order*. Any deviation, such as a movie or restaurant, was reserved for rare occasions when we both had the following day off and was otherwise out of the question due to our semi-narcoleptic states.

Extreme exhaustion notwithstanding, during this time I loved being at Yale in the emergency department. I saw my new friends struggling to survive the stress of medicine and ICU rotations and tried to encourage them, reminding them how much they presumably loved being in the ER there. We were always eager to get our hands dirty, or bloody, as it were—to be the ones to intubate the crashing patient when the shit hit the fan. Since relatively few people were dying each night in the emergency room, I suppose thankfully, I approached Dr. Lathem about attempting to gain access to the anatomy cadaver lab to practice intubating.

"We've tried to get the anatomy department to help us with this," Dr. Lathem said, "but they just haven't been willing. I don't think you're going to get anywhere, but you can try if you want." He sounded slightly hopeful.

Dr. Lathem was the residency director, the same director with whom I had interviewed both years prior. He almost always had a smile beneath his goatee, giving a friendly impression when he was around. The catch was that he was very rarely around. He worked relatively few shifts in the ER itself. Most of his time was working on administrative duty in his office. Despite the excess testosterone that had led to his severe male-pattern baldness, he did not have the bold persona one would expect in emergency medicine. While he smiled amongst his residents, he never seemed completely comfortable. He never stood up and took command when the trauma burst through the doors, never stood back and joked with the guys after the life was saved. But he never said anything harsh if a minor mistake was made, either—and so he seemed like a valuable ally to have in a place that, rumor had it, could be very harsh.

After a few calls, I finally hunted down the director of the anatomy course. He sounded like a hearty man with a deep laugh. He seemed much more friendly than I had expected from a man so obstructive as to keep residents away from the cadavers.

"Sir, I'm Dr. Triton, one of the residents in emergency medicine here. I'm calling because I wanted to propose a cooperative extracurricular activity between our departments. I would like our department to be able to use the cadavers to practice intubating human bodies. We could arrange specific days and times to get this practice, and the procedure would do no harm to the bodies. In return, residents from our department would get together with some of your students and teach them some of the clinical aspects of the anatomy they're learning."

"That is a fantastic idea!" the professor shouted over the phone. "Do you know how long I have been trying to coordinate with surgery and your department to do something like this? All I need to know is when you want to do this and when your residents would be available to teach the students."

"The sooner the better, as far as I'm concerned. What I would like to do is have you talk with my director, as he is ultimately in charge of our schedules. Just call him at this number. I'll tell him to expect you." I rattled off the number and hung up excitedly. I immediately picked up again and dialed Lathem.

"Dr. Lathem, I got the anatomy director to agree to the proposal. We get access to the cadavers, and we get the opportunity to teach their students some of the clinical significance of the anatomy. Maybe a neck dissection or something." I sped through the sentences, hardly able to wait for his excitement.

"Oh."

I waited several seconds for him to complete the sentence and show his elation, too.

"Okay, then," he said with the tone of someone expecting creamed cabbage for dinner.

"Well, I've asked him to call you to help set up times. I think people would be really excited to get involved with this, even if it requires weekend time. And if he asked how many would be interested in teaching the med students, I would really like to."

"All right, thanks." He hung up the phone.

~~~

It wasn't long before the predictable, albeit erratic schedule of ER shifts was done for the month. I had moved on to MICU, the medical intensive care unit (pronounced *mick-you*). This block was referred to as the "Block of Death." It could have been named for the countless patients clutching to life through courses of devastating strokes, sepsis, or pneumonia. They seemed to persevere on a day-by-day basis with only the breaths that we imposed on them and some residual inner drive that we could not quantify. To my dismay, the nickname for the MICU had actually been coined because my predecessors had discovered, as would I, that we would gladly opt for the most grizzly execution in the Orient if it would excuse us from the remainder of the rotation.

The environment gave the impression of being absolutely sterile, to the point of not even sustaining human life. The patients' rooms circled around the central nurses' desk, as was typical of other units I had been on, but the windows into their rooms were wider and peered directly toward their monitors. Their heart rate, respiratory rate, and blood-pressure tracings were almost the sum total of their identity in the unit. It was difficult for us as interns to appreciate the true identity of such people who had not lifted an eyelid since being in our care; nor would they likely ever lift one again.

In some of those few spare moments far removed from the unit floor, we would mourn for their lost lives, even as their pulses persisted. Sometimes we would wonder how the patient might have styled his hair before it was simply projected haphazardly in a starburst pattern, molded to his pillow by weeks' worth of scalp oil and sweat. We watched as retired professors who had once amazed students with their eloquence lost their ability to enunciate, then articulate, then approximate, then even phonate because the strokes had progressed so far. And even though this human side of us existed, it was often relegated to being revealed once every few days on a drive home. In the unit, during the ten minutes we actually spent with these patients, they were little more than their vital signs, their fluid intake and output, and their lab values. We each detested ourselves at one time or another for being so callous, but the psychological lashings that we incurred when we omitted a patient's "ins-n-outs" to mention a discussion with the patient's wife did not promote the humanistic side of medicine.

The formal hierarchy and chain of command was nowhere so appreciable as in the MICU. Even the surgeons who lived to spit on anyone and everyone beneath them would have to acknowledge the strict formula of seniority consisting of smugness, entitlement, and being careful not to over-spice with a sense of duty. The subtle difference was the passive-aggressive approach to demeaning and ultimately destroying the younger residents, as seen in the MICU. I once asked a surgeon how he felt about the MICU's passive-aggressive style of demeaning its residents, and he asked me, "Why bother being passive?"

Three interns were doomed to work the trenches. The more senior residents included residents from the department of internal medicine as well as a single senior emergency medicine resident. The medicine specialists saw the ER residents as docs who didn't have either the brains or the attention to treat a disease for more than thirty minutes, and so we were treated as the ugly stepsisters. However, having an extra senior resident on the unit meant dramatically smaller workloads for the other senior residents, so this was one of the few occasions when an ER doc was actually welcomed.

The emergency resident was a girl who I liked from afar. She reminded me distinctly of the baby depicted on Gerber baby-food labels. Delicate, baby-smooth skin covered her puffy cheeks. Her lips were similarly pert, while her eyes were a nearly fluorescent blue. Her short, curly hair befitted her innocent image. I was thankful to have someone in my corner if things became difficult.

The attending in the MICU was a short, thin woman with dark hair shorn close to the scalp, then waxed with pomade frontward over the forehead. She constantly sipped at her venti latte as we rounded the unit. She would arrive promptly at 7:00 each morning, gathering us all at the first patient's bedside. She always gave her instructions through the pulmonology fellow, the general's colonel in our medical army. In this way, she rarely spoke to me or the other interns. I should have recognized that her speaking to me directly at any time heralded some form of shit of considerable depth heading my way. The interesting dynamic made for what appeared to be frequent brush-offs in the extreme. Per ritual, I recited the patient's case or overnight progress, looking directly at her, of course. Her attention remained directly on me, save for the occasional glances at the chart or computer, almost implying a conversation. But seconds after I concluded each plan of care, she turned her head to the left and instructed the fellow on how to modify my plan.

I can honestly vouch that most of my month in the MICU was a homogenous blur of misery. I was caring for somewhere between six and twelve patients at any point in time. One patient holds the distinction of sharing the longest night of my life. His name was Membe, and he had emigrated from Mozambique fifteen years earlier. Like so many people in Africa, he had contracted HIV and had progressed to full-blown AIDS during his time in America. He had no health insurance in Africa or America and so had started and stopped treatment intermittently as social services could provide. He was not a newcomer to the MICU; he had previously survived all the rare diseases that one only sees in a textbook or a case of severe AIDS. This time, Membe had been in the ICU for two weeks already. We had been greeting each other every morning as I asked him about his fever and cough. Pneumonia, we had decided, was causing his diminished health this round. We pumped him full of antibiotics and crossed our fingers each day that his chest x-ray would improve or his labs would look better. That night, just two days before I completed the rotation, would be the most memorable nights of my training, and paradoxically one of the worst.

That morning, Membe's nurse had noticed some blood on his sheets beneath his bottom. Knowing his history, I was worried even before I saw his labs, which were not due to return for two more hours. As sometimes happens in severe cases of AIDS, and had already happened six months before for Membe, the HIV virus had caused his body to attack the cells that allowed his blood to clot. I was still surprised to see that his platelets had dropped to approximately two percent of what they normally should be.

I paged Gerber and got her on the phone. "Membe is bleeding like a motherfucker up here, and I don't know how quick we're going to be able to stop it. I called the blood bank to get us an elephant's worth of blood and platelets, but they said since he has had reactions to both before, it's going to take a few hours to get him compatible stuff."

"Well, call GI and see if they'll stick a scope up in him and stop the bleeding!" she shouted at me over the phone.

I had been deeply disappointed over the course of the month to learn that Gerber was nothing like the guardian angel I had expected.

"I called them already," I protested. "They said they've looked in his colon a dozen times before, and there's nothing they can fix in him. Apparently his platelets are so low that simply sneezing could make him explode out any orifice."

"Just tell them we need it now!" she screamed. "I'll be over there in a minute. And go over to the blood bank and get that blood. I don't want to have to wait for some transporter schmuck."

The day went much as we imagined it. By noon, Membe had gotten a colonoscopy by the GI specialists and been told there was essentially nothing they could do. He had been transfused several times but was still losing blood before our eyes. After several more trips to the blood bank, and several more bags of blood and platelets, the bleeding finally started to slow down, and his blood pressure started to level off in a region compatible with life.

My breathing had finally slowed from the sprints that I had serially run about three blocks apiece. "How are you feeling?" I asked Membe as I stood in his room.

With the lights off, his room was now lit only by the stray beams from the hall. His eyes opened, and he looked at me. He opened his lips, I think to smile, as he typically did when we met each morning, but he was unable to expose his teeth. His lips were dry and stuck to the enamel beneath them. His eyes closed again shortly afterward.

The room seemed empty, with only his solitary bed standing in dim light. While some rooms allowed for two patients at capacity, Membe's severely immunocompromised state meant that the common cold, or even athlete's foot, could lead to his demise. There were no family members in his room in what might have been his last hours. No one had even visited him in the time I had known him. There were no flowers or pictures on the bedside tables showing his family or loved ones. There was but a single bag of disposed yellow protective gowns marking the extreme contact precautions that were taken; to simply take his pulse, we gowned in Chernobyl-wear. It struck me as I gazed across the blank walls and listened to the nothingness of the background beeps that I did not hear crying. I did not even know if his family was alive, if they were in this country, or if they knew of his condition. Had they been deprived of the right to cry for him?

By 10:00 that night, the black cloud of fortune had rained profusely over me. I had spent every moment I could spare admitting at least three new patients to the MICU. The fatigue from the past four weeks of duty was swelling in me as if in my blood itself. I thought, *My God, if I could just take a small nap to get me through this night…*

Just then, my pager went off. I immediately recognized the number from the MICU.

"Your patient's blood pressure is dropping," Dr. Gerber said, answering the phone without a greeting or checking my identity. "You should really be up here doing something about it." That she was unaware of the irony in her statement was most infuriating. She actually seemed to think I had been lounging in the Bahamas for the past few hours. She was also quick to identify the patient as *mine* rather than *hers* or *ours*. It reminded me that Beaver Cleaver was always Ward's son when he got into some kind of mischief and June's son when he won the spelling bee.

Before I could remind her that I was in the ER and would be right up, she had tossed the receiver onto the cradle and was gone. I walked to the elevators, barely lifting each foot off the ground as I stepped. My neck did not bother to support the weight of my head, and my chin propped on my sternum as I lummoxed down the hall. It was my normal practice to take the stairs if the trip was five levels or less, but the month had worn me to the point that I considered calling transport to shuttle me up in a wheelchair.

No longer for want of visitors but still with a feeling of emptiness, Membe's room now had three yellow-robed nurses surrounding his bed as I looked in. Each was tapping an arm or a leg with her fingers, apparently hoping a vein would jump out and smack them back.

"His IV stopped working, so you need to get another one in him so we can get his blood pressure back up," Dr. Gerber said, looking over the computer screen in deep consternation. "I told them you would get some blood for labs while you were in there."

The chance of successfully digging a well in Egypt crossed my mind as I thought about trying to get an IV in this man who had had more lines in his life than an Academy Awards acceptance speech. His dropping blood pressure also suggested that any vein I might find would likely be very stingy in giving up any blood for me to send to the lab.

I fumbled with his veins for at least an hour before I finally got an IV in place and got two small squirts of blood in the two glass tubes. I connected the lines to his IV bags and started his fluid running again. With the beep that signaled the flow into his body, I rested my eyelids and exhaled. The weight bearing down on each lid, resisting my efforts to open them, was excruciating. My brain felt as if it had settled to the bottom of my skull like a bowl of overcooked spaghetti. I shook my head briefly from left to right and felt slightly more alert, surreal as my wakefulness seemed. And so I walked toward the nurses' desk to send the tubes to the lab.

With the first step outside the room, I felt that warm inner twinge I recognized immediately. I had not felt it in many months, the erotic stroking of my stomach deep inside my chest, and the warm thrill that it just might last this time. The hunger and the satiation were instantaneous. I halted in my footsteps and held my breath at its deepest, afraid that any relaxation might let me slip into some delirious-looking seizure. My eyes moved systematically across the room, focusing intently on anything tangible to hold me in the three-dimensional world. *Clock! Door! Chair!* Previously, I had been under the delusion that simply concentrating on movie quotes was enough to snap me out of this state, until Tara had caught me smacking my lips while I mentally recited Gordon Gecko's "greed" monologue from *Wall Street* one night about six months back.

To my immediate left sat a computer and a chart lying askew in front of the keyboard. I forced myself to notice the stubbled texture of the brown folder of the chart and the slightest imperfections in the penmanship of the patient's name. I glanced upward to the monitor, which was simulating a George Lucas vision of light speed through its screensaver. I quickly swung my eyes from the screen, fearing that it might throw me into an uncontrollable state. My wits were still very much about me, and I fought any urge to think about my stomach or the long-avoided daydreams.

To my right about thirty degrees hung an unstylish white clock face. The little hand was just past the eleven, and the big hand two notches past the three. There was no secondhand to entertain me, and its absence left me momentarily disgruntled. Both hands remained motionless as my brows furrowed in the hopes of making the clock seem more real. The warm emptiness in my stomach returned.

Fuck! I thought. I quickly turned to the right, where one of the nurses was facing away from me, talking, maybe on the phone. I couldn't discern the words from the mumble, and her bleach-damaged hair dangled over the desk as she hovered over some chart. I tried to make out the words, but I repeatedly lost interest over the course of thirty seconds. Then, from that part of my brain that could sometimes speak without my consent, the little blonde girl from my dreams speculated on the nurse's conversation.

I quickly closed my eyes and rubbed them with closed fists.

As the nurse bent over the tabletop, her rump of impressive size became the most effortless diversion of my attention. The cotton fibers woven in Guam had been faced with the formidable challenge of circumnavigating her ass. Under these scrubs, the impression of a distressed elastic band traversed an arbitrary border between gluteus and thigh at an unflattering angle. On the other thigh I saw no such impression, and I hesitated to think of the peril it may have faced and what catastrophe must have befallen it. The strain on the fabric was transmitted to the very hem of the leg as it pulled up taut around her calf. A pink impression marked the gristle of her leg under her raised pant leg. Startling as the image was, the soothing voice and the inviting caress I felt in my stomach were too intoxicating to resist.

I abruptly turned around, realizing that I might not appear sober to the observant nurse. The ICU was surprisingly barren, considering the man rapidly dying of AIDS in the room behind me. I also considered the possibility that there were people nearby who I just hadn't noticed. In either case, I needed to get to the call room, where I could let this pass for a couple minutes. The steps I took seemed stable from my perspective. The gliding sensation made my feet seem immaterial, though. I was halfway to the security of the call room when I looked down and noticed the test tubes of blood still in my gloved hand.

I need to send these to the lab, I thought, enunciating every word in my mind because any abstract thought would have simply vanished into oblivion. *The lab. I can tube it.* A computerized shuttling system could whisk a plastic container of whatever to any section of the hospital in minutes.

I glided over to the tubing system and stared at the keypad. It was no more complex than a phone keypad or an ATM system, and the five-digit code directory for the hospital hung beside it. The letters spelling out locations such as *ADMISSIONS* seemed like Greek nomenclature, recognizable but not decipherable.

To focus my effort, I told myself that the word I was looking for would be spelled *L-A-B*. But my search was fruitless. I paused for a second in frustration, wondering why I couldn't find something so plain. "L-A-B-O-R-A-T-O-R-Y," I spelled slowly and distinctly to myself. The time it took me to spell the word was sufficient to disrupt my concept of alphabetical order as I inspected the headings of *ADMISSIONS*, *AMBULATORY*, and so on. By the time I had reached *CAT SCAN*, I had forgotten what word I was looking for. I paused again, realizing that I had little hope of accomplishing this.

I had a reflexive yet vague sense of desperation that did not require a complex understanding of what was occurring. Although I felt steady as I retreated from the console, my shoulder struck the corner with a solid yet almost unnoticed blow. My pathway to the call room was clear to the right, but to the left a janitor was pushing her cart of mops and trashcans. Her puzzled look was decipherable even in my mental state.

"Can you help me?" I said. "I need this to go to the laboratory. Do you know how to send it?" I had no reason to believe a custodian would tube anything within the hospital, but I had no ability to consider it, either.

"Labo-ratory?" the Hispanic woman stuttered with a strong accent.

Without considering what her less-than-confident response implied, I handed her the test tubes in the plastic bag. "I feel really sick, and I need to go into the bathroom. Just send it to the laboratory," I repeated slowly. Then I turned around and swiftly enclosed myself in the call room.

I leaned back against the door, sighing with some small sense of additional security. By now the warmth that was intermittently stroking my stomach was consistently massaging my entire body from the inside. The vision repeated itself over and over, not like a hallucination that invaded reality, just a thought that I did not want to avoid. The satisfying feeling just beneath my scalp begged my empathy for addicts, if this was what getting high was like. Against my every desire, I pulled myself back to reality and decided that I should call Tara. This was the first time that I had ever lost control when I was at work, and I hoped she could talk me down.

The number pad of the phone was every bit as daunting as the tube console. I had to remind myself after I picked up the receiver that I was calling my wife. The phone number was not to be found in my memory. "My wife is Tara," I said to myself, hoping that the name might spur the memory. "My wife is Tara. Tara's phone number is…" The thought halted as abruptly as it had started.

"My home phone number is…seven-eight-two." I became excited that the number was returning to me, so I quickly reached to dial it. "Seven-eight-two, seven-eight-two…" I repeated fervently. But the organization of the keypad seemed even more foreign than I remembered seeing with the previous glance.

Randomly patrolling the digits, I came across the first desired key. "Seven." I sighed aloud. I looked back at the keypad for the next digit and realized that I had forgotten what it was. I recited the lines rapidly to myself: "I am calling home. My home number is…" Again I paused. My heartbeat sped and strengthened until I could hear it as a whooshing against my eardrum. "My home number is…seven…eight!" I feverishly scanned the keypad for an eight as the loud and obnoxious beep burst from the receiver into my ear.

My back inched and then freefell down the side of the door. My butt crashed to the floor, followed by the phone in defeat. I closed my eyes and submitted to the seizure until it released me. Five minutes or ten, I had no idea.

I stood up slowly, finally lucid. I guessed that I had no sensations in my stomach, but I was afraid to direct my attention to that area for fear it might trigger the seizure all over again. I shook off the drunken stupor and splashed water from the sink onto my face. It had been running in the adjoining bathroom when I became aware of my surroundings, but I swear I do not recall turning on the faucet in my previous state. The cold water had a blunted sting to it.

Several hours of toiling with Membe's health followed. The vacant halls illuminated far beyond what was necessary and became redundant. I was sent on one trivial mission after another, with very little direct contact with the patient. As the night evolved into a one-man relay race, retrieving blood bag after blood bag, I resorted to inventing quests such as exploring abandoned caverns that inexplicably had fluorescent lights and a stale antiseptic smell.

Ultimately, after receiving blood products from no less than thirty-two people, Membe's heart stopped. The mood was somber in the MICU because he was such a nice person and because of the realization that our efforts had been futile as well as costly. As is so often the case, the futility of the situation had eluded us as doctors. Or perhaps we just ignored the obvious futility that never tried to disguise itself at all. I wondered when Membe had recognized this futility, and if he had ignored it. The unceremonious farewell consisted of turning off the light, shutting the door, and watching a hospital technician leave the room with a six-foot-long black bag on a gurney.

The night had been entirely sleepless. But magically I had an ounce more energy than I had previously felt near midnight. The promise of leaving in a few hours inspired me around 5:30 in the morning. I began collecting the numbers that would represent the patients' identities for the morning. Whether my glass was half full or half empty, I was running on a pretty fucking small glass of energy by the end of the night. The blister on the inside of my middle finger had ruptured to expose the pink tissue beneath as I clenched my pen intently.

The activity in the ICU was beginning to pick up. Nurses were moving about, checking on their patients. Thermometers were being placed in various orifices, and blood was being drawn from various veins. I began to tune it out as I approached my last few notes.

"Dr. Triton, what do you want to do about Mr. Johnson's calcium?" one of the nurses shouted indignantly.

"I'm sorry, what?" I was surprised by the intolerant tone of her question.

"I told you that Mr. Johnson's calcium was 7.2 a second ago and asked you what you wanted to do about it."

My failure to hear her or even notice her presence made me leery of my immediate functionality.

"Seven point what?" I asked. Not only could I not remember the number she had quoted, I couldn't remember what the normal range of calcium included. It was clear that I was having another partial seizure, although I only felt tired and had no daydreams or weird sensations going on at the moment.

She repeated the number.

Not able to reach any safe conclusion, I decided to buy some time. "Actually, I'm right in the middle of something with this. Give me a minute and I'll deal with that for you, okay?" I tried to sound as pleasant as possible to avert any attention.

"Just tell me. Do you want to give calcium or not?" she persisted.

"Sure. Go ahead," I conceded, realizing that it must be low for her to question me. Subconsciously and through habit, I knew that the amounts of calcium we gave were relatively harmless.

"Fifteen or thirty?" she asked.

I became increasingly impatient. Fully aware that I couldn't judge how low Mr. Johnson's calcium was, I avoided any reflexive answer.

"Give me a minute. I just need to finish dealing with this first." I became more forceful and abrupt. I propped my elbows on the table and hid my face with my hands. I hoped the façade would create an image of contemplation rather than avoidance.

"Why can't you just tell me? Fifteen or thirty milli-equivalents?"

I exploded from my contemplative posture. "Look! The guy is not going to die if you wait five minutes to give him the calcium. I need to do this. I will deal with that in a minute!"

The nurse turned her head and then her body in repugnance as she strode away.

My awareness improved much more quickly than it had earlier, and I ended the morning soon afterward, thankful that the month of death was over.

Chapter 15

A starving man is exuberant with gratitude as he takes his first bite of an apple but is soon bitter when he finds himself with only the core. A similar surge of emotion ensues when a resident sinks his head finally into a pillow, giving his eyes permission to close. Down or stone, the quality of the pillow is immaterial as he begins to rest. And I was bitter, too, when I woke that evening to the alarm.

The bedroom door cracked open, and Tara's head peered through. Seeing that I was awake, she asked, "Why do you have the alarm set? You should just keep sleeping."

"I wish I could," I said. "I'm starting the next rotation at Bridgeport tonight. My ER shift is at nine."

"Oh, jeez. That sucks! Can't they give you one night off between blocks?"

"I know. But it'll be okay."

"All right, if you say so. You get showered, and I'll get you a little dinner together before you go."

"Thanks, dear."

I later came into the kitchen with my hair still wet and dripping onto my black T-shirt. I reached over and attached my pager and hospital ID to my scrub pants even before sitting down to the dining-room table, where a plate of scrambled eggs sat.

"I didn't know whether to cook you breakfast or dinner," Tara said as she poured a glass of orange juice.

"This is fine. Thanks."

"Actually, I would have made a real dinner for you, but we have nothing in the fridge. So you get breakfast."

"Yeah, I guess it's been a while since anyone had the time to go to the store," I conceded. I ate the eggs in a hurry, drinking the juice in only three gulps.

"How did your call go last night? I imagine it was pretty busy, since you didn't get a chance to call."

"Yeah..." The word trailed off like a piece of taffy pulled from my closed teeth. I thought back to the nightmare of the night before. I also recognized that I was in for a conflict when I explained everything to Tara. "You see..."

"What?"

I paused. "I actually did try to call you last night."

"Really? I didn't hear the phone ring. You should have left a voice mail, silly."

"Well, it wasn't quite that simple. You see, I kinda had one of my seizures last night."

Her eyes widened. "What? Oh, my God. Are you okay? Did anyone see you?"

"Yes, yes, yes, I'm okay. It was just a partial seizure. And no, I don't think anyone saw me. Or, I guess they saw me, but I don't think they realized what was happening. I felt it coming on and went and hid in the call room until it was over. That was when I tried to call you, but I couldn't think straight enough to dial the number."

"Oh, my God. When did this happen?"

"It was around midnight. Oh, and then again around six this morning. But that one was small. I just kinda leaned my head on my hand to look like I was thinking until it passed."

"What the fuck?" she shouted. "You should have called me again. You should have gone home right then!"

"No one was in danger. I knew what was going on, and I wasn't making any decisions while I was messed up like that."

"You still should have gone home. It's not safe for *you,* either."

"I can't go home. I have a responsibility there. I need to do the work if I am at all able. Otherwise, they have to try to find someone else to do it. And they are all just as fucking tired as I am."

She raised her voice again. "But *they* aren't dreaming about *Land of the Lost* characters and talking like they're drunk when *they* get tired! And you definitely shouldn't go in tonight."

"You know I can't call in sick. I never call in sick," I pleaded. "Besides, I got some sleep. I feel much better. If something starts to happen, I will step away when I can and then tell them that I need to leave sick."

"What if you're in the middle of a trauma or a code?"

"If there's that much excitement, I'm not going to start daydreaming and have a seizure. You know it only happens after everything slows down. And, like I said, I'll just take myself out of the situation and ask to be sent home. I don't want anyone to know about my seizures and start feeling sorry for me or treating me differently."

"I still don't think this is a good idea," she added. But I had already hustled into the bathroom to straighten out my hair. Then I kissed her as I slipped past the living-room couch and out the front door.

The lighting in Bridgeport's ER was quite a bit darker than at Yale's. It still had the effect of obfuscating the actual time of day, but the result was that it always seemed about 7:00 at night instead of always seeming 3:00 in the afternoon. I was actually happy to be returning to Bridgeport instead of Yale's ER. While I couldn't put my finger on the actual reasons, it always seemed that there was an atmosphere of conflict at Yale. I wouldn't have said that people were mean or didn't smile. And they did make an effort to teach me. But there were frequently references to protocol, or rank, whose obligation a particular task fell under. A corporal was not allowed to directly ask a commander how a particular strategy should work; he had to give the lieutenant a chance to show what he did or did not know first. Clearly these were questions that needed to be addressed, so it was difficult for me to pinpoint my grievance. But I was much more comfortable at Bridgeport, where the resident worked side by side with the attending, who talked about sports along with medicine.

The attending that night was one of my favorites. Dr. Calicchio's medical knowledge was average at best, but he had a way of not sweating the small stuff—or the medium stuff, and even some of the big stuff, for that matter. More of the work responsibility got placed in our laps when he was working, but we were guaranteed greater verbal encouragement for that work. He was a jovial Italian guy who had grown up and trained in Brooklyn. He always had a joke to tell or a story about his ex-wife, often in the same breath. He had just purchased a new turbo Porsche that he loved to talk about. Sometimes, when the work was slow, he invited one of the interested residents to sit in it and admire various features of the magnificent vehicle.

The nurses there were also nicer to work with than at Yale. Some were younger, working their way up by getting experience at this hospital to apply to one in a nicer area. The county where the hospital was located had a reputation for having the poorest people, highest murder rate, and dirtiest patients in all of Connecticut. As a result of these factors, too, the hospital had notably less attractive décor, less advanced technology, and fewer people working there. The other nurses were slightly older and satisfied with being outside the food chain of Yale. Anything that might have been lost in skill was easily retrieved in personality. Hell, it wasn't my arm that that they needed to stick more than once to find a vein, so what did I care?

Chuck and Erin were the nurses working that night. That was always a blessing because, in their case, there was no compromise in skill to get their lighthearted personalities. They both had come from athletic backgrounds. Chuck was a member of the national guard, and word had recently been sent down that he was soon going off to Iraq for six months. Erin was always either coming or going to an aerobics class when I was working in the ER.

The night began with the car accidents and assault victims that one would expect on a weekend evening in Bridgeport, the kind that had drawn many of us adrenaline junkies into a field like emergency medicine. But I was glad when it finally started slowing down by midnight. The list of patients waiting to be seen had dwindled to two or three, and by now only the less serious complaints remained. The woman with toe pain for a week and the man who thought he had "the clap" were generally condemned to the end of the line in emergency departments. I had been watching several patients since I came on, one of whom was an eighty-year-old man with stomach pain. He had started developing Alzheimer's disease over the past two years and wasn't able to describe all his symptoms well. So, his fifty-something son was in to help describe everything leading up to this night. In an eighty-year-old man, approximately 473 things can cause something as vague as abdominal pain, including mistaking the family cat for leftover fried chicken. As a result, we had talked, pushed, and prodded, drawn blood, and taken x-rays and CAT scans before the night was over. At every stage, I tried to offer the son, who was extremely pleasant, any reassurance I could.

By the end of this ultra-thorough workup, he felt we had developed a rather strong bond.

I sat looking at the computer screen with the CAT scan and the radiologist's interpretation of it, stating that there was nothing acutely wrong with the man's belly. The muscles in my calves cramped slightly and drew my attention to the fatigue setting in again. I realized that this was about the time that I had seized the night before. I thought for a second how thankful I was that I did not feel anything like a seizure now, then quickly changed the mental subject. I was starting to wish I had taken Tara's advice about staying home despite my phobia of missing work.

"Well, I have good news," I told the old man and his son. "We have looked at almost every possibility and haven't found anything. It looks like your dad just has a stomach virus or something small like that."

"Oh, thank you," the son replied. "I was so worried when he started having these pains yesterday."

"So we've given him some medicine that should help with the pain for a while. You guys can wait here for my nurse, who is bringing in the paperwork to let you go."

"Oh, thank you again," the son effused. "It's been a long time since we've had a doctor as nice as you who made my dad feel as comfortable as you have."

I felt somewhat complimented by the statement, but my fatigue allowed it to go largely unnoticed.

"You know, there was one time about five years ago that I had to take him into the doctor because he wasn't eating, and he was losing weight. He had been…"

My mind started wandering. It was relatively normal for me to think about other patients or a pending test when family members decided to talk my ear off. But in my exhaustion, patients were farthest from my mind. I saw the little girl in my dreams as she spoke.

"…but at that time my mother was still alive, and she was still cooking for him. His favorite meal was corned beef and cabbage, and she used to always…"

The warming sensation began in my forehead instead of my stomach this time and did not go away. It gently lowered over me like a veil. The man's lips continued to move, and there may or may not have been sound coming from them. To say that I heard words would give me far too much credit. I considered fighting off the sensation, focusing on his words or something, but fighting it required too much willpower and energy. Frankly, I couldn't find much incentive to break this semi-orgasmic trance that I was in, only to wake and listen to this son ramble on about his father. I just had to let him finish his story and get him out of there. Then I could escape to a secluded portion of the hospital.

He chattered on as my thoughts were massaged within my brain. To taste such beautiful flavors without the effort of taking a bite made the idea of any effort ridiculous. To hear music played as a lullaby behind his voice became an invitation to turn off the lights and nap right then. I watched for minutes more and at some point actively decided that I couldn't tolerate this conversation any longer. I let go. I stopped fighting. The dream consumed my attention. Peace quenched my thirst for rest.

"Hey, are you okay?" Erin looked down at me as she patted my cheeks with small slaps on either side.

My eyes were open. I didn't remember waking and opening them. It was as if time had simply started in that moment. I lay on a gurney being wheeled into one of the larger rooms next door.

"Yeah, I feel okay," I said. "What's going on?"

"Chuck was walking in the room to give that guy his papers, and he said you just passed out right there in front of him. He just barely caught you. He called for help, and then you started having a seizure in front of us both."

I sighed. "Oh, fuck."

Dr. Calicchio walked up to the bed as Erin explained everything to me. "Has this ever happened before?" she asked.

"I have had a seizure before, but only when I got extremely tired."

"Well, I think we should get a CAT scan, nevertheless."

"Look, you guys," I whispered, drawing the two of them nearer. "I really don't want anybody else to know about this. I have a brain tumor. I've had it for years. It's supposedly low-grade. It just does this when I get really, really tired. I was on call last night in the ICU, so I am painfully tired, as you can see. So please, we don't need to get a CAT scan. And I really hope you won't tell anyone."

"Don't worry," Calicchio said. "We won't tell anyone. But I think that, since something new happened, we should just get the picture to be safe."

I gave in and let them put the IV in me. They closed a curtain around my bed so that passing doctors and nurses who hadn't seen what happened would remain unaware. I was granted the benefit of getting a scan within fifteen minutes, which was unheard of.

I had regained most of my senses. The muscles in my right arm and right leg felt like I had climbed a mountain with a refrigerator on one shoulder. The joints in my elbow and knee creaked almost audibly, like those of a seventy-year-old man.

I got off the gurney and tucked my shirt back into my scrubs.

Calicchio came into the room, wiping some imaginary sweat off his forehead. "The radiologist said he didn't see anything at all on your scan."

I had no misconception that my DNET had mysteriously healed itself. Rather, I worried that some patients I had sent home, thinking their brains were normal, had tumors that our Bridgeport radiologist had missed.

"No, it's there," I said. "I'll show you." I walked him over to the same computer I had sat at as the doctor an hour before. "It's right in here." I pointed to the subtle clump of brain folded within the many normal clumps of brain.

"Well, at least we know you're not bleeding in there," he said. "I can have Chuck give you a ride home. He's about to get off shift."

"No, don't bother. I should be back to normal in a half hour or so. I can drive myself home then."

"You know I shouldn't let you do that."

"Don't worry. I'll be fine. And remember, I can't let anyone find out about this."

"All right. You be careful."

I thought about calling Tara before I drove home but decided to prevent any worry during my drive, under the false assumption, of course, that she would have even let me drive. I also wanted to postpone the lecture I would receive until I got home.

The next few days, I had no shifts scheduled and was able to fortify myself with some much-needed rest. It was interesting that I would wake up after a certain number of hours and was unable to fall back asleep despite still being exhausted. It was like trying to quench the thirst of being in the desert for a week with one large gulp. But after the second day, I was able to move around and actually complete some of the neglected errands. After seeing to the food shortage in the house, I ventured down to the faculty office at the hospital. Due to the intense schedule of the MICU, I had postponed talking to Dr. Lathem about something I was very excited by, and I also wanted to see what had become of the anatomy lab.

When I got to the office and approached the desk of Lathem's secretary, she looked up. "Oh, hey, Jeff. What are you up to today?"

"Not too much. I had a couple days off from Bridgeport, and I thought I would come talk to Dr. Lathem. I've been wanting to talk with him about a cool research project I came up with."

"I'm sorry, he's not in today. He's been working on a number of things lately. I'll tell him you stopped by, though."

"Oh, shoot." I paused. "I guess that will have to do."

At just that moment, the door to Lathem's office opened about twenty feet down the hall.

"Hey, Dr. Lathem!" I said loudly to him. "I was hoping you would be in today."

"I wasn't planning on it," he said, "but I had to come in to get some last-minute work done here in the office. There's a big meeting of department heads coming up, and I have to make a presentation. But I'm glad I ran into you. I was hoping to talk to you about something. Why don't you come in for a minute?"

I was excited by his words. I figured that he had arranged the anatomy course on my behalf and wanted to tell me first. Maybe he was going to ask me to teach the medical students. Maybe he would make it an entire elective. I walked into his office, already disregarding the fact that he had faked being out of the office to avoid the residents.

"Have a seat," he said, backing down into his own.

"Okay. But before you tell me about your news, I wanted to bring something new to your attention. A couple months ago, when I was doing the rotation through anesthesia, I came up with an idea that one of the attendings thought was great. I drew up a schematic and wrote a design plan for a digital laryngoscope."

"A digital laryngoscope?"

"Yes, and the chief of anesthesia thought it sounded awesome. This takes the problems that we have with difficult intubations and fixes them completely. Now, some people are using fiber-optics to do the same kind of thing. But that is really awkward, and you have to have special training. To use my scope, you only use the same skills that you already have to put the scope in the patient's mouth. Then, using essentially the same technology as is in your digital camera, it puts the image on a screen about the size of your cell phone. It's perfect, and everyone will be able to use it."

He leaned forward slightly to look at the drawings I had laid on the desk in front of him. "Hmmm. That's not bad. But there must already be something like this, don't you think?"

"When I showed the anesthesia attending, he helped me look up the patents, and we couldn't find anything. He said he would be willing to supervise me in putting the patent application together. I was hoping to make this my research project for the residency requirement."

"Oh," he said abruptly. "I'll have to think about that for a bit." He almost groaned as he said it.

I was perplexed by his response. I had expected him to be elated by such an original idea that would almost certainly make millions. And I knew that anything I produced while I was at Yale would almost certainly get the Yale name on it instead of mine. But that was not as important to me as getting the help to put the project together.

"And, like I said, the chair of anesthesia said that he would supervise—"

"Yeah, you know, after thinking about it, I really don't think you should be able to do this for your research project. You wouldn't be able to get the patent in the four years you're going to be here. Also, you need to get an attending in *this* department to supervise you, not anesthesia. Why don't you talk to Dr. Rogers? She could use you on her breast cancer research project."

He had interrupted me, and I found myself unable to breathe for several seconds. I was stunned to have been turned down so frankly— and for a breast cancer study. Who the fuck comes to the emergency department with their breast cancer? And what the fuck were we doing with a research project on the damn thing? It was not that I was not a fan of breasts, but I certainly had not entered my field expecting to research cancer of them.

"Um. Okay…" I stuttered. "I guess you wanted to talk to me about…the…um, anatomy lab. How did the discussion with the anatomy director go?" It took me half of the sentence to gain my bearings and speak coherently.

"What? Oh, no. That's not what I wanted to talk with you about," he said, quickly shuffling the words under his breath. "I don't know what happened with that. I never got a call from the professor like you said I would. I wanted to talk to you because I received word that they were disappointed with your performance in the ICU."

An arctic sensation swept through my body. I didn't twitch as he spoke.

"What?" I asked with genuine surprise and concern. "What do you mean, they were disappointed?" My hands went numb as I wondered if they had caught me having my seizure and I was going to be put on some sort of disability leave or handicapped duty.

"The attending said that there were times when you did not know relevant data about your patients when asked. I asked Dr. Gerber about it, and she said that there were a few times that this happened." He gazed at me with his hands folded on the desk.

The mood in the room had changed vastly in just a few seconds. I was honestly shocked. "Dr. Lathem, I had eleven patients most of the time," I protested, my voice filled with dismay. "Anytime I didn't know the data about a patient, I just looked it up on my notes. I don't think that should be considered a deficiency. I had twice as many patients as anyone in that ICU!" My red blood cells exploded successively inside my veins as I thought about Gerber not covering for me when she was asked.

"The attending said that you sometimes questioned her management." The pitch of his voice rose in disbelief.

"Questioned her management? When the hell would I have done that?"

"That's what I was wondering. But when I talked to her, she said you questioned her on ventilator settings."

"Questioned her on ventilator settings?" I exclaimed. "I was trying to learn how to set a damn ventilator. Who should I have questioned? One of the other interns?"

"They even said you behaved inappropriately with one of the nurses."

The accusation was reminiscent of something Ken Starr might have said to Bill Clinton. I wondered what he could be talking about.

"Apparently some nurse said you yelled at her one morning at the end of your rotation."

The nature of the accusation became clear. I closed my eyes in understanding. Having listened to the previous charges that seemed so absurd, I had completely forgotten the charges that would have been so apparent.

"Your attending is concerned that you didn't have sufficient experience to meet the ICU requirement of the hospital after that month," he said sternly.

I realized how bad I was looking in his eyes. I felt like these things being said about me reflected poorly on his department, and he thought his best option was to concede to their accusations. He was plea-bargaining to save his reputation, as I saw it. In the process, I had been labeled as incompetent and uncooperative.

I felt completely alone and abandoned. I needed someone to side with me; I had worked so hard in that ICU. I decided that having Lathem as an ally and a friend was the most important thing I needed right then. I needed him on the inside. And if he only knew what had happened, he would do whatever it took to protect me from these unreasonable claims.

"Look, Dr. Lathem, there's something you have to know," I said softly. "Most of that list she gave you was bullshit. I was just trying to work hard and learn through a rough month. The last thing, though— yelling at the nurse. I did do that one."

"She said you told the nurse that a patient wouldn't die if you did nothing about her hypocalcemia. And that is absolutely not true. People can definitely die of low calcium."

"Actually, what I said was that the patient wouldn't die if she waited five minutes for me to get to it. And that patient's calcium was not so low that it would have killed anybody. But I understand it was inappropriate. I needed her to leave me alone for a little bit. I asked her several times politely to give me a minute, but she just kept after me. I couldn't think straight, and she kept badgering me. You see..." I paused. "I was having a seizure."

"You were doing what?"

"Now, I'm not telling you this because I want you to make special exceptions for me. I just want you to understand that I was doing everything I could to keep control of the situation. I did what was best for the safety of the patient by not making any decisions in the few minutes that I felt ill, then I got back to duty when I felt better."

"Why didn't she realize you were having a seizure?"

"I was just having a partial seizure. I kind of zone out and can't think straight. Then I'm okay after a couple minutes when it happens."

"How long have you had these seizures?" he asked me, now seeming genuinely concerned.

"Since med school, I guess. I found out I had a brain tumor then."

"A brain tumor? Oh, my God. Can they do anything?"

"They think it's a DNET. It's a tumor that doesn't grow, so they don't want to do anything about it. I take medication and haven't had a seizure in over a year. It was just the call every three days, and I had been up all night with a particular patient who got the better of me that night."

"Well, that is all a shame. Should I be worried about this happening again?"

"No. It has never happened in a hospital before this. And I don't have any more three-day call rotations left. You really have nothing to worry about."

"I am afraid you are going to have to do another month of CCU so that they feel comfortable about your abilities."

The thought of substituting a cardiac ICU month to improve my skills in the medical ICU was a joke for two reasons: they were nowhere near equivalent, and I liked the CCU so much more. Call was every fourth day instead of every third, and the number of patients was so much less.

"I see," I replied. "I understand why you have to make me do it, and I don't mind. But I want you to know that I don't think I was performing poorly on that MICU rotation."

He nodded. "I believe you."

~~~

A little over a month later, just after a week's vacation, I returned to work. I was to begin my orthopedic surgery rotation by showing up at one of the nearby shoulder clinics. There was a certain irony in beginning the rotation on this day with this clinic. I showed up to the clinic with a shoulder x-ray in my right hand. It was not standard to bring films for the orthopedic attendings (or orthopods, as we called them) to read. And I wasn't doing it for extra credit. You see, the x-ray was of my shoulder—my left shoulder, to be specific. During the vacation the week before, I had been invited to go snowboarding in Vermont with some of the other residents. The trip would have been pretty enjoyable had I not caught the edge of my board in the ice, fallen forward, and separated my shoulder.

After walking down the black-diamond slope, pulling my snow-board behind me with my scarf as a leash, I got my shoulder filmed at the nearby medic outpost. The x-ray was taken by pulling off my several layers of coats and sweaters and then positioning my arm just so, with excruciating pain at the slightest movement of my shoulder. It clearly showed the far end of my collarbone angled up to the sky and closely approximating my ear. Needless to say, I spent the rest of that day and the following in the lodge with a beer in my hand.

This was an inopportune time to get injured, because Tara and I had been planning on making several home improvements. The first on our list was to re-stain the floors throughout the house. We had begun in one of the guest bedrooms next to the master bedroom by sanding it. I assisted like a puppy with a limp, carrying my left arm in a sling and sanding the boards one-handed, front to back. The "do-it-yourself" spirit of a homeowner bestowed itself upon us as we worked for two days solid. We had just begun to stain the floor the night before but had not anticipated the slow nature of the task. The room was not even half complete when we decided to quit for the night. Since each of us had started relatively easy rotations this month, we could finish the job tomorrow.

So I waited in the orthopod's office, early as I always was. I entertained myself by looking at the patient-education handouts. The secretaries were rummaging around their desks getting prepared for the beginning of the week.

The beep from my waist startled me. It was rare for my pager to go off during these outpatient months. The screen read, *13*. I thought it must have been a typo. Tara and I had a code to call each other, in which *11* meant "Call me when you get a chance," *12* meant there was an important issue and to call the other within five minutes, and *13* was the emergency code. It had never been dialed before. I figured it must have been a typo, or maybe she couldn't find the keys and was late for work.

I called her cell phone. It rang three times before she picked up. "Hello," she said with a jittering voice.

"Tara, what's wrong?"

"Jeff…there was a fire."

"A fire? How could there have been a fire? I was just there and left you asleep!"

"I...I...I just woke up because I smelled something. Then I got out of bed, and there was smoke coming from the guest room. When I opened the door, there were flames coming from the rags we used to dry the stain with last night. The fire was small, so I ran to get a blanket to throw on top of it. But when I came back, it...it had spread to the hall. It completely engulfed the doorway and started coming down the hall. The fire alarm didn't even go off! I ran down the hall and turned around, and there was nothing but flames. I thought I might not make it out. But I went out the front door and called 911 from my cell phone in the car."

I had already started running out the clinic and to my car. "Oh, Jesus, dear, are you okay? Did you get hurt?"

"No, not hurt. Just shaken up." She shivered as she spoke. "The firemen came really quickly. Their station is apparently right down the hill. They gave me a blanket. I am out here in the cold with just my pajamas. They had to bust all the windows and spray their hose into all the rooms. The whole house is ruined."

"Don't worry. It doesn't matter. We have insurance. It will take care of it. It's only important that *you* are okay right now. Just give me fifteen minutes, and I'll be home."

"Okay, but hurry," she pleaded.

By the time I arrived, all the hoses had been turned off. Firemen in their heavy uniforms were plodding around the soot with their massive boots.

"You are Dr. Triton?" one of the firemen asked from 'his position near the large tree in the front yard.

"Yes, he is," Tara cried as she ran from the neighbor's house.

"Yes, I am," I said. "Thank you for helping us out." I was in shock as I spoke to him. The clear devastation Tara was feeling forced me to wear a strong face.

"It looks like it started in the back guest room," he said. "You were painting there or something?"

"Yes. We were staining the floor back there."

"And there were some rags left out?"

"Yes, I suppose so. I don't really remember, because my arm was in this sling and I wasn't doing as much of the work myself as I would normally."

"Your wife says they were sitting on top of a cardboard box, and that's where they were when she first saw the fire. It sounds like they spontaneously combusted and started the fire. These acetone-containing chemicals are highly flammable and can do this. We recommend never leaving them out for this very reason."

We spent the rest of the day searching through the damage, trying to find anything of sentimental value. Fire inspectors and insurance representatives all wanted the detailed description of the happenings, and I wished I could give it to them. With each discussion, Tara became more distraught and the tears continued to flow. That night we stayed at a local motel down the street, figuring it would give us the best starting point to begin the business of cleaning up in the morning.

The motel bed was like a slab of limestone, and the sheets were like sandpaper over our skin. We lay in silence, at least our own silence, for hours that night. The noise from the cars speeding past the motel on the main thoroughfare slipped through the papier-mâché doors unimpeded. Tara's breathing pattern let me know that she was still awake.

"What are you thinking?" I asked, wondering if she was worrying about what to do next or dwelling on the images from the morning.

"Nothing," she said in a curt voice, still looking straight up at the ceiling.

The tension seemed more than just ambient fear of our situation. I perceived hostility toward me. Did she blame me for the fire? I didn't remember leaving the rags in a pile, although I probably would not have had the wisdom to explicitly avoid it, either.

"Are you all right?"

"No, I'm not fucking all right. I was just in a fire. Of course I am not all right. How do you expect me to be?"

It had always been nights like these where I prayed or questioned or at least considered God. In my life, I had experienced a childhood awareness of Him, active protest against the possibility of Him, a desperate need for Him, and even a cursed hatred for Him. That night, as I lay there in the still tempest and considered how to approach Him, I could not think of any way. If there were a God in existence, no effort to speak to him could be but fruitless, for he had overtly and unmistakably abandoned me. When He had punished me with my mother's death, it was quite simple to hate Him. But as He had watched me lose so much in the last few days, and months even, the emptiness He left me with as He turned his back was much more difficult to address. A word of ferocity would not be heard by a back that was obviously turned to me and was so far away. Nor would a word of apology, it seemed. I said nothing to Him instead.

The next day, Tara's department phoned her and notified her that she could use a dorm room that they reserved for exchange medical students coming from foreign countries. It was about thirty minutes north of where we lived, but it would be free of charge. They also insisted that she take at least two weeks off and more if she needed it. Meanwhile, I maintained my work obligations, which were at least somewhat lightened because of my shoulder injury.

We broke the silence periodically, driving out to the dorm room that next night. The tension still hung between us, as neither of us could or would verbalize exactly what was bothering us. The SUV approached the freeway off-ramp. The city was not completely foreign to me; I had been to the local mall once or twice. But it had a newfound feeling of desolation as we drove up that night. It had been a large industrial city during the first and second world wars. However, when the manufacturing jobs went oversees, the entire city slowly bankrupted. There were at least twenty tall buildings smattering the hillside, some with smokestacks. Most of them had several broken windows on their faces. The dark red bricks had faded, collecting mold and soot over the years. Their color was now an ash gray.

Abundant snow covered the hills and parking lots, although the main roads had been cleared of snow weeks earlier. The sky was a monotone gray, not from the presence of clouds, but rather from the lack of color's inspiration. Even the billboards of local stores were in grayscale as we drove by. Scant pedestrians walked the sidewalks. Dressed in their gray overcoats and heads tucked down into their colorless scarves, they never turned to acknowledge anyone else's presence. The entire scene looked like the Western vision of the communist life in the Soviet Union: people oppressed, deprived of every human luxury, including warmth and color.

When we arrived at the room on the twelfth floor of our communist tower, we mused that the last occupants were Russian exchange students who had left a picture of their adored president, Putin.

Over the next few weeks, the insurance company agreeably negotiated to put us up in an apartment for the time that we were without a house and arranged to have our home rebuilt.

~~~

Psychologists have studied thousands of people and shown that statistically, among life's stressors, buying a house is the most stressful. Up there among the other great ones such as losing a loved one and changing jobs is losing a home to a disaster. Tara and I found ourselves facing this stress just as we had faced the others in the past year. We bottled it up, refused to admit it, and certainly refused to discuss it. We sat in front of the television in the apartment with our makeshift dinners, even when we were together, and passed the months in silence.

At last, the end of the academic year was approaching. The house was nearing completion, and we had arranged for a week of vacation together in Portugal. There would have been no way that we could afford such a trip, except that Tara's family had a timeshare in the country.

The strain between us had been growing over the past few months. We found incidental things to bicker over: the choice of paint colors for the shutters or what to eat for dinner. The angst reached an almost insurmountable climax as we drove to JFK and took a wrong turn. By the time we reached the airport with a mere one hour to clear security and customs, we were slinging profanities at each other for the first time in our relationship. Even when we had broken up once while dating, we had never cussed at the other. We spent the entire flight in silence. The cold, dry airline chicken was more enjoyable than each other's company.

In the condo, perfectly built and decorated for such a glorious summer as this, we made not a single positive comment to each other. We spent day after day in deck chairs on opposite sides of the pool, our view blocked from the other's face by various magazines. We would not likely have spoken to each other the whole trip had we not been forced to put on an act for her relatives visiting from Ireland. At their request and expense, we traveled to the beach and restaurant which made the area so highly regarded. We walked behind her aunt and uncle, holding hands in a façade of happiness. We watched them as they looked so peaceful ten steps ahead, their pant legs rolled up to their knees.

"Do you think this is worth saving?" Tara asked.

These were perhaps the first words we had uttered that weren't for the express benefit of witnesses. The first words, and I cannot deny that they conveyed the same skepticism and disdain that I felt.

"I'm not sure," I replied.

We were discussing divorce, if this could be considered an actual discussion. We were speaking of divorce, and I couldn't even have told you why we were so angry. That fact alone may have been the source of half my anger. But we continued the evening without further mention of our plans. We feigned a love and appreciation we wished we felt. We ate a dinner that had likely been made by one of the top chefs in the world, and it stood not a chance of tasting good in our state of mind.

The flight home emulated the trip overseas.

Chapter 16

In every story of a long-term struggle to be successful or make right, the hero will hit bottom, or so he thinks. The heroin addict will overdose and almost die, and the white-collar criminal will find himself being investigated by the FBI for conspiracy or insider trading. In each of these cases, our hero thought he was above such things all of his life, only dabbling in the drugs in a fast-paced, high-society world where everyone was doing it, or only getting involved in the dirty deal to make it ahead and impress his superiors. *Something* just went wrong.

As for me, I am not so glamorous as a celebrity living on the edge or as powerful as the businessman. But you have looked into the window of a man living in a house not so different from these cutthroat worlds. No, I had not always wanted to be a doctor, but I had always wanted to be something. Not just something, but *Something*. Somewhere along the way, I got a taste of success with a hint of failure driving me to seek that full-bodied flavor of ultimate success. When I reached that level I had sought for so long, the illusions slowly peeled away. For, like the celebrity or the businessman, my world was not what it seemed from the outside. My friends would call and ask how wonderful Yale must be. My father would list the people to whom he had boasted about his son being an emergency doctor at Yale. In my quest for this power of celebrity or the stature of business, I saw myself losing my home, my wife, and my self.

But I recognized my dilemma, as do the addict and the white-collar criminal. I saw that I would meet with no favor as I tried to achieve superstar status at Yale. I saw that my success would mean egg on the face of those above me and would come with a cost, the collateral of which I could not afford. I resigned myself to simply working hard as a resident and fostering the relationship I had with Tara.

Giving up on this image of fame and notoriety, I resolved to simply fit in, at work and at home. I hoped that by not obsessing over work day in and day out, Tara and I could salvage our marriage. We sought marriage counseling when we returned from Portugal. The gap between us was ultimately closed, however, only when we realized that we were *both* struggling with the same feelings directed against the same foe. Our lives in Connecticut had been filled with disappointment, and after each incident, we found ourselves arguing and somehow blaming each other.

After coming to terms with our joint discouragement and communing over our situation, we began to grow slowly closer. We were soon able to laugh about each trip to a different barbeque restaurant advertising "Voted Best Ribs in CT!" and dining on desiccated plywood covered in an unsavory tomato sauce. We laughed about our New England Ivy League friends who mourned their own poverty as they wore last year's Gucci sunglasses and Prada shoes to their summer home for the week.

As our outlook started getting a little better, we actually looked forward to the hour of television we watched together most nights. What was previously a wasted moment in front of the TV was now a stolen moment relating to drama we both enjoyed. We began going to a local church that Tara had found. She had gone a few times when I was stuck in the hospital on Sundays in the past, but only now had I agreed to go, too. The church was a cute little white building in the middle of a small town square. The steeple reached high from the single room of the church, and the bell rang right before the sermon started, usually just before we walked in.

The chemistry of churches is interesting and unique, almost like relationships. There are several parts to each, and the casual observer can often pick out the flawed components. For example, when the voluptuous blonde walks down the street with the older, homely gentleman, we are often quick to perceive the asymmetry and draw conclusions. The minister at this church was a dynamic speaker who was able to relate his sermons to the woes of the day or even to his individual church members. The members of the church were also friendly and dedicated, making sincere efforts to say hello on each day we attended.

The church choir, however, was a collection of about eight senior citizens whose hearing aids had exceeded warranty years ago. As the organist played the introduction, the parishioners rose up, one at a time, in random order. No one seemed to want to be the first or last one to stand. But they also seemed to fear standing at the same time as anyone near them, as though it were a childhood superstition akin to stepping on a crack in the sidewalk. The choir included two women pushing their eighth or ninth decade of life, each of whom thought that they were, or at least should be, the soloist of the group. And with every song, their voices rang out louder than the rest of the group, and with total disregard for tone or pitch. Their vibrato was operatic and made them clash with the other members serially throughout the songs. As we watched them sing, no less than four times in each sermon, it was difficult not to wonder if they actually thought they were talented. But as the weeks passed, we more often wondered if someone had died when one of the enfeebled members did not show up.

By now, I had come to appreciate anything that appeared to give Tara strength. We were doing so much better together, and although we rarely spoke of it, I know her faith was a strong factor. While I personally found the sermons interesting, I looked inward for the strength to get through the stress rather than upward.

I was currently on the surgical ICU rotation (SICU), which, like the cardiac ICU, only required me to stay overnight every fourth day. It required a great deal of work, as did many rotations, but like the trauma rotation during my first year at Yale, the worst part of working in the surgical ICU was dealing with surgeons. It seemed that Dr. Koker, the trauma attending, had been promoted to director of the SICU after only one year at Yale. It baffled me that he still had not come up with a more socially acceptable way of greeting me each morning than actually putting me in a headlock. It is difficult to take pride in ones work in the midst of shouting and degrading comments, all of which Koker was notorious for. But it is near impossible when one is dragged around the SICU with his head bound in the armpit of a 5'4" surgeon with a Napoleon complex.

The team consisted of Dr. Koker, me as the ER resident, two anesthesia residents, and a surgery resident. The anesthesia residents were a year ahead of Tara, who now worked in their department, but they already knew of her. They seemed to have reached the same state of Zen as I had and realized that there was nothing we could do to turn surgeons into real people. So we all put up with the monsters and provided each other with support and solace.

Two SICU fellows had each graduated from residencies in other countries, Brazil and Argentina. My assumption was that Yale had searched the far reaches of the globe to get the best and most promising applicants to run the ICU. These two had not been in the Yale system long enough to be corrupted by the sinister malignancy that is Yale, and so they were still relatively friendly.

The rotation had actually progressed well. I was three weeks into it and still had not had a day with more than five patients at a time. Granted, these patients were sick enough to have tubes coming out every orifice of their body, some of which they hadn't even been born with. I was on call this particular Thursday, which was a blessing of blessings because I could plan on having most of Friday, Saturday, and Sunday off. Yale had become hypervigilant about enforcing rules of going home early after call once the program had been threatened with closure for several violations.

I was pretty confident going into the day, because Mr. Chen was the only patient who would stay in the SICU. My other two patients were to be transferred to the standard surgical floor.

Mr. Chen was a sixty-something man who suffered from severe heart failure. He had been brought into the hospital this time for a coronary artery bypass graft, or "cabbage," as it is known. He was seven days out from the operation, and his heart had been functioning extremely poorly. It had taken several days to get him to breathe on his own after the surgery and to take him off the ventilator. Now he lay in his bed with his head raised to a 45-degree angle, just to let gravity help the fluid get out of his lungs. His face was puffy, and his body equally swollen. The entire picture reminded me of my mother as I watched him day after day, struggling with each breath. So much had been done for this man, and each heroic procedure had bought him only one day to a few weeks more.

Mr. Chen's daughter was a pharmacist in Yale Hospital and would come visit him on a daily basis. She would sit by his bed reading to him from a small book that appeared to be the New Testament in Chinese. Not once did he turn his head or open his eyes, but she continued to come to his side to read. She and I had formed a strong bond when he was on the ventilator and she had constantly asked me why he couldn't breathe on his own. I knew that her education as a pharmacist was strong enough to understand even without my explanation of why he was doing so poorly. Nevertheless, I always offered her my best and most gentle explanation of what was going on. There is something in the relationship of a parent and child that allows knowledge and understanding to be superseded by fear and hope simultaneously. I had sat by this same bed, years before, with this same hope.

When he was finally able to breathe on his own, I had called her up from work to be there. And after we removed the tube from his airway, he successfully breathed on his own for several days. His heart was holding on to life by a thread, and this was discussed regularly on rounds. We knew on Thursday morning that Mr. Chen's heart was failing again, and the fluid was backing up into the lungs faster than the heart could pump it out. The decision would have to be made as to whether to intubate him again if he stopped breathing or simply let him pass away at that time. The decision would ultimately lie with the daughter, but the collective sentiment was that his chances of ever coming off the vent would be zero.

I called her office down on the second floor after rounds. "Ms. Chen? I'd like you to come up to talk in the ICU when you get a chance."

She came up immediately, and I remembered how completely the failing health of a loved one consumes your time as well as your stamina.

"Dr. Triton, is everything okay?" She was a slim Chinese girl with a heavy accent. We had never discussed how long she had been in the country or where she had gone to school. She was obviously glad to be working at Yale, at least for the benefit of having her father in the hospital nearby.

"Everything is about the same, but we are starting to worry," I said, sitting her down in the chair outside her father's room. Inside, her father continued to labor with each breath, occasionally pausing for several seconds and then sighing with a single deep breath.

"What are you worrying about?"

"You know your father has had many heart attacks, and the operation he had is just not allowing his heart to function as much as everyone hoped." I paused, watching her face for understanding and the strength to hear more. "He is still in serious heart failure, and there is a very likely chance that he will need the tube put back in to breathe for him."

"Oh, no. He's going to need it again?"

"Yes," I said. "But that is what I wanted to talk to you about. You see, his heart is so bad that we don't think it can get better. And if we put the tube in his lungs, we don't think we will ever be able to take it out without him dying."

She gave a soft sob before any tears showed in her eyes. I remembered the feeling of that sob myself.

"I know you want to take care of your father, and that's why I wanted to ask you. Right now, we have your father listed as a 'full code,' which means that if he stops breathing, we will put the tube in his throat, and if his heart stops, we will shock it to make it start again. And even after all that, his heart is still going to be dying, just like it is now. It would likely only give him a few more days of life after doing all of those things to his body. I wanted to give you the choice of withholding those treatments and simply letting him go peacefully."

"You mean you would just let him die?" She looked up at me, her eyes twice as big as usual.

"He is already dying, Ms. Chen. I'm sorry, but there is nothing else I can do for him to prevent that. We have tried every medicine and surgery we could. But he is dying. Now I want to give you a chance to choose whether to let him go smoothly now or let him go after we have put a tube in his throat and shocked him." At times, I felt guilty about the subtle manipulation we, as physicians, used to promote our own viewpoint, generally based on our clinical experience.

She shook her head sadly. "I don't know. What would you do, Dr. Triton?"

I leaned toward her. "I want to tell you a secret, and that is, I had to do this for my own mother just a couple years ago. She was very sick with sepsis and had to have many operations to try to get rid of it. But none were successful. The doctor explained that the infection was getting too bad and that her heart might stop." I spoke in a whisper. "I looked at all she had been through and saw that her time had come. So I chose to let her go when her heart stopped."

As Ms. Chen looked up at me again, I saw that tears had gathered on her cheeks. "Is there anything we can do?"

"The best thing you can do is be by his bedside and make sure you tell him that you love him," I said, stepping back. "Nothing else is as important."

She wiped the droplets from her face and sniffed. She looked back into the room where the oxygen mask sat over his mouth and nose, blowing a brisk breeze up through his hair. I looked up at the monitor, which showed that his oxygen level was continuing to drop at a slow but steady pace.

She turned back around. "Okay…I will sign the paper."

I nodded. "I think that's the best thing for him, and I think that is what he would want. I promise I will call you if anything starts to happen."

The night was rather quiet, although I was careful not to violate resident superstition by saying so. I had admitted only one patient during the day, and there had been very little excitement going on around the ICU. It was quiet enough that I did not mind that the SICU fellow had left for the night to moonlight at the local VA hospital to make a little extra cash. Officially, a fellow was supposed to be on the ICU floor at all times to assist with any emergencies; ours was kind enough at least to wear his pager while he worked two blocks away at the VA.

At about 9:00 that night, I got a call from one of the rural hospitals an hour north of New Haven. Apparently the patient they were calling about had suffered a severe car accident a few days earlier that had ripped out his diaphragm and left him with no abdominal muscles. The surgeons at the rural hospital did not believe that they had the facilities to perform the surgery to correct this and stated that Dr. Koker had agreed to perform the surgery tomorrow. They were planning to send the patient by ambulance tonight.

The first image that came to mind was what a patient with no abdomen or diaphragm would look like. The second thought was how late I was likely to be awake just waiting for the patient to arrive. I gave the okay to send the patient, then called my fellow, who apparently had not been made aware of the scheduled surgery, either. He told me to page Koker to confirm everything, but after three tries, there was still no reply. I decided just to treat the situation as I would any other admission and deal with it when it came.

I strolled around the circular floor of the ICU. Unlike the MICU, whose lights remained bright 24/7, the lights dimmed every night around 8:00 in the SICU. It was largely for show, as the same percentage of the patients were heavily sedated and could have slept midday in the Sahara with gale-force winds. But I appreciated the effect, as it made things feel calmer.

Mr. Chen's oxygen monitor had continued to fall, but even more worrisome was that his heart rate had begun to fall as well. This suggested that his heart was starting to give up the battle. I personally did not know whether the end would last ten minutes or ten hours, but I saw it coming. I called Ms. Chen on the cell-phone number that she had given me.

"Hello," she answered in a polite and surprisingly sprightly voice, for nearly 10:00 at night. Before I spoke, I couldn't help but reflect on the call I had received that Saturday morning while I was in bed.

"Ms. Chen, this is Dr. Triton. I am calling you because I think your father is starting to get worse, and I think you should come in to be with him. Is there anyone who can bring you to the hospital?"

"No, it's just me. But I am coming in right now." The *click* of the phone and the emptiness on the line was haunting, as it left me alone with this dying man and his daughter's sorrow pressed to my ear.

She arrived in less than twenty minutes and was next to his bed before I was aware. I noticed her kneeling beside his bed as I paced the floor, looking at the patients' vital signs. The small, brown, leather-bound book was closed in her right hand, her head reposed at his feet, she repeated the same words over and over. I never learned what they meant, but the sound of her words whispered as poetry remains with me to this day. I wondered if I would see a prayer answered that night.

Meanwhile, the transferred patient was being pushed in by the EMTs. They were chuckling over each other's fantasy-football prospects as the gurney clanged against door handles. One EMT, in charge of the ventilator, was an overtly obese man who could hardly keep up with the other. The ventilator tubing was taut and the patient's head was angled back, almost looking straight behind him. I ran over and took over for the technician, who looked more grateful than ashamed.

We entered the room and began to get everything set up. The ventilator he was attached to looked like those I had seen in the black-and-white photos of surgeries conducted in large auditoriums in the 1920s. It was a simple box with a single switch labeled *ON/OFF*. A knob could be turned to adjust the pressure in the lungs, and the only corresponding gauge showed a dial moving from white to red. The entire setup seemed antique, in the way that a rusting Chevy Nova on a front lawn in southern Mississippi is antique.

The three of us lifted him over onto the bed. I left to call the fellow. He was slow to answer my page, but after several tries I reached him.

"Jorge, I'm calling you because this guy looks like shit," I said immediately, before he even identified himself. "The only thing he has for an abdominal wall is some gauze and some surgical tape. Why the hell did Koker agree to cut on this guy?"

"Koker figures he has nothing to lose. But wait—I'm getting hammered over here right now and can't talk much. Is there anything specific that you need?"

Someone who knows what the fuck to do with this guy, I thought. "The equipment he came over on was ancient," I said. "It only had a setting for pressure. How should I get him set up on our vents?"

"Just do the standard stuff for his size and weight. He'll be fine." He sounded rushed. "Anything else?"

"No, I guess not."

The *click* beat me to my last word.

By contrast, the ventilators in the SICU had the computerized monitors for pressure, volume, and moisture. We could adjust almost any and every variable involved in a patient's breathing. I could have probably adjusted his breathing pattern to coincide with that of Pavarotti singing *La Traviata* if I wanted. But I had always been partial to Puccini over Verdi. Instead, I placed him on the settings that corresponded to ninety percent of the patients in the ICU and left it at that.

As I left the room, my attention was drawn to the red light flashing over Mr. Chen's room. Usually this would be accompanied by fairly loud and obnoxious ringing, but this had been disabled after his daughter signed the "Do not resuscitate" paperwork. I peered through the window and saw that his blood was only carrying fifty percent of the oxygen that it was supposed to. He was dying.

I felt myself choke up. Even my hope had been rekindled when I had seen Ms. Chen praying with her father earlier. As I walked toward the room on the far side of the floor, she came running out of it.

"Please, he's dying!" She grasped my shoulders with both hands. "You have to do something!"

Her words were quivering with each sob. I could read every painful thought in her mind by her face alone.

"Ms. Chen, we knew this was coming," I said gently. "We talked about it before. You said you didn't want him to go through extra pain."

"We can put the tube in to help him breathe. Let's just do that."

"I can do that if you really want to, but it will only help for a little while." Again, I found myself whispering to her. My hand was on her shoulder now. "I think you should go be with him."

"Is there anything I can do?" she asked.

"Just make sure the last thing you say to him is 'I love you.' That will be the most important thing when he goes. I promise you." I silently questioned myself as I sent her to be with him.

She crept back into the room.

Thirty minutes later, the oxygen saturation had drifted down to zero, and the heart tracing was completely flat. There were no bells or whistles, no hustling around his bed to push his daughter away and thrust needles into his chest. When the line went flat, she merely kissed his cheek. She sat there in complete silence for fifteen minutes, her head across his chest. She said no more prayers—aloud, at least.

After that, she walked peacefully out of the room. She was still taciturn as she stepped toward me. She did not look up as she approached but kept her head tucked down. When she reached me, neither one of us said a word as she hugged me. I considered what to say, but nothing came to me. I wanted to calm her, to ease her pain. I wanted to convince her that her father had gone peacefully, that she had made the right decision. But still, I said nothing. As her arms released, she spoke in a meek soprano voice, "Thank you." Then she walked out of the ICU with her head still down.

It is perhaps the most powerful gesture of bonding and the starkest reminder that we are alive to be privy to another's pain and sorrow. I don't mean the type of pain one gets with their arthritis, as any Joe on the street will speak ad nauseam about his endless suffering from rheumatism. But when someone is truly suffering from loss, it is rare to see inside their soul. There are a million emotions which cave in on you at once, and when they subsequently lift from your shoulders, you are left with a feeling of vitality that is not easily matched. That is what I felt that night I spent with the Chens.

It continued to be a rare night, in that I got to sleep shortly thereafter. I slept through the night, no less. I awoke to the alarm setting on my pager, reflexively scrambling to see who the fuck was waking me up this time.

When Koker and the rest of the crew arrived to round, he greeted me with the customary headlock and noogie. The post-call noogies were always the favorite, leaving my hair in an awkward state of disarray, with the help of stress-induced oils as pomade.

"Anything happen last night?" he asked as I straightened my black T-shirt, tucking it into my scrub pants.

"Mr. Chen passed away last night."

"Hm." (Notice that this is not the traditional 'hmmm' that might denote reflection or concern. His "hm" was just one short syllable. I suspect his meager response was more impressive even than his actual empathy.)

"And that guy you had sent in from BFE to reconstruct his abdomen and diaphragm came late last night."

"Good. How is he doing?" Koker asked.

"He's fine. The vent he came in with was archaic. It only had a pressure-controlled setting. I don't know what they were doing with him out in the boonies."

"What did *you* put him on?" he said with a scowl.

"I put him on AC, thirty-five percent oxygen, rate of sixteen and five of peep," I said, starting to feel more insecure as his scowl grew with each word passing from my mouth.

"Goddammit, Triton, are you some kind of fucking retard? Should I be carrying around a towel to wipe up your fucking drool? Or maybe we should get you a little white helmet with a strap so you can walk around here like the other 'tards. You used the assist/control setting on this patient? Don't you know when you're supposed to use pressure-fucking-controlled ventilation?"

"I thought you were supposed to use it only when someone had severe pulmonary hypertension and acute lung injury." I tried to quote from the emergency textbooks I had read.

"You thought. You thought? I don't want to know what you thought! If you don't know, you should have asked! Why didn't you ask Jorge?"

Jorge had been completely silent during my scolding. I knew that if he were caught, it would mean stern disciplinary action against him. Not termination, mind you. I had come to learn that Yale was hard up for workers who would put up with the kind of ridicule they took, the long hours they suffered, and the low pay. He would probably have been forced to give up the moonlighting position and do extra menial labor around the hospital. I also knew he was doing it to support the family he had brought from South America, so I was not eager to point my finger at him.

"I just thought I knew—"

"Jesus Christ, Triton! There you go thinking again. If I catch another thought coming out of your mouth, I'm going to take a scalpel and cut your gonads off and stick them in your mouth to plug up that thought spout of yours!"

In retrospect, his words seem somewhat humorous. But he yelled with sincerity. And no one on the team would dare laugh for fear of being his next target.

"Jorge, tell him what the other situation requiring pressure-controlled ventilation is."

Jorge's head was humbly bowed, not knowing if I would rat him out. "When the patient has no diaphragm or stomach wall," he said quietly.

"When a patient has no diaphragm or stomach wall," Koker echoed firmly.

What textbook he expected me to find that trivia in was beyond me. I was more than slightly resentful of Jorge for not coming forward and confessing his absence, but I still kept his secret, as he was one of the few people of seniority who were friendly toward me.

After rounds, he approached me and said, "Thanks for not saying anything to Koker. And don't worry about the patient; it's not that big of a deal."

"Not that big of a deal? I never have to be worried about constipation again—Koker ripped me so many new assholes there!"

"He just makes a big deal because he can. The patient is no worse off. He's still going to die on the table."

"Why do we put up with this shit?" I asked. "I came here because I wanted to do something impressive. I wanted to learn more than I could at an ordinary hospital. I wanted to be a part of a great team. I thought it would be better to be from Yale. Instead, I just take shit from everybody who thinks they deserve to be at Yale more than I do. I get stepped on by anyone above me who thinks that my hiccup challenges their authority."

"I know what you mean," he said. "You really have to lay under the radar to survive around here. It's pretty random who gets picked to be the golden child in each department or class. But if you aren't that person, you're better off not being noticed at all."

I shook my head, infuriated. "That is just fucked up beyond recognition."

"You were right about one thing though, in a manner of speaking." He stopped me before we parted. "It is better to be from Yale. That is, it's better to be *from* Yale than *at* Yale."

~~~

I had made it to the winter of my second year at Yale. An entire year after the month of death in the MICU, I had not had another seizure since the public one in Bridgeport. Amazingly, news and rumors had not propagated after the event. The story had made its way to the director of Bridgeport's emergency room, who showed some sympathy and understanding, but I was never confronted by any of the other residents or Lathem regarding the event. I had been performing well academically, scoring at the top of my class on all examinations. So, for the most part, I thought I had slipped back under the radar, which is where I decided I wanted to be.

This month, I had been working in the pediatric emergency room at Yale. In many hospitals, the children are treated in the same room as the adults, but in an institution with such self-congratulatory pride as Yale, this would be unconscionable. However, the situation resulted in a turf war, as was so common at Yale. In this case, the war was between pediatrics and emergency medicine over who was more qualified to treat these children. The pediatricians thought their education made them better suited to treat these children who happened to be having an emergency, whereas the ED docs thought they were better trained to deal with these emergent situations that happened to involve tiny, wiggly people. Much like French diplomacy, the ED threw up their hands and a white flag at the first sign of conflict with other departments, and our residents were treated as visiting doctors in this room directly adjacent to the ER proper.

The disparate background of the residents did not, in itself, create an atmosphere of alienation. In fact, the nurses were happy to work with residents who had been humbled by years of being shat on by other departments. The attendings were more patronizing than insulting, as the surgeons generally were. The average day was spent evaluating babies with fevers and treating kids with broken bones. It is impressive to see, really, how resilient children are. Of all the children I saw and treated, ninety percent would have probably gotten better all by themselves. Often our treatment was just for the anxious parents.

This was an interesting month, not so much for the cases I saw or the facts I learned, but for the relationships that I formed. "Relationships" is perhaps too respectful a label. "Affectionate conspiracies," I think, is a more applicable term. During this month, it became widely known that the surgical resident who had recently broken up with a close friend of mine was now dating another emergency resident. The obvious scandal was that there was likely more temporal overlap than had been openly declared. Residents dating nurses, attendings fooling around with nurses and/or residents, these things were nothing new.

By far, the most important conspiracy to be revealed was between the pediatric emergency fellow and Dr. Gerber, the ER resident who had worked with me in the MICU. Dr. Gerber had been elevated to the level of chief resident in the ER since then. This was an elected position achieved by vote, wherein the faculty each get a vote and the residents collectively get one vote, which can be easily overturned if the residents are deemed to be misguided in their selection. The principal qualification for chief resident was thus a tremendous skill in the art of ass-kissing. A willingness to give the buttock a peck like your mom would on your cheek was not nearly sufficient. A breathtaking enthusiasm as seen in *Gone With the Wind* had to be demonstrated when establishing this romantic relationship with the faculty's collective sphincter. It was unclear to me whether Gerber had achieved this position by portraying me as an incompetent fool, but it certainly wasn't for supporting her intern when he needed help or when such claims of incompetence were made by MICU faculty.

I will call the fellow she was seeing Book, because he had the distinct appearance of one who had spent his childhood as a lanky bookworm getting teased on the playground. He had failed to outgrow the crew cut his mother had given him weekly with her barber shears, and his blonde hair made him look bald. After surely suffering years of being called names like "dork" and "nerd" and likely avoiding most social interaction, he had made it into medical school, where at least no one would begrudge his study habits. Somewhere along the way, his belly had grown a bit rounder and his glasses a bit thicker, and he had developed a little confidence when he gained favor with some pediatric attending. Like the nerd that becomes a prison guard and gets a baton, he treasured the opportunity to make others' lives miserable—especially those who in any way resembled the kids who had teased him as a child.

With Gerber's new title of chief resident, she spent much more time with Lathem. Rumors of her active role in defaming me in the MICU had made it to a friend of mine in the residency. Lathem and Gerber's dislike and mistrust of me was self-propagating. Now with her dating Book, targeting me became a sexually transmitted disease.

Every night he was on duty, I tried to avoid him, but he made my every move his responsibility to oversee. The abbreviations I used or my description of a wound were common targets of criticism by Master Book. This is not to say that I didn't make mistakes; all residents make mistakes, and some can actually affect the patients. Actually, I made more mistakes working with Book because I was consistently worrying whether he would scold me about some minor incident.

This was the tone of much of the pediatric ER rotation. It was fast-paced, and I saw many kids with minor infections or injuries.

It was the third week of the block, and my shift started at 7:00 at night. The traffic jam on the Connecticut freeway even looked appealing as I passed it going the opposite direction. The sun was just about to set, and nurses from various departments passed by me, walking to the parking structure. When I finally walked into the peds ER, my jaw tightened and my teeth gnashed slightly when I saw that Book was on this Wednesday evening. The attending to start the night was a sweet young lady who had a reputation for having a gentle touch with the children and the residents. I would see little of her with Book on, though.

It was unusually busy for a Wednesday night in the winter. Few organized sports were under way at the time, but somehow kids in the area were finding new and unusual ways to break arms and legs. There was always an assortment of parents bringing their toddlers in for fevers, mothers thinking this sore throat was strep because the last one was, and the always-regarded "My baby has diarrhea." I tried to move quickly, seeing as many as I could, figuring that the more I saw, the less time Book would have to prod me. I jumped in and out of rooms within five to ten minutes after asking all the pertinent questions and feeling the pertinent spots, then ordered the x-ray for whatever arm or leg the child had injured. From there, it became habit: call radiology, get results, call orthopedics, let them handle it.

But when things become routine and mundane, mistakes slip through the cracks. The patient was a seven-year-old girl who had broken her leg ice-skating. She looked much like the girl before her who had broken her arm in the driveway, and more like the girl after her, who had fallen off her bike.

"Triton, did you check the x-ray on room 5?" Book said to me, passing me on the crowded ER floor.

"Yeah. It's broken. I called ortho already. They're on their way down."

"Displaced or nondisplaced?"

"Non," I said, walking in to get started on the next patient.

Five minutes into the next patient interview, the curtain behind be swung open abruptly.

"Dr. Triton, can I talk to you for a second?" Book said with a disposition that feigned professionalism but mimicked the disgruntled mother calling her son "mister."

"You told me that the leg in room 5 was nondisplaced!" he growled sternly at me through his wire-rimmed bulletproof glasses.

I thought back to the radiology room that I had rushed in and out of at least fifteen times over the course of fifteen minutes, usually to find out that the x-ray had not been read yet. I realized that when I finally got the news that her leg was broken, it had quickly triggered my call to ortho when I had only personally looked at one of the three pictures of the leg.

"Oh, I'm sorry, man," I said, backing up. "I looked at it quickly, and radiology told me it was broken. I didn't pick up the displacement, I guess." My heart was visibly pounding against my chest. I knew I had been careless because either result—displaced or nondisplaced—would result in the ortho call. *Careless.* It is not a word that doctors tolerate well, in others or themselves. "I'm sorry. I will go apologize to ortho and take another look at the films."

After going back to see the films, I couldn't be certain whether I had looked at someone else's x-rays, looked at only one of the x-rays, or what. But it was clearly displaced. Not by a mile, but obviously. The reason didn't matter to me, or to them, for that matter. I spent the rest of the night with my heart pounding like a bass mallet in my throat.

The pace started to mellow later that night. Book had apparently been working most of the afternoon and went home a few hours into my shift. I was still on edge about my mistake and took extra time with each patient, clarifying every symptom, making sure of every vaccine they had gotten or missed. I was like a senior citizen on the freeway.

A boy came in that night whose primary-care doctor had sent him into the ER because he had been experiencing headaches. The doctor was concerned about a brain tumor, and the lethargy of the bureaucratic medical system prevented a quick CAT scan unless the boy went to the ER. He was three years old, and to all observers a normal kid. He had been having headaches and sometimes vomiting for no reason. I spent a great deal of time discussing the possibilities with the mother as well as reassuring her that tumors were very rare, as we waited to get the scan.

By now, only the attending was left to supervise me. As I told her the story, the concern was obvious on her face. She had recently been on a tropical vacation, and I had not had the chance to see her personality in action. By now, there were only two or three patients in the ER, so she and I had the opportunity to discuss tumors in children.

After some time, the child was brought from and then returned to his room, his mom holding his hand each way. I was quick to go see the CAT scan on the computer monitor for myself, not just to prevent my earlier mistake from recurring, but also because I had an interest in brain images for obvious reasons. The radiology resident sat up quickly from her reclining position when I entered the dark room.

"Jesus Christ! I thought it would never slow down," she said, sitting up.

"You're telling me," I breathed. "Can we take a look at the head CT?"

"Sure. Let me pull it up here." She clicked the mouse around. I wondered why I had not gone into this field. The soft chairs and the computers seemed like the perfect environment for a kid who had grown up playing video games.

The screen was black initially. Then, as we looked at slices of the head starting at the very apex of the scalp, the reassuring fluffy look of healthy brain greeted us.

"Everything's looking good," she said as we scrolled down.

Simultaneously, both our brows furrowed when we hit the sixth slide. The stark appearance of a dark and empty spot where there should have been more light and fluffy stuff made us both withdraw for a few seconds. We scrolled down even more. With each screen, we saw that this spot was not just a spot, but a hole. It was a hole in his brain, starting just above his left ear and going down to his jawline. The diagnosis was clear, but neither of us would say it.

"Oh, crap," I said with a sigh.

I walked out to talk to my attending. This was the glioblastoma that I had assumed I had when the neurologist first saw me at Empire in medical school. This was the picture in the textbooks to describe brain tumors, and this was my every fear. I felt so much pain for the mother of this child with every step I took back into the ER. I wanted to be the one to tell the mother what we had found; I wanted to be the one to ensure she received compassion and empathy along with information from her doctor. I feared that the "efficiency" of an ER environment might evoke the same feelings of abandonment and resentment I'd had during that trip with Tara to the neurologist.

When I asked my attending, she replied, "I think I should talk to them, since this is such a serious condition."

We walked into the room together. I stood behind her, much as I had done as a medical student. The mother looked up at my attending with frightened eyes.

"Ma'am, I'm sorry to hear about your son's headaches. I'm the supervising doctor here, and I wanted to come in and talk to you about what we've found on the CAT scan." Her words were soft, and her tone reflected compassion as well as authority. She continued on, explaining exactly what the tumor looked like and why the boy had the headaches.

"Is my son going to die?" the mother pleaded.

This is the question that doctors fear as much as politicians fear questions regarding abortion. It is one step away from telling someone how long they have left to live. The chances are, if you have some reason to ask the question, you are not going to like the answer.

"I have to be honest with you, ma'am. He might. But we can't be sure of that until we do more tests. And you are in a place with some of the best neurologists and cancer specialists in the country. There might be something that they can do to help him. And there are definitely things that they can do for his pain."

I was impressed with the way she spoke plainly to the patient and explained the dire nature of the situation, but she never took away the last piece of hope. The importance of hope is beyond question, and I felt good about the hope that she offered.

We walked out of the room to a nearly empty ER. Neurology had been called and was shuffling out of bed to see the CAT scan.

"Can I talk to you?" I asked my attending.

"Sure." She faced me. She was a small woman with a youthful yet motherly quality about her. In the short time I had worked with her, I felt a bond between us. Though her kind words were directed to everyone and not just to me, I was able to convince myself that she liked me in some capacity.

"I just wanted to tell you that I thought you did a great job discussing the brain tumor with that patient's mother. I have seen it done so poorly by others. And your compassion when you addressed it was really impressive."

"Oh." She tilted her head in apparent surprise. "Thank you. I think empathy is important when we talk to patients."

I was aching inside to tell her. She had shown me that she was a person of feeling. She had spoken gently to me. She seemed, in every regard, different from the rest of the Yale physicians. She seemed like a friend, and I needed a friend. I wanted everyone to be a friend, but she was the first person in whom I had seen character.

"I have actually had personal experience with this," I said. Just saying it brought some relief. I felt the pressure release from my chest as I shared my secret with this new friend.

"What happened?"

"A few years ago, I had a seizure and was diagnosed with a brain tumor. The first neurologist who saw me was extremely curt and unfeeling. He didn't explain things at all. I found myself confused and distressed for a month until I saw a neurosurgeon." I continued to explain things to her as we hunched in the corner by ourselves. When she left at 2:00 in the morning, I was heartbroken to see my new friend go home. Our farewell was unpronounced, but I was left with a childlike anticipation of our next meeting.

I went back into my inconspicuous mode after she left. There were no patients at all, and the new attending entertained herself by discussing careers and department gossip with the pediatric residents. Hoping to seem motivated while not drawing attention, I opened up one of the pediatric dermatology books on the side of the office. The pictures in these books were amazing and told stories of disease without needing to use a single word. I was able to peruse the text uninterrupted until morning broke, and the first three children hoping to miss school showed up at the same time.

Chapter 17

It was a quiet morning in the office. The false claims of warmth from the sunshine outside were exposed by the frost still on the window from the night before. Its light helped to remedy the feeling of loneliness and inferiority of sitting in the waiting room. Seeing the heavy stone frame of the main hospital across the street made me truly feel the mongrel as I sat in the makeshift shanty building reminiscent of the special-education classrooms from junior high.

The walls rattled as the ambulance screamed down the street toward the ER I had been working in five days before. It was that day when the attending approached me with the word that Lathem had called him asking that I be taken off duty to meet with him.

The meeting went something like this: "Yes, I wanted to talk to you about your peds ER rotation. I just spoke to—" Lathem interrupted himself midsentence and pursed his lips for a second. "Actually, how do you feel it went?"

"It went fine. I learned some things here and there. Everyone was pretty nice." I specifically left out my feelings about Book and the one tyrannical attending.

"Because I just got your evaluations, and they were really disappointing."

The same way the impulse to sneeze can be stolen by someone offering a "Bless you" too soon, my inclination even to breathe was stolen from me. I stuttered to ask what he was talking about. I'd had only the one bad night and never another negative word spoken to my face.

"Disappointing?" I asked. "You're kidding, right?"

"No. The director over there said that you were uninterested and irresponsible. She said that you stood by while three patients sat on the board, and did nothing."

I remembered back to that hellish night. The kids' names had been written on the board for no more than a few minutes, and I couldn't see them from where I was reading the dermatology textbook. Only she could see the list from where she was engaging in office gossip.

"I wasn't avoiding work, I was looking something up in a textbook. I came as soon as the patients were brought to my attention," I said, almost trembling as I looked across his desk and saw the multiple-choice circles under the *2* filled in with pencil, reflecting their opinion of me.

"And apparently you lied about some x-rays?"

"Lied? I haven't lied about anything!" I thought about that motherfucker Book, who must have patted himself on the back when he explained that I was untrustworthy and a liar. "I confused one patient with another and made a mistake! How can they say I'm a liar?"

"Didn't anyone give you a sense of how you were doing during the month?"

"Absolutely not. In fact, I asked for feedback three weeks into it, and the director herself said she didn't want to spoil the surprise. Well, that was a great freaking surprise!"

"So it sounds like they had a conference to discuss your performance, and mention was made of your seizure disorder," he said.

I was stunned. I had trusted the wrong person again. I couldn't believe that she would sell me out in a discussion around some committee table over coffee. She had seemed so kind and genuine when she spoke to me. I could almost taste the metallic flavor of blood in my mouth as I thought of the figurative knife in my back. Maybe she was trying to protect me from the defamation of character she was watching. Maybe, but it was difficult to trust anyone at this point.

"When they mentioned the seizures, I guess they started speculating as to whether you were having seizures when all these things were happening."

"I wasn't having any seizures! I haven't had a seizure in over a year. I can't believe this!"

"We have been talking about what to do about your situation, and we aren't quite sure." The mysterious *we* he spoke of was worrisome. "We're going to take you off duty for a while so we can get a neuropsychiatric evaluation and an MRI. After that, we will just have to see."

~~~

I suppose I should be thankful. I had never gotten a medical appointment so quickly before. The nurse called my name and walked me back into the office, where I sat down. The doctor soon entered and began the testing. It wasn't the first time I had undergone the testing. The previous time had come a year earlier, when I had been concerned about my poor memory, forgetting names and details. Just as before, she showed me a series of sentences to correct, puzzles to solve, and words to define. The tests lasted for over two hours, the bulk of which were obvious and easy. I faltered on one of the drawings she showed me. I was supposed to name that stupid little folding armed device with a needle and a pencil I had once used in geometry class to draw a circle. It looked like the sextants the old navigators used to use, but she didn't let me call it that. It wasn't a protractor. It wasn't a compass, or maybe it was. The word sounded right somewhere in my mind, but the rest of my brain discounted it. This was the same fucking picture I couldn't remember the name of last time. This time I actually said "compass," and we continued on, not revealing whether I was right or wrong. The uncertainty of whether my final answer was right haunted me through the rest of the test as she flashed her pictures of random faces. Why couldn't she have just accepted "sextant"? It looked the same as whatever the fuck that was. And why couldn't I think of the name in the first place? Had some remote section of my brain that happened to be in charge of obscure high school mathematical devices been obliterated by my tumor? Oh well, I've never liked math anyway.

The second she pulled out the photographs, I knew I was doomed. She held each of the photographs of people's faces in front of me for three seconds. After about thirty faces, she showed me new pictures with various lighting and shading and asked me to identify the ones I had seen before. There was no doubt in my mind that I had failed this part the last time I took the test, even though I was told my memory was perfectly normal. As before, she flashed the pictures of them. The Asians, the Africans, the Hispanics, the Caucasians. Then she flashed the shadowed pictures. Often there was only a silhouette, maybe a mouth, sometimes eyes, sometimes not. Rarely could I see but a sliver of a nostril to tip me off.

"Yes. No. No. Yes." The shrouding darkness made some look like the Phantom of the Opera.

"No. Yes." Apparently it had never occurred to the inventors of this stupid test that robbers wear ski masks for a reason.

"Yes. Yes. No." After some number of these faces, I became discouraged and soon distracted. I started to find some of the female faces attractive. Even some of the less attractive faces became appealing when the shadowing seemed erotic.

"Yes. Yes. Yes." *Shit, that was three yeses in a row. They wouldn't do that, would they?* I worried that the entire department would decide that I had a horrific memory. Or that I was racist and thought that all Asians looked alike.

Either way, it felt like the enemy forces within Yale were closing in around me. Lathem, the director, may have been against me from the start. Maybe the anesthesia director had forced him to accept me into the program so he could get Tara. I certainly knew Lathem would bend to that kind of pressure. Or maybe my early attempts to change the residency threatened him. The seizures, of course, couldn't be discounted. Was he trying to cover his ass? What about these other rotations? Was I really doing badly, or were the residents above me truly trying to get ahead by making me look bad? And why had I met such resistance with every attempt to create an amazing project?

I realized I had been worrying about the conspiracies for several pictures instead of paying attention to the faces. Whatever was going on, and whether or not there was a conspiracy to get rid of me, I sensed I was in trouble. "No," I said quietly, and she showed the last card.

~~~

Remediation, they called it. My neuropsychological tests had shown that I was "intact." So while they could not, in the strictest sense, say that I was retarded, my department concluded that I was stupid. This remediation program was to be the solution. The label was a tragic misnomer, however. One might expect that extra teaching might be involved to fill in my perceived deficiencies. Instead, the next four months tended more toward parole. I worked only in the emergency room, during the shifts scheduled to have an overabundance of faculty. Those faculty members would then be responsible for directly oversee- ing my work. At the end of each shift, I was to get written evaluations from the doctors I worked with. My work was not much different than before this probation. The patients were just as sick, the shifts were just as long, and the pace was just as fast.

Unfortunately, the difference was in everyone's attitude toward me. There were no more casual conversations in the pause between cases. The mother attending stopped mentioning her children in front of me. The academic attending stopped mentioning his research in front of me. The eccentric attending stopped making his off-color jokes in front of me. But there was no extra teaching in these voids. No tips, pointers, or advice. Nothing.

At the end of each shift, I approached the attendings, who were often in a hurry to get out. I cannot fault a man for wanting to get out of the ER as soon as possible after a long shift. But the often clan- destine appearance of their getaway made me wonder if it was me, particularly, that they were trying to avoid. Most of the time, I caught up with them and reminded them I needed a written evaluation. Night after night, I asked for specific feedback and got vague replies telling me I was "doing fine" or "doing much better." I was confused, because I really hadn't seen much growth in myself over that time and thought that I had been doing equally well before. But no one had paid enough attention to me to notice.

Nevertheless, the four-out-of-fives were being checked off. The oc- casional attending would give an abundance of fives in the evaluations, even though the avoidant behavior was as typical with him as in the others. Quite frequently, the attendings would slip out before I caught up with them, or they would ask to fill out the cards later and turn them in. Such requests cannot easily be denied, since an unenthusiastic attending might throw in a rating of two if I offended him.

I treaded ever so lightly around the attendings, dreading the pos- sibility of being perceived as uninterested. I asked questions at every opportunity and never complained about any amount of scut thrust upon me. But the responses were tantamount to the hesitation of shak- ing the unwashed hand of a man just out of the restroom. They always answered the questions. But just as the man hesitates and looks at his hand sourly before and after the shake, so too the attendings would respond with reluctance.

As much as I tried to impress and befriend them, all my efforts seemed in vain. It was bizarre to me at the time, because making friends had always come easily to me. But now I was like the person with tuberculosis whom everyone worries might expose them to an infection. Some attendings could and possibly did literally hold their breath for the moments they spent in one-on-one conversation with me.

Every day was more lonely, in a room crowded with people. To be friendless in a room full of "friends" left me with the sensation of something stuck in my throat that would not go away, despite the hundreds of times I tried to swallow it down during the walk into work each day. Even without hypothesizing about conspiracies, I felt like the only enemy in a world of paper allies.

I did maintain true friends within the residency. They were residents in my class and a few in years above who were not competing for positions of power. While likely not a direct causal relationship, there was a clear association between one's kinship with me and a lack of ascension to positions of power. Our respective brutal schedules kept us isolated, and they heard of my problems largely through rumor. When we did meet, I was repeatedly briefed about conversations overheard in private and sometimes even public settings, about Lathem's desire or plan to "get rid" of me. Again and again, the plotline seemed akin to Mafia subterfuge. None of my sources had specific information on what he was planning. I was performing relatively well in the ER. They had even "allowed" me to take the nationally standardized emergency medicine exam during this time, and I topped my class and most of the class ahead of me. But I felt far from safe. If a jet-black Lincoln Town Car with tinted windows and personalized plates reading GDFTH_ER had peeled around the corner and began shooting, I would not have been surprised.

Meanwhile, at work the vibes of alienation were being emitted from the nurses, too. Even the younger ones, who had always wanted to make the best of a long work day with a good joke, had become more aloof. My desperation was becoming apparent even to me as I made pathetic efforts to entertain them with some form of humor or another. Sometimes things seemed so hopeless that the jokes were merely to entertain myself, as no one else appeared to be even listening. Now the nurses excluded me from their conversations of bad dates and failed relationships. At one of my lowest moments, I had to interrupt my nurse in the midst of a tirade over a man who had not called her after a first date. "What's wrong with these jerks?" she exclaimed to one of the other nurses. When I tapped her on the shoulder and asked her to draw blood on the patient in room 3 for cultures, she audibly sighed in exasperation and rolled her eyes. With no hope to exert any authority in my current position, I tried to defuse the tension, joking, "It's your enthusiasm that really gets us guys hot, though." She shook her head and went to draw the blood.

I became wistful for the days of Mon Gracia, when friendship was a given, even amongst competitors and frank enemies. I had taken the kindness and charity that they had offered so freely for granted. Their naïveté seemed more like worldly insight and wisdom, now that I was in an environment of harsh isolationism. The jokes we had shared were of chickens crossing roads, but we shared them. I had been different from them in many ways, but never so different that anyone would hesitate to smile. They would have offered their food, their homes, or just a prayer without a second thought. At Yale, nothing was offered to me or anyone. Everything was earned—not through discipline and effort, but through deference and unspoken agreements. What I would have given for an unsolicited prayer then.

What I got instead was a letter stating that I had committed sexual harassment with my joking statement. I was forced to sign the letter, in effect admitting my guilt without being able to face the nurse who was accusing me. If I had been able, I would have asked if she *really* felt offended by my comment. Did she feel that I was making advances or taking advantage of my fictitious power? How could she feel any of this when her conversations about these men were more explicit than anything I had said? But there was no one to speak to. No face to question. Lathem presented me only with the page to sign.

My embarrassment when I explained everything to Tara goes without saying. I feared that her perception of the harassment would foster images of Monica Lewinsky. While she shouted at me, slapping my shoulder with alternating sides of her hand, she did not waste her time being angry with spurious ideas of what had gone on. She chastised me for my stupidity in saying anything that could possibly be misconstrued or held against me. She argued that I knew the department was out to get me, and that jokes of any sort gave Lathem the perfect excuse to fire me. I could only remain silent, as I knew she was right. *Stupid.*

The incident did not result in my termination. I continued on in the emergency department until the end of my probation period. I spent each shift in the crowd of unfriendly faces, worrying about which ones were watching me behind my back. The back of my head seemed to have an amazing ability to detect the radar of others' eyes better than my actual eyes.

As I began a shift one Friday night early in the last month of my second year at Yale, Dr. Lathem pulled me aside to notify me that I had finished my time of probation and passed.

"There was some concern among members of the academic committee about your abilities, however," he said after we had sequestered ourselves in the empty trauma room.

"I see," I replied with as little emotion as I could. My aggravation welled up inside me. I decided not to bring up the strength of the daily evaluations I had gotten over the past three months, because challenging anything had repeatedly gotten me into trouble before.

"I explained to them that you had met all the goals of this probation period, but they just felt something else had to be done." His acting skills rivaled those of a low-budget actor in a made-for-TV movie. The fact that he now said these things to my face made it all the more clear that he had not supported me in this or anything I had done since I had come to Yale. His act was not transparent, however. Something must be clean to be transparent, and he was anything but clean.

I became more livid with each word he spoke. As he put his hand on my shoulder with his makeshift sympathy, I thought back to the identical gesture he had made when I had interviewed two years before, explaining how surprised and disappointed he was that I hadn't gotten into Yale the first time I applied. I began systematically reviewing and questioning the sincerity of every word we had ever exchanged in those few moments.

"In the end, we decided that you should progress to the third year of the residency," he said, "but you won't serve in a supervisory senior role for the first two months in the ER."

Realizing that this would mean two more months of longer shifts and extra work, his verdict didn't even matter to me. What *did* matter was the realization that I would continue to be treated as the bastard child, just as I had been for the past three months. I would be watched like a suspected terrorist. Regardless of my supervisory or subservient role, I would be ostracized and unhappy. I would submit to this because it was my duty and what I needed to do to move on with my life one day. But I couldn't continue to talk to him under the pretense of any respect between us.

"I'm sorry. I really tried to support you," he said.

I had already turned to leave as he spoke. In a voice that hopefully reflected an undertone of repugnancy as much as the obvious discouragement I felt, I softly said, "I'm sure you did."

Once outside the room, I noticed the headache that had almost surely been brewing during the entire conversation. This was more than the low-grade heaviness behind my eyes that I had become used to through my depression the past few months. I disregarded the pain and began my work, hoping that the momentum of a busy Friday night would alleviate the pressure.

Butch was the attending the rest of the night. She was a recent alumnus of the program and had been a chief resident in her final year. While she clearly was not above kissing ass to get ahead and could likely expect to go places in the Yale system, she had actually come back to work at Yale because her wife wouldn't give up her job as local police officer. Butch was a lesbian who had worked as a fireman—or firefighter, if that is the politically correct way to phrase it—before going into medical school. She had met her then-girlfriend at some fireman's ball, and they had been together ever since. Such devotion was nice to see in someone who was an otherwise unpleasant person. It was typical for young attendings to be very cautious and nervous, but Butch took micromanagement to a new standard.

The first wave of patients to come in on such a Friday night were typically those who had been having problems for days and couldn't get a last-minute appointment with their primary doctor before the weekend, so they came into the ER. The tradeoff, as far as they were concerned, was a three-hour wait in the waiting room. Each was genuinely concerned that the three trips to the toilet yesterday, the slightly thick gunk when they coughed, or the two-day hangover that didn't follow a drinking binge were life-threatening conditions. All were fine in the end. And if the wait didn't convince them not to come back the next time they had these simple problems, sometimes the only marginally necessary rectal exam would serve as a more convincing deterrent.

The next wave tended to be the motor-vehicle accidents, a mix of the late commuters and the youngsters going out to party for the night. Tonight the halls were lined with them because there were not enough rooms for each. One, I could tell from across the room, was looking for a payday. She sat up in her bed with a neck brace on, looking around like a parrot. As I walked up to her bed, she began wailing in pain and grabbing the back of her neck. The agility in her neck was much more impressive than her acting skills, but she demanded that x-rays be taken for her lawyer to review. Normally I would have refused, but tonight Butch's head was within a two-inch proximity of mine as she looked over my shoulder, and she agreed to get the x-ray for me. Others had come in complaining of neck pain two days after getting bumped from behind.

"Doc, I got rammed from behind in my car two days ago. I came into the ER, and all they gave me was this Motrin. And it ain't doin' shit for my pain." At least three patients quoted the exact same monologue to me on this particular night. "Doc, I need to get something real for this shit. I'm in pain, man."

Over and over again, people came in for a magic pill that would, with one dose, take away all the pain, stop all the coughing, and solve all their problems. I guess we are all looking for this on some level. And when these people come to the doctor, they expect such magic in the blatantly cryptic signature. Unfortunately, many doctors, including both primary doctors and emergency doctors, don't take the time to create realistic expectations by simply talking.

Another person who came in with the accident crowd was a teenage boy who was driving to a party with his girlfriend. She had made it without a scratch, but he had gotten knocked out by the collision. He was awake by the time he reached the ER, but was being combative with the staff, trying to get out. We planned to get a CAT scan of his head, but the line for that was particularly long because of the number of accidents tonight. He lay strapped to the gurney in his neck brace, trying to convince his girlfriend to undo the bindings. Finally his mother showed up and demanded that if he wanted to go, we should let him go. I wondered how people survived being so stupid as I tried to convince her to keep him in the ER. I tried to convince him that he could be bleeding inside his head and that we could not stop it if he left. Ironically, when I needed her, Butch was not around. She was picking over some other resident's *I*s and *T*s.

"Can I interrupt you and get you to check on a patient situation for me over here?" I said, to the relief of the other resident. "A patient with head trauma is trying to leave against medical advice."

"Yeah. I'll be there in a minute," she said without looking up.

"Okay, but try to hurry. He's getting anxious and his mother is not helping the situation."

She looked up this time. "I said I will get there when I can!"

I crawled off to the teen and his mother. "Just give us a few minutes," I said. "My boss would like to talk to you. And if you still want to go after that, we won't stop you." And, in truth, we couldn't stop them legally. They had the right to leave, and apparently had the right to be stupid. I supposed I had exercised that very right years before when I was the patient who had been knocked out and left "AMA."

Ten minutes later, a nurse approached me as I was seeing another patient. "Dr. Triton," she said, "the patient that was over there in the hall just walked out with his family."

"Oh, well," I answered. "We tried."

Just then, Butch turned the corner with her palms up in front of her. "Where is that patient you mentioned?"

"Apparently he walked out."

"What?" she screeched. "When? When did he walk out?"

"I don't know. I was seeing someone else."

"How could you let him get away? He needed a CAT scan!"

"He wasn't a prisoner. I told him and his mother all those things, and they still left."

"If they were that anxious, you should have gotten me over there right away!"

I looked puzzled for only an instant. I had grown to expect this kind of transference of culpability at Yale. It is a difficult situation to face, because disagreeing with the boss guarantees a confrontation there. If I were to let her comment slide as I normally would, there was always the hope that no conflict would arise from it. But I had seen too many bloody battles be merely postponed, and my fate had always been devastating.

"How dare you!" I shouted in the middle of the ER as nurses and patients looked on. "I came to you and explained exactly what was happening. *You* chose not to deal with it promptly! Don't even suggest that this was my fault." I turned around and walked back to my patient.

The next string of patients tended to be the alcohol-related patients. It had gotten late enough that people were passing out on the street with their bottles of Jack Daniel's or getting in fights in the bars themselves. The homeless, who chose to pay for liquor over a loft, lined the back hallway as usual. One masculine patient had gotten into a brawl over an ex-girlfriend, and the other guy had sliced his face up with a broken beer bottle. I spent over an hour stitching up his face, tolerating his vodka-laden insults. It is surprising that someone would insult a person holding a needle to his skin. It is also humorous to me that the larger the man is, the more likely he is to whine like an infant when given a shot.

When I had finished suturing the guy's face at last, the ER had quieted down. Last call had brought in the patients an hour ago, and now there were but a few stragglers. My head was pounding by now. The *thump* was clearly out of sync with my heartbeat, which was going much faster.

The silence of the room and the rhythm of my throbbing head were interrupted when a large black man with a Jamaican accent ran into the ER. The security guards stood up, seeming to notice him only after he was twenty yards past them.

"Help me! Please. You got to get dem out!" he shouted, standing within arm's length of me.

The whites shone above and below his dark brown eyes as they shifted left and right and then left again. His muscles clenched, and the veins in his arms and neck postured visibly from where I stood. His hands alternately rubbed and then clawed his chest, not in the manner that one scratches an itch, but rather as a man tears through his pockets looking for his lost keys. The bright red divots appeared in his ebony skin next to the darker crusts left previously.

Eager for a thrill to perk up my night, and but two feet from being a victim rather than a doctor, I took the man on as a patient before his chart was drafted.

"They in me, Doctah! You gotta do somthin'," he repeated.

I looked at him, realizing that he was clearly out of his mind— whether from drugs or just from birth, I didn't know. I was not as worried, though, about his mental status as I was the remote chance that he actually had lice or some other vile creatures burrowing into his skin. "Gross" quite easily trumps "insane" and "dangerous" on my list of motivators. Besides the veins, there were no other marks on his arms suggesting infestation with fleas, ticks, lice, leaches, or other repulsive creatures. He didn't even have track marks down the veins of his arms. Between the frequent flyers with multiple medical problems who get a new IV every two weeks and the heroin users who can find a vein better than an ICU nurse, finding a virgin vein had become a rarity.

"Where are they?" I asked him, shouting mostly because he was.

"They're here! And here!" he screamed as he pointed to various points on his arm. "And here! And here!" He pointed around his chest. "And there!" He pointed toward my arm.

Admittedly, I looked for a second. But then the psychosis that was involved became clear. I started speaking more calmly. "Okay, sir. We are going to take you back here and get a look at these things. I know we can get them out. You just have to calm down. Are they itching or hurting?"

"They itching! And hurting! Oh fuck, they itching!" He began to slash his fingernails across his chest again.

"It's okay. I can fix it, sir," I said, backing away. It's funny how the use of the words "sir" and "ma'am" is generally inversely related to our actual respect for the person to whom we are talking. Even the boss we call "sir" we generally revile as a slimeball.

I called the nurse in to sedate him. After the Haldol plunged into his shoulder, he swung his arm wildly. "Whatchu doin', lady?" He stared at her without making a move toward her as she backed away.

"Don't worry," I said. "The medicine is going to help you with your itching."

He began to calm and look around the room in a more curious than agitated way. Soon, he was simply standing there in the middle of the room, staring blankly into space. With the phone on the wall next to me, I called back to our psychiatric evaluation center. The center was open twenty-four hours a day for such psychiatric emergencies or suicide attempts. A nurse and a psychiatrist manned the locked unit. ER residents have to serve a month rotation back in the psych unit during their third year, so I had not spent any actual time back there.

"Jules. Hey, I have a guy up here who is whacked out of his mind. He thinks he has bugs crawling under his skin. Some of the nurses know him and say he just gets like this, and that he never has any drugs in him when he gets tested."

"You don't even say hi anymore?" she said with playful sarcasm in her voice.

"I'm sooorry. Hi, Jules. How are you tonight?"

"Pretty good. It's been quiet back here tonight. So what's up?"

"That's all I get after that?"

"Yep. Is that Mr. Miller with the bugs?" she asked.

"I don't know. He hasn't gotten a bracelet or told me his name. He just keeps yelling and scratching his skin."

"That sounds like Mr. Miller. You can bring him back."

As I walked him back to the psych unit, I noticed Mr. Miller's head slumped down. He was no longer scratching himself or thrashing about. It took only my fingertips between his shoulder blades to encourage him to walk back with me. The entire hospital staff looked similarly sedated as we walked by. Butch had ventured up to the front desk near the waiting room, where she was flipping the pages of a magazine, laughing with the front secretary. I wondered whether the men's or women's fashion magazines gave more suitable romantic advice for a woman like Butch.

Miller walked back with me past the drunks, silent in their beds. He sniffed with disgust as he looked over them, as though *they* should be ashamed. At the back of the hall, we came to the locked door with the large plastic window next to it. I pressed the button next to the door and pulled the handle, just about jerking my shoulder out of socket.

"You have to wait for me to buzz you back," came Julie's voice, sounding metallic over the intercom.

"Okay."

I waited.

"Could you buzz me back?" I asked, half laughing.

"Oh. Why didn't you just say so?" A loud buzzer sounded overhead, and a *clack*ing came from within the door.

I opened the door and saw Julie sitting to the side, eating popcorn.

"Just put him over there in the first room," she said as I shuffled him in and left him lying almost asleep on the bed.

"'Night," I said as I walked out, too tired to make small talk this evening.

The headache had somehow gotten worse over the last few hours. I questioned whether the tumor had started growing, like a muffin being baked. I knew that wasn't even remotely plausible; I wasn't having any sense of seizures, so I was fine. It was just a fucking bad headache.

I looked to the front of the ER and saw the clock with two hours left in my shift. Not a single patient in the waiting room. I crept back to the physicians' lounge to sit down with the lights off.

Thirty minutes later, I woke from my somewhat unintentional nap. My head was still pounding without remorse, but I had a bit more energy to face whatever might come in the last hour.

"Where have you been?" Butch said from the same seat with the same magazine in her lap. "We've been looking for you."

I turned my head momentarily and confirmed that no one was listed on the white board to be seen. "I stepped away to sit down for a minute. Is there a problem?"

"I just wondered what happened to the bug guy. And you should always tell me where you're going."

"I took him back to psych. And I still have my pager, so you can get me if I'm not immediately in sight."

~~~

"Jeff, I called you in here because I have gotten several complaints regarding your behavior in our own emergency room."

I was in Lathem's office again three days after that ferocious night of pain.

"Complaints?" I asked rhetorically. I had grown so accustomed to the surprise complaints that they were about as surprising as a rerun of *Gilligan's Island*. "Who this time?" I sighed, rolling my eyes.

"I have four recent complaints. Apparently you let a patient leave against medical advice without telling your attending?" he said, as though his statement was interrogative.

I resisted the urge to stand up and shout directly into his face. "That's garbage. I told her exactly what he was doing. She chose not to come very quickly. And actually, he didn't sign anything saying he wanted to leave AMA. He just ran out while nobody was looking. There is *no way* that can be considered my fault."

"It says here also that you yelled? At your *attending*?"

"Because she was accusing me of the same crap you are. It's completely ludicrous. I can't just sit by while everyone keeps slandering me."

"It doesn't seem like slander to me. I also have that you took a psychotic patient back to the lockdown unit without security?"

"Yeah, I guess. So what? I had chemically restrained him."

"You can't just take a mentally ill patient back there to the lock-down unit where there are two females alone. He could have seriously hurt our nurse or someone else."

"I didn't know that! I haven't worked back there yet. Nobody explained that to me. I would have been happy to let him take the guy back there, but your security guard, along with everybody else, was sitting on his ass in the waiting room!"

"I guess we can forgive that one, since you haven't done the rotation yet. But it seems that there was a twenty-minute period where you were unreachable?"

"Unreachable?" I shouted. "I was twenty feet away in the lounge, just sitting down. Nothing was going on! I had a headache. I came right back. People take more time eating their freaking lunch, which I never stop to take, by the way."

The accusations and the threats were totally out of control, and I wondered where they would go from here. Lathem repositioned himself in the chair with his elbows resting on the leather-covered armrests.

"I really didn't want to have to go this way. But—" He paused with his lips hidden behind his folded hands. "As I see it, you've given me no choice. I have written a letter of resignation that I think you should sign. If you don't agree to it, the committee will have to consider terminating you."

He wasn't quite within arm's reach to strangle, as he should have been. I thought about him and his committee and thought about the relentless way they had targeted me for so long. I wondered again if it was out of fear over my seizures and liability. Was it because of my arrogance, which I thought I had lost with all other self-esteem long ago?

"It will be much more difficult for you to obtain another residency position if it is mentioned that you have been terminated. Almost impossible, I would say."

It is a frightening moment when a simple wooden desk keeps a professional from becoming homicidal, rather than his conscience. I had no regard for right or wrong; morality was incomprehensible. I sat in shock, attempting to look like I was contemplating options rather than his murder.

"I will take the letter home and consider it," I said in a deep monotone. There was no anger left. No will.

Chapter 18

I wonder what the world looks like to a turtle. Does the FedEx-paced, text-message-me-on-your-Blackberry, traffic-updates-on-the-twenties lifestyle seem nonsensical for the stress it creates? Did the tortoise eventually speak to the aged hare and offer some sage advice? If he did, I imagine he might say, "Christ, man! You are fifty years old." (In rabbit years, of course). "You are over the hill; you have all that fur on your back, and you are still racing around like your tail is on fire. All that stress of racing through your life, not taking time to appreciate everything you have, and what has it gotten you? I think even the tortoise driving the Hyundai whipped your ass in the end, didn't he? Granted, all that action you got with the bunnies deserves some recognition. But after all is said and done, you aren't going to remember the races you've won. That is, assuming you keep racing me."

Maybe, however, he doesn't have such a placid perspective on his place in the world. Perhaps even the senior citizen in the slow Cadillac driving in the fast lane is a reminder that he is just a turtle. The restaurant serving him would be the most frequented at the bottom of the food chain, were the service not so bloody slow. Clearly he would have to develop a strong sense of security, or a tough shell, if you will, to fight off self-doubt as the world passed him by while he watched. I suspect that evolution gave turtles Coke-bottle nearsightedness in order to protect their self-esteem. That way, they could not see all those passing them by and could therefore continue to feel good about themselves.

I heard a tale once. It was a sequel to *The Tortoise and the Hare*. Not the first or second sequel; the tortoise didn't seem to catch on very quickly. I believe it was *The Tortoise and the Hare, Part VI, the Final Reckoning*. After several rematches in the preceding episodes, the hare finally understood the lesson the fable was meant to teach. He demanded one final rematch with the tortoise, which he intended to win. Having learned to take his time and be methodical about the race effort, he decided he would force himself to do just that. He crafted an elaborate tortoise-shell body gear that he would wear during the race. In the shell, he placed several large weights that would force him to plod along at a turtle's pace. Still having the competitive spirit and racing skill of a rabbit, he would certainly emerge victorious.

When the day of the race came, the two lined up at the starting line and wished each other luck once again. The gun went off, and the two bolted off at a rate that would make only a snail proud. By mile two of the ten-mile race, the hare had achieved a whopping ten-meter lead over the tortoise. He thought that his skills would surely pull him through this tough time, and he would overcome the weight he had put upon himself.

The hare's friends had grown tired of watching the race, which, in their experience, should have been over by now. They continued on with their lives to become successful, just as Hare had always expected to be. His friend Bugs went on to employ illegal immigrants to harvest carrots in central California while he became the poster child for a Beverly Hills cosmetic orthodontia firm. His ex-girlfriend Jessica went on to star in movies, to walk the red carpet annually with various rock stars for years to come. Another friend of his adopted a pseudonym and was rumored to have gotten a job modeling in a *Where's Waldo* manner each month within the centerfold of some risqué men's magazine.

Hare saw all of this happening, his friends leaving him behind as he was forced to go so slowly. He felt absolutely alone. He was still in front of the tortoise by mile four, but the pace he was traveling at was devastating him emotionally. By mile five, nobody was watching the race, and despite all his efforts, the hare did not feel like he was making any advances toward the finish line. Although he was winning, he saw only the things he had given up. He remembered the days of sprinting frantically and sometimes needlessly from one activity to another. He remembered the dreams he had of one day meeting his idol, the

Cadbury Easter Bunny. But these dreams seemed impossible, as he had been left behind.

By mile six, no rabbits were watching, and only turtles lined the roadside. The hare saw this and fretted that he had lost everything he wanted to be. From his shell he pulled out a semiautomatic pistol and shot himself in the head. The turtles observing, shouted, "Noooooooooo!" and attempted to jump in front of the bullet. But, as you can imagine, what appeared to be slow motion was directed by biology rather than Spielberg, and a tortoise acting as a human shield is not as effective as one might hope. Hare died that day realizing that he could not force himself to live his life as a tortoise.

As I stood in line, I empathized with the tragic hare. It had been four weeks since I had signed the letter of resignation in Lathem's office. The sense of urgency that had come after the shock was equally overwhelming. I needed a new job, and I needed to finish my training. I frantically searched for any programs across the country that had open positions to fill. Applications went out within an hour of my hearing of the positions.

The first position was in the emergency department of George Thomas Olmsted Hospital, located in South-Central Los Angeles. GTO, or Ghetto, as it was referred to in the emergency field, was named after an unsung hero in the fight for racial equality. As frequently is the case for those hospitals, schools, and parks named after those fighting for racial equality, it was in the worst part of town and was the most under-funded in the state. It could be compared to the MASH units in Korea during the war, with very little technology and surgeons who resorted to using chopsticks from dinner to perform emergency thoracotomies in the ER. That being said, I could not complain about the education I would get in such a trial-by-fire environment as GTO. The worst part would be moving back across the country, leaving Tara behind. But desperate times called for disparate locations, and there was always the possibility that Tara could get a position at one of the other Southern California hospitals.

I was invited to interview also at Brooklyn Hospital's emergency department. I was surprised when I received a call from Slash, my old classmate from Mon Gracia. After taking a year to volunteer in Jerusalem as a medical worker, he had gone to Brooklyn Hospital and was about to begin as chief resident in their ER. I would never have doubted his ability to achieve a position of power, but the coincidence

.

that he was in Brooklyn Hospital was remarkable. It was even more so because all the boroughs in New York seemed alike on television—everybody was poor and talked like De Niro or Spike Lee. But Slash had been doing well there. He and I spoke at length about the stresses and injustices I had experienced at Yale. And he was confident that he could get me a spot in his program. Working in Brooklyn would mean an hour-long commute to work, but again, it was something I had to do to finish.

The spirit was desperate when Tara and I discussed the options we had, and every conversation was a blunt reminder of my failure. The commute or the distance that would separate us across the country was daunting, but our fear easily prevailed when we thought about how to proceed. The time we had to discuss it was far greater than we had hoped. Both programs were asking for three letters of recommendation before they accepted me.

The difficult part of the interviews was explaining why I would want to leave a place like Yale. *Everyone has to realize that it is better to be from Yale*, they must have thought. This became my burden to overcome. I knew I couldn't simply bash the faculty as though it were a congressional election, because I would come off looking poorly. Trying to express that I was looking for a program that was less cutthroat, I explained that I was looking for a program that was focused more on the clinical work and was less academic than Yale. Each of the programs seemed eager to recruit me, praising my board scores and goals. The letters, however, were not so easy to come by.

My voice must have sounded as desperate as I felt by the third call. I had already called attendings who had been relatively nice to me in the past. I called the associate director of the Yale program who had been pleasant around me, never making accusations. It was thanks to her that I had actually felt part of the program at all over the past year. "Hmmm. I'm not sure I can write you a letter," she said.

"Can't write me a letter? Can't write me a letter!" I exclaimed over the phone. "You and I have worked together a hundred times, and you have only corrected me a few times. And now you can't find one decent thing to say about me so that I can finish my training somewhere else?"

"I'm sorry. I just don't think I can write it," she said. The tone in her voice was much more unfeeling than I had ever heard it before. Even when she had spoken of the prognosis of the heroin dealers that had been shot, she had more compassion in her voice than now. "You should probably ask someone else."

I found the same response when I sought out anyone with a somewhat official title, such as "associate director" or "assistant director." I never really knew the difference, nor did I understand why either position was needed. But they shared the commonality of each trying to become the actual director. And, in trying to gain favor with those in charge as the chairman, they could not do anything to support me. I couldn't determine whether the black mark next to my name was explicitly drawn or simply inferred. But anyone hoping to move up the chain of command at Yale observed it without question. I was finally able to get letters from some of the attendings at Bridgeport who had already achieved the positions they wanted and did not subscribe to the Yale politics. A letter from the director, Lathem, was non-negotiable, though. Beyond the absolute lethargy with which he wrote it, I couldn't predict what defamation his letter might bring upon me. I had no expectation that he would spin my less glorious moments in a positive light. But would he attack me or describe me as unhealthy and unfit for clinical duty? Everything happened behind closed doors.

I only learned that Lathem's letter had been written when I received an email from the director at Brooklyn apologizing that they would not be needing my services. I later spoke with Slash, who explained that his director was concerned that I was looking for a "less academic" program. It occurred to me that stating this as a prerequisite for a new residency was about as smart as approaching a random girl on the street and saying, "Hi, I am looking for a girl who is just a bit more of a slut than my last girlfriend. Want to go out?" Nevertheless, it took them the three weeks waiting for Lathem's letter to decide that they were insulted by my comments that far back. Clearly, "glowing" was not a word to describe the reference he had provided for me. It surprised me that he was not trying to facilitate my happiness elsewhere, inasmuch as I was contemplating suing him for my unhappiness at Yale.

GTO was not so forthcoming with their verdict on my application. I felt more confident about my chances in the ghetto because there had been a vacant position listed on their website since my second year in medical school. I had never considered applying there before because their reputation was so poor. The weeks went by, still with no word from them. Later, after speaking to my father back in California,

I found out what had become of *my* position in the ghetto. The hospital had been fined several million dollars because residents had been left in charge of the floors and emergency department while attendings lazed in diners across the street or beds in adjacent offices. The hospital was ultimately closed down after funding for inner-city hospitals was cut for those who were losing money so dramatically.

With my other options exhausted, I stood in the county unemployment line one morning. In front of me stood a small Southeast-Asian man in olive green utility pants. The stains on his trousers looked more like vomit than paint or caulk or some other work-related blemish. His hands were in his pockets and his head tilted forward. He never looked up in the time that I followed him. I pondered with some concern how long he had been on welfare. The sympathy for such a social leech would not have entered into my consideration just a year before I stood in this line for forty-five minutes to place my own request.

The man in front of him was a middle-aged white man dressed in a short- sleeved checkered shirt. His hair was an ash gray and his face a ruby red. Unlike the man before me, the grayed gentleman's anxiousness was apparent. He looked about the office as if to find the one person who could help him, or possibly the one place he could hide from his troubles. Like the man before me, though, he too had his hands in his pockets, jingling the keys or coins intermittently. When he was called to the desk, at last, I heard him explain his story of being laid off as a drafter when his company downsized. He was nearly in tears as he related his difficulty finding a job at his age.

"Have you thought about looking into a new field, Mr...." The woman at the counter said as he finally broke into tears. As I watched, I felt an emptiness for this gentleman, as well as a fearful void of my own.

When I reached the front of the line, the same woman looked at me with puzzlement. "You're a doctor?" she said.

"Yes, ma'am."

"And you are here for unemployment?" she asked.

"Yes, ma'am."

"And you lost your job?"

"Uh-huh," I responded as the questions became more painful.

"Well, you are going to have to join our resource class this afternoon before we can give you any unemployment money. We have to be sure that you know how to find a job before we can pay you for not having one." She directed me to the room to the left, where several computers sat with chairs before them.

I was one of the first ones to arrive as I sat down near the back of the computer room. The others filtering in seemed about as enthusiastic as I imagined they had been to come to class in high school. The vast majority of the clothes were filthy, and the occasional pair of jeans was unbuttoned. Some of the men laughed to one another in a familiar manner. Another man sat off to one side of the room, seemingly oblivious to the rest of us, picking his nose. The dried white trail down his cheek looked like either milk or snot. Up at the front of the classroom sat the graying drafter who continued to fidget as we sat waiting for the class to start.

The smell of their failure was pungent, and so was mine. If they had just given a shit in high school and tried a little harder, if they had they cared and not been lazy at work, they might not be here. But I was here, too, suckling on the teat of society. And the taste was sour. Just as I loathed them for their assumed faults, I found myself equally vile. Was I stupid? Was I lazy? The guilt of my arrogance was evident even to me. It was so difficult to comprehend as I considered that I had no strength without confidence and no opportunity without initiative. Yet over and over, throughout my life, I had heard reference to my hubris. The paradox was almost too great to overcome, like a round Earth must have seemed to Columbus' crew taking his word while sailing ahead into what looked like a flat sea. But the logic was irrefutable.

"Good morning, everyone. Let's start by turning on our computers." A large woman walked into the room and proceeded to explain the basics of the Internet and job searching. Within ten minutes, I was able to keep up with everybody else who might have to resort to applying for a telemarketing position. Scrolling down the list that morning and several mornings to come, I wondered if my education and background would make me an appealing applicant to the pharmaceutical companies as a sales representative or for the barista position at Starbucks. Or would it simply make me a cocky prick, sight unseen? But the feelings of rejection and worthlessness led me to seek out anyone who would have me. In college, a similar situation was referred to as being "on the rebound."

~~~

"Gosh, I'm sorry, Dr. Triton. I think this would have been a perfect position for you. If only you had gotten in touch with us a month ago. We just hired a nurse practitioner to work the hours that we posted in the journal. I would have much rather had someone of your experience and competence working for us."

It was early September. I was surprised to have gotten the interview at Elk Grove Community Hospital. *It couldn't hurt*, I thought as I called regarding one of the job openings listed in the back of the emergency medicine journals that were still arriving in my mailbox, adding insult to injury. But I left the small hospital in quiet, wooded central Connecticut as discouraged as when I had walked in.

Despite the empty hand and empty heart I drove home with, I felt a piece of my hope renewed as I realized that perhaps someone might find value in me after all.

The changing of the leaves still did not garner any favor with me in my third autumn in Connecticut. Like trash of any other color, it gains little appeal, especially when *you* have to clean it up. I exited the freeway and drove past the supermarket. My trips there had become more frequent over this summer because they were no longer squeezed into the few hours I had off work, but rather an elective trip to fill the time I spent waiting for a prospective employer to call. A left turn, up the back road, past the cemetery. The stones there were all well over a hundred years old, yet I often saw fresh flowers left on the graves. Even in their long absence, the departed had value to someone. The houses here, every thirty meters, were so quaint—not inviting, but presumably home to someone. The flower arrangement outside each door meant something to someone, and it made that home in Connecticut feel like theirs. The perfectly trimmed grass abutting a neighbor's unruly lawn, a cute little fall harvest display or scarecrow on the porch of the house thirty yards from the previous one. These things made someone feel at home and a part of Connecticut. In contrast, nothing had made Tara and I feel comfortable in Connecticut. Relationship difficulties, fires, firings...all of these had made us feel like the unwelcome morsel of food that causes indigestion until it is finally expelled. On the right stood the free library's supply of videos, which I had exhausted over the course of the past three months.

I finally pulled into the driveway. I felt the lump in my throat as I swallowed. The slight optimism I had felt initially after the interview had faded, and I remembered nothing but the rejection. I surveyed the enormous yard and the fence I had constructed over the summer and realized that the work and accomplishment meant nothing to me. I walked inside and changed out of the gray three-buttoned suit. The fabric whispered and gave as I released the metal clasp on the pants.

Fuck, I thought. The sweat of mowing the yard had not been enough to burn the extra calories, I realized, as I saw that the conciliatory eating had brought along several pounds of comfort fat. I pulled the sweatpants up my legs and lay down on the couch with no shirt in front of the television. After thirty seconds of remorse over my developing love handles, I got up and microwaved some leftover desert. Just as the commercial began, the cell phone in my leather bag rang. I scurried to it, searching through the inconveniently numerous pockets until I found it.

"Hello, Dr. Triton?"

"Yes, this is Dr. Triton."

"Dr. Triton, this is Jim Ranier, the chief physician in the emergency department in Brattleboro, Vermont. I received your application and hoped that you might come out and interview with me in the near future."

"Absolutely, Dr. Ranier," I said, trying to hide my desperation. "When would you be interested in meeting?"

"How does tomorrow sound for you? I will be working a shift, but I don't expect it to be busy in the morning."

I paused and silently counted to three for effect.

Yes! Okay. You bet. Fuck yeah! I said all these things in my mind, but I maintained my silence. "That sounds perfect, sir. 9:00? Excellent." We hung up calmly.

When Tara got home, I had prepared dinner. The sirloins grilled outside next to the vegetables were no evidence of celebration, as they were used more frequently to placate our sorrows with food.

"How did the interview go, sweetie?" she yelled as she walked in through the garage.

"I didn't get the job, but the interview went okay."

"How can the interview go okay and you not get the job?" she asked as she walked out onto the patio, where the smoke billowed up into my face.

"He said he had just given the position to a nurse practitioner a couple weeks ago."

"Then why the hell did he interview you, if he had given the spot away?" she yelled, her arms flailing above her head.

"He said it was in case the NP fell through. He said he might have a part-time position for me, anyway. He asked if he could keep my number."

"Well, I guess that's something. I'm sorry, sweetie." I heard the genuine sorrow in her voice. She had seen my optimism be extinguished progressively since resigning from Yale. Somehow the stress and distress of our situation had not led to the bickering that our stress in the ICU had the year before. We kept it inside, silent and unspoken. Yet both of us knew that I was dying inside.

"There is some good news, though," I said, closing the cover to the grill. "I got an offer for another interview."

"Another one? Where is this one?"

"This is the one in Vermont. This is the one that would pay over $200,000 dollars per year. We could totally have a bunch of money saved up by the time you get done with residency."

"And do they know you haven't finished residency?" she asked.

"Yeah. I put it in my application. I guess they really need someone to work those weekend shifts out there in the boonies."

"Yeah, I guess so."

The next morning, the frost was plastered across the windshield, hoping to claim a few last hours of sleep before the sun climbed over the mountainous form of a sleeping giant. But I had risen even before Tara today, and the ice sealing the driver's-side door crackled like twigs in the fire as I pulled the handle. No streetlights were lit on the quiet cul-de-sac, and I could only see my breath by the moon still hovering by night's string. The motor growled as I turned the key, but at this hour it sounded more like the snort of a spouse refusing to wake up when nudged. The slightest press on the gas pedal, and the spouse was more cooperative and purring like she should. I pulled the seatbelt over my shoulder and sighed as the buckle clicked.

The freeway was morbidly empty. It seemed peculiar for a weekday, despite the 4:00 news flash that shouted from the radio. I hated that advertisers and newscasters felt like the previous few minutes of music that had interrupted their previous commercials and news clips had also rendered me hearing-impaired, and they therefore needed to shout. The enthusiasm was transparent as rain, and under any other circumstance, I would have been annoyed and wanting to relax. But

318

this morning I was worried and had no intention of relaxing. This worry was not the casual worry of going to an interview. Christ, I had been through countless interviews throughout my education. This worry was like the man who wagers his final dollar on black—only, I had not bet on black. This job in Brattleboro was a bet on red thirty-two. I felt pressure in my bladder, although I had just gone before I left.

I knew my career options were dwindling rapidly. In my search for residency programs with spots to fill, Tara had even urged me to look at positions in Kansas or Wyoming, knowing that we would see each other only during the infrequent vacations. I had applied for the internship match all over again, realizing it would not lead to a job until the following summer, if at all. I applied to match in residency programs in family medicine and internal medicine, hoping that the high number of positions and the relatively low pay of the specialties would give me a chance to compete, considering I saw myself as an ex-con from Yale.

The drive should have taken three hours. I feared traffic would get heavy in Massachusetts, so I had left plenty of time to spare. With the barren roadway, however, I reached the Vermont border in two and a half hours. Brattleboro was the first exit across the border and the last for the next ten miles north. The skyline from the freeway as I exited showed hundreds of thousands of acres of unending spruce and pine ebbing and flowing in the distance. The roads could not even be made out beneath the dense wood.

The right turn off the freeway led me down the single road, with no obvious traffic intersections for miles. I read and reread the directions from the computer as I drove on, looking for the turnoff. I felt the sweat bead start to form on my temple as well as in my shirt as I questioned my ability to download directions, follow directions, or even understand directions. I directed my attention temporarily toward willing the droplets to resorb back into my skin. I think the droplet above my right brow was beginning to vanish back into the skin when I noticed something by the side of the road. A deer was rolling spastically on its back, thrashing about dramatically as if in pain. I slowed to see if some venomous snake had grasped its neck. When the car slowly approached the animal, it quickly sprung to a sitting position with its head upright. It looked up at me calmly, its head turning as I passed. Its eyes were a bright white until I was beside him, then they became a quiet gray. The deer remained there in its recumbent position for a few moments and then returned to its back scratching or cleaning. Obviously, it was not frightened of me. I wondered what significance this might hold regarding an emergency department in Brattleboro.

I finally reached the left turn that the directions spoke of. They did not describe the lack of a right turn option, and thus I still seemed to be on the solitary road that ran through Vermont. The radio reception was remarkably clear, considering the lack of any other signs of civilization nearby. As the morning DJ greeted his crew and listening audience, I approached an actual fork in the road and signs directing me to the right toward Brattleboro.

The town thoroughfare was a mix of buildings from the 1970s and the 1770s. The city hall doubled as a courthouse and was built of red brick with three-story-tall white columns. Next to it stood a collection of small shops, including a Laundromat, video store, and a diner. The deep forest behind the buildings enhanced the lonely feeling of the empty parking lots. The grocery on the opposite side of the road was the size of a convenience store from any town I was accustomed to. A few other similarly utilitarian buildings spanned the boulevard. At the far end of the road stood a stone church with a towering steeple that rose above even the tower of the courthouse down the road. The stones that built the church were massive and impressive unto themselves. Above the looming cherry doors was a stained-glass pattern of immense size with a complex collection of colors. I considered stopping and looking more closely, but the fear of being late still consumed me, although I was scheduled to meet in two hours.

The hospital was less than a mile down the road from the town center and consisted of a single story not much bigger than a large warehouse. The parking lot was vacant and stretched out in every direction, leading me to wonder why so many people would come here and how they might all be squished into the small building. The emergency-room entrance was perched on the side, away from the sea of parking spaces. The few spots that sat in front of the emergency entrance were too exposed to anyone who might look out. They would see my car and wonder why a random freak would park there for an hour before walking inside. Granted, I would introduce myself, but I would have to overcome the preconception that I was the "random freak" applying for the ER position. Instead, I parked the car on the opposite side of the lot.

For an hour, Howard Stern interviewed the latest couple to be spawned from the growing reality-television trend. In my repugnance for the characters, I ignored them completely and focused on the interview approaching.

"He is going to ask you why you left Yale," I said to myself. "Don't say too much shit about the place. That doesn't look good.

"Focus on the positives.

"Sound confident, but not too confident.

"Sound eager, but not desperate.

"You can do this job. There is no reason you shouldn't get it. Show your commitment. Let him know—"

"Those are fake boobs, right?" the caster bluntly asked over the airwaves.

The flow of motivation was lost. I shook my head and reached for the keys.

"Just make me believe that those are real knockers!" he shouted to the aging and years-past-appealing pseudo-celebrity as I turned the car's power off. Outside the hospital, I paced for the last thirty minutes before the interview.

When I was introduced to Dr. Ranier, he led me around the small emergency department as though he was trying to sell me the job rather than the other way around. He showed me the critical-care rooms, which doubled as trauma rooms when the occasional chainsaw accident took place, tripled as the intensive-care unit of the hospital when the two ICU beds were full, and quadrupled as the paramedics' napping area when it got too cold in the Vermont winter. He pointed to the ten emergency beds, partitioned by curtains. The nurses' station faced all of these beds, while the doctor's office was an offshoot of one of the hallways. It had a television and a bed next to the desk with the computer atop.

"So we would need someone to work Friday, Saturday, and Sunday nights," Ranier said as he sat on the bed and faced me. "There would only be one shift that was twenty-four hours continuous. The rest would be twelve hours long."

I nodded as though this seemed an obvious arrangement; meanwhile, I calculated how many hours I would spend on the road only to turn around and come back. I didn't give a fuck. I could find an empty bed in the hospital or get a motel room even, for the money they were going to pay.

"Now, there will be times that you are the only doctor in the entire hospital," he explained. "There are approximately 200 beds. So if anything happens, you will be responsible for running codes or writing orders. Most of the time the primary doctors just give orders by phone, but there are a few occasions when I get called."

"That sounds fine. I feel comfortable with inpatient management, too." I began to grow a little nervous thinking about how many patients I might actually be responsible for. I also wondered where the hell they fit these patients. In the mulch heap behind the hospital? I also began to worry about the long hours over a weekend. Even if I stayed in a motel or a call room for the weekend, then went to Connecticut for the week, I would still be pushing the limits that my brain could handle.

"Most of the time it is pretty slow, and I can get a few hours sleep even on a shift. And the nurses are pretty good about letting you get sleep when there's a break in the action."

I hid any signs of the relief I was feeling, but inside I was doing cartwheels. I thought I just might have a chance of doing the job without having a, shall we say, embarrassing seizure in front of everyone.

He went on to tell me a few more details about the job, while all I could do was calculate over and over the sixty hours he wanted me to work per week multiplied by the salary he was offering. Not for a long time had the prospect of a career in emergency medicine seemed real. And even when I was on the traditional path to such a career, I had been indoctrinated to accept salaries less than minimum wage because I was said to be training. It is quite convenient to academic medicine that so many hours must be worked in the name of training. But if it must be done, "Who are we to complain?" they might say.

"You know, I'm really pleased with everything I've heard," he said, "but I would like to ask you one thing, if I may." His request seemed odd, since I didn't remember answering any questions or disclosing any information to begin with. But I knew it had to come sometime.

"Of course," I said. "That's why I'm here."

"I was wondering…why would someone leave Yale, of all places, from a specialty they enjoy as you seem to? And forgive me if this question is too personal."

His courtesy was out of a Jane Austin novel. I wasn't quite sure how, exactly, to respond. "Allow me to be frank, Dr. Ranier."

"Please," he responded. "And call me Jim."

"Oh. Thank you." I stopped, again surprised by his friendliness. "I have to say that Yale is not the most pleasant place to work. I came into the residency with such high goals and expectations, hoping to one day teach residents somewhere. And I took off from the starting line with a great vigor, but I stepped on a few toes out of the gate."

"How do you mean?"

"I created research projects and teaching labs for the residents and medical students. I did all of these things to make it big and impress my superiors along the way. But people were not impressed, and I began to meet resistance from faculty, including my director. My actions began to be seen in a negative light. I was seen as arrogant, when I was simply trying to be confident and decisive. The questions I asked frequently were only an effort to be active in my learning, and I performed very well on my exams as a result. But they were perceived as confrontational. Only later did an alumnus explain to me that my number one, two, and three responsibilities at Yale were to shut up and do what I was told."

Ranier nodded. "I've heard things like that about Yale."

"I suppose I had heard it was brutal, but I really thought I could make them proud of me," I said, somewhat touched that he seemed to be identifying with my struggle as he looked knowingly at me. "Anyway, by the time I realized how big the pit was that I had dug for myself, I was unable to climb out despite my efforts. I actually changed my behavior dramatically to fit their goals for me. But I already had a scarlet letter on my scrubs, and I hate to even consider what letter they would have placed on my chest. So the working environment became too uncomfortable to work in. I felt like my evaluations were not reflective of my knowledge, performance, and effort. Others had felt similarly. We had four people leave our emergency program from my class alone."

"Out of how many?" he asked, sitting back to a more erect posture.

"Out of ten."

"Jesus," he gasped. "That's terrible."

"Don't get me wrong. I don't take my role in this for granted," I said. Immediately I was mentally kicking myself in the ass for not stopping. "I realize that I seemed cocky to people because I was trying to do so much." At that moment, it occurred to me how to spin my personality flaw that had gotten me into so much trouble over the years.

"But I had merely failed to appreciate my role as a young resident, and that was to do the work and learn the way that *they* wanted to teach me. Now I understand that I must recognize the priorities of the position I am in. Take this job, for example." I could see his interest perking up. "I have no goals of changing the department here, or blatantly impressing anyone. I understand what *you* need, and I am coming here to do just that—work hard, be reliable and pleasant. I will work hard and take care of the people of this area. And if you want any more, I am willing to hear those needs and try to do that, too."

I was almost out of breath as I finished talking. I had not reached the point of ranting, but grandstanding would not be an unfair assessment of my speech.

"Hmm," he said, closing his eyes and furrowing his brows. "I have to say...I really admire your honesty in telling me about your time at Yale. Most people would not have told me that story. They would have made something up to make themselves look better."

He paused, and my sphincter tightened as I waited for the "but."

I couldn't tolerate the silence, and the joke slipped out. "Actually, I had my lie all planned out, and then I stumbled over the part about the alien abduction, so I just went with what came to me. Thankfully, I had this truth thing handy."

"Okay, well, I probably would have gone for the alien thing, too, but I was really impressed. I would like you to come work for me here."

I couldn't believe it. Even though I had heard the words and understood the meaning of the sentence, it seemed remote.

I had a job.

I was an emergency physician.

I was an attending emergency physician.

And I was fucking *out of Yale!*

"All I will need is a letter from your director discussing your training there," he said.

The request was like a quick thump to my chest.

"Umm. Okay," I said, slowly drawing out my words. Had he not heard anything I had said in the last ten minutes?

"Don't worry. I don't need a letter of recommendation. I just need a letter stating you did the training there and saying that you didn't commit any crimes or anything." He chuckled to himself.

I chuckled along with him, but wondered inside if Lathem would find new and different ways to thwart my attempts to succeed.

"Meanwhile, you can start getting your Vermont license and DEA number to prescribe narcotics in the state. We should be able to have you working by December or January."

His cavalier tone as he stood from the bed and offered me coffee, showed me he did not consider this such a major hurdle as I did. We spent no more than an hour discussing the logistics of starting work and joking about current events over the java. The coffee had been made in an automatic maker in his office, and I laughed to think of the Dunkin Donuts refuse still being consumed on a daily basis in the Yale ER.

After walking out of the emergency department at Brattleboro with Ranier's personal number in my hand, I noticed for the first time in months an unfamiliar malleability to my face. The stress, anger, and fear were no longer binding, and a grin was no longer a challenge. I smiled easily at the dramatic turn my life had just taken. The ease of the muscles in my cheeks simply rising was miraculous. And they stayed elevated, almost obstructing my eyesight. I remembered forcing social smiles in the past few months, and transient smiles in response to a joke. But they always seemed to pass when I stopped attending to etiquette or expressly thinking of the joke. This smile seemed like such a natural state. Why would anyone leave such a state of euphoria?

I did not go to the car directly. I walked toward town. I walked first past the church I had noticed on the way in.

First Baptist Church, Sunday sermon at nine, the sign read. I thought casually that this was the same title of the church where Tara and I had been married...the same church where we had gone occasionally when life seemed so much simpler...the same church we attended on Thursday nights, when I could ask her questions and we would have genuine conversations about her understanding and my curiosity. It had been a long time since I'd had the emotional energy to consider a feeling as effortless as curiosity. Our conversations had become more tense.

It had been even longer since I considered God. There had been so many times that I thought He had failed me, if not directly spurned me over the years. I had gradually forgotten about Him in my own depression. I had not reached enlightenment during my several months of unemployment; I had not found God, nor had He spoken to me in a way that I could understand. But I had found *myself*, and I understood my own vulnerability. I had reached the trough of my own hell when I could not work. I was lost in darkness and felt worthless to all. In that darkness, I could not see enough to ask for help or pray to any god, so alone I had sat.

There I had sat, until that day when I found myself released from my prison. Who had granted me this absolution, I didn't know. But I was so overjoyed and grateful for this gift, I was willing to discard any skepticism I held out of principle.

I opened the heavy, dark cherry door and walked into the chapel. Candles at the front lit the room dimly, and the dark beige hue of the walls created a peaceful and somber atmosphere. I walked quietly to the third row of benches in the vacant auditorium. I knelt down before the bench and prayed in front of the elegant gold cross that hung from the ceiling.

In my life, I had faced the threat and reality of a brain tumor and possible death. I had seen my mother succumb to a devastating infection. I had faced each of these wondering what role a god might play in them but had refused to resort to prayer. Even when I tried to call upon God to show himself to me, I did so within the depths of my mind and then rescinded my words when I got no response. Through all these hardships, only in my state of futile worthlessness had I prayed. Today, I prayed aloud. I admitted to my skepticism and uncertainty but asked that anyone listening try to understand my reasoning. I apologized for the hatred I had felt when my mother had died. I confessed that I did not even know whether a God was listening to me as I spoke, with both tears and laughter interrupting me. I didn't know if anyone was listening, or if *that* someone was responsible for this fortune bestowed upon me. But I needed to share my gratitude with anyone who might be involved.

I continued to speak aloud with God until the last tears for my mother and for my own suffering and for the near loss of my marriage were exhausted. I continued to thank Him, thinking ahead to the possibilities this might hold for my future. I made no promises about my future or praying or church-going, but I promised to remain grateful. I promised to remember where I had been. I promised to consider.

Chapter 19

To blame Lathem or not? The question was difficult, because he had sent the letter to Vermont relatively quickly. But the Vermont medical board required a letter from him as well. By mid-December, the board still had not decided whether to issue me a license. Under most circumstances, it would be obvious that Lathem had said something to stop me, either about my seizures or claiming I was unfit in some way. But apparently the population of Vermont was small enough and the doctor requirement equally small such that the Medical Board of Vermont was merely a night job. Actually, they met only twice a month, and the application process could easily be delayed without any effort by Lathem—not that I thought he was above it.

A month had passed since the interview, and I was beginning to feel uneasy. I called Brattleboro intermittently to let them know I was still waiting for the license, but often I was forced to leave a message with the secretary. Days continued to pass, and all I could hear from the medical board was an answering machine with no way of leaving a message. Each time the voice message chimed in after the ring, I put the phone down on the console, along with my head in frustration. I thought of the regret Ranier must have had over hiring me, even though I was not at fault.

It was a Thursday morning when I got that call. Tara was on call at Yale, and I had gone to the Indian casino an hour north of New Haven to play poker and take my mind off my worries. I acted excited to hear

Ranier's voice, but it was actually the call I had been dreading for the past month.

"Jeff?"

"Yes, this is Jeff Triton," I answered.

"Jeff, this is Jim Ranier out at Brattleboro. I wanted to call you and see how your license application was coming."

"It seems to be going fine according to the board. The problem is, they only meet twice per month, and very little gets done."

"Yes, I guess I remember that," he said. "I have a friend who works on the board. Anyway, I wanted to call and let you know. I had to give some of your hours away to someone else. I simply couldn't keep waiting in the dark. The doctor is one of the locals from the neighboring county. He is only working part time, so we should still have maybe twenty-four hours per week for you if you still want it."

"Yes, certainly," I said quickly. But I could not escape the thought of the money I would lose by working only twenty-four hours a week—if I ever got the license, that is. And if there were really twenty-four hours left for me. "I will keep on the board to try to get this license application hurried up."

"Yeah, give me a call when you hear from them," he said as we hung up.

My optimism shrank immediately tenfold. Never do twos and sevens fall as often in poker as when you are already depressed. I left, several hundred dollars down, and more so in spirit. The traffic had accumulated on the ninety-five highway such that the drive home was two hours instead of one. When I got back to New Haven, I pulled off the freeway. I had planned to play poker all night in Tara's absence, thus mitigating dinner. But with the swing of bad cards and bad luck in general, I had to stop off at the bank and then the market.

The cell phone rang as I sat in line for the drive-through ATM. It didn't seem as threatening, since it was 5:00 p.m., too late for the board to be calling. It was not likely that Ranier would be calling back to take away even more hours. I expected to hear Tara on the other end of the line, venting her mid-call stress.

The number on the ID, however, was again unfamiliar. I answered it in my serious tone. "Hello, Jeff Triton."

"Hello. Is this Dr. Triton?"

"Yes." I answered tentatively. I wondered how a telemarketer would have gotten my cell phone number.

"This is Dr. Neill, from the University of Pennsylvania Family Medicine Residency," the man explained in a slow voice. "You submitted an application for a position we had available for a second-year resident a couple months back."

I remembered the many mornings I had spent in the county unemployment office, writing letters and making phone calls. There was a brief sour taste in my mouth. While I recalled submitting countless applications to many programs, this program did not stand out in my mind.

"I'm sorry it took me so long to get back to you," he continued. "We've been in the middle of a number of changes around here. So, I've been reviewing your application and credentials. I've been looking at your publications and your experience, and I think you might be perfect for this program." His voice had a smooth, mellow flow until he emphasized the word "perfect," then paused before finishing the sentence. "We have been looking for someone like you to fill a void here in our program, and when I saw you, I thought, *Ya know, this might just be the guy.*"

The calming tone of his voice, like something out of an evening drama, morphed into the sound of a Sunday-morning infomercial. But I was flattered by his enthusiasm over me.

"Might you still be interested in the program?" he asked.

"Well, actually I have accepted a position and am just awaiting a license in Vermont."

"Have you signed any contracts? And when might you start?"

"It's still up in the air due to this license issue," I revealed.

"Tell you what. If you haven't committed to anything, why don't you just come on down to Philly and check out our program. If you don't like it, nothing's lost. But if you do, this might be the start of something really exciting."

I thought for a second about breaking a commitment to Ranier. The thought of disloyalty chilled me inside. But he had just broken his word to me, so there couldn't be any hard feelings. But where the fuck was Philly from here? I had applied to places across the country and stopped thinking with reference to distance. But this Neill had a charm and enthusiasm that I liked.

"All right," I conceded. "That sounds good to me."

"Perfect. I will email you the directions, and we will meet tomorrow at, say, nine?"

"Excellent. Then I will see you at nine tomorrow. I'm very glad you called, Dr. Neill."

"So am I, Jeff. Have a good evening."

~~~

I still keep it there, pasted above my desk in the residents' room, above the engagement photo of Tara and me sitting together on a beach in Newport, California. With each letter in different colors, red, orange, blue, yellow, green, and even some of the pastel colors that don't come with a standard Crayola box, the sign reads, *WELCOME JEFF!!!* Each of the exclamation points is in a different color as well. I keep it there to this day.

When I first saw the sign back in early January, I thought back to the night of the interview with Dr. Neill. I had just arrived home in Connecticut after the four-hour drive, walked through the door, and flopped on the couch. I was explaining how well I thought the interview had gone and how amenable the Penn doctors had been to my feelings about changing specialties.

"When do you think they will decide? Did they tell you?" Tara asked from her reclined position on the adjacent loveseat.

"I don't know exactly. They seemed pretty eager to—"

My cell phone rang from the breast pocket of my winter coat in the hallway. I lugged myself up halfheartedly to start and then sprinted to the phone after overcoming gravity.

"Hello?"

"Jeff, this is Richard Neill."

"Dr. Neill, hi. How are you doing?" I rattled off reflexively, realizing that not much could have changed since I had seen him last.

"I'm doing fantastic. Listen, I'm calling you this evening because I want to offer a position in our residency. Everybody who met with you agrees that you would be a perfect addition to our program, and we would like you to start ASAP."

It had been such a whirlwind transition from getting that call to renting an apartment in Philadelphia and beginning work at Penn by the beginning of January. Tara and I had to rapidly adjust to the new paradigm of living separately and visiting each other every other weekend. We had to get used to discussing our stresses and renewing our devotion and concern for each other over the phone. We had to get used to the idea that the other was *there for us*, even when they weren't literally there with us. There were many nights of tears early on, and I cannot deny there have been some as time went on. But throughout this treacherous journey, we've learned the value of hope and faith. In those times when we have found it difficult to remember on our own, we try to help each other realize that we are doing this so that we can soon be together.

I think it is easier for me most times, because I, as a man, can create an illusionary nobility, honor, and glory out of suffering, which makes the prize of finishing more valuable. Not to mention the fact that I had been the one suffering when I was not working, feeling lower with every unemployed breath. Tara is still living in our house, still beautiful from the post-fire renovation. She, to this day, avoids movies with house fires, and will not leave a room even to go to the bathroom without blowing out and relighting the candle when she gets back. I still tell my jokes and silly puns to her over the phone, and I can hear her eyes rolling on the opposite end of the line. These are the quirky moments we share that keep us going during our time apart.

I still keep the welcome sign above my desk to remind me to appreciate the inspirational kindness and warmth that I found away from Yale, here at Penn. Within days of beginning in January, I was avidly welcomed by everyone. Working in the clinic, I was complimented on my work on several occasions. "Nice workup on that bad diabetic patient, Jeff" and, "Thanks for seeing that man with the chest pain for me; I knew you would be the one to read the EKG." When I first heard statements like these, all action and thought temporarily shut down for me. It had been so long since I had heard a compliment that I nearly didn't recognize one, and I certainly didn't know how to respond. I kept waiting for the negative statement to follow. But it never came. I found myself just smiling, until the smiles became almost axiomatic. This self-esteem concept could be natural rather than wishful, I realized. I was thankful for every day I worked with these people.

The interactions were not limited to the clinic where I saw the bulk of my patients. Delivering babies was a large portion of our practice, and my experience began in my first week at Penn. Men and women often vary in whether they refer to the process of birthing first as beautiful or as gross, although both usually come around to the beautiful side after the birth of their own. One thing that does not vary, however, is that people delivering their first few babies describe it as terrifying. And this is how I felt as I stood between the bent legs of a seventeen-year-old black girl from west Philadelphia as she pushed and breathed in her panting fashion. I had paged my attending, who was seeing his own patients, to let him know that we were about to deliver. Meanwhile, her contractions were strengthening, and the baby's head was slowly inching its way toward the light. I directed the nurse to gather the gowns and equipment as I donned my blue smock and protective eye shield.

"Oh my God!" the patient screamed as her mother and two younger sisters sat quietly on the sofa across the room. Her face crinkled and her teeth ground against one another. She gripped the hands of the two nurses on either side. Meanwhile, the baby's head crowned just as the latex snapped onto my hand and my hand snapped to her perineum. At that moment, the door opened, and my attending walked through the door as calm as a ballad.

"Oh, boy! Looks like someone's having a baby," he cooed from across the room. "I wish someone had invited me to the birthday party." He stepped behind me and looked over my shoulder. "Excellent. Just keep going."

My heart was pounding faster than either the mother's or the baby's. Dr. Michaelson seemed very calm and confident. But despite being a pretty good goalie growing up, I had dropped an occasional ball, which had not been covered in blood and snot.

"All right, when you feel the next contraction, you are going to push," he said over my back.

With that, the mother produced a loud grunt and squeal. A few seconds passed before the baby's head, shoulders, stomach, and legs had passed through. Although it felt awkward, the baby landed face-first in my hand and then slid onto my forearm. I don't remember whether I was more worried about the landing or the sliding, but both seemed to turn out well.

"Here is your son, Mom!" he jubilated while nudging my arm to place the baby on the mother's chest. Because the father was not there, the baby's grandmother walked from the side and cut the cord, crying all the while. The baby had let out some early screams and was becoming progressively pink as he lay on Mom's chest.

With all the family celebrating at the bedside, I sat on the stool at the foot of the bed to deliver the placenta and stitch up a few small tears. Although I had sutured countless lacerations in my life, the difference between suturing cuts in the skin and lacerations in the birth canal is like the difference between sewing up a tear in a pair of jeans versus sewing up a tear in a pound of raw ground beef. Everything looked alike, and as a result, I could see nothing.

"That's perfect. Just like that," Dr. Michaelson whispered in my ear. "Get that one over there, too," he directed as a matter of course.

Minutes passed, and I became more aware of the number of relatives and nurses whom I was certain could read my lack of experience. But they kept on cradling the baby and tickling it at the side of the bed.

"I would like to talk to you outside when you get done with this," Michaelson said, slowly removing his gown and throwing it in the laundry. "Just clean up before you come out."

My streak had ended. *Fuck!* I thought. I wondered if I had caught the baby wrong, sewn the cuts wrong, or just taken too long. It could have been anything, but the blunted way that he had said it warned me a scolding was about to ensue. I wiped the blood off the patient and sorted the instruments I had used, making sure the sharp tools were disposed of. I attempted to help put more tools away, but the nurses assured me that they could do it for me, despite my reluctance to step out of the room. Finally, my blue paper robe came off and went into the trash as I walked out of the room. I breathed a sigh of relief, at least to be done with the delivery. But I continued to walk slowly toward Michaelson, who was completing his notes on the procedure.

"Well, the baby looked healthy," he said to me, briefly glancing up, then back down at his note.

"Yes. He looked great," I replied in a staccato fashion.

He signed his note with a single swirly design and, in a similarly swirly arm movement, closed the chart and placed it back on the desk. He stood up and began walking down the hall toward the elevator, perhaps assuming I would follow, or perhaps assuming I wouldn't.

I followed and caught up to his side. As we approached the elevator, I cleared my throat and said, "Ah, Dr. Michaelson, in the room you said you wanted to talk to me?"

"Mm? Oh. I just wanted to tell you that watching you in there…" He paused and shook his head slightly. "I think you have it. I think you have what it takes to do OB."

I was breathless. I was expecting an execution, and instead I had gotten an exaltation. He left the conversation with those words, and I thanked him for the comment as he boarded the elevator. I stood there alone for ten minutes.

These personalities for which I was so thankful were not infrequent, but abundant. Dr. Neill, the director who had been the first to call and interview me, proved himself an amazingly pleasant person to work with. A balding man in his young forties, he maintained his beard as though it were an 11:59 p.m. shadow. He was a Southern man with Southern values, who liked to subtly interject or imply those values in the way he taught. He was ever the professional, but never relinquished his smile and his subtle humor. He had a certain mystery to him in the way he prefaced his response to a question or comment with a three-second pause. His head would tilt and his grin would widen, only to lead into his usually serious remark. I always wondered whether he was fighting the urge to tell an off-color joke, scheming in the back of his mind, or thinking completely off-subject about Southern-style barbeque. But with Dr. Neill, I found it easy to trust that any scheming was nothing more diabolical than where to get the best Jamaican food in Philly.

This was the trust and kinship I felt with the residents I worked with at Penn, too. It would be an exaggeration to say that I was immediately intimate friends with everyone. But I can honestly say that I would have trusted any of them not to insidiously attempt to hurt me, as was so common at Yale.

There was one woman with whom I had a relationship best described as powder-keg-cordial. She had transferred to the program several months before me but had come from a surgery residency where she had felt similarly persecuted. I truly felt sorry for her, because the extent to which the surgical mind-set had invaded her brain was evident in the way she interacted with everyone. As the only female in the surgery residency, she felt alienated by the attitude of the male surgeons and targeted by the malevolence that, in my view, makes surgeons surgeons. Despite rejecting the field, she couldn't displace the surgical demeanor that had been embedded in her. Her traumatic reflections on her previous career had left her skeptical and suspicious of anyone around her. She directed her patients, nurses, and colleagues with an iron fist. I felt sorry for her, knowing how such a stressful experience could change someone's perspective, as it had mine. I wished that somehow she could see it as an inspiration to be grateful rather than cynical.

One of my first experiences with her occurred after a long night I had spent delivering babies. As I sat down to my desk to pack up my belongings for the day and walk home to sleep, she stormed out from a nearby cubicle.

"Did you come in here recently?" she shouted in an accusatory manner. A heavyset Korean lady, she had a habit of standing with a hyperextended back to rest her folded arms on her belly. I had learned inconveniently that she was Korean when I incidentally referred to a patient as an Oriental female. I was sternly notified that the term was outdated and offensive, as was the term Asian. As she explained, there are significant differences among Koreans, Chinese, Japanese, and other Asians. (Whoops!)

"No," I replied. "I've been on call delivering all night." I was perplexed why she would care of my whereabouts, but didn't even consider asking her.

"Because I left some food in the refrigerator," she said, "and someone took it out and threw it away!" She shouted all of this, emphasizing every second or third word in a punctuated, discordant voice. It was like a child persistently striking random combinations of piano keys with all his might. "They just got in there and took it out. And I think it was an act of racism!"

I had to fight off my laughter. "Racism? How on earth could this be an act of racism?"

She crossed her arms smugly. "Because mine was the only Asian dish in the refrigerator."

Seeing how infuriated she was, I fought the urge to correct her on the politically incorrect term "Asian."

"And that refrigerator has been stinking for weeks," she continued. "So someone goes in there to clean it out, and they assume it was the Korean food that was smelling up the place. It is totally racist! How would *you* like it if I just assumed it was your…your…whatever stinking up the refrigerator? You wouldn't like it much."

"I might not like it, but I don't think I would jump immediately to concluding there was a governmental conspiracy to abduct my pizza."

"Still! I think this was racist. And I am going to let everyone know that I am not happy about it."

The very next morning, an email had been sent to everyone in the residency outlining her theory on the racist theft and disposal of her

Korean meal. In elegant formal prose, she made a blanket accusation of anyone and everyone in the residency being racists and robbers. Most people discarded the email and forgot about it before they became angry. The brash nature of her accusations was revealed when the perpetrator turned out to be the unit secretary—a woman so petite of voice and innocent of heart that sinister motivations were completely unimaginable. I found myself quite angry in defense of the secretary, who had been trying to help the residents by tidying up, but kept my silence to keep the peace. Surprisingly, not much verbalized protest came from the rest of the residents, who had been equally impeached. A response from an anonymous staff member, however, came in the form of a letter posted on the bulletin board:

W.S.

Associate Director

American Civil Liberties Union

Philadelphia Branch

Dear Sirs, Madams, and all those insufficiently addressed by the aforementioned,

As associate director of the Philadelphia branch of the ACLU and resident of Philadelphia myself, I was appalled to hear of this egregious display of blatant and obvious discrimination. The ACLU wishes to express our deepest sympathies to all those food items who have been oppressed in this instance and to declare that we shall make it our explicit goal to stamp out culinary prejudice in this city. We call on all citizens to join us in this struggle, because it is not just the freedoms of the wonton that are at stake here, for your food may be next to be targeted by the great evils of this world. Be cautioned that gastronomic racism is a deep-seated problem which will not resolve on its own; we must band together to prevent its progression.

Those responsible for this tyranny would have you believe that it was an isolated incident, perhaps a mistake even. Their propaganda tells us that it "smelled funny" or "seemed to have something growing" or "was barking." Such excuses should not be permitted; you probably just ordered it medium rare that time. If we allow this to go on, before you know it, signs will appear on some refrigerators stating, "All egg rolls and fried rice should yield to other foods and move to the back of the refrigerator if a non-Asian food should board the appliance." How dare they make mention of *mistakes* as we march down the pathway toward "separate but equal" refrigerators! They will cite Bacillus cereus and Step 1 and 2 of the USMLE board exam as justification for these acts of naked aggression. But in truth, it is simply their profound hatred of soy sauce which drives these actions. We have seen this happen all too often. But we now refuse to stand by quietly, watching what could be the beginning of a fortune cookie holocaust, knowing that *we* could have done something about it.

We at the ACLU have constructed a plan which we feel adequately establishes the Sweet-N-Sour Chicken in the multicultural society of groceries as well as offers reparations for the abuse inflicted on him and his relatives, General Tzo and Teriyaki Chicken. We call our plan *Affirmative Distraction*. In this plan, a minimum number of Chinese, Japanese, and Thai dishes must be granted admission to the refrigerator for the electric bill to be paid. If there is insufficient chow mein representation, electricity will be denied that appliance for the month to follow, and all cuisine shall suffer. In our plan, all Asian food shall be granted special privileges once inside the refrigerator and in finding a consumer once out of the appliance. Each of the aforementioned benefits shall be granted to all Asian foods with the exception of sushi, because it is just too fucking trendy already.

We at the ACLU are glad to have been of service and hope that we have encouraged you to continue finding dirty, disgusting, intolerable, filthy, Hitlerian oppression and racism in everything around you—even something as simple as a lost pair of chopsticks.

> Humbly Signed,
> Wisheed Shuddafuggup, ACLU

I also keep the welcome sign above my desk to remind me of where I have been…to remind me that not all the world can smile and joke freely…to remind me that there are places like Yale, where people will consider the cost and the benefit of something as simple as a smile before offering it. I keep it to remind me that there are such places where a friend is merely someone who has not had the opportunity to stab you in the back or someone whose treachery you simply have not discovered. I keep it to remind me, most importantly, that it does not have to be that way. I can share myself with the people around me. I remind myself to welcome everyone on a daily basis.

Now I find myself preventing a heart attack in my friends through hours of effort rather than treating one in strangers through thirty minutes of effort. Now I care that my patient has a heroin addiction because it can ultimately ruin his career, his marriage, and his health, instead of it simply increasing his risk for drug-resistant sepsis. Now I find myself greeting patients by asking how they have been rather than asking why they came in. Now I find myself in a profession where not the least important half of my job is making eighty-year-old women feel beautiful and young and making 280-pound men feel empowered to change their lifestyle. The results I achieve are a bit more subtle but no less critical than those times before. I do sometimes miss the thrill of placing a tube directly into someone's lungs and then shocking them back to life. I miss the excitement of calling for an amp of epi as a patient's blood pressure drops. I occasionally miss the euphoria of being God to the person I just brought back to life. But it seems to me that the people who find God because he saves their life often lose him within a relatively short amount of time, whereas those who find a friend in God tend to keep him for life.

I had settled into my position after the first few months and was taking call on a Saturday night. The few patients who remained on the service for the weekend were relatively stable. There were only two patients: a thirty-year-old woman with heartburn mistaken for a heart attack and a seventy-year-old man waiting for Monday to be transferred to his new nursing home. I found myself able to relax for a short time. It was not uncommon for the doctor on call for the weekend to venture out to a nearby fast-food restaurant, where he could respond quickly to any nurses who might page him during dinner. It being so quiet, I decided that this was a perfect opportunity to walk to the Mexican food joint a couple blocks away.

Typically, I would be blasting heavy metal music through the headphones, fostering my hardworking but aggressive attitude. On this night, I listened repeatedly to a CD that I had been introduced to just the previous weekend. Unlike the fast and furious sounds that I usually preferred, this was a mellow collection of ballads, most with deep messages beyond what I could pick out of the lyrics. But I was deeply ensconced in the music and actually enjoyed the tranquility of walking down the urban street of west Philly with an enormous burrito and giant Mountain Dew in hand.

As I walked out of the elevator on the sixth floor on my way to the office, I was startled by a worker in a dark blue jumpsuit. I was embarrassed that he must have heard me singing along with the tune in the headphones. But he didn't budge as I approached him from behind. He just stared at a gaping hole in the wall that I didn't recall being there an hour before, when I left.

"What the heck happened here?" I asked causally, before I had even removed the headphones.

He looked sideways at me with exasperation and, I thought, blame. His lips moved, but the chords of the piano were too loud for me to make out his words. I was nervous that he thought I had broken something electrical or plumbing-related that required him to tear down the wall to fix. The dust from the drywall covered his navy pants and his heavy work boots. Only the pipes within the wall were exposed as I tried to come up with what might have broken.

"I'm sorry, what did you say happened?" I said after I had removed the headphones.

"You wanna know what happened here?" he said rhetorically. The angle of his head seemed to insinuate that I should already know. "I'll tell you what happened. What happened is you gonna gimme yo' money."

I chuckled lightly, humoring his not-so-clever joke. "What?"

"You gonna gimme yo' money. I don't wanna have to shoot you," he said in a low, monotone voice while reaching around to his right rear pocket. He held his hand there, motionless, not exposing the weapon.

Never in my life had the tone of a situation changed so dramatically and so abruptly. I stood motionless, not scared but in utter disbelief. I stared at his face blankly, studying each of the features I intended to describe to the authorities. I examined his clothes and any feature I could discern. I thought about the credit cards in my wallet and wondered how quickly I could cancel them after he left.

"Look, man, I don't have any money," I said. "I just went out to get a little dinner and took a few bucks."

"You a doctor. You got a wallet on you. Give it to me."

"I don't have a wallet. I just—"

He interrupted me by cocking his elbow behind his back, about to pull the gun out.

"All right, all right. Here!" I shouted while reaching into my heavy blue coat. I tossed the black leather billfold with several credit cards and various licenses.

He hunched over like a rodent breaking open a nut. He turned his back to me and began to pace.

"Man, you only got three dollahs in here!" As he circled around the hall, his right hand remained concealed by his blue coat.

As he paced, rummaging through the wallet and its compartments, I considered my options. I could let him go with the wallet and just cancel the credit cards. Or I could try to jump him and get to his gun or his hand before he could get to it. I debated the two for what seemed an eternity as he circled and gazed like a hyena. If I jumped him, I would risk being shot. But I had seen the moves performed in movies time and time again. He wasn't much bigger than I was. On the other hand, it might be safer to just let him go with the wallet.

He continued his pacing in wider circles. He seemed to be getting angrier as we each stood in the hallway. I wondered if he realized that I had seen him long enough to identify him in a lineup. Would he just shoot me to prevent me reporting him?

"Man, how can you only have three dollahs in yo' wallet," he repeated. "You a doctor!"

"Look, I am a resident here. I get paid less than minimum wage. I stay here over the weekend for free and take care of floors full of really sick people in the hospital, just trying to keep them alive. These are your friends that are sick up there, and I'm just here trying to keep them alive because I want to help."

I was giving greater consideration to attacking the man as he paced closer and closer to me. His breath was heavy, and he scowled past me. He kept looking up at me as if trying to plan my fate. This was it, the moment of truth.

Just as he approached me again and I was about to dive toward his concealed arm, I smelled a hint of alcohol on his breath. I halted for a second before making any noticeable movements. I didn't give it the same consideration or forethought I had given the previous plans. I just began talking.

"Why are you doing this, man?"

"Whaaat?" he shouted.

"Why are you doing this, man? This isn't like you."

"What you mean 'this isn't like me'? You don't know me!" He continued to shout and swiveled at the hips again to emphasize his hand on the gun.

"Tell me I'm wrong then," I said. I realized I was gambling. But I was still breathing. "You're not the kind of guy that goes around stealing shit from people and shooting them. I can see you're stressed out."

"Bitch! You don't know shit 'bout me!"

"You probably went out drinking before this. What got you so depressed that you had to resort to this?" I asked, tapering down to a whisper.

"Man," he repeated, no longer shouting. He was crying as he turned away from me again. "I lost my job a week ago…my woman kicked me out of the house fo' days ago. Man, I been sleepin' on the ground fo' days, man." He was sobbing repeatedly.

"Jesus, that's terrible. Couldn't you go to a shelter or something?"

"Man, I went there the first night she kicked me out…I couldn't take it. There is guys in there that been there fo' long time. They bullied me and took my money the first night just so they could get crack. Then they raped me."

"Oh," I gasped in horror.

"Do you know what it's like to have two guys raping you?"

"No, I don't, man."

"They just hold you down." He looked up at me as the tears fell profusely. "And they say all sortsa shit, like, 'You ain't worth nothing, so suck my dick, bitch!'" His voice deepened as he recounted their taunting. "So I had to leave there. I just couldn't take it. So I been livin' on the streets for the past fo' nights. I ain't got no clothes besides these on. I haven't eaten in fo' days, either."

Somewhere in his story, I forgot that he was explaining why he was robbing me and going to shoot me. He became just another destitute patient who needed someone to help him.

"Well, here," I said. "Why don't you take this? I just went and got this burrito." I lifted the bag toward him.

"Man!" He began shouting again. "I don't need yo' food!"

"Actually, you know what?" I said abruptly, almost interrupting him. "Let's do this instead. You and I are going to split this."

"What?"

"Come on." I continued to speak rapidly so he didn't have a chance to interrupt me. Meanwhile, I hoped it didn't occur to him to just shoot me. "We'll go into this room and split this. I think there are some paper plates and glasses in here. Follow me."

I opened the door to the conference room nearby and sat him down with half a pound of burrito in front of him. He watched me walk to and fro, getting glasses and pouring the soda before him. His look of sadness and agitation had morphed into one of puzzlement, and he was absolutely silent as I walked by him.

"So, tell me what you wanted to do before all this shit happened to you," I asked him, sipping on my drink.

"I was a carpenter," he said.

341

"No, I mean, what was your dream? You didn't just want to be a carpenter. What else did you want? Did you want a family? Did you want to travel?"

"No, I had a dream. I wanted to be a writer."

"A writer! That's cool! What kinds of things did you want to write?"

"See, I had this great idea that I could make a picture book for kids. But it would be with Bible stories. And I would do a whole series of books with Bible stories in 'em."

"Now that sounds like an excellent dream," I said. "Maybe now that you're not doing the carpenter work, if we can get you settled a little, maybe you could pursue that dream. Do you have any family who might be able to help you?"

"Yeah, I got a cousin who could help me. You know, Jesus was a carpenter, too."

"As a matter of fact, I do." I thought back to my late Christian education in medical school.

Our heads turned at that moment as we both heard the elevator doors open. I thought it was almost certainly the security guard making their evening rounds. She had to realize something was wrong from the hole in the wall and my CD player and gloves lying on the floor. The last thing I needed was for her to open the door and provoke a violent scene when I felt it was coming to a peaceful close.

I placed my index finger to my lips as we looked at each other.

The elevator door opened again, and I figured she was gone. Although I was relieved, I thought how stupid it was for her not to investigate all of the rooms, considering the signs of foul play.

After we heard the door close, the man in blue stood up and threw my wallet down on the table. "I can't take this from you. You've been too kind to me. Like Jesus in the Book of—"

I interrupted him. "I'm not like Jesus. You just need some help. So just stay here for a minute, and I'll be back."

I left the room, wondering if he would be there when I returned. I thought he must be wondering if I would return at all. I came back into the room with a few spare crewnecked shirts that had been lying in the office for a fund-raising event. I also brought out my Oakland Raiders sweatshirt, my one remaining vestige of California memorabilia.

"Take these and put these on in many layers. That will keep you warm out in the snow," I said commandingly. "Here is what you are going to do. I want you to head down this street." I pointed out the window. "That will take you to the bus station. Along the way, you will surely pass a church. Tell them what you have suffered and that you have a relative in Florida. They might be able to give you some money to help. You cannot threaten to shoot anyone at the church or bus station. Do you understand me?"

"Yes. I ain't gonna shoot anyone," he pleaded. "I'm sorry. I didn't mean to hurt anyone here. I thought everyone had left, and I was trying to get into the pharmacy to get some pills to sell."

It was clear he had mistaken the residents' office as a pharmacy.

"Now I am going to have to call our security people to explain this hole," I said. "Otherwise, I am fucked. But I'll give you fifteen minutes before I do it. That will give you enough time to get to the station and get out of here. I won't let on that I know where you went. But you *cannot* come back here, or they will be all over your ass. Understand?"

"Oh, yes. I understand. Thank you. Thank you." He walked down the stairs and out the front door.

Of course I didn't give him fifteen seconds let alone fifteen minutes. I called the security officers who then called the police. I was never notified of his capture. Nor did I care to be. I had felt a little fear for a few seconds after the shock wore off, but then came a strange sense of calm that I couldn't explain. I never saw a gun that night, and I choose not to wonder whether he actually had a weapon. He was a mugger for a few minutes. After that, he was just another man in need.

That was a month ago. Dr. Neill still speaks of the incident when the mood strikes him, and somehow it's always with a chuckle. The interview season continued today. Prospective family medicine residents strolled the halls as Neill pointed out the call room, the cafeteria, and today, the slight divot in the wall near the residents' room. I thought about the man in blue and wondered if he had begun writing his children's book in Florida. I also wondered if he became a Raiders fan after our night together. I have told Neill several times that it is probably not the strongest advertisement to mention that I got mugged in our lobby on a weekend, but he just chuckles as if this were one of those myths I heard when I was applying for medical school or residency, and moves on.

Tonight, after the interviews, a social hour was held at a local bar. Ten medical students tried to gain recognition, and ten residents tried to lose meaningful cognition as the blue and red lights danced through the room. The excitement of the applicants and the genuine interest of the residents and faculty was a refreshing change from the elitist routine I had grown accustomed to in years past.

"What year are you?" a young woman asked me. We had caught eyes earlier in the day, but this was the first time we had spoken.

"I'm a second-year. I'm Jeff." To say that I was a second-year, after all the time I had dedicated, did not hurt as much in the friendly environment as I had thought it would.

"I'm Reese," she said as we began speaking of medicine and residency. I kept many of the secrets and mysteries of residency to myself. And while she was no stranger to the horrors that internship would bring her, she smiled as she recited every apprehension. She explained that her fiancé was a year ahead and would be moving out of town before she did, but the hope was more lucent than the blue of her eyes. She laughed as she spoke of the terror of call and beamed as she wondered how she would wake up so early day after day. We smiled together as she told me of Philadelphia, a city that loves food, loves art, and loves its people. She reminded me tonight that even in the loneliest and most frightening times, there is always so much left to see, that it would be wasteful to face it without hope. I looked at the things she saw and even those she didn't, and I marveled at how easily she smiled into the unknown.

As I left the bar, I simply walked. The fastest route home would have led me west, away from the city. Instead I walked downtown, just to reflect. The enormous skyscrapers of Center City hovered above the foliage of other buildings. Reese's attitude was inspiring. Thoughts that might have otherwise worried me, did not as I walked. The brain tumor that was most likely benign no longer seemed menacing, not because I trusted the MRI from a few months back, but because I had hope for the future. I think this was the first time I had ever smiled while thinking about my tumor. I thought about the two years I would spend away from Tara, and what previously had seemed like dauntless isolation was just a stepping stone to our inevitable time together. I don't know what will come of anything any more than Reese does, but I trust that it will be for the best.

I thought about the changes that I had seen, and those I had seen in me. I smirked as I thought of the drive-by relationships of early medical school, and what I had come to value since. I smiled as I wondered at what times God might have peeked his head into my world and what he must have thought. And I thought of that young boy who had such a different impression of what was important in life and in a career—that boy who sought notoriety, that boy who thought it must be better to be from Yale. Now he wanted only to be back with his wife and family, and to appreciate every day of life along the way. Ironically, I think only now does he have the strength and faith to achieve those things.

As I walked, I noticed some of the buildings that Reese had mentioned to me. The glass edifice of Wharton loomed beside me. The snow had almost completely melted on the grass of the quad, but spring would be some time in coming. The breeze gently crossed my path as I approached the river's bridge. On the corner, a bearded man in an overcoat sold bouquets in random assortments. He hollered at the cars passing as well as the people exiting the subway. His shouts faded into the background of my sensorium as the soft breeze carried the fragrance of the irises in my direction. The sweet smell of honeysuckle added brightness to his collection. Even the ferns he crowded in to add bulk offered a scent that could be smelled when the heart was not overburdened.

As I set foot on the bridge, the roar of the passing cars was but a whisper as the steel of the bridge swayed beneath me. More profound was the waft of brine that teased me as the wind came across my coat and traced up my neck. The air was sweet, as if from a virgin shore and not from the stagnant pools hugging the sides of the stream. Above the tones set by the wind, I also smelled the reeds as I approached the opposite side. I stopped and breathed deep. It had been since that moment several years before as I walked past the flowers on the college campus. It had surely been there plethora times since that day, but the inner peace required to appreciate it had eluded me.

Today, I could smell the breeze again.

Preston Stone, MD
Author's Bio

Preston Stone was born in California, where he studied all the way through medical school. After training on the East Coast, he now practices family medicine in Encinitas, California. He has published several academic articles in the fields of science and medicine. *It's Better to Be from Yale* is his first fiction work and is based on his observations and experiences as he personally grew through his medical training. Today he finds his greatest passion within medicine is to treat his patients with education and inspiration as much as medication.